Mr. ~~Right~~ Write

Mr. ~~Right~~ Write

International
Bestselling Author

Monica James

MR. WRITE

Cover Design by Perfect Pear Creative Covers
Edited by Editing 4 Indies
Design and Formatting by

E.M. TIPPETTS
BOOK DESIGNS

www.emtippettsbookdesigns.com

Follow me on:
monicajamesbooks.blogspot.com.au

Other Books By
Monica James

THE I SURRENDER SERIES

I Surrender

Surrender to Me

Surrendered

White

SOMETHING LIKE NORMAL SERIES

Something like Normal

Something like Redemption

Something like Love

A HARD LOVE ROMANCE

Dirty Dix

Wicked Dix

The Hunt

MEMORIES FROM YESTERDAY

Forgetting You, Forgetting Me

Forgetting You, Remembering Me

SINS OF THE HEART

Absinthe of the Heart

Defiance of the Heart

STANDALONE

Mr. Write

Dedication

To my Mr. ~~Write~~ Right.

In the beginning…there was conflict (noun)

1
One

I hate airplanes.

And I bloody well hate Christmas.

The two combined are my ultimate hell, wrapped in a single-serving nightmare.

It's scientifically proven that at high altitudes, our taste buds are saluting us with the middle finger. The low humidity dries out our nasal passages, and the air pressure desensitizes our taste buds. That might explain the god-awful food, but I wouldn't hold my breath. On second thought, better for one to pass out from asphyxiation than breathe in the recycled, acrid air.

Shifting in my minuscule seat, I subtly reach down to rearrange my strangled balls, diminishing the prospect of me ever having kids by the second. Not that that matters any longer, seeing as my soon-to-be ex-wife is a lying, cheating, psychotic she-devil who decided shagging Eduardo the pool boy took precedence over staying faithful to her husband of ten years.

Thoughts of the succubus has me raising my hand to alert the forty-something stewardess of my dire circumstances and need to get completely and utterly wasted. But just as she did three times prior, she ignores me.

"This will be good for you, Jayden," said my agent, Nick West. "Get out in the real world and socialize with normal people."

"I socialize," I retorted, not liking the direction of this conversation.

"Seeing a different woman's vagina every night doesn't count as socializing."

"It's not *every* night," I pitifully argued.

"Every second night then."

Touché.

Nick West is my literary agent and best friend. We have been best mates since I moved from London to Seattle with my family when I was sixteen and was paired up with him as lab partners. He was the best man at my wedding, and he was the better man when he stopped me from committing double homicide when I found Eduardo doggy paddling Elizabeth's arse.

Tugging at the collar of my white shirt, I peer across the row, desperate for some fresh air. But thanks to the illusive windows, mocking me with false freedom, I'm bound to suffocate before this flight ends.

With limited legroom, I contort my six-foot-four body and hunt through the bag stowed under the seat in front of me. Yanking out my laptop, I decide to work on my latest novel. The flight from Seattle to Connecticut will give me a few hours to hopefully unearth the inspiration I've so desperately craved for the past six months.

There are endless reasons why I would throw a weeklong celebration if Elizabeth Evans contracted Ebola and died a slow, painful death. At the forefront is the fact she was an adulterous wench, but in true Liz fashion, it wasn't enough that she ruined my home life. She had to go and take it all.

My name is Jayden Evans. I'm a thirty-three-year-old Sagittarius who used to write about the miracle of true love and finding your forever soul mate. I'm a *New York Times*, *USA Today*, and *Wall Street Journal* bestselling author with over twenty-five million copies of my books sold worldwide.

My first novel, *Lost in Love*, was written when I was twenty-two and inspired by Liz's and my whirlwind romance. By twenty-four, I was one of the world's most beloved authors. All of this, all my accomplishments were because of Liz because she was my muse. She was the reason I was able to write sappy dribble and renounce my manhood by using the words "make love" instead of "fuck."

But now, she's my muse of a different kind—the kind of

muse that has me wanting to write about what utter bollocks "true love" is. There is no such thing as true love. It's an illusion we fabricate because we don't want to die alone. Well, screw love and all the pussies who believe in its existence. All I believe in is whiskey, Manchester United walloping Liverpool, and partaking in unspeakable nasties with anyone who can make this constant ache go away. So far, no one has succeeded, which should be my cue that this life of promiscuity is not for me.

It's been six months since the love of my life tore out my heart and set it on fire, and I haven't written a single word since. I'm a bestselling author who has severe writer's block because I've lost my passion to write…and to live. Every time I stare at my screen, I see Liz's striking blue eyes, but then those eyes are transformed into her arse cheeks as she yells for Eduardo to spank her *culo*.

That dirty, dirty *puta*.

My publishers are riding me hard, asking for the first five chapters of my next "bestseller." All I've sent them is a title.

I Never Should Have Loved You.

It goes without saying, they've asked me to resubmit something less disheartening. What they don't understand is that this is the best I can assemble. The original title was *I Hope You Burn in Hell.* So they're lucky they got option B.

Every time I go to write about how wonderful love is, all I want to do is add a footnote that all love does is break, burn, and end. Love is an optical illusion for unknowing twats. I've lost that connection in the real world, and in turn, I no longer can relate in the fictitious world either.

So the reason behind my newfound debauchery is to find inspiration in someone…something…anything. I need to find my passion again, and to do that, I'll try, *do* anything to find my groove because if I can't write, I may as well give up on life now.

"Not a good flyer?" asks a soft voice, snapping me from my woeful troubles.

Turning to my left, I see an elderly lady smiling kindly at me. She bagged a window seat while I'm in the aisle. The seat between us remains empty, and I'm hoping it stays that way. But I'm not optimistic, thanks to the holidays—fucking Christmas.

"Love, I don't think anyone is a good flyer. What, with thirty thousand feet between you and plummeting to your death in a horrific, fiery explosion, what's there to enjoy?" She pales, and her fingers tug at the cross around her neck.

I know she's only trying to make conversation, but I'm not interested in conversing with anyone. Not little old ladies, soccer moms, or lonely men desperate to talk about their midlife crises. I don't discriminate—I hate everyone.

"Are you on the way to see family?" she asks, in no way deterred by my apathy.

I'm on this early morning flight bound for Connecticut thanks to the fact I can't keep it in my pants. On one very drunk and disorderly night at a fellow author's book launch, I thought it would be fun to shag Daisy Bell. I didn't know she was the daughter of Axel Bell, the CEO of my multi-billion-dollar publishing house until I saw her photo, sitting pretty on her daddy's desk—the desk which I defiled her on—over and over again.

Shagging Daisy Bell definitely did not give me the inspiration I sought. All it gave me was a headache and the desire to neuter myself. After one, well, BOOM, three orgasms, she claimed I was the love of her life and turned up unannounced, offering to do my laundry or make me lunch. If she were anyone else, I would be telling them to hit the road, but thanks to my oversight, I now have to man up and try to pull myself from the mess I've made.

I've seen her for no more than a handful of "dates," trying my absolute hardest to deter her from liking me further. But the meaner I treat her, the keener she seems—it appears the saying rings true. So now I'm shite out of luck. I have no book or balls, as both are in the hands of one Daisy Bell.

I have told her endless times we're nothing but friends who occasionally hook up, but she doesn't seem to listen. I can't be any clearer. She said she's fine with whatever I have to give—which, honestly, isn't a whole lot.

But the predicament I find myself in is if I end things with her, she'll run to Daddy, detailing what a rotten scoundrel I am. And I'm quite certain he won't take too kindly to me breaking his little girl's heart as I had no qualms breaking her virtue in unspeakable ways. I'm already skating on very thin ice because my brain decided to close up shop and not deliver on the awaiting deadlines. If Axel were to find out that I was failing epically at being a human being *and* a writer, I have no doubt I'll be standing on a street corner wearing a chicken suit and handing out flyers for KFC.

Don't get me wrong, Daisy is a nice enough girl, but as I previously stated, I'm not interested in conversing with anyone, and that's all Daisy wants to do. She wants a relationship while I just want to be left alone.

"No," I blankly reply, giving this woman no further need to talk.

The only reason I'm on this damn plane is because Daisy invited me to spend the holidays with her family at their lake house, and ingenious me believes if I can sweet-talk Axel, allowing him to see what a great guy I am, then he might not want to murder me when I break his daughter's heart. I'm a bastard, but I'm not a fucking bastard. I need to end this now. Hopefully, the truth will set me free, and if word gets out about my current mental drought, he'll go easy on me and not terminate my existing contract.

I will not allow Elizabeth to ruin all aspects of my life. She's taken my heart, house, and money—but I'll be damned if she takes my career too.

Thankfully, my fellow passenger gets the hint and turns to look out the window. I bet she's wishing she could change seats with the chatty blonde in front of her.

Looking down at my watch, I see that it's past time for takeoff—how predicable. The holidays roll in, and everyone's sense of time takes a vacation too. Jolly travelers in full festive spirit continue to board the plane while the only spirit I want is a damn Jack Daniel's.

The neighboring seats are occupied, so I'm hoping for a Christmas miracle, and the seat beside me remains vacant. However, when a woman with an oversized floppy sun hat waddles down the aisle, I know Saint Nic is flipping me off and high-fiving baby Jesus.

No one likes sitting near strangers, especially in a space that makes Barbie's Malibu dollhouse look like a penthouse. This is Nick's fault. He was the one who told me I should live a little and not fly first class, as stepping outside my comfort zone may inspire me to uncover those hidden words. I should have told him to sod off because the only thing I'll be uncovering are my eyeballs from the peak of that hideous hat.

Her gaze drops to her ticket, then overhead, ensuring she's going the right way. When her eyes land on the number above my head, I sink in my seat, cursing Christmas, the Easter Bunny, and the entire human race.

She does a double take when she sees me, her full lips tipping up into a sassy grin. My mojo may be nonexistent when it comes to writing, but it's definitely in full swing when it comes to the opposite sex. It's like a lid exploded off my sex appeal because I'm never short of female attention. But maybe it was there all along.

Elizabeth used to tell me I was ruggedly sexy and far too fit, muscular, and tanned to be a writer. I run five kilometers every day—rain, hail, or shine. If I didn't, I'd be an out of shape vampire addicted to coffee and M&M's.

She said my blue eyes were electric. They constantly sparkled as they were the window to my graceful soul—*what a load of shite*. My dark brown hair is probably a little too long to be called conservative but not long enough for me to be labeled a hoodlum. It's shaggy on top with shorter sides. The mussed top matches the bottom as my jawline is never free of scruff. I always have a five-o'clock shadow even after I shave. Another aspect Liz said made me a man. Too bad I wasn't man enough for her.

"Excuse me."

Snapping my head up, I see that hat lady is blocking the aisle as she stands by me. She has an enormous bag strapped to her shoulder overfilled with god knows what. She looks at the spare seat beside me and then back at me, playing visual charades that I'm to move so she can squeeze past me.

Sighing, I quickly stow my laptop and move into the aisle so she can invade my privacy for too many long hours. She looks at the small space, then down at her handbag, which could technically have its own seat. "Here, let me put that in the overhead compartment for you," I offer as there is no way I'm having her *and* the bag encroaching on my space.

"Why, thank you. What a gentleman." She bats her eyelashes before hurling the bag at me as though I'm her own personal bellhop. I grumble under my breath as she shuffles down the row, her robust frame giving the unsuspecting passengers in the row in front of her whiplash as they jolt forward.

As expected, the overhead compartment is crammed full, so I move down a couple of rows, but no luck there either. Looking over my shoulder, I see a line of impatient people waiting to get past me. Apologizing, I buck my hips forward and suck it all in so they can pass. After I get bumped and shoved repeatedly, my patience is about ready to snap.

Just as I'm about to bowl this ridiculous arsenal I'm still holding down the aisle, a small giggle has me pausing, the air from my lungs escaping in a strangled whoosh. Every hair on my body stands on end, and my dick stands to full salute. "That's your color."

Looking down to where the mischievous yet sweet voice is coming from, I see an elegant creature with the warmest hazel eyes peering up at me from under delicately long lashes. Her cupid bow's lips form a sexy, pouty smile as she boldly meets my stare. A navy knitted beanie sits loosely on her head, her long, wavy dark auburn hair tumbling around her slender shoulders.

Her natural beauty is completely organic—no heavy makeup. I can see every freckle sprinkled across her rosy, heart-shaped cheeks and button nose. She looks young, maybe twenty-five, but either way, she stirs something inside me—

something I lost six months ago.

Now that I'm somewhat coherent, I see that my crotch is inches away from her amused face, eager to get acquainted with that sinful mouth. If this was any other woman, I would probably make some lewd remark; a remark which would probably get me laid. But not with her, and I don't know why.

"I am so sorry." I swiftly shift my hips back but end up connecting with an ankle biter who tumbles down the aisle. His lower lip trembles before he bursts into melodramatic tears, pointing his stubby little finger at me as his mom turns over her shoulder to see what the commotion is.

I'm standing guiltily, gripping the stupid pink bag as if that'll save me from the mommy bear jacked up on Christmas cheer. Thinking on my feet, I discreetly point behind my palm to the oblivious, angelic nun across from me reading a copy of *Jesus Saved Your Soul.* I pull a staged, horrified face, while shaking my head at the sister's alleged brutality. That magical giggle sounds once again, leaving me winded and slobbering like a desperate fool.

Jesus really does save.

Once my dilemma subsides, I return my gaze to the anomaly. Who *is* this fit lass? Instead of standing around, dick in hand, I smile. "So you think pink is my color?"

She nods animatedly, tonguing her rich lower lip. "Most definitely. Brings out the crazy in your eyes."

Her comment catches me off guard, and I actually laugh—a

full-bodied, genuine throaty chuckle. It's a sound I haven't heard in a very long time, and it surprises me.

"Well, you know, the holidays do bring out the best in everyone." My comment is accentuated when a passing smell that can be comparable to soured sauerkraut permeates the air.

Unpleasant odors aside, this is, by far, the most stimulating conversation I've had in months. It's also the first time in months I've actually wanted to know someone's name. "I'm Jayden." I have no idea why I just gave her my real name. In the past, I've given my random hookups my nom de plume, which is J.E. Sparrow.

Why did I choose that name? *Jayden Elizabeth Sparrow*. Sparrow was Liz's maiden name. She thought it was only fair I carry her maiden name, seeing as she adopted mine. Thinking about what a pussy-whipped joke I was, I clench my teeth, disgusted I happily handed her my balls on a silver platter.

Just like always, thoughts of Liz ruin my day, and I realize I have no business wanting to know this girl's name. I promised myself I was D. O. N. E. with love. Actually, I was done with feelings altogether. But this exotic sampling has my mouth watering, wanting a taste. I've avowed the only tastes I'll be having are meals on the run. No wining and dining, which is exactly what I want to do with this mystery girl.

I'm not looking for love. Been there, done that. All I'm looking for are single-serving friends who are uncomplicated and want what I want—to connect on a physical level—and nothing more, nothing less. Some girls just want to feel special while me, I just don't want to feel. Hence, why my mind is drier than the Sahara Desert.

I ignore the palpable tension bouncing between us because that crackle is what got me into trouble in the first place. I felt that undeniable pull when Elizabeth Sparrow walked into the Starbucks I was working at and changed my life forever from the first moment I laid eyes on her.

My gaze drops to her glorious chest, and traveling back up, I see a small letter C hanging off the end of a delicate silver necklace. She'll forever be known as C because this ends right here. Just as she opens her tempting mouth, I cut her off. "Merry Christmas."

Who the hell wishes someone a Merry Christmas? Especially someone who'd rather the twenty-fifth of December didn't exist.

She opens and closes her mouth, not hiding her surprise of my brush-off, seeing as seconds ago, I was clearly interested. I don't wait around to hear her reply because I wouldn't blame her if it consisted of the words "fuck" and "you."

As I turn to leave, the sugary smell of strawberries and cream catches on the air, punching me straight in the solar plexus. I need to leave. Now.

I just did this girl a favor. Believe me, she doesn't want to get messed up with the likes of me. Even though she's sassy and bold, I sense a layer of purity and innocence lying just beneath the surface—a layer that I'd soon destroy with my apathy and arseholeness.

"Sir, let me get that for you. We're about to take off." The unhelpful stewardess decides now is the time to do her job. I pass her the bag and make my way to my seat, ignoring the fact my fellow passenger is using my headrest as her pillow.

The only way I will be able to get through this flight is to revert to my original plan of getting completely and utterly wasted. I suddenly feel like a Malibu Swirl. I know what this is. My sense of smell is secretly controlling my mind.

Squeezing into the seat, I close my eyes and grind a fist to my temple. This is my karma for screwing daddy's little girl. It's also my karma for screwing *a lot* of daddy's little girls around Seattle and its neighboring cities.

I'm not a full-blown manwhore—well, not yet, anyway. But what's the closing number that confirms you're a man-slutosaurus? I have no doubt I'm marching toward the victory line, a fact that sickens me more than I care to admit.

I need to forget I ever saw a girl named C because C can only lead to fuCking trouble.

2
Two

"I *love you, J.E. Go write me a bestseller.*"

The signs were there. Cracks were starting to show. I was just too blinded by love to see them.

I should have known something was off. It was an unusually chilly morning in Seattle, after all, and Liz was lazing about on a floatation ring like she was Queen Elizabeth herself.

The sunlight drew out the gold in her hair, the hue giving her an imaginary halo, confirming she was an angel…of death as I was soon to discover on that fateful morning. She blew me a kiss goodbye, wishing me a good day at work.

I hadn't been able to find my groove at home as the words were slowly drying up. My mind was parched, and no cocktail could quench my thirst. Liz suggested finding a new environment to work in, so I made the Starbucks where I once worked at my hub.

Being away from home helped me concentrate, but now I know it was being away from *her* that was the solution.

I didn't realize it then, but my house was no longer a home. Liz and I had slowly drifted apart because she couldn't fall pregnant. Testing proved everything was in working order, but Liz was certain it was me. God forbid, anything was wrong with the perfect Elizabeth Sparrow.

I jumped into my Mercedes, adamant that today was the day I wrote something I didn't hate. I deleted more words than I wrote, making writing almost a chore. Liz was on my back to finish this novel because the sooner I started the next one, the more money we made. My advances were generous, and Liz loved the money. She lived like royalty, and I was happy to provide for her, to be her king.

Just as I turned out of our street and cruised down the highway, I remembered I left my MUFC mug on the kitchen counter. We writers are superstitious creatures, and we must have a specific item or follow a certain routine to ensure we don't disturb the "flow." Whether it is wearing a particular pair of underwear, or no underwear at all, never ending a chapter on an odd-numbered page, writing drafts in pencil, steering clear of the number thirteen, or drinking out of a certain football mug, we all have our rituals to help us get into the zone.

Seeing as I was slipping way, *way* out of the zone, I didn't want to take any risks, so I turned my car back around. As I climbed the back steps, I heard a faint whimper—the unmistakable sound of Liz in the midst of pleasure. I paused, turning my ear to ensure I was actually hearing her breathy moans and it wasn't my sex-starved mind conjuring up the sounds as we hadn't had sex in over two months. Every time I tried to touch her, she said she had a migraine or felt unwell. She was desperate to have a baby, but she wasn't exactly trying to remedy the situation.

I envisioned her slipping her hand between her sculpted thighs and stroking herself, spreading her arousal as she slithered two fingers inside. Liz was a gluttonous lover. Her ravenous appetite for sex was every man's wet dream. Too bad that dream was soon to become my nightmare.

My body instantly became hard, desperate to feel that intimate connection with my wife once again. I charged up the stairs, a man on a mission, but as I rounded the corner, I choked on a sight that will be scorched into my brain forever. I believed the sounds were of Liz pleasuring herself, not someone else doing the job for her. I trusted her, so not in a million years did I ever think I'd walk in on some wanker fucking my wife six ways from Sunday.

Both were too lost in their grunting to notice the intrusion, and honestly, I needed a minute to figure out what the hell to do. Sure, my characters had cheated plenty, but this wasn't fiction. This was real life. It was *my* life.

I silently and calmly walked into the kitchen, remaining unnoticed as I grabbed my mug and coolly poured myself a cup of coffee. As I watched my wife being shagged in our hot tub, I wondered if her face contorted in pleasure like it did now when we made love. I also wondered if he was a better fuck than I was. He *was* younger and probably knew some new move I was too old to become acquainted with. Was that why she cheated? Did I bore her?

She looked to be enjoying herself, shouting that he fuck her harder, groaning as he palmed her fake tits—the tits I paid for. She was perfect to me without the surgical enhancements, but the more money we made, the more she became obsessed with her looks. Claiming she couldn't have any flaws, she said the wife of a millionaire had to always look her best. She didn't have any flaws. That was, until now.

The fucking I could deal with, but when that sodding arsehole bent down and kissed her, and she kissed him back, I lost it. A kiss was most treasured, more intimate than shagging, and when I saw her kiss him like she meant it, like she enjoyed it, I finally snapped.

I stormed out and hurled my mug across the yard. It smashed into a million pieces—just like my heart—inches from Liz's face. She screamed, stunned at what had just happened. But when she saw me standing before her, fists clenched and ready to murder anyone who stood in my way of justice, she pulled the card no cheating spouse should.

"I did this for us."

Her words hurt more than her actions.

"*Lo siento*!" Eduardo exclaimed, detangling his body from my wife's.

His erect todger was like waving a red flag in front of an angry bull as he emerged from the hot tub, pleading for me to forgive him. He proved who had the bigger balls as he dropped to the floor, crying like a little girl when I head butted him and broke his nose.

As my world, my entire life emerged from the water, her skin still pink from another man rutting into her, I was baptized—my eyes were opened to who this woman really was.

She was my past.

"Let me explain!" she entreated.

But there was nothing to explain. I knew what I saw. I didn't need a diagram.

"I did this for us," she said once again. That excuse didn't stick the first time around, and quite frankly, she was just making things worse.

I scoffed, turning my back, unable to look at her.

"Jayden."

The moment her flesh touched mine, I pulled back, burned by her betrayal. "Do *not* touch me!"

"I want a baby!" she cried, tears streaming down her cheeks.

"And it appears anyone's baby will do."

She had the gall to recoil and appear hurt. To add to insult, she proclaimed, "I think there's something wrong with you."

"With me? You're delusional. I wasn't the one caught

cheating with a boy just out of diapers!"

I instantly felt like an arsehole when her lower lip trembled uncontrollably, and she choked on her strangled sobs. As much as I loathed her, she was still my wife. And she was still naked. I literally gave her the shirt from my back, and she thanked me by insulting me further.

"I think you're sterile."

Had her voice always been this irritating? "What?"

"That's the only explanation."

"No, that's not the only explanation. How about you're not as perfect as you believe yourself to be?"

She blinked once, incredulous of my claims. "That's impossible. Look at me."

And I did. For the first time ever, I looked at my wife, my beloved, and all I saw was a stranger. "I *am* looking at you, Elizabeth, and I don't like what I see. You'll be hearing from my attorney."

When she realized I was dead serious, she pleaded that she'd leave to give me time to think about my decision. When that didn't work, she said I could have it all. The house, cars, money—all of it was mine. She just wanted a second chance. But what she didn't realize was all that I ever wanted was her.

I was the nice guy, but nice guys finished last with their dick in their hand. So I told the love of my life it wasn't her, it was me. I finally realized what a shallow, self-centered bitch she was, and I never wanted to see her again.

Whether it was because I smashed my lucky mug, or discovered my wife was screwing the pool boy, I deleted every single word I'd written, and I haven't written a word since.

♥ ♥ ♥

My eyes pop open.

It takes me a moment to find my bearings and realize I'm stuck in a different sort of hell. Looking down at my watch, I see I've been asleep for a measly forty-five minutes. The snoring giant beside me has no qualms invading my personal bubble. As she inches closer and closer to me, I have no doubt she'll soon be drooling on my shoulder.

I need to find another seat.

Stepping out into the aisle, I allow my eyes a moment to adjust to the dim lighting. Most travelers are making use of the darkness by either happily sleeping or watching their TVs. Stretching overhead, I ignore the need to seek out C because I should not, will *not* look at her.

I had good intentions for all of point two seconds before I subtly seek her out. It doesn't take me long to find her. I'm drawn to her, and I don't know why. The glow from the screen lights up her gentle face, highlighting the deep frown lines crinkling along her brow as she concentrates on the flickering TV in front of her.

I begin to wonder what she does for a living, where she's going, and if she's happy. Ridiculous thoughts to be wondering about a mere stranger, but something about her leaves me curious.

I become conscious that I'm staring when she lifts those eyes and knowingly meets my gaze. She doesn't appear embarrassed or offended, just curious. So much is going on behind those mesmerizing hazel eyes. She intrigues me.

Remembering who else intrigued me, I lower my gaze and quickly walk down the aisle, purposely looking straight ahead. By the time I reach the lavatory, I'm talking myself out of going back the way I came because what would I say? *"Hi. My life is complete and utter shite. I'll pay you one million dollars if you slip poison into my JD."*

"Excuse me."

"Huh?" I very inarticulately reply. A female's giggle fills the small space. Peering up, I see a pretty brunette before me.

Her lip biting, hair flicking, and doe eyes all point to one thing—it's a look I've become acquainted with. I've come to appreciate that women have just as ravenous an appetite for sex as men do. I've also learned that things have changed since I was last in the game. It's completely acceptable to screw one's brains out and not know their name. No one wants romance anymore—romance is dead.

"You're J.E. Sparrow, aren't you?" That phrase is my pickup line. The funny thing is, I don't have to use it. It works for me without me having to open my mouth.

I run a hand through my mussed hair, smiling a "you got

me" look.

"I knew it!" she half whispers, half yells. "The girls owe me twenty bucks." She looks down the aisle where two of her colleagues are staring, giggling, and masking their grins behind their palms.

Returning her attention my way, she licks her red-stained lips. "*A Whisper of a Kiss* is my all-time favorite book. I've read it like ten times," she confesses, tucking a strand of hair behind her ear.

"It's one of mine too." *Was* one of mine, rather, as Liz was the muse for the heroine. Goes without saying, I now wish I'd killed her off.

"I've always wondered," she says, taking a step forward while I stand my ground. "What a whisper of a kiss felt like." She boldly runs her fingernail along the collar of my shirt. "I don't suppose you could show me?"

This girl isn't unattractive by any means, it's just, is it always this easy? Before my recent long list of women, I only ever craved the touch and feel of one woman. And it was enough. I didn't care that the only person I ever fantasized about was my wife because I had no interest in being with anyone but her. But after I exposed her affair, I felt pathetic. I was a bestselling romance author, and the only romance I'd ever had was with a home-wrecking tart.

"I suppose I could," I reply, returning to the here and now.

My response seems to bring out her inner temptress

because before I know it, she's latched onto the collar of my shirt and pushed me inside the cramped, foul-smelling lavatory. The door clicks, revealing to fellow flyers that this stall is busy and will be for some time. There is hardly room for one person inside this lavatory, so I begin to feel claustrophobic when she leans toward me with a ravenous grin. "Your book gave me my first orgasm."

The back of my knees hit the toilet, and I fall backward, landing on the seat with a loud thud. With no place to hide, I sit tall, trying my best to appear confident and turned on, but I'm just not feeling it. Whether it's my surroundings or the fact I'm about to join the mile-high club with a horny stewardess, everything below the belt is numb. I suddenly just want to get out of here because this scenario is definitely one I'm not proud of.

I open my mouth but don't know what to call her as she didn't tell me her name. This hasn't bothered me in the past, so why am I hit with a sudden case of guilt?

"I touched myself while reading *A Whisper of a Kiss*. I used to imagine Franco was making love to me."

"*Bloody hell*." I don't hide my surprise at her attention to detail.

When she rolls her glossy lip between her teeth, I know my unexpected coyness is seen as a personal challenge. "I love your accent. It's so sexy." Her voice lowers on the last word, hinting things are about to get nasty. "Are you South African?"

Thanks to me living half my life in the UK and the other half in the USA, I have adopted an accent which combines both nations' unique way of speaking. On any given day, I can sound American or British. Or a variation in between.

"I'm British actually, but…"

"That's even hotter," she cuts me off, not interested in what I have to say.

I need to leave…now.

Sadly, all plans of fleeing are put on hold when the air hostess draws up her tight skirt, revealing an innocent, white cotton triangular cloth between the apex of her thighs. This is all an optical illusion as I know nothing chaste is behind what I'm seeing. The moment she straddles my waist, I gulp, cursing the fact I didn't suck it up and stay seated.

"I'll be quick," she purrs, reaching for the belt on my trousers.

She can be as quick as she wants because this will be a one-man, or woman, show. Absolutely nothing is stirring within my pants. The fact I'm questioning my manhood has nothing to do with the overeager air hostess, but rather, I'm slightly disgusted that I've found myself in yet another predicament that has me hating myself more than I already do.

"Love, look…" I try to reason with her, attempt to stop things before they get out of hand. The only thing in hand, however, is my dick...in the air hostess's palm. I jolt upright, staggered by her forwardness. She grins as she begins to massage my pathetic excuse of a prick.

No matter how hard she tries, I stay soft. This is beyond embarrassing, and I can just see the headlines now…*Air stewardess mistakes J.E. Sparrow's penis for a peanut.*

I shudder at the thought as this is exactly what Liz would want to read—that I'm losing my manhood because of her. With that as my driving force, an animalistic rage takes over me, and I grip the air hostess's wrist, stopping her from searching for something that isn't there. I'm a hairsbreadth away from her quivering lips, growling in bitterness over what I've become.

She yelps in surprise, her eyes widening, her chest heaving in breathless anticipation. My aggression turns her on. "Show me what you got, you big, British brut." She wiggles her arse, attempting to seduce me. I wish it was that easy.

There is an explosive tension humming from her body, eagerly waiting for what comes next. As I'm panning through the pros and cons of whether to shag this helpful hostess, she makes the decision for me. She swoops forward, intent on kissing me, and I almost give myself whiplash when I jerk my head back. I bump my skull on the wall, but better a concussion than feeling her lips on mine.

I may not have high principles when it comes to shagging, but when it comes to kissing, I'm a fucking saint. No woman's lips have touched mine since Liz because the thought of kissing someone other than her makes all this real. A kiss is more valuable, most precious, and to share a kiss with someone you don't love or don't even particularly like is just downright sad.

Liz, however, doesn't share the same ideals as she had no qualms snogging someone who wasn't me. I thought I was happy, but my wife sucked the joy right out of my life. She's a succubus, feeding on my happiness, and she won't be satisfied until she bleeds me dry.

"J.E.? Is everything all right?"

No, everything is not all right, and it never will be again.

Just as she attempts to kiss me again, I become a different being, detaching myself from what's right and wrong. To do that, I switch my feelings off. That's the only way I can do this and look at myself in the mirror afterward.

Her lips are like tentacles as she smacks them together, desperate to latch onto my face and not let go. I need to put as much distance between us. With that thought in mind, I launch up off the toilet, taking the stunned girl with me. I slam her arse onto the basin, not giving it a second thought as I reach out and rip her innocent white underwear clean off.

Her big brown eyes widen, but that surprise soon turns to desire as she shuffles backward, exposing her glistening center when she brazenly opens her legs and places her heels on the sink. This woman is like a human pretzel.

She's open to me, a silent invitation to do whatever I please. I've made my bed, so it's time I lay or squat in it. Dropping to my knees, I contort my body to fit in the cramped space. Her smooth entrance is my view for the next few minutes. Here's hoping her prediction of being quick was, in fact, true as I don't think I can stomach a long-winded affair.

I hook my arms behind her knees and drag her forward, not seeing the point in beating around the bush—so to speak. Her fingers clench the edge of the basin as she hooks her legs around my shoulders and draws me in to the point of no return. Formalities are long forgotten when I lower my head and devour this woman like she is my last meal.

I've come to learn that I'm a mixed bag lover. Depending on the consumer, I can be gentle or rough, charming or aloof, attentive or casual. I can be whatever they want me to be, but the one thing I can't be is their one and only. Once we've both gotten what we came for, I'm out the door, not interested in making promises I can't keep. Up until Daisy, this rationale worked just fine, but now, here I am in yet another bullshit predicament that could have been avoided had I just kept it in my pants—which could have been avoided if my wife followed the same set of principles. Looks like we're both stupid prats.

The feel of another woman on my tongue, my lips, has me appreciating we all come in different shapes, and sizes, and tastes. For over a decade, I've been dining on the one flavor, but now, I've been offered an entire smorgasbord of tastes. As I bury my head further, I can only hope this flavor will have my mental taste buds singing in delight as I need to unlock some form of inspiration and soon.

Her well-sated moans reveal I've unlocked something.

Sadly for me, it's unlocking a trip down misery lane as I'm suddenly craving Liz's familiar floral bouquet. Thoughts of my wife have me physically burying myself deeper and deeper, wishing to escape this nightmare.

My self-loathing is this woman's gain because I consume her with a ferocious appetite, intent on ending something that should have never started. I lick, suck, and consume, stopping only when I feel a thundering quiver beneath my tongue. She clenches while I circle her ripened clit.

I splay my fingers at the small of her back, encouraging her to ride my face, but this devil doesn't need the encouragement as I doubt I'll be able to pry her off me. She bucks her hips wildly all the while screaming in an over-exaggerated manner. I move faster, more aggressively, showing no mercy, but she likes it. Her body begins to tremble, her sharp stilettos dig into my back, and her flesh explodes into a fireball as she screeches out her release for deafening seconds. She digs her long fingernails into the back of my head, ensuring I don't escape until she's milked dry.

After what feels like an hour, she finally releases me, and I take two much-needed deep breaths. She slouches backward with her eyes sealed shut, a docile grin tugging at the corner of her slack lips. She looks well satisfied while I stand, rubbing at my lips, eager to leave. Reaching between her splayed thighs, I turn the tap to cold, scrubbing away the evidence as I splash water on my face and lips. Looking at my reflection in the mirror, I see someone I'm despising more and more each day.

"That was…so incredible." Her pause for dramatic effect grates on my nerves. Her eyes slip open, dropping to the front of my flat pants. She lowers her leg and massages her foot over my pathetic excuse of a bulge. "It's now my turn to return the favor."

Just as she hops down from the ledge, I gently secure her wrist in my palm, stopping her from proceeding. She cocks an eyebrow. "Honestly, I'm good." When she frowns, I add, "I'm sure your mates have covered for you for long enough. I wouldn't want you to get into trouble."

She licks her glossy lip, my answer seeming to appease her. However, there is one favor she can help me with. "I wouldn't suppose you could switch my seat? It's a little…cramped where I am."

She smiles, happy to be of service. "78A. It's reserved for emergencies. Maybe I'll pay you a special visit." She accents her promise with a wink.

I hope that doesn't happen. However, if it does, I reply, "Feel free to unload the drink cart my way."

She giggles, her cheeks a rosy hue from the mind-blowing orgasm she just had. When she begins to straighten out her appearance, that is my cue to leave. Bending, I pick up her now useless underwear, but offer them to her just the same. She accepts them with a twinkle in her eye. "I know this is completely ridiculous, but do you think you could sign them for me?"

I've been asked to sign some ludicrous things before, but underwear I tore off? That's a first. When she offers me a pen from her pocket, I know she's serious. This is completely insane, considering I was all up in this woman's personal space moments ago, but I sign without a fuss. I hand them over to her, feeling the need to flee now even more urgent.

"Thanks, love. For the seat," I clarify.

"No, Mr. Sparrow, thank *you*." She holds up her underwear, grinning victoriously. "I'll make sure your belongings are brought to you." I give her half a smile, desperate to escape this claustrophobic space.

I unlatch the door, impatient to take off and never look back. Sadly, with eyes solely on the prize, I don't look back or forward and run straight into a delicious smelling being who has my mouth watering. My sense of smell gets caught up in the sweet bouquet of…strawberries and cream.

Horrified, I peer down and see C inches away. Thankfully, she is still standing, but her curled lips reveal she knows exactly what I was doing inside that lavatory, and I'm suddenly beyond embarrassed.

"I…" I attempt to deal with this situation by dropping a witty, charismatic comment, but all I'm left with is a mouth full of nothing.

Just as I endeavor to save face once again, C calls bullshit, leaving me a blubbering twat. "I hope you washed your hands."

My mouth falls open.

This delicate creature stands confidently while I feel like I'm seconds away from doing the walk of shame. I don't know what it is about this girl that leaves me tongue-tied, but I'm suddenly desperate to find out why. Her striking beauty is unlike anything I've ever seen before, but her wit, in the few sentences we've exchanged, whets my mental appetite. Looking at her, breathing in the confidence she exudes, inspires me to… write.

Goddamn!

A jumble of words floods my starved mind with sentences and paragraphs of…stuff. I don't know if it's any good, but regardless, this has not happened in a long, long time. I have the sudden urge to yank my laptop out and allow my fingers free rein.

Regrettably, my sudden inspiration goes up in a ball of flaming doggy doo when the air hostess saunters out of the loo, winking vivaciously at me. Her reaction confirms what a rotten bastard I am, and all I'm left with is white noise.

C stands back, not interested in making contact with the woman who was screaming out my name minutes ago. Before I have a chance to make up some pathetic excuse as to why we were both inside the lavatory, C brushes past me and slides the door shut. The lock flashes red, confirming she's not interested in hearing my excuses. Sighing, I run a hand through my snarled hair.

The only good thing that has come from this nightmare is that I snagged a seat on my own at the back of the plane. I buckle my belt, thankful when another air stewardess passes me my laptop and bag. Her coy smirk reveals my shenanigans have provided in-flight entertainment.

"Can I please have a bourbon?" When I see her colleague loitering a few seats away, I add, "Make that two." She nods and thankfully leaves me to wallow alone.

Deciding to try my hand at this thing called writing, I place my laptop on the tray table and wait for it to power up. I really wish I had my lucky mug. Stretching overhead, I crack my neck from side to side, ready to beat this writer's block's arse. It feels good to be sitting in front of the screen with a sense of hope that today is the day I write something that doesn't suck balls.

Opening a new word document, I look at the flashing cursor. Each blink taunts me, cementing what a complete failure I am. I'm verbally constipated. How am I supposed to spill my heart and soul onto this blank canvas? I swallow and grind my fists into my eyes. Why is this so hard? It used to be so easy, but now, I'd rather donate a kidney than write a paragraph.

Hunting through my bag, I find my black rim glasses. Maybe the extra seeing power will help. It doesn't. All I see is my failure with 20/20 vision.

Just as I'm about to press the call button and request a bottle of every hard spirit they have on board, the seat beside me depresses. I spin, ready to tell whoever this is to sod right off, but I gag on the words when I see who is sitting pretty beside me.

"Hi," C whispers, leaning in close to see what's on my screen.

I'm staring at her like a total tosser, but my brain needs a second to process what's going on. When she smirks and tucks a strand of auburn hair beneath her beanie, I know I'll need a minute. She reaches across me, her perfume doing something to my insides akin to an atomic bomb exploding. I hold my breath, watching her mutely as she drags my computer to her lap. Her slender fingers work deftly at the keys, then her lips twitch, and she passes me the laptop.

I remind myself that staring is not only rude but incredibly creepy and pull my shite together. Peering at the screen, I can't help but smile.

`What are you writing because you better hope the wind doesn't change? I'm Carrie, by the way.`

Alas, she has a name. Finding this form of communication a lot easier to deal with, I respond.

`One can wish. If the wind did change, I'd be first in line, ready to liberate my lungs. And nose. Nice to meet you, Carrie. I'm Jayden. That hasn't changed since I told you 30 minutes` ago. I pass her the laptop, unable to wipe the smile from my cheeks.

She reads my reply, and a magical laugh escapes her, making me think of sunshine and wildflowers. A sentence suddenly hurtles into me out of nowhere.

A gentle wind catches in her long auburn hair as she bounds through a field of tall wildflowers. The golden sunshine is her beacon of light. With her freedom, she brings hope.

I can see it vividly, the scene clearer than any others before it. It's one I don't hate.

Just as Carrie attempts to type something, I yank the computer out from under her fingers and desperately type out the sentence before I forget it.

I'm like a madman, my fingers sparking with electricity, ecstatic to be writing something that has a small bubble of energy swirling around my belly. Reading it over once, twice, three times, I know that this is half decent. Finally, I've written something that isn't rubbish, and it's all because of someone who I actually know nothing about other than her name.

Carrie leans across me, reading what's displayed on the screen. At this moment, I don't care what she thinks about it because I'm immersed in the soft touch of her skin against mine. Our forearms touch wrist to elbow, and the sensation pleases me more than I care to admit.

"Wow, that's good. Are you a writer or something?" She tilts her slender neck to look back at me.

"Or something," I say, thankful I managed to get out half a sentence while lost in her brilliant eyes. She smirks before turning back around to look at the screen.

I'm too lost in her to realize what she's doing until it's too late. Boldly, she minimizes my screen and helps herself to a folder labeled DO NOT, UNDER ANY CIRCUMSTANCES, OPEN. In hindsight, probably not the best title to label an item you don't want anyone to see. It's the ultimate temptation to any aspiring snoop.

I endeavor to stop her, but the moment I see a picture of Liz and me on our tenth wedding anniversary, looking nothing but in love, my hand freezes midair and my body contorts with rage.

It was a lavish affair—quite superficial if you ask me—but Liz insisted we celebrate and invite anyone who was a somebody. I would have been content to take a quiet holiday instead since I was burning the candle at both ends, but Liz was so adamant and never one to shy away from attention, so I gave in. At the time, I thought she was overjoyed to celebrate our love, but now I know she was only interested in celebrating and showing off the expensive gifts I bought her.

"Ex-wife?" she asks, peering at me over her shoulder.

"Soon to be," I reply, clearing my throat. "How'd you know?"

"The fact you look seconds away from setting your laptop on fire gave it away." A ghost of a smile plays at my lips. "Sorry, I didn't mean to pry." She appears genuinely apologetic.

"It's fine." I wave her off, refusing to look at the screen. "It's my fault for not being a little more creative with my choice of words when naming that folder." She smiles before repositioning in her seat.

Leaning her head back against the headrest, she turns her head to look at her. I truly am fascinated by her beauty. She is in no way my "type," but my "type" was a blooming slag.

"What happened? You looked…happy."

"I was, but Liz decided to find happiness elsewhere." I clench my jaw, not finding it necessary to elaborate where.

Carrie shakes her head, her lips pulling into a thin line. "Happiness isn't out there." She circles her finger, before stating, "It's in here." She gently touches her chest over her heart. "I have a feeling she'll never be happy anywhere," she wisely adds as an afterthought.

She's right. Liz had everything, but it still wasn't enough. She wasn't happy within herself, and nothing I could do would change that.

Holy shite—I feel like I've just had an epiphany.

Deep down, I knew it was Liz's fault, yet I questioned myself every day, wondering where I'd gone wrong. My only fault was that I loved her unconditionally and was blinded to her manipulative ways.

"I could use a stiff drink. Can I get you one?" I raise my hand while peering over the seats to seek out the air stewardess.

"I don't drink," Carrie replies. "As of"—she pauses, looking down at her watch—"eight hours, twenty-seven minutes, and nine seconds ago, I have decided to approach the new year with a different mindset."

Lowering my hand, I cock an eyebrow, completely intrigued.

"So what happened eight hours, twenty-seven minutes, and nine seconds ago?"

She sighs, sinking low in her seat. "I failed at yet another attempt to find Mr. Right." She scrunches up her nose, appearing defensive. "But honestly, is there such a thing? Finding *The One* seems so…final. No offense," she quickly adds. "I know you were married, so I guess at the time you thought you'd found your soul mate. But I don't think I believe in that concept anymore."

"Why? What happened?"

"Which time?" She laughs softly.

"How about we start with eight hours, twenty-seven minutes, and nine seconds ago."

She toys with a frayed thread peering out from the rip in her jeans. "My asshole radar obviously short-circuited because Donny was the poster child for the kind of man your mom warned you about. He was a total bad boy, and I knew he would lead to heartache, but why is the unattainable so desirable?"

I shrug, as I've been trying to figure out that riddle myself.

"Anyhow, we dated against my better judgment. It wasn't really dating, more like him calling me up when he was drunk and horny. The next morning when he sobered up, he couldn't get out the door fast enough. Each time, I promised myself this was the last time, but then he would do something nice like buy me flowers or send me a cute text message about how much he missed me." She mistakes my silence for disgust. "Pathetic, right? Allowing this to continue for months."

"Not at all. I was thinking what a fucking twat Donny was."

Her mouth falls open, then she bursts into melodious fits of laughter.

How could any man treat her with anything but respect? Not only is she beautiful, but she appears kind and intelligent, topped off with a witty sense of humor. She is the perfect package, but it seems she's been settling for deadbeat losers who really should be kissing the ground she walks on.

"Surely, you've had some luck in love?" When she stops laughing and shifts uncomfortably in her seat, I know the answer is no. "You've never been in love?" I can't believe it.

She shakes her head and pulls in her lips.

"Ever?"

She raises her shoulders in a feeble shrug. "What can I say? I'm a hopeless romantic. I'm looking for butterflies, but all I've found is indigestion."

This is completely none of my business, but my inquisitive mind needs to know. "There wasn't one man who captured your heart?"

"Nope, and it's not from lack of trying either. I guess I'm a serial dater, trying to find true love. After"—she appears to do the math in her head—"twenty…no, sorry, twenty-one boyfriends, you'd think I'd have some luck, but I'm convinced I'm doomed to live alone with fifty-five cats. I thought Donny may have been 'the one,' but I was wrong."

Wow, that's some track record. I wonder if she's slept with

them all. But who am I to judge?

The air stewardess who I know far too well saunters over with my drinks in hand. When she sees Carrie, her eyes narrow into slits, and she doesn't hide her contempt. She places the drinks on my tray table, arranging the white napkin so her number written in red pen stands out like dog's balls. "In case you stand under mistletoe, feel free to call." I give her a strained smile, regretting my deplorable actions. Thankfully, she doesn't linger.

Reaching for my drink, I toss it back, relishing the bitter burn. I don't make eye contact with Carrie as I'm ashamed she knows the reason I have some random woman's number on my cocktail napkin.

"So," Carrie says, breaking the silence. "My New Year's resolution is to quit booze, boys, and sex."

The liquor goes down the wrong pipe, and I choke. Thumping my chest, I cough loudly while Carrie giggles beside me. "That's some list. Are you planning on joining the nunnery?" I manage to get out between wheezes.

Her giggles grow louder. "I've traded in my chastity chips, Jayden. There aren't enough Hail Marys to save my soul."

Just when I think I've composed myself, I gag on…air. I need another drink. I have an incredible, beautiful woman telling me she's decided to abstain from sex, and all I can think about is having sex…with her…right now.

"Wow, that came out completely wrong and slutty," she

whispers from behind her hand. "I didn't mean I sleep around. I mean, I have had sex..." Her cheeks instantly blister, and she bites her lip. "Just...I need to stop talking," she quickly backtracks, shaking her head in embarrassment.

"It's fine. There's nothing to be ashamed of. You're an adult. The number of partners you've had is..."

She holds up her finger. "Partners? Why plural? It could be partner?"

"Yes, yes, of course," I correct quickly, afraid I have offended her. "I just meant if you had multiple partners, then that's completely fine."

"What if they were at the same time?"

I hiss in a strangled breath, certain I'll choke to death by the time this flight ends. Just as I'm about to affirm that I'm not here to judge, a mischievous grin touches her lips. "I'm just messing with you, Jayden. What do you think, I'm some loose woman or something?"

"Good god, no!" I'm quick to reply, horrified.

She giggles, appearing amused by my sudden coyness. "Besides, why is it morally acceptable for a man to sleep with as many women as he likes and he's labeled a stud while a woman is labeled a slut if she sleeps with more than a handful of men?"

"Some parts of society still live in a prehistoric era, that's why. For the record, you can sleep with whomever you like, and I'd still find you the most interesting person I've spoken to in quite some time."

I shut up quick smart, concerned I've crossed some line, but when Carrie smiles, I breathe out a sigh of relief. "Thank you. And ditto. Hypothetically speaking, if you were a complete manwhore, I'd still choose to sit near you over anyone else on this plane." There is nothing hypothetical about that sentence. We both know that.

"Thank you. I think," I add a second later. Her lips twitch, which awakens a stirring down low. Needing to change the subject as all I can think about is her admission that she's a naughty, naughty girl, I ask, tongue in cheek, "So what's a nice girl like you doing in a place like this?"

She looks at my lone drink, appearing wistful she can't have a sip before revealing her secrets. "It all comes down to eight hours, twenty-seven minutes, and nine seconds ago. And for the record, I'm not a nice girl."

"The twat?" I question, refusing to use his name.

She nods with a smile. "I work at The Lonely Bird pouring drinks and waitressing. I had a late shift. Donny texted, asking what time I finished as he wanted to come over. This was a first because he usually just turns up on my doorstep unannounced. I thought maybe he'd finally come to his senses and was turning over a new leaf.

"It was a quiet night, so I asked my boss if I could go home early. I was thrilled when he said yes. I couldn't get out of there fast enough. I decided to surprise Donny and not tell him I had finished early. But I was the one who was in for a surprise. The moment I opened my front door, I knew what was happening. I shared an apartment with my friend from art school. Natalie. She knew all about my woes with Donny. She was the ear I chewed whenever he did something to piss me off. She also knew that regardless of everything, I liked him. But it appears she liked him too. Well that or maybe she disliked me enough to hurt me by sleeping with him—in my bed to add to insult."

I shake my head disgusted. Does nobody have any decency anymore? "I'm sorry you had to see that. I too witnessed something very similar to what you did." I tug at the collar of my shirt, suddenly feeling smothered.

"Thank you, but I'm not sorry," she firmly states.

I frown. "I don't follow."

She replies without pause. "The only thing I'm sorry for is wasting six months of my life on someone who didn't deserve my time. I needed to see what I did to pull myself from a toxic situation. If I didn't, I'd probably be sitting home alone, waiting for Donny to call. How sad is that?"

This woman, she is truly remarkable. This entire time, I've been looking at what happened with Liz as a bad thing, but Carrie is right. Wasn't it better I found out the truth than live a lie? Liz wasn't always a superficial cow, but people change—some for the better and some for the worse.

Maybe Carrie is onto something. Maybe there is no such thing as a soul mate because can one person really fulfill every need you have? Perhaps there is more than one "The One," and we find that person with change. It's very possible that they are "The One" at one time, but with change comes new needs and different views on love and life.

I toss back my drink, my mind running circles around this very plausible concept as it's one I've never had before. I was happy with Liz, therefore, I didn't question my beliefs, but now I see that I was living blind.

Words, names, sentences, phrases begin materializing in my head, all amounting to a story that has never been told by me before—a story inspired by my new muse.

"I'm sorry, I'm boring you."

"What?" I shake my head, clearing it. "No, not at all. I just… when you asked if I was writer, well, I am. And honestly, after finding my wife shagging someone who wasn't me, I've had a hard time writing anything that doesn't involve the words 'die, you traitorous cow.'" She covers her mouth, muting her magical cackles. "But talking to you, I actually am inspired for the first time in months. I've tried to find inspiration elsewhere…" I don't need to elaborate where. "But I think I too might make a New Year's resolution."

"Oh, yeah? And what's that?" She leans in close, eager to hear my pledge.

"Don't let yesterday take up too much of today."

"That's a great resolution."

I can't help but smile. "Thank you. So how does your story

end, Carrie?"

She blows out a loud breath, raising her shoulders. "Well, after finding my roomie shagging"—she attempts to mimic my accent, which has me smirking—"in my bed nonetheless, I decided to pack up my stuff and not look back."

"You moved out?" I don't mask my surprise.

"Yes."

"Wow." My eyebrows shoot up into my hairline. "That was fast."

"Life is too short for hesitations. I'm technically homeless, so I thought while I'm figuring out my life plan, I'd visit my old holiday home in Connecticut. What better way to start the new year than with a loving family." Her sentence is dripping with sarcasm. "So the answer to your question is… my ending is pending."

I like it. It's honest, and it's a future with endless possibilities. And I suddenly feel the same.

"You have brains in your head. You have feet in your shoes. You can steer yourself any direction you choose."

"Dr. Seuss! I love him." Just when I thought she couldn't get any more amazing, she professes her love for my favorite author. "My dad used to read those books to me when I was younger." I hear the longing in her tone, revealing their closeness has faded.

I want to ask her what happened, but when she appears lost in a memory before switching on the TV screen and reaching for her headphones, I don't press.

Looking at my computer screen with nothing but a sentence, I suddenly feel hopeful that my story has only just begun too.

3
Three

Carrie is sound asleep beside me, her light breathing surprisingly soothing. I haven't been able to stop thinking about what she said. A weight I didn't even know I had has lifted from my shoulders; the weight which stopped me from writing. Looking at the word count, I can't help but feel a sense of accomplishment. I've written 587 words. It's not much, but they're words I don't hate. Words I won't delete. And that's all thanks to the mystery girl beside me.

Carrie is the first woman I've wanted to talk to because I actually am interested in what she has to say. She mentioned art school. I wonder what she's studying. I begin to wonder a lot of things. Who are her family? Why can't she find Mr. Right? How can she still be single? How many men has she slept with? I hiss at the last thought. I find her both physically and intellectually attractive, a combination bound to lead to trouble.

I feel a comfort around her, and a connection I can't explain. I've only felt this way with Liz, but this feels different.

I'm different.

The air hostess saunters past, garbage bag in hand. "Do you have any trash, Mr. Sparrow?" I pass her my cups along with the white napkin with her number on it. Her eyes widen when she sees that I have just thrown her out with the rubbish, but I'm sure she'll move on in no time.

The pilot's message over the speakers announcing our descent wakes Carrie, who peers around, gathering her bearings. When her eyes land on me, she smiles, appearing thankful that I'm still here.

"I thought you were a dream."

"More like a nightmare," I correct, playfully.

Yawning, she stretches above her, not bothering to fluff her sleep-laden form. Her unguarded nature has me liking her even more. If she were Liz, she would be dashing to the bathroom to ensure not a hair was out of place. I once thought she just took pride in her looks, but I now know she was a stuck-up, conceited diva.

"So what are your plans for the holidays?" Carrie innocently asks. And just like that, my original plans of staying away from her are affirmed.

Shifting in my seat, I try to act cool. "Just working." She waits for me to elaborate. "I'm actually escaping Seattle." Which is true in a roundabout way. "I don't want to say I have a stalker, but let's just say, if I had a bunny, I'd ensure he slept inside."

Carrie's mouth twitches. "You guys dated?"

"Not exactly," I confess, not wanting to lie. "I've tried to tell her I'm not interested, but..." I extend out my palms and shrug—the universal gesture of I'm royally screwed.

She seems to feel my pain. "Some girls won't take no for an answer."

"Yes, this girl is proving to be one of those girls. Any advice?"

She moves her lips from side to side in contemplation. "You could always turn up with another woman on your arm. There's nothing like that sight to send a message."

I ponder over her suggestion. "That theory is great; however, I have no doubt I'd be singing falsetto as she sports my balls for earrings."

Carrie bursts into laughter, the sound truly magical. "She sounds crazy."

"Believe me, she is." If only she knew just how crazy things were—like me spending the holidays with her.

"What's her name?"

"Jasmine." For some reason, I don't want to taint this memory with Daisy's name. "I'm hoping by the end of the holidays, she'll set her sights on some other poor bugger and leave me alone." One can only hope.

Carrie smirks, and the sight leaves me a slobbering fool. "I wouldn't be too sure. I have a feeling you're not someone easily forgotten."

I open my mouth but close it soon after. Her comment could be construed in so many different ways. Am I unforgettable because I've charmed her with my debonair smile, or am I unforgettable in the restraining order kind of way?

Again, she leaves me questioning something that would be a no-brainer with any other woman. But Carrie isn't like anyone I've ever met before.

"I'll take that as a compliment."

"Good." She doesn't elaborate. She simply smirks, leaving me to question my manhood once again.

As each minute ticks by, I know I'm wasting precious time. I want to ask her for her number, but there are so many reasons I shouldn't. I need to sort out my shit with Daisy first because I don't want to drag Carrie into my mess.

"So you plan on laying low over the holidays? Catch up with family?"

She shifts in her seat. "Something like that."

Her vague response has me wondering what she's hiding. "They don't know you're coming?"

"They do, but they probably wish I wasn't." Her confession has me frowning, but she waves off any sympathy. "It's fine. I'm used to being the black sheep of the family. With a star athlete for an older brother, and an airhead, little Miss Goody-Two-shoes who can do no wrong younger sister, I had no other choice but to fill the shoes of the rebellious middle child."

I'm intrigued. The more she divulges, the thirstier I become. "In my experience, perfection is overrated. Where's the fun in predictability?"

"I'll remember that when I meet my sister's new boyfriend. He's apparently 'dreamy.'" She uses air quotations while rolling her eyes. "Who even uses that word anymore?"

"Your sister apparently," I quip, unable to stop from smiling.

"I can't believe we're related. When I was younger, I used to tell everyone I was adopted. And it wasn't hard to believe because I'm nothing like my family. My parents are high school sweethearts, and so are my brother and his Pollyanna wife. My sister has fallen in love about five hundred and seventy-two times, but this time is different apparently. He works with my father which means…I'll probably hate his guts. My father and I disagree on a little thing called morals. This guy is rich, drives some eurotrash car, and is in love with my sister, so it's safe to say we won't be having any heart to hearts anytime soon."

"This guy sounds like a complete and utter wanker."

She nods, curling her lip in disgust. "Yes, he really does. He better steer clear of me because I'm nothing like my sister…and for that, I'm glad. The fact he even likes her…" Shuddering, she doesn't need to fill in the blanks.

"Your Christmas sounds as enjoyable as mine."

"Maybe we could trade families? Or better yet, boycott our plans and fly to Paris."

If only she wasn't joking because that sounds far more appealing than spending the holidays with someone who is completely nuts.

If I wasn't already on this plane, I would have texted Daisy and told her that whatever this is, is over. It's what I should have done when she invited me to spend Christmas with her. Too bad I didn't grow a conscience before I thought shagging her would be a good idea.

I was an utter twat to think this would work.

"Paris is looking far more appealing by the second," I say, running a hand through my snarled hair.

"So your stalker doesn't know you've left for the holidays?" Carrie innocently asks. She doesn't know that in roughly twenty minutes, I'll be at her mercy. Once upon a time, I would have relished at the thought, but now, the only mercy I want is for my soul.

"She knows, but I'm hoping the time apart will have her seeing that we're not soul mates, or in love, or with any luck, she'll eventually get the hint that I don't want what she does." Harsh but true. "I made no false promises; she knew what came with the package deal."

Carrie's gaze falls briefly to my lap, which has everything standing to full salute. "So you're spending it alone? Working?"

There is no pity to her tone, only curiosity. I could tell her the truth, tell her how I'm regretting my idiotic idea, or I could lie. "Yes, completely alone." I may have deviated from the truth, but I can't allow her to see what a downright bastard I am.

Watching her innocently wet her lips and nervously brush strands of hair behind her ear awakens me. I haven't felt this in so very long, and the feeling is almost new. I'm seeing the world with fresh eyes, and all I want to do is write about it. But I'm afraid if I tell her the truth, this newfound mojo will die in the arse, and all I'll be left with is a blank screen—literally.

Something about her stirs something in me I thought was long dead. But the reason I'm on this plane headed for hell in the first place has me quashing down the urge to ask for her number. She's had her fair share of arseholes; I don't need to add to the shite pile.

I will have to commit her to memory and hope that once this plane lands, that'll be enough inspiration to finish this damn book. Just looking at her has me itching to pull out my laptop.

As the winter-kissed landscape comes into view, a bout of reality kicks me in the nuts. I can't believe I agreed to this. I must have been high. There is no way I can pull this off. I may as well say goodbye to my career now.

"Are you okay?" Carrie whispers into my ear.

The harmless question has me jolting in my seat because her closeness has the sleepy lion within me raising its very interested head. Nothing good can come from this. "I'm fine." I man up and grow a pair. I don't elaborate and simply stare out the window, wishing that the pilot would turn rogue and change the flight path.

Lost in visions of sunbaking on sandy white beaches in Australia, I don't realize we've hit turbulence until my fingers begin to lose circulation. Peering down, I see Carrie clutching at my hand, and her eyes are squeezed shut. She's breathing steadily as one on the brink of a nervous breakdown would.

"Carrie?"

She shakes her head, sealing her lips shut as if she's afraid to speak.

"I would ask if everything is all right, but the fact I'm losing feeling in one hand confirms you're not."

A strangled chuckle escapes her, and she loosens her hold—only just. "Sorry," she pants. "I'm not a good flyer especially when there is…" She doesn't finish her sentence because the pocket of air we hit does it for her. She yelps and buries her face into my arm, clenching both her hands around mine.

"It's just a little turbulence. It'll pass." I hesitate for a mere second, then wrap an arm around her slender shoulders, attempting to console her. The moment we make contact, she shivers, and a small whimper slips past her lips. The sound is merely innocent, but it arouses a craving deep within.

A need to protect her overcomes me, and I surprise myself at this very uncharacteristic trait. Liz was never a damsel in distress, a quality I once liked about her. But now I see I mistook her cold-heartedness for independence.

"Thanks for being so kind. It's nice to know that not all men are lying, cheating assholes." I wish I lived up to her impression of me because little does she know about the true Jayden Evans.

For the rest of the bumpy journey, I keep my arm wrapped around her while she holds my hand. When her grip loosens, I expect her to release me, but she doesn't. This simple act of handholding may seem juvenile, but I would trade every woman's body I've lost myself in for this single moment. I suppose I'm an old, soppy romantic at heart, and I've lost that thanks to Liz. It's no wonder I haven't been able to write.

"Thank you."

Shaking my head, I peer over at Carrie, thankful the color has returned to her cheeks. It's only then that I realize we've landed. "Oh, sorry." I quickly unhook my arm from around her, not wanting her to think I'm trying to get fresh.

There is a sudden charge to the air. I know what it is, and so does she. Now that the crisis has been averted, memories of her lithe body pressed up against mine have me gripping both thighs to stop from reaching out and touching her.

Her lips part, then she wets her bottom lip quickly. The harmless motion has me leaving dents in my upper legs.

She shoots upward, banging her head on the ceiling. It appears we're both affected by whatever this is. "Thank you," she repeats, rubbing the top of her head with a smile. "I'm sorry I invaded your personal space."

"You can invade my space anytime you want." It's out before I can stop myself, and it sounded even seedier aloud than it did in my head.

What's going on? I've had no issues flirting in the past, but now I feel like an utter twat, and I need to rectify the situation immediately. Thinking on my toes, I reach into my bag and pull out a copy of my book. Not wanting to encroach on her no boys rule, I can't allow her to leave this airport without knowing I'm within reach if she wants to find me.

Passing her my novel, she accepts, but her confusion shows. "You asked if I was a writer. Well…" I leave the sentence hanging, not needing to fill in the blanks.

She turns the book over, perusing the blurb, before turning it back over again. I cockily wait for the usual gushes about how awesome it is to be in the company of an author, but none of that occurs. If anything, she seems repulsed by my offering.

"That's my book," I clarify, just in case she thinks I'm a librarian.

"I figured," she replies, reaching for her bag under the seat in front of her and placing it inside.

"I wrote it," I reiterate. Are we lost in translation? But we're not.

"You must be proud." The air drops about five hundred degrees.

"I can sign it if you want?" Even I cringe at how conceited that sounded. She shifts her gaze awkwardly to look anywhere but at me.

I have no idea what went wrong, but that was a major kick

to the balls. With most women, that line would have sealed the deal, but I should have known that Carrie wasn't like most women.

Just as I'm about to apologize for being a pompous arse, she pulls a camera out from her bag and snaps a picture. The flash blinds me, and it takes a moment for my eyes to adjust. Blinking quickly, I'm thankful when I see she's no longer scowling.

"Something to remember you by." The book was meant to convey that token, but she obviously has something against paperbacks. Maybe she's an e-book girl.

It's more than obvious she's not interested in exchanging numbers. I knew this from the start. So why am I suddenly so disappointed?

"Well, I hope you took my good side," I tease, reaching down to snare my bag.

"I'm pretty sure that's all you have." She's quick to quip, but when I lift my eyes, surprised by her comment, she blushes a sweet pink.

In a roundabout way, she's just confessed she finds me somewhat attractive. My inner Casanova primps his collar and struts his shite. I need to think of something witty, something funny to say, but all I'm standing with is my mouth hanging open like a useless muppet.

"Well…"

"Well…" I repeat, my lingual skills apparently nonexistent.

I've never had to put so much effort into talking because I've never really met anyone who didn't know who I was. Being in the limelight has turned me into a lazy conversationalist. I'm so used to talking about writing, or when I'm not writing, talking about what I'm reading, that normal, everyday discussions have left me with a mouth full of air.

My conversations with Liz were based around work and money, and anything in between were skimmed over, deemed unimportant to people like "us." When did I turn into such a conversational snob?

As the crowd on the plane begins to thin out, I know it's now or never. "Not wanting to disturb your resolution, but I thought maybe once the new year starts, we could grab…" I never get to finish my sentence, however, because Carrie places her pointer finger to my lips.

"Don't spoil it."

"You don't even know what I was going to say," I say from around her finger.

She arches a brow. "I can guess." No isn't a word I hear too often, so I've forgotten the sting associated with it.

It appears Carrie is full of surprises, and I'm apparently a masochist because I keep coming back for more. "Just in case you change your mind…"

"I won't," she replies matter-of-factly as she lowers her finger.

I've obviously done something to piss her off, but what? I was her knight in shining armor minutes ago, but now it appears she wishes I'd left her stranded in the tower.

"It was nice meeting you. Merry Christmas." I haven't been that long out of the game to know a brush-off when I see one. Again, it's not a concept I'm too familiar with, and I don't plan on becoming too acquainted with the notion.

When she makes it clear she wants to push past me and escape this sudden suffocating space, I could stand my ground and turn on the charm. It's worked in the past, but from my earlier experience, I know it'll just tick her off further.

With ego in hand, I step out into the aisle, gesturing for her to go first. No matter if she suddenly thinks I'm a leper with two heads, I remember my manners. My mom would have my hide otherwise. The moment she steps past me, someone in front of her tosses his backpack over his shoulder, resulting in her losing her balance as it whacks her in the face.

My arms shoot out to steady her, but the moment we make contact, she pulls out of my grip. Raising my hands in surrender, I assert, "Whoa, love, I'm not going to bite."

"Good, because I wouldn't want to catch whatever diseases you have," she snaps.

Before I get a chance to ask what the hell crawled up her arse and died, she storms down the almost clear aisle. I could follow, demanding to know what I said or did to provoke this state of craziness, but I don't. This just confirms my earlier affirmation that I'm to steer clear of feelings. It's probably best if I added the opposite sex to the list too.

Shouldering my laptop bag, I shake my head, wondering at what precise moment this entire thing went cock-up. Women are a strange species, and I don't pretend to understand them. As I amble down the aisle, I can't help but feel a little rejected and a lot like the hunchback of Notre Dame.

The air hostess gives me a flirty smile as she bids me happy holidays, which strokes me a tad, but it isn't her attention I want.

Seeing Daisy doesn't seem quite so bad now. After Carrie left me standing alone, knob in hand, my bruised ego could use a little fawning over. Pathetic but true.

As I step off the plane and walk down the passageway, I straighten out my shirt and run a hand through my mussed hair. As I peer up ahead and see a hoard of people with cameras surrounding the exit, I remind myself why I'm doing this. I don't fancy being elbow deep in chicken grease as I work for minimum wage.

"There he is!"

The flash of cameras and the roar of the excited press somewhat comfort me. It's like coming home—coming home to the land of the crazy, but coming home nonetheless.

"Mr. Sparrow, what are your plans for the holidays?"

"Are you spending it with someone special?"

Flash. Flash. Flash.

Shielding my eyes, I make a quick beeline to collect my bags but am stopped in my tracks when a nosy reporter asks, "Just who is Daisy Bell? We hear you two are getting married?"

"Have you set a date?"

"How do you know about Daisy?" I bark. I know better than to allow them to bait me, but I don't want this leaked to the media. That's the last thing I need.

The reporter seems like all her Christmases have come at once as she shoves the tape recorder in my face. "Do you confirm you're engaged to her?"

"What? *No*," I reply, unable to hide my repulsion. "How did you…?"

I don't need to continue because all my questions are answered at once. "Pookie bear!"

Before I have a chance to curse whatever god is laughing at my expense, Daisy Bell propels forward and launches herself into my arms like we're in some sodding romance flick. The press have a field day, their cameras capturing every uncomfortable moment.

With no other choice, I embrace her, wishing I could squeeze a little harder. "You tipped them off." It's a question intersected with a statement because I know that she did. This is so typical of her—always wanting to shine in the spotlight.

"Hello to you too. Is that any way to thank me?" she whispers, kissing my cheek for dramatic flair. There's no point in arguing.

After we're done hugging like long-lost lovers, she lets me up for air. She poses for the cameras, flicking her long brown hair over her shoulder and pouting her glossy lips. With soft wavy curls, chocolate brown eyes, and a fit body with all the right curves, there's no denying she's every man's dream girl.

But I was surrounded by this for years, and I've grown tired of it. I want a change.

Linking her arm through mine, she snuggles into my side. "I missed you, pookie bear."

"Please stop referring to me like I'm a prop from Sesame Street," I berate through clenched teeth, trying my best to smile. She giggles, oblivious to the fact that I'm deadly serious.

When she's done posing for the press, she leads the way toward baggage claim. A few photographers follow, snapping last-minute photos, hoping for the money shot. "How was your flight?" she asks, her heels clacking against the floor.

"Long." I don't see the need to elaborate.

"Oh, poor baby. I'll give you a massage if you're lucky." She accentuates her promise with a wink.

Bags fill the carousel as impatient holidaymakers eager for their vacation to begin wait. I scan the area, wondering if Carrie is one of those people. Her abrupt exit has left me curious as to what went wrong. For a moment there, I thought we connected, but I was obviously mistaken. Not that I can blame her. She did catch me post copulation, and then I acted like a fucking idiot by offering to sign her book.

Whiskey is needed to erase the past six hours or, better yet, the past six months.

"What color is your bag?"

"Black."

This shortness between us is so atypical of our conversations. I thought she'd tire of it, but the less I speak, the more she talks. "I can't wait for you to meet the family. I know you've met Daddy, but my mom is dying to meet you. It's going to be so much fun. I can't wait for you to unwrap your Christmas present. If you're a good boy, maybe I'll give it to you early." Her voice turns husky as she reaches down and fondles my balls, uncaring that we're in a very public place.

I grip her wrist and push her away from my family jewels. I want her nowhere near my junk. "My dear, you're embarrassing me." She giggles, keeping her hands to herself—for now.

Fortunately, my bag emerges, and I step forward, thankful for the breather. I've been in her company for roughly five minutes, and I already want to kill myself.

"The driver is waiting outside," she declares, leading the way. I follow, slipping my Ray-Bans on as I've had enough of the cameras.

Wearing sunglasses indoors in the middle of winter makes me look like a total wanker, but I've already crossed that line by being here. I drag my bag behind me, half listening to Daisy detailing the Bell family traditions.

I have no doubt I'll be a raging alcoholic by the end of the week. Reaching into my pocket, I pull out my cell, needing some moral support. Nick replies on the third ring.

"I thought you'd be balls deep in Daisy by now."

"You have problems, mate." I chuckle, his crudeness never ceasing to amaze me. "I need you," I whisper, lagging behind. Daisy doesn't even notice my retreat.

"I'm flattered, but I don't swing that way. If I did, however, I'd be all up in your man parts."

"I can't believe you went to Yale." I shake my head, amused. "You need to get your arse on a plane and come save me. I can't believe I let you talk me into this."

"I talked you into screwing Sweet Cheeks on her daddy's desk?" he rebukes. I hear him open a beer bottle. Lucky bastard.

I pinch the bridge of my nose, not needing the visual reminder. "I was drunk and shouldn't be held accountable for my actions. You know I have a weakness for girls in red."

"And yellow and pink and green," he singsongs, unsympathetic to my cause.

"You are the worst literary agent ever, not to mention best friend."

"C'mon, old chap," he says in his staged British accent. "I could think of a dozen worse ways to spend my Christmas. You're vacationing at a million-dollar secluded property along the shoreline with a woman who would do anything, *anything* you ask, and you want me to feel sorry for you? Did you misplace your balls on the plane ride over?"

"Goodbye, Nick. I stand by my earlier affirmation."

"Don't do anything I wouldn't do!" he shouts, needing to get in the last word before I end the call.

"That doesn't leave me with many options," I mock, before hanging up. That was a waste of time. I should have known he'd enjoy my pain.

Once we step outside, the cool breeze is a welcomed reprieve, and I take a moment to absorb my surroundings. I wish I was here under different circumstances as Connecticut is one of my favorite states.

The driver tips his hat when Daisy saunters over to the door he's holding open for her. The fact we have a limousine picking us up instead of a taxi displays the type of treatment Daisy is accustomed to. I've always been thankful for having such luxuries at my disposal, but now, I wonder if I was always such a pretentious jerk.

"Mr. Sparrow."

"Hello."

I stop, bracing my hand on the doorframe as Daisy pats the empty seat beside her. I almost ask the driver if we can switch places but suck it up and hop in. The door shuts, sealing my fate. There's no turning back now.

This limo is one of the nicest I've been in. There's ample room, and no expense is spared. The black leather seats and top shelf whiskey give me insight on what's headed my way. Our chic surroundings don't seem to make a difference to Daisy because the moment the car pulls into traffic, she rockets onto my lap, making her intentions clear when she wiggles her arse.

"Hi," she huskily purrs, interlocking her hands around my

nape.

"Hi." I humor her.

"Did you miss me?" She pouts like a sulky child.

Reminding myself why I'm doing this, I nod. "Sure."

"Good 'cause I missed you too."

I pull backward when she encroaches on my personal space. Her target is my lips, but it'll be a cold day in hell before I allow her anywhere near them. "Daisy, we agreed to take things slow. I've told you numerous times we're not together. Or exclusive." Or however they are phrasing it these days.

She sighs dramatically, her sweet breath bathing my cheeks. "I know, I know. A stallion like you cannot be tamed."

I screw up my face because I would never refer to myself as some steed. Images of a bare-chested Fabio riding a white horse into the sunset assault my brain, and it takes all my willpower not to throw her off my lap and reach for the whiskey.

I try another tactic. "On the plane, an air hostess—"

She interrupts me, not allowing me to be honest. She shakes her head, proving that denial is bliss. "I don't care, Jayden. You're here with me now. And I don't plan on letting you go."

I gulp.

Images of Daisy calling me Paul and shattering my bones with a hammer while I'm tied to a bed suddenly don't seem so farfetched.

"After the holidays, you'll be so in love with me, you'll never want to leave." I grin, thinking she's joking, but when she makes it clear she's serious, I fear for my safety.

There's no point in bursting her bubble because the odds are I won't last long. I need to make headway with Axle, and soon. I don't know how long I can partake in this little charade without losing my sanity.

"So is your father at the lake house already?"

She nods, toying with the curls at my nape. "Yes. He flew down in his private plane yesterday."

That's not all bad news then. Her admission confirms why I'm here, and what I have to do. "Great, I'd love to talk to him about my new book and…"

Daisy slaps her hand over my mouth, surprising me with the harsh whack. Leveling me with a dogged stare, I don't dare speak, afraid she'll take my insolence out on my balls. "There will be no business talk while we're away. I've already told Daddy. These next ten days are all about me."

"Splendid." I don't bother checking my sarcasm at the door.

"Now…" When she reaches over and presses the button to slide up the privacy shade between the driver and me, I know things are about to get dirty. "It's time I showed you just how much I missed you."

She advances forward, but I'm too fast, and she's too predictable. My turned cheek is where her lips land and where they'll stay. "Sorry," she teases. "I forgot about your no kissing rule."

She can mock me all she wants. I have no intention of

breaking that code—ever.

"Poor baby. She broke your heart, didn't she?" No guessing to whom she's referring to. "What a silly woman. Oh well..." She slips a hand between us, rubbing over the front of my slacks. "Her loss"—untangling herself from my lap, she slithers down my body—"is my gain," she concludes when she comes to a stop on her knees between my splayed legs.

She peers up at me from under her lashes, wetting her lips—she's mastered the art of seduction. It's times such as these that it's easy to forget that Daisy is only twenty-four. She knows how to work a man, and when she walks her red painted nails up the front of my legs, coming to a stop just an inch away from my groin, she reveals what a true seductress she is.

I need to stop this, but when she unbuckles my belt with deft fingers and snaps open the button on my pants, all I can do is lean back and try to forget. I can try to forget that there is no part of this scenario which doesn't end in me going to hell. I can disregard the fact that hours ago, I was nestled between the legs of a stranger much how Daisy is nestled between mine. But what I can never overlook is the reason I am where I am. No matter how hard I try, Liz will always be the shackle that I will never break free from.

Losing myself in the rhythm of Daisy's hand working its way into my pants, I close my eyes and lean back against the headrest. Each lewd act is tearing me further and further away from who I once was, but I don't even know who that person is anymore. My entire life was mapped out for me, but now, I have no idea what comes next.

But right now, right this second, all I want to do is get laid.

Daisy goes straight in for the kill, bypassing my boxer briefs. A hum escapes me, the feeling of surrendering unburdening a small part of my regret. She increases the speed and friction, working my length with skill. My body has become accustomed to her touch and craves a release like an addict seeking his next fix.

She isn't gentle, and it's exactly what I need. Her hand pumps me in an almost hypnotic tempo, and nothing else matters but crossing the finish line a winner. Soft, breathy moans slip past Daisy's lips, and it's a turn-on knowing that she's as into this as I am. "I love every single, hot, hard inch of you." She pauses between each word, accentuating her love by stroking me faster and faster.

The L word bothers me somewhat, but she's used it in a context I can deal with.

Daisy is a master manipulator and the ball, well, balls are in her court when she suddenly slows down, revealing I'm at her mercy. "I really like you, Jayden."

"Thank you," I reply with strain. I'm in physical pain, and she decides now is a good time to have a heart to heart.

She slides her hand up and down my knob, dragging out my release. "I know we agreed to take things slow, but I lo…" My eyes pop open, and I peer down at her, shaking my head.

However, Daisy's sentence remains unfinished because I'm saved by the bell.

The cell vibrating in my pocket isn't exactly the vibrating I was counting on, but it's suddenly the throbbing of the best kind. "Sorry, love. Duty calls." I lift my hips and retrieve my cell, not bothering to look at the screen. I'll talk to Satan himself if it means I never have to hear those three little words slip past Daisy's lips. "Hello."

Silence.

"Hello?" I repeat, worried that whoever was on the other end has terminated the call.

Just as I'm about to see who the caller is, blackness overcomes me, and I get metaphorically kicked in the balls. "Hi, Jayden." I've never hated my name more than I do right now.

I haven't heard her voice in over three months, but the pain it brings is like I only heard it yesterday.

"Please don't hang up," she pleads. "I just want to talk."

Elizabeth Sparrow is the opposite of Viagra. My hard-on goes into hiding, not interested in listening to whatever lies she wishes to spew.

"I'm hanging up now. Please feel free to lose my number."

"Jayden! Please! Five minutes is all I ask for."

Her plea touches a small, annoying part, and I sigh, frustrated that piece still exists. "You have two minutes. Use them wisely."

Daisy is still on her knees with her eyebrows knitted together.

All she knows of my past is what she's read in the papers, which has been utter bollocks. She knows I'll soon be divorced, but the reason will always remain a mystery. I obviously don't have a convincing poker face because she somehow knows that my ex-wife broke my heart.

"I'm sorry."

"One minute and fifty-five seconds left," I mock, not at all interested in her hollow apologies.

"How can you be so cruel? I've said I'm sorry. What more can I do?"

"You can stop calling me, for starters, and sign the damn divorce papers."

She ignores my insolence. "I love you, Jayden, and I know that you love me too." It seems I'm the center of everyone's affection today—lucky me.

A chuckle escapes me, but it's anything but joyful. "You love me? Is that why you fucked the pool boy in our home?"

Daisy gasps, but I don't want her sympathy. I just want to be left alone.

"It was a mistake. One I wish I could take back every day."

"Well, guess what? You can't," I bite back, angry she has the gall to call me and expect me to change my mind.

"I want my husband back, and I'll do anything to make that happen." I'd forgotten just how arrogant she can be.

"What's the matter, Liz? Run out of money and boys to keep you entertained?"

“You’re just angry. This will pass,” she says. She must be trying to convince herself because nothing will change my mind—ever.

“That’s right, I am angry.” Daisy is still on her knees, biting her lip nervously. The sight gives me an idea. Threading my fingers through her thick hair, I suddenly yank her head backward, exposing the length of her soft neck. She mewls, now licking her lips for a different reason.

“Of course, you are. You have every right to be. But you’ll forgive me.” Always so presumptuous. Some things never change.

Ignoring her arrogance, I decide to hit her where it hurts. “And to deal with that anger”—I tug harder, eliciting a moan from Daisy—“I’ve taken a page out of your book and decided that shagging anything in sight is the only way to remedy that rage.”

Liz’s gasp is a small victory for me. “You’re lying. I’m the only woman you’ve ever been with all these years.”

I tsk her. “You were, but now your quim is a distant memory, one which has been replaced by many, many others of different shapes and sizes.”

“I don’t believe you.” Her sniffles are my gain.

Daisy is still my prisoner, and I wish to punish her in ways we’ll both enjoy. “Believe what you want. Just like always, you know how to ruin a good time. For old time’s sake, I thought you’d like to know that before you called, I was seconds away from getting a blowjob from a smashing, perky twenty-four-year-old."

"Liar!" she snarls.

"On the contrary, love."

Releasing Daisy, I skim my hand down the side of her neck, before running my finger along the top of her breasts which are spilling from her low-cut blouse. It's made of silk. A soft peach in color. Too bad it's soon to be destroyed. I suppose there are always victims in war. With a sharp tug, I rip it from her body.

"Much better," I hum, admiring her bountiful breasts which overflow from her black lace bra.

"Fuck me, Jayden," she moans loudly. It's the response I wanted from her because Liz has heard, loud and clear.

"Oh, I plan to, darling."

"You pig," Liz spits, disgusted.

I scoff mockingly. "That's the pot calling the kettle black, but whatever makes you sleep easy at night. As pleasant as it's been, I must go. Unless you want to wait? Although"—unclasping the clip at the front of Daisy's bra, her breasts escape their lacy confines, stirring my interest below the belt—"I might be a while."

"I won't give up on you. On us."

Her words are ones I wished I'd heard long ago, but now, I wish she'd just give up—period. "That's a pleasant story, but if you'll excuse me, I have a bang tidy woman who can't get enough of my coc…" She doesn't allow me to finish, and the line going dead is my victory.

Petty, but still rewarding.

My good mood has definitely done something to my libido because all I can think of is stripping Daisy bare and having my way with her very willing flesh.

"Come here," I command, leaning back in my seat. She moves without pause, and I plan on that being the precedent for the remainder of this car ride.

She straddles my lap, going to work on the buttons of my white shirt. My pants are already undone, and thanks to my victory, I'm standing at full salute. Daisy's hands glide up the center of my chest, pushing the shirt from my shoulders in one smooth sweep. Her eyes widen, appreciating what's on show.

"You're so damn hot." She continues her journey, stopping at the tattoo on my side. It sits diagonal across my top rib, just under my pec. It's in honor of my soon-to-be ex-wife.

Dum vita est, spes est

It's Latin for where there is life, there is hope.

She may have sucked the existence from my veins, but I will never give up hope that I will rediscover that vivacity once again.

Running her fingers through my hair, she tugs at the longer strands as payback for my earlier exploits. Swooping forward, she buries her face in my neck, her small teeth biting over my pulse. The sting is phenomenal—a well-balanced combination of pleasure and pain.

When she bites me again, harder this time, I can't help but grin at her cheek. Speaking of cheeks, I snatch up her skirt and slap her on the behind. She yelps, but it's followed with a well-sated moan. "No underwear? You cheeky thing."

"They just get in the way," she pants, rocking gently, making her needs clear. She reaches into her purse and produces a condom. Good to see one of us has come prepared.

Once I'm suited up, I don't see the point in delaying the inevitable, so I lift her, molding her curves to my hands perfectly as I lower her unhurriedly. Her body trembles, anticipating what's to come. It's somewhat empowering to know I can drag this response from her. But it's a two-way street when we connect, and she allows me full rein of her supple flesh.

She clenches, hugging me tight, and I hum low.

"Bloody hell." She sighs, appearing to adopt my native tongue.

"Bloody hell indeed," I concur, gripping her hips and rocking her slowly.

My body certainly likes hers, and although this is purely physical, I can't help but admire everything Daisy has to offer. Her breasts are heavy and full, accented by perfect pink buds. I lower my head, still coaxing her to ride me as I take one of those pearls into my mouth.

She moans, tossing her head back and increasing her tempo. "You're incredible."

"Thank you. You're not too bad yourself." She matches

me stroke for stroke, her sexual prowess a complete turn-on. It's moments such as these when I wonder if maybe I'm being unfair to Daisy. Maybe if I stopped being such a killjoy, things with her might flourish. But deep down, I know that'll never happen.

So for now, I cherish this woman how she deserves.

Daisy is a greedy lover, and she isn't afraid to take what she wants. She arches back, allowing me to control the speed with my hands on her hips. The view is spectacular. Her concaved stomach quivers each time I delve deep inside her. Her breasts sway from side to side, pendulums lulling me into a trance. This sight has all the trademarks an author needs to get the creative juices flowing, but as she continues to bounce up and down, taking everything I give, I'm drifting further away from my words.

The reality is I may never get close to them ever again. It could be that I've had my time in the spotlight, and it's now someone else's time to shine. I growl at the thought, taking my frustrations out on Daisy as I snake my hand through her hair and curl it around my wrist.

Maybe I'm a washed-up writer who's had his heyday, and now it's time I accept my failures and leave with my head held high. I haven't written in over six months. If that isn't a sign, then I don't know what is.

"Jayden?" Daisy breathlessly asks. "Is everything all right?"

"Yes, fine," I lie, concentrating on the task at hand. At least

I haven't lost my mojo when it comes to this.

I thrust my hips, showing no mercy as I drive into her over and over again. She screams in delight, surrendering her body over to me and growing lax in my hands. I started down this road hoping I would unearth some form of inspiration, and yes, it feels sodding amazing, but the only time I felt inspired was when I did something I haven't done in a very long time—I actually spoke to someone, and sex wasn't involved.

Thoughts of Carrie have me wondering what went wrong, and that longing I felt when I first laid eyes on her stirs within. She's been the only woman who provoked me not only physically, but emotionally as well. But now that she's gone, all I'm left with is white noise.

I'm pissed off she left the way she did because what if she was the key to unlocking this mental drought? Her mischievous smile, buoyant laughter, and smashing body ticked all the right boxes, and like an utter twat, I let her go.

Anger courses through me, along with a newfound hunger that has nothing to do with the woman riding my lap. I remember Carrie's strawberry and cream scent and how it lingered. I can almost taste it on my tongue.

As I go on to recall her lips, the length of her smooth neck, and the way her touch left me a salivating fool, I plunge into Daisy harder and harder, unable to stop. Daisy's breathless moans hint that she's close, and suddenly, I am too. But it's not because of the woman who's riding me like a stallion. Instead, it's the woman inside my head, invoking memories far hotter than actually getting laid.

Carrie has left me frustrated and angered, and surprisingly, it's a match made in heaven because as I pound into Daisy and she cries out her release, I am hit with words and sentences, just like on the plane. I have finally found the inspiration I've sought. Yes, it came to me like an epiphany as I was buried inside a warm body, but Daisy had no hand in unmasking my revelation. It was Carrie.

Just her name is enough of a tipping point and sends me over the edge in a loud, hungered growl. Lunging forward, I bite Daisy's neck, imagining I'm surrounded by strawberries and cream instead of vanilla musk.

Daisy falls forward in a heap, pressing her bare breasts to my chest. It feels amazing, but I'm a fucking bastard because it's not her body I want pressed to mine. I'm officially screwed—in every literal sense that there is.

"That was unbelievable," Daisy hums sleepily, snuggling into me.

"Yes, it actually really was." But not for the reason she thinks. I'm still buried inside her, and all I can think about is someone who isn't her.

The world can go to hell...and I'll happily drive the bus.

4
Four

As we arrive at the steel gates and the driver opens his window to speak to the security guard in his tower, I regret that I didn't pack more suits. I had no idea what I was in for, but looking up ahead, I see that the soaring Gothic-style mansion displays nothing but elegance and class. I shouldn't have expected anything less from Axle Bell.

We're granted entry, and as the gates slowly swing open, a sense of dread fills me. I have no idea how I'm going to pull this off. I didn't plan on ending things with Daisy here, but spending ten whole days with her is going to test my acting skills.

As we ascend the steep driveway, I take a moment to appreciate this remarkable property. It's a four-story building with wraparound white balconies so one can venture outdoors during the warmer months and appreciate the views of the water from every angle of the house. Off to the right is what appears to be a boathouse. I wonder if I could sneak off and find a reprieve in there when I'm close to losing my mind.

There are three garage doors, one of which is opened. As I take a closer look, I see a tall man with a sailor's hat packing fishing rods into the lavish boat. When Daisy giggles beside me, I know that man is Axle.

I've never actually sat down with Axle Bell—no one has. I've seen him in passing, but actually coming within ten feet of him or having a conversation are things no one can say they've done. There's no need for him to liaise. The two hundred-plus employees he's hired do that for him.

He looks in great shape—tall, sturdy, and a head full of graying hair. His navy polo reads Ralph Lauren, and I'm sure his khaki slacks and leather boat shoes match the designer tag.

"Daddy just loves to pretend he's the skipper." Her affection for her father cannot be mistaken, which makes this situation even more difficult as I have no doubt the feeling is more than mutual. When he sees the limo pull up, he waves happily.

Daisy hunts through her oversized handbag and produces a compact. She dabs at her neck, covering the small mark left behind by my bite. It's a reminder of what a sodding bastard I truly am.

"Don't worry," she coos. "I like that you branded me." I attempt to smile, but wheeze instead when she fondles my balls. I really hope this isn't a preview of what's to come.

Thankfully, she releases me when Axle strolls over to the door, eager to welcome his little girl home. "Daddy!" she gushes, bouncing from the limo and throwing her arms around him.

"Princess!"

The driver lowers the screen and gives me a knowing look in the rear-view mirror. I almost beg him to take me away. Growing a pair, I run a hand through my hair and let out a deep breath. Time to shine.

Stepping from the car, I lower my shades and wait for the father and daughter reunion to end. It's quite chilly out, but it's nothing compared to London's tumultuous winters.

Once they've embraced, Axle peers at me over Daisy's head. I stand tall and proud, knowing this man doesn't appreciate weakness. "Hello, Mr. Bell. It's a real honor." I extend my hand.

Daisy pulls from his arms and smiles, appearing delighted that we're finally meeting under these circumstances. Axle pulls back his shoulders and glances down at my hand, unimpressed. "Daddy." Daisy nudges him in the ribs, laughing. "He likes to give all my boyfriends a hard time."

The B word kicks me in a B of my own, but I don't allow it to show as this introduction has gone a little pear-shaped. Mercifully, he puts me out of my misery and steps forward, shaking my hand firmly.

You can tell a lot by a person's handshake. If weak and uncommitted, I believe it's a reflection of the person's character. However, if it's strong, firm, and commanding, like Axle's, then I can only imagine what his hands could do if they were wrapped around my neck. Especially if I ever broke his little princess's heart.

"Hello, Jordan."

I peer over my shoulder, wondering if he's addressing someone else. But when I don't see anyone there, I have images of being used as bait.

"Daddy! Stop it!" Daisy seems to be finding this highly amusing while I'm wondering if I'll receive my hand back in one piece. "You know his name is Jayden."

"What kind of a name is that?" he scoffs, letting my hand go.

"Well, you may know me by J.E. Sparrow?" I interject, hoping the name rings a bell and he remembers the vast sum of money I've made for his company over the years.

My plan backfires. "Sparrow? Seems fitting. You have arms like a five-year-old girl."

"Daddy!" Daisy admonishes.

I clear my throat, wondering how I missed the memo that my boss was a complete wanker.

"His arms are fine. Great, in fact." Daisy smirks a smile that will only lead to me leaving this place a eunuch.

Axle glares down his nose at me, and it's instant hatred. I have no doubt he knows I'm shagging his little girl, and I'm not exactly being a gentleman about it. My plan has backfired and coming here has almost definitely cemented my fate.

“I’ll just grab our bags.” Even though our driver has been kind enough to pull them from the trunk, I need an excuse to get far, far away from the Bells in fear I’ll lose a limb if I don’t.

“I don’t suppose you need a caddie?” I half tease to the middle-age man who is unloading three humongous pink suitcases from the trunk. I lend some help, hardly believing Daisy needs this much stuff for ten measly days.

“I could always put in a good word for you with the boss?” he quips with a smile. If only it was that easy.

We finish unpacking the luggage, and I know I can’t avoid Axle or Daisy the entire time we’re here. All I can hope for is a miracle because I have no other choice but to bank on my backup plan. The only problem is, I don’t have a plan b. I was convinced this would work.

“I have your bags, Daisy. You catch up with your dad. I’ll meet you inside,” I call out to her, hoping to buy some time.

She gazes at me as though I’m her knight in shining armor while Axle glares at me like I’m the devil reincarnate. He isn’t going to make this easy for me.

“Okay, pookie bear.” She departs with a wave of her hand, before looping it through her father’s arm. I hold his stare, not intimidated by him because if I want to earn his respect, then I have to be a worthy opponent to play his game. When he leaves, I thankfully have all my parts intact for now.

Once they’ve entered the house, I blow out a trapped breath. “I need a miracle. But a stiff drink will do for now.” The driver laughs; no doubt he's seen many poor suckers in my shoes. I wonder what their outcome was.

He helps me roll the suitcases through the garage. "Be careful of Mr. Bell's Hummer. It's his prized possession."

This obnoxious eyesore is obviously making up for something Axle is lacking in the pants department because this thing is blooming huge. As I attempt to squeeze past the side panel with Daisy's overstuffed suitcase, something gets caught, and I come to a jarring stop. The inertia propels me forward, and to stop myself from face planting, I let go of the suitcase and grab onto the closest solid thing, which is the side mirror.

"That was a close call," I cry out in celebration, but that festivity is short-lived when I hear a smash and the undeniable sound of my balls being laid out to dry. The sound in question is Daisy's dead weight suitcase toppling forward and scratching the living hell out of Axle's car. "Oh, fuck me." I turn, and I suddenly see my funeral played out before me when I hear another crash, followed by something shattering.

"You have to be shitting me." I drop my head back and peer up, flipping off any godly intervention looking down on me. The side mirror which kept me afloat has now just dragged me under as it lies in a broken heap on the garage floor. "It's not that bad." I attempt to convince myself, but when I see the driver's face scrunch up in horror, I know it's not bad—it's fucking cataclysmic.

The entire quarter panel has a zigzagged scratch engraved

into it. And the side mirror? I don't even want to go there. Shrugging, I whistle and sweep my foot outward, brushing the evidence under the tire. "It was like that when we got here," I practice aloud. The driver runs ahead, wanting no part in my imminent demise.

As far as first meetings go, I suppose I'm still standing, but for how long?

The moment we enter the side door, all thoughts of longevity are forgotten because this house is as remarkable on the inside as it is on the outside. With high, ornate ceilings, and pristine white polished floors, I admire the delicate pieces of art adorning the grand foyer, setting the vibe for what's to follow.

I've visited nice homes before, but I can't help but appreciate the elegance this mansion has to offer. I really shouldn't have expected anything less from Axle, considering his social standing, but this place is the Taj Mahal on steroids.

A beautiful woman I presume is a maid runs to my aid, offering to take the bags off my hands. I politely decline her assistance because there's nothing wrong with me. I can carry my own luggage. She wrings her hands in front of her, obviously torn. "Don't worry. I won't tell Mr. Bell." She appears relieved and bows graciously.

I tug at the collar of my shirt. This place would be paradise to my ex-wife, but to me, it's hardly a vacation I can enjoy. It seems unfair this lovely lady can't spend the holidays with her family because she's here serving tea and scones to wankers who drive Hummers.

"Ms. Daisy is with Mr. Bell. I will show you to your room." I nod as I have no doubt this place will be a maze.

She leads the way, passing countless doorways and passageways. It seems a little unnecessary. From what Daisy has told me, it's only her and her brother. I have no idea why this many rooms are necessary, especially since this is their holiday home, and they only use it once in a blue moon.

It shouldn't surprise me, but after growing up in the poverty-stricken streets of Enfield where we didn't have two quid to rub together, I won't ever forget where I came from. All of this can be taken away in a blink of an eye and what will the Bell Family be left with then? A scratched-up Hummer and a loose cannon for a daughter.

We stop at the bottom of the circular staircase and I peer upward, wondering which room is mine. Even though I think the space is unnecessary, I do find the multiple doors a godsend because that means I won't have to share. After the icy reception I received, I'm certain Axle will insist Daisy's and my rooms are miles apart, which suits me just fine.

"What's your name?" I ask as we make our trek up the stairs.

"Sue," she replies, appearing hesitant at first as if divulging her name is against the rules.

"It's nice to meet you, Sue. Have you worked here long?"

"About twenty-five years. I was Ms. Daisy's nanny," she reveals, piquing my interest.

"Oh? So I suppose you know all there is to know about Daisy Bell then?" She doesn't respond, but she doesn't have to. "I know you're most likely sworn to a code of silence, but has she brought many men home for the holidays?"

Our footsteps are the only sound filling the sudden stagnant air. Is she afraid to reveal the truth?

Just when I think this conversation is a one-way street, she replies in a whisper. "No, Mr. Evans. You're the first one."

Bugger.

No wonder Axle wants to castrate me. This is bound to end in tears—my tears, that is.

I follow Sue the rest of the way in silence, attempting to strategize a plan to dig my way out from the mess I've made. When she stops in front of a door, I glance from left to right, wondering which room is Daisy's. She reads my mind.

"Ms. Daisy's room is down the hall."

There are five doors between us. "Excellent. This room is perfect then." I don't care if Sue tells Daisy about my apathy. She'd be doing me a favor.

Opening the door, I stand outside, taking in the complete, over-the-top extravagance. The sizeable bed can fit a small army. It's draped with black and gold silk. There is a walk-in closet, and off to the side, an opened door reveals an en suite. I wonder if there's a hidden kitchen. If so, I'm all set.

When Sue leaves me, I'm almost certain she's headed to unpack Daisy's things as the spoiled princess probably can't do it herself. Strolling into the room, I holler when I see a bottle of whiskey sitting pretty on a long dresser. A crystal glass sits by it, but I reach for the bottle instead.

Uncapping it, I leave my suitcase in the center of the room and look at my surroundings. Once again, no expense is spared. The furniture, linen, fixtures—everything is the best of its kind. Taking a sip from the bottle, I push back the lace curtain with two fingers and peer outside. My view is stunning. My window overlooks the lake and the tennis courts off to the left.

Two row boats are tied to the wooden dock—a means of transportation if I need to escape in the dead of night.

Pinching the bridge of my nose, I mumble, "What am I doing here?"

Taking a long sip of whiskey, I know it'll only take another bottle or two for me to forget the woes of my life. I should have known this trip was going to end badly. Liz calling was just one of many bad omens.

I need to come up with a game plan. I think it's safe to assume Axle wouldn't look twice if he ran me over with his scratched-up car. So I need to find some common ground. Daisy most definitely is off-limits as I have a feeling he'll skin me alive if her name slips past my lips.

Groaning, I fall backward onto the soft mattress, nursing the liquor like it's my new best friend. If this were a story, the writer would be setting up the main character for an abysmal plot twist. Lucky for me, I'm the writer in this story. But I have no idea what to write next.

Each strike of the clock on the bedside table is marching toward my demise. I know I can't hide in here forever. Throwing a forearm over my eyes, I sip my whiskey, my only friend till the end. I decide to down another pint or two before I face the music.

"Quick." I don't have time to hide because she's on me before I can scream bloody murder. "We have five minutes."

"Five minutes for...? Whoa!" I scramble up the bed to get away from Daisy's prying fingers. "What on god's green earth are you doing?" The headboard stops me from fleeing.

She pounces forward, her arse wiggling high in the air. "I think it's fairly obvious."

I smack her hand away from unbuckling my belt. "Stop it. I don't want to give your dad more of a reason to hate me." *And therefore, firing my sorry arse*, I silently add.

Her inner sadist shines as she grins at my troubles. "I promise I'll be quiet."

When she lunges for me once again, I leap off the bed, fending her off with my trusty bottle of whiskey. "We need to set some ground rules."

When she sees I'm indeed serious, she pouts. "You're kidding?"

"No, I'm dead serious." This is genius. Why didn't I think of this sooner? "While we're here, I think it's best we refrain from..." My words die in a garbled mess when she rolls onto her back and begins fondling her chest. "That," I conclude, my eyes growing wide. She pinches over where her perfect nipples lie, partaking in a theatrical moan.

Shaking my head, I refuse to be steered down this shady path that will end in me losing all resolve. "While I'm under this roof, I won't touch you."

Daisy continues her staged cries of passion, uncaring of my rules. "That's fine," she pants. "You can watch me touch myself then." To emphasize her point, she sashays her hands down her torso, landing between her legs.

"Stop that!" I scold. But it's like a train wreck—I'm unable to look away.

I watch with interest as her small hands work their way under her skirt, zeroing in on my weakness from the beginning. If I want to survive this in one piece, I will look away now.

Taking a swig of whiskey, I manage to turn around and denounce my manhood even though my feet feel like they're rooted to the ground. My slander doesn't seem to bother Daisy in the slightest because the sounds coming from her reveal she's completely okay for this to be a one-woman show. This woman has no shame—a quality I once liked about her.

"Oh god, Jayden. I want you."

I gulp down the whiskey, the burn reminding me why I'm doing this. I'm here to save my career, not to get laid. "Well, I want an everlasting bottle of Jack Daniel's, but we can't always get what we want."

"You're just making this hard on yourself…hard being the operative word," she moans while I count to ten.

I need to get out of here. "It appears you have your hands full, so I'll leave you to it."

"Jayden!" Her surprise is clear, but she'd best get used to it.

Just as I'm about to turn the handle, there is a knock on the door. "Ms. Daisy?" Sue's hushed tone reveals she doesn't want Axle to know she caught his baby girl mid masturbation on my bed.

"What do you want, Sue?" Daisy yells, obviously not bothered with discretion.

"Your father is looking for you. Your brother has arrived," she adds. I can hear the hope in her voice that she'll come downstairs, so Sue won't have to report back to Axle what she found. I turn over my shoulder, fearful of what I'll catch a glimpse of.

Daisy's legs are spread, her hands mounted over her sex, and her cheeks a warm rose in color. She appears as if she was on the cusp of something incredible, but now she's come crashing down. With an exasperated huff, she rises, rearranging her clothes so she appears semi composed. "You owe me."

I cock a brow. "Owe you what exactly?"

As she steps toward me, I have an instinctual urge to cup my balls. "Owe me an orgasm. Or two. I'll come collect later."

She leaves me standing with my mouth agape as my warning has fallen on deaf ears. When she lurches forward to kiss me, I recoil two feet back. Daisy is without a doubt going to be the death of me.

She smirks, my rejection having the opposite effect as she now sees me as a challenge, one she wishes to conquer. She yanks open the door, giving poor Sue a heart attack as her ear most likely was pressed to the door.

"Sue, I thought I told you it's not nice to eavesdrop," she reprimands, brushing past her like she is nothing but a nuisance.

"Sorry, Ms. Daisy." Sue bows, only rising when Daisy's annoyed footsteps trample down the stairs.

I gingerly meet Sue's eyes. "She came on her own accord," I explain, holding up my palm in an oath style promise. My words are a double-edged sword however.

Sue shakes her head, not in disappointment, but rather, she appears to feel sorry for me. "She does that a lot," she divulges sympathetically.

"Thanks for the word of warning. I don't suppose there are any rooms with locks on the doors and bars on the windows?" I ask, half teasing.

She laughs but quickly covers her mouth, embarrassed to be caught laughing at her boss's expense. "I've heard the boat house is quite comfortable."

"Thanks. I'll keep that in mind." She leaves me to guzzle down the remainder of my whiskey. The empty bottle is a sign of things to come.

Not bothering to groom my unkempt appearance, I stagger

down the stairs, hoping the eldest Bell child doesn't take after his father. I'm rather unsteady on my feet, and when I hit the polished terrazzo in the grand foyer, I realize I'm a little wasted.

Maybe if I spend my entire time here a little—or a lot—intoxicated, I'll be able to survive this house of horrors. When Daisy's shriek pierces through the halls, I wonder which way will take me to the kitchen so I can snag another bottle of booze.

"I missed you, Tanner!"

"Missed you too, little sis. You breaking any hearts?" he says, tongue in cheek.

"She's breaking something," I mutter aloud.

Putting my game face on, I enter the living room, surprised to see it filled with an abundance of people. I assume the tall guy Daisy is hugging fondly is her brother. He's build like a brick shithouse, and her arms barely fit around his robust frame. The pretty blonde who stands off to the side trying to control four rug rats running amuck must be his wife.

The regal looking lass standing by Axle's side is no doubt his wife as Daisy is her spitting image. I can feel every organ being perforated by Axle's death stares, but I choose to ignore him because something suddenly attaches to my calf. Peering downward, I now see where the phrase ankle biter comes from. One of the screaming kids clings to my leg, hugging it like a deranged koala on crack.

I attempt to shake him off subtly, but his vise-like grip is similar to his aunt's. "Ah, hello, little mate. Think I can have my leg back?"

The little tyke peers up at me, grinning an innocent grin, before he opens his mouth and bites me—hard. "Bloody hell!"

My outburst highlights the fact I'm now shaking my leg as if I'm doing the rumba with this sodding maniac still clinging to my calf.

"Justin, language! We're in the presence of children."

"Daddy! His name is Jayden."

"I am so sorry! Teddy, get off him!"

"My turn! My turn! My turn!"

An uproar of voices filters through the air, overlapping the one before it. As Tanner comes to my rescue, his wife fends off the other three spawns of Satan to keep them from latching onto my remaining limbs, and I see Daisy march over to her father and give him a mouthful.

Axle is being an utter dick, but I keep my cool because it's nice to know I get under his skin. As Daisy lectures him about his manners, no doubt, he glares at me, hating that someone out there can tarnish Daddy's perfection.

"Teddy, come to me." I'd almost forgotten I had a child fixed to my leg as watching my boss squirm was far more enjoyable than I thought it would be.

Tanner has dropped to a squat, coaxing his son off with a stuffed bear. He waves the bear at arm's length, hoping it'll bribe the little critter to let go. The tattered toy is obviously far more tempting than my flesh because he thankfully unlocks his jaw and waddles over to where his father is.

"I'm so sorry," Tanner says, peering up at me with a smile. Unlike his father, he appears genuine and to be a good guy. "He's teething."

I wave off his apologies. "Yes, I felt that," I quip.

Tanner passes the bear to his son before standing and extending his hand. "I'm Tanner, by the way. Daisy's brother."

I'm impressed by his handshake. "Hi, I'm Jayden." I don't wish to elaborate just who I am to Daisy because I want my hand returned in one piece.

Tanner doesn't press, but I can see the faces of everyone in the room wondering what the hell I'm doing here. Being bitten by a toddler seems far less painful than being stuck here with the Bells.

"Hi Jayden, I'm Nora. Nice to meet you." Daisy's mom is first to break the ice as she advances to me. I'm pretty certain Axle's blood pressure just shot through the roof as Nora is more than the hospitable host and kisses both my cheeks.

I lean into the embrace, turning on the charm. "The pleasure is all mine. I can see where Daisy gets her remarkable looks from."

Nora turns a pretty shade of rose pink, before lowering her eyes with a lascivious, wanton smile. Looks like Daisy got something else from her mom.

"Well, seeing as we're doing the rounds, I'm Brooke, Tanner's wife." She steps forward, kids hanging off her, but I manage to shake her hand without losing a finger. "And these little terrors are Victor, Theo, Chandler, and you've met Teddy."

"Yes, I don't think I'll ever forget meeting him," I assure her as my leg begins to throb.

"Don't worry, he's had his shots," Tanner teases, bumping me with his elbow. I almost catapult to the other side of the room.

Everyone erupts into laughter, bar Axle who folds his arms across his chest, appearing angered he was upstaged. Maybe I'll like it here after all.

"We're still waiting on a few people to arrive. How about we have a drink in the den?" suggests Nora, toying with the pearls around her neck while glancing my way. I know that look. Things just got interesting.

Brooke takes her little monsters upstairs, while the rest of us follow Nora into the den. The fireplace is lit, emitting a blanket of warmth through the room. An enormous plasma hangs on the wall, and a leather sectional sofa offers seating for a modest fifteen people. Numerous team jerseys in glass frames decorate the walls.

Axle makes his way over to the bar, tight lipped. I wonder what he's thinking. I bet he's wondering how he can slip cyanide into my whiskey undetected.

Daisy has been surprisingly unclingy. She has been since I failed to mention just who I am to her and why exactly I'm here. But Nora seems to fill her daughter's shoes perfectly. "So you're a writer?" she asks, sauntering over with a glass in her hand.

I accept the offering, raising it to clink my glass with hers. "Yes, I am. Your husband has been quite supportive over the years."

She sips her drink, appearing to weight up what to say. "Don't let the name on the building fool you. I doubt my husband even knows you're one of his authors. He has his minions do all the hard work for him."

Her comment surprises me. "I suppose in his position, he can do whatever he wants."

She scoffs, peering over at Axle with nothing but contempt. "You can say that again."

It's blatantly obvious that the spark fizzled from Nora and Axle's marriage long ago. This just confirms my original thinking that Axle is a twat because Nora is beautiful. I know looks aren't everything, but from what I can tell, she seems relatively normal and down to earth.

"I've read all your books. After Daisy told me who you were, I was intrigued." She skims her red painted fingernail along the rim of the glass while tonguing her top lip. "You didn't disappoint."

She is brazenly flirting with me, and the slits Axle's eyes have shaped into are a sure sign he knows it too. "Thank you. I'm pleased you enjoyed them."

"Are you working on anything new?"

I try not to cringe as I gulp down my scotch. "Yes, I am. I'm hoping to be done by summer." That's wishful thinking.

"Well, I can't wait to read it. Your leading men are so"—she places her hand to her chest—"swoon worthy. I can't help but wonder if they're based on you." She winks over the rim of her glass.

I'm flattered, but I'm also a little concerned for my well-being because if she continues to flirt, I'll be leaving here in a wooden box. "Well, they do say the first rule of writing is to write what you know," I reply, hoping my lightheartedness will reveal I'm not interested in a holiday fling.

"Well, you know your art well," she purrs, not at all deterred.

"What are you two whispering about?" Daisy asks, and I've never been happier to see her.

"Just about what a great author Jayden is, honey," Nora replies without pause.

Daisy snuggles into my side as if marking her territory. "Yes, he is. I'm sure I've given him enough inspiration to finish this new next book in record time." If only she knew the half of it.

I simply smile and gulp down my drink.

"When are we eating? I'm starving," Tanner says, walking over to our circle carrying a beer.

"We're still waiting on everyone to arrive," Nora says with a small laugh. "And besides, I don't think you'll be starving to death anytime soon." She steps up on tippy toes to kiss his cheek.

Daisy rolls her eyes while Tanner pretends to fend off her affections, but it's clear he loves his mom. "Do you play ball?" he asks me.

The jerseys on the walls reveal that this family loves to play. Maybe this is my chance to impress Axle. I may be a writer stuck indoors most days, but I pride myself on my physical prowess. "Yes."

Axle finally graces us with his presence, but of course, it's only to mock me. "I highly doubt you can keep up with us," he boasts, practically beating on his chest like a gorilla in the wild.

Daisy huddles into me, blowing out a small, frustrated grunt. This egomaniac act is really growing old, just like Axle. He's in good shape, but if he thinks he can beat me, he's got another thing coming. I've always been an overachiever, and now is no exception. "Challenge accepted."

Tanner hollers in excitement, enjoying the friendly competition, but I know blood will be spilled. Axle grins, limbering up as he stretches his arms in front of him. "Very well then. Let's make things interesting. How about a wager?"

"Daddy," Daisy scolds, shaking her head in warning. "It's freezing out. Hardly suitable weather to play football." But her cautioning goes unheard.

"Sounds like my kind of game." My confidence isn't an act. I'm determined to whip Axle's arse.

He grins smugly because in his head, he's already won. "If I win…" He peers over at Daisy who is clutching onto me tightly.

"My daughter is off-limits."

"What? That's ridiculous!" she protests in horror while I'm suddenly beginning to come to terms with my future loss.

This is a win-win. If I lose, Axle feels like a big man with the bigger cock, but his ante is my get out of jail for free card. This is the out I needed. I stroke his already enormous ego, *and* I'm Daisy free. Where do I sign up?

But I simulate confliction and hold off on my victory dance for now. "And if I win?"

Axle appears humored, as if that prospect is too ridiculous to fathom. But he indulges me nonetheless. "If you win…I'll triple your current advance and sign your next three books."

Now that changes everything.

If I win, I can go home and forget this charade ever took place. But by winning, that will make Axle the loser, something he doesn't like being.

My career is pretty much saved thanks to Axle's arrogance, but by saving myself, I have to step into the lion's den and deal with the repercussions. I know without a doubt that Axle will make my life hell if I upstage him, and he's declared the loser. But if I lose, I may gain his respect for playing with the big boys.

Respect usually equates to some form of peace treaty, but pretending to lose would make me a cheater. I think I've done enough of that lately.

Observing Axle's arrogance, I know there is only one answer—I'm going to wallop his smug arse.

"You have yourself a deal, Mr. Bell." I offer my hand, and he shakes it without appearing to want to reach for the hand sanitizer once we're done.

A macho energy palpitates in the air, and I almost suffocate on the old man testosterone Axle is emitting. I sneak a peek at Nora, who raises her glass with a nod. She's celebrating my courage. Or maybe she's toasting me luck.

"Jayden, what are you doing?" Daisy whispers frantically into my ear. "Daddy doesn't like to lose."

Unable to mask my smirk, I reply, "Well, neither do I." Her mouth pops open because she knows what this means.

Not giving her a chance to chew off my ear about my decision, I head upstairs to change into something a little more appropriate. As I'm rummaging through my bag, my cell chimes, and I know it can only be one person. His scheming radar has probably short-circuited.

Nick: How's Daddy?

Me: Daddy is a wanker. He's also a presumptuous twat.

It takes Nick roughly three seconds to reply.

Nick: He's also our gold mine. And you're also screwing his baby girl whom you don't even like. Do you hate me?

I can't help but chuckle at his melodramatics.

Me: That's debatable. I think I'm neutral.

As I change into black sweats and a University of Washington T-shirt, I know that whatever happens today will change everything. I came here to show Axle that I can be a great guy...on most days, but it seems he called bullshit within seconds of meeting me. Maybe the saying rings true—don't bullshit a bullshit artist.

He doesn't care if I'm a great guy or not because *he* isn't one. If I were a manipulative egomaniac with a god complex and exchanged strategies on taking over the world with him, then I would be his people because misery loves company.

Nick: Jayden, whatever you're thinking, stop it right now.

Me: Sorry, mate, can't talk. Have a decrepit old fart to beat. This could have been avoided, but idle hands...

My cell chimes twice, but I ignore it. Tying my laces, I can't wait to show Axle Bell just who I really am.

5
Five

"Got it?"

I only just refrain from rolling my eyes when Axle explains the rules to me a second time as though I'm some imbecile.

Eight of us are playing. The neighbor and his two teenage sons chose the wrong time to deliver their Christmas gift as no one says no to Axle Bell. Nora's brother and his twentysomething son also got roped into playing. They didn't even have a chance to unload their Mercedes before Axle was dragging them out to the yard.

On my team is the neighbor Ron and his two sons, Hamish and Thomas. They look to be in great shape, but compared to our opposition, we may as well throw in the towel now. Axle's brother-in-law, Damien, and his son, Trevor, look like they were warriors in their former life.

Daisy sits on the sidelines with her eyes hidden behind enormous shades, but I can feel the daggers from here. I technically don't have to play nice with her—I don't have to play with her at all. Once I win this ridiculous wager, I'm on the next plane out of here, bidding sayonara to the Bells for good.

I'll deal with the repercussions once I return to Seattle because now, I have a game to win.

"Right, remember what I told you?" I say to my fellow huddled team members. They all nod, but I don't feel confident.

We break apart from our circle, and my gaze drifts to Axle who is revving up Tanner. They're doing some ludicrous war dance and bumping chests like two blooming buffoons. To all other players, this is just a friendly game, but as Axle narrows his eyes and challenges me with a lopsided smirk, I know this is war.

We take our positions on our makeshift playing field, bending low as the football is placed between us. I insisted on being quarterback. Not because I'm interested in being the big man on campus, but because I have every intention of running circles around Axle.

"This is your last chance to back out," he goads while I grin smugly.

"I hope you have a pen handy because my agent is emailing over the contracts as we speak." Tanner finds our bickering hilarious, not realizing how serious I am about winning.

"All right, boys, let's keep it clean," he says, slapping his dad on the back playfully. But that word doesn't exist in our vocabulary.

Axle's team won the toss, but with my eyes on the prize, I bend low, waiting for the call. Tanner is star quarterback, and I wonder if those jerseys in the den are his. Taking a deep breath, I put all thoughts out of mind and focus.

"Hut, hut, hike!"

The moment those words leave Tanner's lips, both Axle and I are suddenly possessed. We spring forward, appearing to both be on the same page as we charge for the other. The ball is Axle's head, and all I can think about is taking him down.

We collide into one another at full force, not holding back an iota. If I didn't think he could take it, I would have gone easy on him, but built like a brick shithouse, the old bastard gives as good as he gets. But I give better and almost holler in delight when Axle topples onto his arse.

"It seems my arms aren't like a five-year-old little girl after all," I call out with a winner's grin as I leap over Axle's crumpled form and chase after Tanner who has the ball. I'm too late, and he scores, but I've already won.

Damien offers Axle a hand, but he swats it away, his ego bruised enough. He stands, wiping the dirt from his now ruined pants. I jog over to my team who look at me like I've gone mad. Their uneasiness only fuels my need for annihilation.

We stand in formation, and Axle glares at me, his pride

clearly wounded. My response is a grin, which only adds salt to the wounds.

When it's kickoff time once again, Axle doesn't even wait for the official word before he tears toward me, a war cry piercing the air. He catches me off guard and smashes into me. I lose my balance, but if I'm going down, so is he. I latch onto his arms, and we both tumble to the ground with a solid thud.

I'm winded, but Axle wheezing beside me is music to my ears. "I'm sorry," I pant, clutching my side. "I didn't see you."

"Give up now and save yourself the embarrassment." He knows he can't beat me physically, so he's trying to intimidate me instead. I'm sure this tactic has worked in the past, but to me, it only highlights the fact I've won.

"I think you'd best take your own advice," I rebuke, standing to catch my breath.

"That was a hard hit. Are you okay?" Tanner asks us both. He knows better than to help his dad. "Did they swap your blood pressure pills with crack? The ball wasn't even in play."

Axle stands, and there's no doubt I've knocked the wind from his sails. But he pulls back his shoulders stubbornly. "You call that hard? I barely felt it. You have to try harder, Jordan, if you want to take me down."

"I was just warming up, old chap," I quip, which infuriates Axle further.

For the next twenty minutes, the same pattern follows. The moment the ball is in play, both Axle and I run toward the other like two rabid dogs. And the outcome is the same—Axle falling to his arse while I edge closer and closer to the victory line.

I'll give the old man credit; he's a stubborn son of a bitch. But with each hit, it's getting easier to bring him down.

"Let's take a five-minute breather," Tanner declares, helping Axle up, who surprisingly accepts the assistance this time.

He's unsteady on his feet but quickly regains his balance. His pride won't allow him to show weakness. He wears the dirt and grass stains with pride as he limps off to no doubt lick his wounds.

I slap my teammates on the back. We're leading. I have no idea how, but I'm not questioning it. From where I stand, he's bound to throw in the towel after a few more hits. Either that or he'll be leaving this field on a stretcher.

I'm quite parched—victory does that—so I decide to head inside and grab a beer. However, when Daisy comes stampeding over, I know I'll need a whiskey instead. "What are you doing?" she hisses, latching onto my bicep with her icy cold fingers to stop me from walking away.

"Playing football," I reply without pause.

"You know what I'm talking about."

"No, I really don't. Now, if you'd be so kind to release me, Jack Daniel's is calling my name."

"This isn't funny, Jayden," she exclaims. "Daddy doesn't like to lose."

"I never thought it was. I thought your father would

appreciate a little friendly competition. Not to mention the fact if I lose"—I lean in close, causing her to suck in a tiny breath—"we can't finish what we started." Not that, that is going to happen anyway, but I'm trying to get her to let me go.

It works.

"If you think I'd abide by my father's stupid rules, then you don't know me at all." She closes in on me, like a predator hunting its prey. She circles me, and I comply, turning with her. With her back facing the crowd, she makes her intentions clear in seconds. "Besides"—she cups my junk, and I inhale sharply—"sneaking around is half the fun."

She doesn't care that her family and friends are feet away. All she cares about is leaving me with a severe case of blue balls. I should relish her touch because after I win, I plan on telling her that my time here is done.

Using that as my driving force, I go limp, figuratively speaking, and allow her full rein. She pulls her red-stained lip between her teeth, my surrender turning her on. I shouldn't be enjoying this for so many reasons, but the fact Axle's daughter is giving me a discreet hand job only yards away from him does surprising things to a man's libido.

"I want to blow you," she whispers, giggling when I groan low.

"Right here?" I fake horror.

She nods, increasing her strokes.

"What if Daddy saw?" I mock, hissing when she unzips my fly.

"I can be very sly when I want to be."

"You cheeky little fox." I never break eye contact with her, hoping that to onlookers it appears like we're merely talking.

As she palms my swollen shaft, I'm certain I have everyone fooled; everyone, that is, except Axle. As I'm marching toward another victory, I feel an invisible punch to the solar plexus. Looking to my left, I see Axle glaring at me, his cheeks a bright red. If I didn't know any better, I'd say he was on the brink of having a heart attack.

"Love…" I subtly coax Daisy's hand out from my pants. She frowns irritably. "You obviously aren't sly enough."

She raises a brow, confused, so I gesture with my head toward Axle's direction. When she turns over her shoulder, she gives a surprised squeak but doesn't appear embarrassed. "Oops."

"Caught red-handed," I state, unable to keep the humor from my tone.

She stands on tippy toes and kisses my cheek, taking another ten years off her father's life. If I didn't know any better, I'd say she was enjoying every minute of this. Once I think I can turn around without poking someone's eye out, I make a beeline for Axle. Nora's standing beside him, sipping her wine. When she sees me mosey over, a smirk tugs at her lips. "Sorry to keep you waiting. Your daughter is a real handful."

Nora drowns her laughter in her glass as she throws back the contents, and the corded veins in Axle's neck pulsate in rage.

"Let's play ball." I ignore the fact I just confirmed what they both know to be true and meet my fellow teammates in the middle of the yard.

"You have a death wish," Ron says with a smile. He does appear happy that someone is upstaging Axle, though. I bet he hasn't seen that before.

"I'm still standing," I reply with an arrogant shrug. "Keep up the good work, lads." I slap them on the back before we take our positions.

Axle is looking a little worse for wear, and I can't help but chuckle at the sight. He brought this on himself. If he wasn't such a bloody jerk, we could have been civil and broken bread. But he chose to judge me before even getting to know me.

My conscience reminds me that I came here with a not so innocent pretense myself. I may have been open to getting to know Axle, but that was for my personal gain. But I tell my guilty conscience to take a hike because I have a game to win.

Squatting low and getting into position, I never take my eyes off Axle. He knows it's do or die. As I'm waiting for Tanner to retrieve the ball from his wife who is holding it hostage, I notice movement from the corner of my eye. I ignore it, however, as I don't have time for distractions.

Tanner finally pries the ball from her, but not before she

steals a kiss. He kisses her back with as much passion, and there is no doubting their love for one another. It leaves me slightly nostalgic as I can barely remember what that feels like. Hence, why I'm here.

But that's sure to end. Now that I have the assurance that my next three books have found a home, I can stop beating myself up and just write. It takes the pressure off. But that niggling feeling returns because that was never the issue. I want to write, but I can't…that is, until today when I met someone who got my creative juices flowing.

"Carrie!"

Whoa, what?

Before I can question my sanity, Tanner runs over and places the ball between us. But suddenly, playing is the last thing on my mind because I'm kicked in the guts and left with a heavy, disconcerting feeling. I get an awful sense of déjà vu. I scan the grounds and see a woman walk toward Nora, her face obscured behind dark sunglasses. She bypasses Daisy, who jumps from her lounge, stomping after her while moving her mouth a hundred miles a minute.

The girl ignores her, a smirk tugging at her lips. My dick instantly stirs, and it's a feeling I experienced hours ago. Not with the air hostess, but with the girl who has barely left my mind since she left me standing alone like a complete chump.

"Hut, hut, hike!"

I've heard the call, but I'm frozen to the spot. "No," I mutter under my breath when she removes her sunglasses and gives Nora a familiar hug. "No *fucking* way."

But when she slips off her beanie and shakes out her hair, I know I'm not seeing things. My mind has not conjured her up because here stands a woman who I knew would lead to trouble all along, but I never knew just how much fuCking trouble she would bring.

When she meets my eyes, her pretty mouth falls open, but it's quickly covered with a whip of her hand when she covers it, and screams, "Watch out!"

That's not exactly the reaction I was expecting, especially since she left me without an explanation of why she ran off like I was the Antichrist.

I have no idea what she's warning me about and am certain this lass has lost her mind, that is, until I'm hit with a ton of bricks and face plant into the ground.

❤ ❤ ❤

I wake with the world's worst hangover.

Groaning, I attempt to piece together what I remember. With my head pounding the way it is, it must have been some night. However, as I pry open one eye, I see that it is daytime, and that I'm in a room which looks familiar, but I can't remember why.

"Oh, thank god. I thought you were dead."

Those words partnered with that voice leave me wheezing, and memories of why I'm here and how I got here collide into me. I know this nasty throbbing in my head has nothing to do with whiskey, but everything to do with Carrie.

As I piece together the fragments of what I can recall, I suddenly wish I couldn't remember anything at all. I also wish I didn't remember the reason Axle knocked me out cold. Peering to my left, I see the reason sitting by my bedside, wringing out a white washcloth into a ceramic bowl.

When I think I can move without throwing up, I rise slowly, propping myself up against the headboard. The silence speaks volumes as we're waiting for the other to talk. I can barely look at her, so the odds of actually having a conversation with her are slim.

Why is she here? Did she follow me? As flattering as that concept is, I know that the tender hug she shared with Nora reveals she knows the Bells well. Clearing my throat, I decide to find out what the hell is going on.

"So…" Manning up, I turn to look at her. But when I do, I wish I was still passed out. If possible, she's far prettier than I remember. My mind has done a poor job cataloging the depth of her hazel eyes, the fullness of her pink lips, and the sweetness of her strawberries and cream scent. But pushing that aside, I attempt to get to the bottom of why she's here.

"So…you're here to apologize for running off like a deranged lunatic?" I decide to put forth every reason she's sitting in my room until I get some answers.

She scoffs and rolls her eyes. I guess I can cross that reason off my list then.

"Don't flatter yourself," she says with bite. I wait for her to fill in the blanks, but she simply places the cool cloth to my forehead.

Why is she tending to me? This situation gets far more complicated by the second.

"Carrie…" I pause, arching a suspicious brow. "If that even is your name. What are you doing here?"

She appears to weigh up what to say next, which makes me a touch nervous. "You got me." She raises her hands in mock surrender, waving the cloth as her peace flag. I have no idea what she's talking about. She sheds light a second later. "My name is Svetlana, and I'm here to harvest your organs. Although, after the airhead blonde you screwed on the plane, I may have to rethink my decision. I'm pretty sure you're a poster child for chlamydia now." She shivers in repulsion.

Unable to contain my laughter, I chuckle even though she just insulted me. "I'll have you know I didn't screw her." She appears relieved until I reveal, "I merely went down on her."

She screams and throws the washcloth into my lap. "Yuck! You're disgusting."

"You owe me an apology for insulting my character," I say, tongue in cheek.

"I owe you nothing," she replies playfully. "I nursed you back to health. We're even. Now if you'll excuse me, I need to take a bath…in bleach."

My hand shoots out when she goes to stand. She looks down at where my fingers have latched onto her wrist. “I don’t have cooties,” I state very seriously while she bursts into laughter. I let her go, thankful she sits back down.

Now that the ice is broken, I decide to ask her once again. “Carrie, what are you doing here?” I love the way her name rolls off my tongue. I could think of at least five other things I wish for my tongue to be doing to her right now when she leans in, gesturing I’m to come closer so she can share her secrets with me.

When I’m close enough, she cups her hand to my ear. “I’m pretty sure you’re my sister’s Mr. Dreamy.” She doesn’t hold back on the sarcasm while I choke on air.

“What?” I manage to get out as I thump my chest to kick-start my heart. “Daisy is your…*sister*?”

“Sadly, yes.”

When she confirms my nightmare as being true, I pull back, horrified. “You’re joking.”

“Nope, I wish I was. I’ve been tested, twice.”

“This is…how can this be?” I’m finding it hard to breathe. I tug at the collar on my T-shirt, hoping I don’t pass out from lack of O2.

She bites back a smile. “Well…when a man and a woman like one another, or in some cases, they don’t even have to like each other, they…”

“All right, stop right there.” I wave both hands out in front of me, not interested in having an anatomy lesson of Axle and Nora bumping uglies. "I just…Daisy never mentioned you."

Carrie shrugs and leans back in her chair. "No surprise there. There is no love lost between my sister and me, and if I died a suspicious death, let's just say I'm pretty sure she'd be hiding the cyanide."

How is this possible? What are the odds? Slim to none. But it appears I'm up shit creek without a paddle.

"So…now it's my turn." She appears thoroughly entertained by the clusterfuck that is my life. "What happens if Jasmine finds out you're here? If what you tell me is true, her stalking skills are probably buying a red-eye to Connecticut as we speak." She cocks a brow, waiting for me to reply.

Choo choo. I can hear it. The karma train is stopping at all stations.

"I…um…er." I know she doesn't give a rat's arse about Daisy, but I'm suddenly embarrassed to tell her the truth.

Rubbing the back of my neck, I think on my feet, needing more time. "Why did you run off on me?"

"Why are you being so evasive?"

"Why are you?"

"Why are you answering a question with a question?"

"Why are you asking so many questions?" This conversational ping pong flows so naturally, I can't help but laugh. "By the way, you never mentioned your dad was a complete and utter twat."

"I'm pretty sure I did." She taps her chin, meditatively. "Now stop avoiding the question."

I owe her the truth. "Okay, I'll make you a deal. On the count of three, we both answer one another's question. Deal?"

She ponders my suggestion, making me squirm as she moves those plump lips from side to side. "Deal," she finally says, putting me out of my misery.

"One..." The pause is excruciatingly long, but I'm trying my hardest to prolong the truth. "Two..."

Carrie taps her fingers against her cheek, huffing impatiently while I grin at her adorability. "And three," she finishes for me, her impatience getting the better of her.

This is it. With nothing left to lose, I confess, "Daisy is Jasmine," while she purges at the same time.

"Because all authors are obnoxious, arrogant asshats with a god complex."

"Wow," we proclaim in union as both our expressions mirror the other.

I fold my arms across my chest. "You judged me based on my occupation? I'm highly offended."

She shrugs with a devious grin. "I was right, wasn't I?"

Touché.

We're at an impasse. She's right for the most part, but I thought we shared something. She's the first woman I've actually wanted to be around in a long time, but it appears she wants nothing to do with me based on a stigma associated with my profession.

"So Daisy is your stalker. No surprise there." She shakes her head in sympathy. "I feel sorry for you. The last guy she was this hung up on…it didn't end pretty."

I gulp.

"Why did you agree to come?" she asks, piecing it all together. "It's fairly obviously you don't particularly like her. So why did you agree to spend the holidays with her?"

Nothing slips past her.

Her large eyes sparkle in inquiry, waiting for me to shed some light on this extremely fucked-up situation.

My head is now throbbing for a different reason. Unable to sit still for a moment longer, I kick my legs and stand, thankful I'm not arse over tit. Stretching overhead, I feel an ache in my ribs. I'll be sore tomorrow.

When a strangled hum fills the air, I pause and listen closer because I have no idea where the noise is coming from. At first, I think Daisy is spying on us through a crack in the door, but when the sound is clearly coming from inside the room, I look at the only person who's in here with me.

I blink twice to ensure I'm not seeing things, but it's clear as day—Carrie is tugging at her bottom lip while her gaze rakes up and down my frame. The hungered noises are coming from her. Her confidence has simmered, and in its place is an innocence that has my inner alpha beating his chest in pride. There is no mistaking that sound—Carrie likes what she sees, and what she sees is me.

Although my profession repulses her, my body obviously doesn't.

I clear my throat melodramatically, wanting her to know that I'm aware of her watching me as closely as I'm watching her. The sound snaps her into the now. Her cheeks blister, but the sweet pink has everything below the belt piquing in interest. "Thank you for tending to my wounds."

"I-it's fine," she says with a tiny falter.

"Not that I'm ungrateful, but why did you? I would think Daisy would be first in line to tend to my unconscious form. I can't say no, you see."

Carrie remains seated, toying with the edges of the washcloth. "I offered to help. She's downstairs talking to our father. That hit was intentional. What did you do to piss him off?"

Blowing out an exasperated breath, I know she won't let up until I tell her the truth. Walking over to the window, I look outside and see that the battlefield has calmed. The still waters are untouched by any holidaymakers. A few water birds are all that are game enough to invade Axle's private oasis.

"I'm here because ever since I caught my wife shagging someone other than me, I haven't been able to write a single word…that is, until I met you."

Carrie's silence reveals I've caught her off guard. I don't see the point in sugarcoating anything as she'd just call bullshit anyway.

"Your father can ruin me," I continue, still peering out the window. "I came here with the grand plan of having him see what a great guy I am. But it's backfired, and I'm pretty sure he wants me dead." Carrie giggles, and the sound is too perfect for words. "The only good thing about being knocked out cold is that I lost our bet. I now have to stay away from Daisy, which suits me just fine as I'm seconds away from maiming myself if I hear her call me pookie bear one more time.

"The bad thing is I now have to convince your dad not to drop me from his publishing house because if I won, he was going to sign my next three books, which really took the pressure off. But now, I'm screwed."

"Let me get this right." She finally speaks after digesting everything I've just said. "You came here because you're seconds away from dumping my sister, who you aren't really dating, but you know if you do that, she'll run to our father, and in turn, he'll most likely ruin your career. You wanted to try to sweet-talk him into liking you, but that's completely turned to shit. You're now stuck with writer's block, a boss who hates you, and a woman who has already named your unborn children." She blows out a breath once she's done.

I turn to face her with a smile. "Yes, that pretty much sums up my life."

She pulls in her lips and shakes her head. "You're right. You're screwed."

All I can do in this situation is laugh. It's either that or I change my name and move to another country. "I was crazy to think this would work. I should just dump Daisy and get used to frozen burritos. I have no idea why I thought I could talk my way out of this. I can't even construct a coherent sentence, and that's my job."

I hate to sound desperate, but it's the god's honest truth. There is no way I can carry on with this charade with Daisy a moment longer. But if I leave now, I have no doubt Axle will sever all ties with Nick and me. I suppose I could always pitch to another publishing house, but seeing as I have no new material to show them, I don't see that working. There are whispers among the houses that I've had my five seconds of fame. I wish my name alone would sell my books, but the market's changed—it's now a competitive, saturated jungle out there.

"Your silence is making me nervous," I tease, waiting for her to speak.

Her lips tug at the corners as she stands. I've forgotten how lithe she is. "I've got a plan."

I don't hide my surprise. "A plan? Does it involve fireworks, clowns, or decaffeinated coffee?"

She scrunches up her nose, confused. "No?" She replies as a question, unsure if that's the correct answer.

"Okay, I'm in." Her laughter brings me hope, and I pray this plan of hers works. No one knows family better than their own family. "So what's this grand scheme of yours?"

She shakes her head. "All in good time. I need to make a few calls."

That sounded so out of left field, and I love it. "Well, you know where to find me. If you can't find me, however, odds are I'm tied to your sister's bed with broken kneecaps."

She bursts out laughing. "It serves you right for hooking up with my sister." She shudders in disgust.

"In my defense"—I hold up my finger while stepping toward her—"I didn't know she was completely bonkers until *after* she turned up on my doorstep sporting nothing but a bull's-eye painted on her..."

"Ugh! Enough!" Carrie shrieks, covering her ears and singing loudly. She's just too adorable.

Putting her out of her misery, I walk toward her and uncover her ears. The moment we make contact, the burn has me growling low, and an adrenaline punch shoots straight through my body, ending in my pants.

I swallow deeply, caught off guard, but I release her, not making a big deal over something that can never happen. She's sworn off men, especially men like me. Not to mention the fact I'm plotting with her to break things off with her sister, who I'm not even really dating. If that isn't an episode for *Jerry Springer*, then I don't know what it is.

Her cheeks glimmer in that delicate pink, leaving me wetting my lips. "I'm going to hit the shower. Thanks for saving my arse."

She nods quickly, averting her eyes.

Her confidence has diminished, leaving a vulnerability in its wake that suits her as much as her confidence. There are many sides to Carrie Bell, and so far, I've liked each one far more than I should. And it's because I do that I leave her standing in my room, untouched and alone.

6

Six

After a cold shower and jacking off twice, I feel somewhat better. There is no question who the inspiration for my in-shower action was.

From the get-go, Carrie fascinated me. But I'm surprised I find myself attracted to more than just her looks; it's her personality too. I find myself admiring things like the way her nose crinkles when she laughs, or the graceful pink she turns when she lets down her guard. No man should be noticing these things about someone they've just met, and most men would never even acknowledge such trivial things, but I'm a writer. I've come to appreciate true beauty, and Carrie is the epitome of the word.

If I was a believer in fate and all that philosophical shite, I could say that our meeting was pre-destined in the stars. But since she busted me post-coitus and caught me in a lie involving her sister, I have no idea what exactly we're predestined for.

The whole idea has me thinking about destiny and just how it did on the plane, I'm hit with the urge to write. Not questioning it, I make a mad dash for my laptop on the edge of the bed. I turned it on earlier to check the football scores, but now my fingers can barely keep up as I type frantically.

`This wasn't supposed to happen. I had given up, or so I thought.`

I stare at the single sentence, the flashing cursor taunting me to type more. I'm not one to back down from a challenge, so for the next hour, I type. There is no method to my madness, but when I pull away to rub my tired eyes, I don't have that sense of desperation nipping at my heels.

With the words I wrote earlier and now this new addition, I have over two thousand useable words. I still have no idea of the middle and ending, but I have a beginning, and that's better than having nothing at all.

As I'm reading over my work, I'm left vulnerable and exposed and don't hear the door close until it's too late. A warm body settles behind me, scaring the living shite out of me. Before I have a chance to move, a pair of arms wind around my chest.

At first, I believe it's Daisy because I know how much she loves to break the rules, but as I take a closer look, I almost rocket off the bed when I see red fingernails clawing down my bare chest.

"What the bloody hell!" I exclaim, turning over my shoulder to see a smirking Nora on her knees. Her hair is down and wild, and her eyes are hungry. I know this look far too well.

"Hello," she purrs while raking her nails farther down my body.

I suddenly feel violated. "Nora." I latch onto her wrists to stop her from venturing any farther. "What are you doing?"

The unmistakable sweetness to her breath reveals she's had one too many glasses of wine and is clearly not thinking straight. "What does it look like?" she replies, leaning forward and nibbling my earlobe.

"Whoa! Time-out!" I carefully pry her hands off me and launch off the bed as though it's on fire. "Your husband's room is down the hall. How about I show you to it?" I suggest, giving her the benefit of the doubt.

She pouts and shakes her head. "I know where his room is, but it's not where I want to be. I want to be right here with you." My eyes drop to her chest as she begins to unfasten the buttons on her silk dress. "I saw the way you were looking at me."

I curse my cock. The infernal thing needs to have a restraining order placed against it where all women are concerned. Backing up, I raise my hands in surrender. "Please stop, Nora. This is so, *so* wrong." However, my words fall on deaf ears when she unfastens three buttons and peels the dress over her slender shoulders.

The dark, fragile lace complements the milky suppleness of

her skin. Her breasts are full, her pink nipples ripe and hungry. "Like what you see?" She palms herself, showing me she is more than a handful.

"Yes, you're lovely. But that's not the point," I quickly correct. I need to look away, but when she reaches around and unhooks her bra, I'm glued to the buoyancy of her soft breasts, and the manner in which they fall from their lace confines.

My dick is telling me to stop being such a pussy and give in. But a voice I thought long buried between D cups and XXX waxes screams at me that this lady, this hot woman currently tweaking her nipples and moaning my name in delight, is Carrie's mom. The same Carrie who has been nothing but kind to me and inspired me with her honesty and spirit.

I grit my teeth when she glides the hem of her dress up her thighs, exposing her bare, honeyed center. "Nora, I just, please stop. That." I point at her bottom half, finally lifting my eyes from the erotic but equally dangerous sight and look at nothing but her eyes.

"Why? We're two consenting adults."

"What about Axle? And Daisy?" I attempt to play the family card, hoping she sees reason.

She curls her lip at the mere mention of Axle's name. "What about him? His dick is merely for decoration purposes. He wouldn't know what to do with it, unlike you. I've read your books. I know how you like it." She unfastens the last few buttons and strips bare.

Holy shite. Her body is fan-fucking-tastic.

She is an undoubtedly magnificent sight, but regardless, I take control and stop things before they get out of hand. "My characters aren't me." A mistake many readers make. Authors may or may not write from personal experience. In most circumstances, we're just a vessel for whatever stories are rattling around in our heads. Some may be based on reality, but in most cases, it's fiction—that's what makes it a story and not an autobiography. "I'm truly flattered that a smashing, hot woman like you wants to offer yourself to me in that way, but I can't. For so many reasons, I just can't." At the forefront is Carrie's magical laugh and smile.

Nora frowns, her fire beginning to simmer down. "W-why not? You don't find me attractive?" Her insecurity is clear when she quickly wraps an arm around her chest.

"Are you kidding me?" I scoff. "You're beautiful. If your husband doesn't worship you daily, then he's more of an idiot than I thought he was."

She snuffles out a laugh. "When you've been married for as long as we have, you tend to forget the other person exists."

Still semi concealed, I take a step forward as I think I'm safe from being molested. "You're a stunning woman, Nora." Her cheeks tint pink, reminding me so much of Carrie. "Maybe Axle needs reminding."

"I wouldn't even know where to start," she gushes, brushing back her hair embarrassed.

"Well, what you did there"—I circle my finger toward the bed—"is a good start." She giggles; the fire has thankfully burned out.

"I'm so sorry, Jayden. Can you ever forgive me? I'm so embarrassed."

"Don't be. There's nothing to forgive." Who am I to deny this plea when her quim is still exposed to me? "What's a little nudity between friends?" I wave it off, but I really wish she'd put on some clothes. I'm a gentleman, but I'm not a sodding saint.

She seems relieved, but I can sense something else is playing on her mind. "Do you think we could keep this between us?"

"Of course. Let's never mention it again."

She brushes the hair behind her ears before carefully stepping down from my bed. I back up, afraid she's changed her mind because if she rubs those outstanding breasts against me again, I won't be held accountable for my actions.

"Thank you, Jayden. Best I stick to water from now on." Before I can speak, she steps forward and hugs me. I'm like a rigid lamppost, too afraid to move in the wrong direction because she's still very nude.

"It's all right. No worries." She clings to me, nestling her nose into my chest and inhaling deeply.

I spread my arms out wide, and if this were charades, one couldn't be blamed for guessing I was re-enacting a tree, but this is a safe zone, and I don't care how ridiculous I look. I have no chance of rubbing, touching, or bumping into anything that

I shouldn't. I've already seen enough.

"Ah, Nora?"

"Yes," she mumbles happily against me.

"You're kind of very naked."

"Oh, my god!" she yelps, mortified. She releases me and quickly hunts for her clothes. I do the same and slip into a shirt with many buttons just in case she gets any ideas.

When she fastens her bra and rearranges her copious breasts, my dick has had enough of this saintly act and demands we take the high road to hell.

Quashing down the urge to act how I've acted in the past, I spit out, "I'll leave you to it." I don't even wait for a response and run out the door.

As I charge out into the hallway, my mouth waters the moment I bump into a delicious smelling mass. I know without looking who it is because my body seems to be in sync with hers. "Where are you running off to in such a hurry?"

"Hurry?" I scoff, leaning my arm against the doorjamb to prohibit her from opening the door. "I hardly call exiting my room at a steady pace a hurry."

Carrie scrunches up her nose. "I have no idea what you're on, but please give me some. I welcome anything that will numb the next two hours of my life."

Now that I'm somewhat composed, I take in her extraordinary appearance and scold myself for not admiring her sooner. Her long wavy hair falls softly around her face, elongating her creamy smooth neck. The small scripted C hangs off her thin necklace, falling between the low, V neckline of the royal blue silk dress she's wearing.

Unable to stop my visual feasting, I descend, my mouth salivating when I see a dainty sparkly anklet secured around her ankle. Her feet are bare, which actually sets off her spirited pixie look beautifully.

Her entire person is stunning, but I can't help but give her amazing chest a second glance.

Now it's her turn to clear her throat. "My eyes are up here."

She's completely busted me checking her out, but it'd be a shame not to give them the attention they deserve. "Oh, I know where your eyes are, dove," I reply, meeting them a second later.

The term of endearment just popped out, but it seems fitting because Carrie is free-spirited and delicate. I've also never felt freer than I do when I'm around her.

Her glossy lips part, and a breathless whimper escapes her. A pink hue creeps up her nape as she nervously toys with her pendant.

There is no denying the attraction we feel for one another, but underneath that pull is the fact I'm a dirty, rotten scoundrel, and Carrie wouldn't touch me with a ten-foot pole. I'm no better than what's-his-face. Speaking of whom.

"Heard from the fucking twat?"

My obscenities sever the invisible tether between us as Carrie scrunches up her nose. "Who?"

"Donald?" I reply, knowing damn well that's not his name.

It takes her a second to realize who I'm referring to, but when she does, she bursts into that magical laughter. "Donny?"

I shrug, placing my hands into my pockets nonchalantly. "Personally, I prefer fucking twat, but yes, him."

She raises her eyebrow as I didn't exactly mask my touch of jealousy. "No, I haven't, and I don't think that'll change anytime soon. He probably lost his phone in Natalie's vagina anyway."

I splutter up a cough intersected with a laugh as I was not expecting that response. I should know by now to have my guard up when Carrie is involved.

"Let's get tonight over with." She sighs, her pain palpable.

Daisy gave me a brief rundown about what dinner with the Bells would entail. Apparently, Axle sees himself as quite the chef and doesn't half arse any meal. As expected, no expense is spared, and it appears we'll eat as though it's Christmas every night. And tonight is no exception.

Realizing Nora is still hidden inside my room, I decide to continue this conversation downstairs. I sweep my hand forward, gesturing for her to lead the way. I'm thankful when she does. "Your dad is some sort of genius in the kitchen, I hear?"

Carrie's scoff reveals Daisy is full of shite. "More like a Nazi. He only puts on a big show and dance to show off to all his snobbish friends. They're in competition with everything—who has the biggest house, the most expensive car, whose wife has the biggest implants. The list is endless."

I follow her, smiling as she descends the staircase, not masking her contempt for her family. I can see why she believed or, rather, wished she was adopted. She's nothing like these loony tunes. "It goes without saying we're to get totally pissed to deal with tonight's proceedings then?"

She turns over her shoulder with a sultry grin. "You twisted my arm." As she steps onto the polished terrazzo, she shakes her head as if remembering something. "You can't drink. You're probably concussed."

"All the more reason to drink then," I counter without pause.

"Did you want some Tylenol?" Her concern catches me off guard, but I shrug it off and don't read into something that isn't there.

What is there sadly is someone who I almost forget was here. "Pookie bear!"

Daisy rounds the corner, her happiness to see me making me feel like an even bigger arsehole because the feeling is most definitely not reciprocated. Her absurd red heels click against the floor as she charges over.

Leaning into Carrie, I ignore her delectable scent as I whisper, "Forget the Tylenol. You wouldn't happen to have any Valium or Oxy on hand?" She mutes her giggles behind her hand while Daisy narrows her eyes.

The claws come out as Daisy saunters over, hooking her arm

through mine. "I missed you." Before I can speak, she thrusts her tongue into my mouth and kisses me with a dramatic flair.

Carrie snickers because she knows what this is. This is her sister all but cocking her leg and taking a piss on me. She is clearly marking her territory, or what she thinks is hers, because when I gently push her away, I make it clear that I don't appreciate being treated like a piece of meat.

Wiping my lips with the back of my hand, I don't shy away from that fact. "I need a drink." Daisy doesn't hide her surprise when I don't fall for her advances. Her arrogance is a complete turn-off, and I plan on telling her tonight that whatever this is, is over. I will figure out another way to salvage my career. I'm done being her chew toy.

Nora chooses this moment to come sweeping down the stairs, and thankfully, she's totally clothed. Her cheeks turn a soft pink when we lock eyes, but I smile, hinting it's water under the bridge. "Come on, girls. Your father is waiting." She locks arms with Daisy, but she seems to know better than to do so with Carrie.

They chat up ahead while Carrie and I lag. It's hard to believe she is related to these people. I can understand why she believes she was adopted. However, the moment she leans in close, all I can focus on is her sweetness. "You're in so much trouble."

How I wish she was proposing we could rectify this situation by taking me over her knee, but I know she's referring to her sister. "I need a lifeline," I whisper, her heady fragrance punching me low.

"This isn't *Who Wants to be a Millionaire*," she replies, a sudden hitch to her breath. I ignore what the sound does to me and focus on what's important, which is leaving this house with all my parts intact.

"Well, at the moment, I feel like *Slumdog Millionaire*. Please help me." She bites that full bottom lip, eliciting images sure to send me straight to hell.

She doesn't have time to put me out of my misery because when we turn the corner, I'm fearful we've stepped onto the set of *Iron Chef*. Carrie sighs, vocalizing my exact thoughts that what we're seeing is bordering on ridiculous.

The dining room is a flurry of madness as servers rush around, ensuring the mammoth table is set with military precision. The crystal sparkles, and the gold-rimmed plates look like they've been polished within an inch of their lives.

The guests in the crowded room all hold glasses filled with bubbling champagne as they talk about the latest pretentious headline among themselves. I can't believe I used to be one of these wankers.

Axle is in the midst of the commotion, forever the show pony. He's mid conversation with someone who looks to be a bigger tool than he is when he spots Carrie and me standing awkwardly by the door. She's toying with the C around her neck, and when Axle makes it clear he's gloating over kicking my arse today, a word beginning with C, which describes him to a T, tempts to break free. But I rein it in. Only just.

He slaps his chum on the back before making a beeline to where we stand. This should be fun.

"I didn't think you'd be up for tonight…after me kicking your ass and all." *Oh, I could have been all up in your wife tonight,* I silently reply, but instead, I smile quietly. "You snooze, you lose." He's cocky while I bite my cheek to stop the cursing from erupting.

Carrie, on the other hand, has no qualms about filling in the blanks. "If you're done with your macho bullshit, Dad, I need a drink. Jayden?"

My mouth moves in wordless animation as I feel an even bigger attraction for Carrie. "Lead the way."

Axle's eyes narrow, which pleases me beyond words. It appears Mr. Macho doesn't like to be upstaged and ignored, which is exactly the hand he's been dealt. Carrie rolls her eyes before taking off after the waiter who holds a tray full of champagne glasses.

I go to follow, but Axle's hand snaps out, securing my bicep. I peer down at it with my jaw clenched. He has five fucking seconds to remove his hand before I remove it for him. "That little wager…that extends to *both* my daughters. Hands off."

This guy has some nerve. I am done playing nice. I am done playing—period.

Jerking my arm free, I drop all pretenses and grin, smartly.

"I'm a man of my word, but I don't think your darling daughter will abide by your hands-off rule. I think you've just created a monster." I shoot him a wink, all but confirming that Daisy will be giving me a not so discreet hand job the moment his back is turned. "As for Carrie, she knows better than to get involved with someone like me."

Touché, motherfucker.

Axle's mouth hinges open as he could interpret my comment in many ways. His poker face is obliterated because he's currently scanning through what exactly "someone like me" entails. I leave him to stew over the many possibilities, most of which are probably correct, and seek out Carrie. She has two glasses in her hands, scanning over the room and looking as impressed as I feel. I need to get out of here.

Once this dinner is done with, I'm calling Nick and demand he put me on the next flight out of here. I'm fearful for my sanity if I stay here a moment longer.

"J.E. Sparrow?" Turning, I see an older man peering at me with uncertainty. I have no idea who he is, and when he sees my confusion, he shakes his head with a smile. "Sorry, I'm a little star struck. I'm Gerry Williams." He extends his hand, and I shake.

Gerry Williams? Why does that name sound so familiar?

"Gerry, I don't mean to be rude, but have we met?" We continue shaking before Gerry severs the connection, appearing embarrassed.

"I'm the G in A&G Publishing," he reveals while I piece together where I know his name. He's my fucking boss. Now, I'm the one who's embarrassed.

"Please accept my apologies," I say while Gerry shakes his head once.

"It's completely fine. Axle and I have remained on the sidelines for a long time, much to my distaste." My ears prick at his comment because it was intentional. Just what is he playing at?

When he comes in close, gesturing whatever he wants to say is in confidence, he reveals a whole different ballgame. "Please keep this between us because it's early days, but I haven't been happy with the direction A&G Publishing has moved. Because of this, I have decided to go out on my own."

Well, I certainly didn't see that coming.

"I know your loyalties lay with Axle…" I don't bother correcting him as I'm intrigued to where this conversation is headed. "But I was wondering if you'd sit down with me and listen to what I have in mind. You're our biggest author, and I have always, always seen your talent since day one, which is why I wanted to offer you a contract at Williams Publishing."

"You want me to jump ship?" I ask, unable to keep the surprise from my tone.

Gerry sweeps the room, ensuring no one is in earshot. "Yes, I do," he states very matter-of-factly. "I want you to be the first client signed to Williams Publishing, and I will do anything to make that happen. I have big plans for you. A whole new rebrand and different marketing plan. We have no other choice but to keep up with the changes in the publishing industry. We have to stay current in an everchanging world; a fact Axle won't acknowledge."

Running a hand through my hair, I billow my cheeks with the strangled breath caught in my throat. This is big, and I can't deny I find it very tempting.

Reaching into his inner suit jacket pocket, he produces a crisp white business card with a royal blue W as the header. It appears this plan is well in motion. Fingering the corner, I see the address is not too far from where A&G Publishing is located. This should be interesting.

"Think about it. Talk to your agent. But please know that if you decide to sign with us, your next four books will be secured in a very lucrative deal."

Pocketing the business card, I nod calmly. "I'll talk to my agent."

Gerry smiles, appearing relieved I didn't tell him to bugger off as I waved the A&G Publishing team colors. "Excellent. Please call me anytime."

He slaps me on the back lightly, before joining a blonde across the room who I presume is his wife. She looks awfully familiar, but I can't place where I've seen her. As a server zips past with a tray of champagne, I snare two glasses, needing all the booze I can get. I watch closely as Gerry whispers into her ear before she seeks me out and smiles.

"Pookie bear." And just like that, my moment of happiness fizzles out. I down my drink with the other following soon after. "I feel like we haven't had any alone time. Maybe we can change that tonight," she purrs, running her fingernail along the collar of my shirt.

There is no maybe about that equation.

Sighing, I know what I have to do, and it has absolutely nothing to do with the conversation I just had. Yes, the offer is tempting, but I need to discuss this with Nick. Although he's a questionable best friend most of the time with his uncouth behavior, he's a bloody good agent.

"Daisy, look…" She purses her lips, faking innocence because she knows what's about to come. It's a conversation we've had before. "You know I'm not ready to see anyone after what happened with my"—I swallow past the lump in my throat—"ex-wife. I think I've been very clear of that fact. But I feel you're not listening. So I feel it's best if we…" But my sentence remains unfinished.

She launches forward, pressing her finger over my lips to silence me. I shrug out of her hold because this is happening, whether she wants it to or not. But when she closes the distance between us, pressing us nose to nose, I know I'm wasting my breath.

"It's my sister, isn't it?"

"What?" I recoil, unsure how to respond.

"She's always been jealous of me, so it doesn't surprise me the moment she arrives, you begin questioning your feelings for me." She snivels while I wonder if I've stepped into an alternate universe. "What did she do? Offer to blow you? Is that it?"

I'm fucking insulted. Is that what she thinks of me? But more importantly, is that what she thinks of Carrie? That fact angers me more than her judgment over my morals.

"You're not listening. There are *no* feelings for me to question." Harsh but also very true. I've tried to spare her feelings, but the fact she's blaming our "relationship" woes on her sister has me desperate to set the record straight. "We had a good time. That's all. I never promised you…"

Whack.

The stinging in my cheek confirms that Daisy just slapped me. Rubbing my face, I move my jaw from side to side. I suppose I deserved it for allowing this to continue for as long as it has.

"Good time?" she spits, her crazy lashing out of control. "I know how much of a good time you had when you fucked me in the limo coming here!"

"Lower your voice," I hiss as we've drawn the attention of almost everyone in the room.

"Oh, you weren't complaining about how loud I was when you were eating me out on my father's desk! Or when you came all over my face!"

Speaking of faces, I screw mine up into a contorted mess because *that* never happened. "That wasn't me, love. Maybe you're mistaking me for somebody else." A lady gasps beside me while her husband appears to want to fist bump me.

Bodily fluids aside, this is far messier than I anticipated. I won't entertain her melodramatics a second longer. Just as I'm about to tell her we're done, she looks over my shoulder and then suddenly bursts in crocodile tears. "You're breaking up with me because you don't think you're worthy. Stop putting me on some pedestal. I'm not perfect. I know you think I am, but I'm not."

My mouth hangs open because she has clearly gone completely mad.

However, when Axle's voice sounds from behind me, it proves to me what an evil genius Daisy Bell truly is. "What's going on here?"

Daisy shoots me a sly wink, which is akin to witnessing my own death, before sobbing a tearless cry and shielding her face with her hands. "Jayden doesn't think he's good enough for me. He said I'm perfect, and he doesn't deserve me."

"Finally, we agree on something," Axle says while I glare at Daisy. That conniving little harlot.

She is doing this, all of this, because she believes if her father thinks we're no longer a thing, he won't be watching her like a hawk 24/7, which will mean she can use my cock as her personal pogo stick, uninterrupted for the duration of our stay.

This is my fault for not giving her credit. Daisy is an evil mastermind.

"So you're broken up?" Axle asks, the hope clear in his tone.

"Looks that way, Daddy. You have nothing to worry about. Jayden has made his feelings perfectly clear. He would rather become a saint than touch me ever again."

All I can do is stand mute because I actually don't know what to say. By trying to be honest, it appears, if possible, that I've dug myself an even bigger hole. "I think it's best if you leave, Jayden."

"Fine by me," I reply, finding my voice as this is the best suggestion since I arrived.

But Daisy won't have that. I won't be leaving until she says it's time. Being tied to her bed doesn't seem so farfetched now. "No, Daddy, let him stay. It's the holidays. No one should be alone."

Not only is Daisy the victim, but she's also the martyr. I underestimated her. She knows how I feel, how I've felt this entire time, but it's clear that it's over when she says it is and not a second sooner.

I have no idea what she wants from me, but I don't feel like such a rotten bastard knowing she was playing me this entire time. Most would be angry, but I'm not most. If anything, I'm relieved. I just have to get to the bottom of her reasons, and then I'm home free.

She brushes past me, ensuring we touch, just in case I haven't clued on to her game.

This is all for show. To throw her dad off the scent. When I turn over my shoulder and witness his suffocating smugness, I see that it's worked like a charm.

This would be a turn-on if the joke wasn't on me.

Daisy huddles into her father's side, sniffling as he escorts her far, far away from the villain who just happens to be me.

Everyone attempts to be polite and not stare, but what better scandal for them to discuss with their spouses over Christmas Eve hor d'oeuvres? Not interested in being the topic of discussion over dinner, I relieve the server of his tray of drinks and leave the room with no intention of ever returning.

Each step requires a celebration, and by the time I reach the top of the staircase, I'm well and truly on my way to being pissed. With a tray filled with empty glasses, I shoulder open my bedroom door and begin gathering my belongings, not that I really unpacked.

I send Nick a text, telling him to book me on the first flight home. Until then, I'll be staying in a hotel. I decide to leave out the predicament I found myself in with Gerry for now. I will tell him that when I talk to him next.

Once I'm packed, I call an Uber and am ready to bid sayonara to this house of horrors. However, when I open the door, I almost run into Carrie, who stands about to knock. She lowers her hand when she fixes her gaze on my bag. "You're leaving?"

"Yes, I am. Feel free to come with me. This place is Stephen King's dream come true." I attempt to push past her, but she steps to the left, blocking my escape route. Peering down at her, I arch a curious brow.

"What about your contract with A&G Publishing?"

"Screw the contract. I'll figure something out."

She purses those supple lips. "I don't want to say I told you so…but I told you so."

A chuckle escapes me. "Yes, I know. I completely deserve it. It's time I start making amends for the error of my ways."

"So what was with Daisy's Oscar worthy performance? She's always been melodramatic, but that was something else."

Indeed. "She wants to fool your father into thinking we're broken up so he'll call off his hounds, meaning she can have her way with me whenever she wants." I don't mean to sound cocky because it's the god's honest truth.

Carrie turns a lovely shade of pink while I wonder if every part of her does the same. "My god"—she shakes her head—"you must be *some* lay for her to go to all that effort."

This time, however, I can't keep the cocky at bay as I shrug with a grin.

"Your sister isn't as…innocent," I opt for, "as she looks. She knew what this was, and when I was about to end it once and for all, she reminded me that the ball or, more specifically, *my* balls are in her court, and she's not done playing—not by a long shot."

Carrie's lips move from side to side in thought while I focus on anything other than their fullness.

"I don't have any proof, but I have an inkling she would play with me until she gets bored and then feed me to the sharks—aka your father. She comes across as the martyr for allowing me to stay, all the while she's blackmailing me into literal submission." I shudder at the thought. "I clearly know how to pick them. Between my ex-wife and your sister, I am wondering if maybe I should just settle with the companionship of thirty-seven cats."

Carrie snorts a giggle, which is the most adorable sound in the world. "Under most circumstances, I would feel sorry for you, but well, I told you so."

She's right.

"Daisy doesn't like taking orders." I don't bother correcting her because I'd rather burn those images from my mind for good. "She's punishing you for even thinking you could end this, whatever this is, without her consent. You're her new shiny toy. Lucky you."

"Yes, lucky me," I quip. "And I think you mean chew toy, which is exactly why I need to leave."

I attempt to push past her once again, but Carrie extends her arm, holding the doorframe. I can't help but admire her supple flesh and the defined shape to her arms. She must work out. Thoughts of her all sweaty and in skimpy gym wear leave me with a raging semi. But I need to focus.

"But you leaving means she wins," she says, reminding me of my dire circumstances. "She comes out looking like the good guy while you're the bastard who broke her heart. My father will be sure to see you never publish with him ever again."

All she says is true, but I have an ace up my sleeve. Gerry Williams.

When a lopsided smirk which can be labeled as nothing but trouble tugs at Carrie's lips, I know she too has an ace in the hole. "Oh, dove." I lean forward, relishing in her small intake of breath. "You are positively evil. Please share whatever diabolical thoughts you have racing around that pretty little head of yours."

She licks her lips, closing the distance, while I almost come in my pants. "How about I just show you?"

Sweet baby Jesus.

She can show me whatever, whenever because I am a salivating fool when it comes to Carrie Bell. The air pops around us, and the small space between us sparks with an energy that leaves me desperate for so much more.

"I'm at your mercy," I reply, meaning that in every way there is.

"Careful. The last time that happened, you ended up here." She circles her finger with a smirk.

Unable to help myself, I close the distance between us until we're only inches apart. I'm mesmerized by the rise and fall of her chest. "If I never came here," I declare, moments away from throwing caution to the wind and sealing my mouth to hers, "then I would have never seen you again. So I suppose it's not a complete disaster."

Her breath hitches, and her cheeks turn a lovely shade of pink. "Thank you. I'm glad I can be your silver lining." At this moment, Carrie is my muse because, out of nowhere, I get hit with words and visions, and all I want to do is write.

"This is fucking incredible," I push out on a breath, brushing back a piece of her auburn hair. The move wasn't intentional. I just had to touch her.

I'm expecting her to shrug from my hold and call me a creep, but she does neither. Instead, she leans into my palm, and a tiny mewl slips through her parted lips. I don't understand what this is with her, but either way, I don't care. Something about this woman inspires me to just…live.

She peers up at me through her long lashes, and I instantly get kicked by her beauty. She is fragile, but I make no mistake in thinking she's some damsel in distress because she's not. She's strong, and she's also fierce and independent, and suddenly, I am so attracted to her, I don't know how I'm going to play this off.

Caressing my thumb over the apple of her cheek, I pry my hand away before I throw resolve to the wind and act on the desire thrumming through my veins. When she opens her mouth, I am ready to hang on her every word, but then I hear the unmistakable voice of Daisy gushing downstairs, and she simply smirks.

The gesture is filled with utter villainy.

"Are you ready for me to save your ass?" she says, still beaming.

It's out before I can stop myself. "You can do whatever you wish to my arse, dove."

Her grin widens, and my god, this flirting is going to leave me with a serious case of blue balls. "I'll keep that in mind. Come on." She gestures with her chin that we're to go downstairs.

I don't particularly want to go back down there, especially since whoever is there has Daisy either sobbing or squealing. I can't really tell. But manning up, I close the door and follow Carrie.

There is a lithe movement to her, and I know that's just her natural grace. She doesn't have to wiggle her arse or thrust out her bountiful chest; her beauty is reflected in every step she takes because she is herself. There are no smokescreens with her, and I find myself drawn to that honesty. Maybe that's what I've been lacking these past six months—being honest with myself.

Food for thought because as Carrie descends the last step, my entire attention is focused on the tall man Daisy is groping and calling lamp chop. Poor guy. I feel his pain. But when he reciprocates the molesting, declaring how much he missed his "cuddle muffin," I wonder if he's high.

Axle stands on the sidelines, watching on in approval. I have no idea what's going on, but there is no doubt this is Carrie's doing.

On cue, Daisy clears her throat, severing the long-lost lover's embrace. When she meets my eyes, she bites her lip guiltily. "I'm sorry, Jayden. This won't work."

The blond beau by her side who looks a little like a Ken doll wraps an arm protectively around her shoulders. Is he marking his claim? I'm barely able to retain my laughter.

"This is Isaac." She offers no other explanation, but I can connect the dots.

Axle's smugness is near suffocating because it's clear he thinks Isaac is worthy of his daughter while I am merely a bug he could squash with his Italian loafers. Carrie turns over her shoulder and throws me a subtle wink.

So this was her plan—to reunite Daisy with the Ken doll, whom she clearly cares for. I don't know why they ended, but I don't particularly care. This is the out I needed. I would applaud Carrie for her wickedness, but it seems for this to work, I have to appear at least somewhat upset.

Shaking my head, I swallow while turning my cheek. "It pains me, but I can see you're happy with Isaac. Best of luck to the both of you." And I mean that in every way possible.

"I know you'll miss me," Daisy says in a patronizing tone, "but we will always be friends."

Clenching my teeth, I rein in my temper because that's all we ever were. I'm using the term "friends" lightly, but I don't bother correcting her because I don't deserve anything less. I never should have come here. It seems Daisy was using me as much as I was using her, and that fact doesn't make me feel any better. If anything, it just makes me feel like an even bigger wanker.

Once again, Daisy is the martyr, but this time, I'm really home free, and I intend to take advantage of that by fleeing from this house without ever looking back. Carrie shifts to the side, allowing me passage, and although a front door has never looked more appealing, I don't want to leave because I don't know what that means for her and me.

Will I ever see her again? My heart kicks against my ribcage in protest, demanding I man the fuck up and ask her to come with me.

Setting foot on equal playing field, I turn to look at her. I know her family is watching closely, but screw them. I need her to know that I won't accept this as goodbye. "Well then, it was lovely meeting you." I use my hug as a guise to whisper into her ear, "Westpoint Hotel."

She freezes as I no doubt have caught her off guard, but there is no way I'm leaving this house without giving her option to follow if she wants. I can only hope that she does.

We break apart, and the reddening of her cheeks reveals she wasn't expecting me to disclose the name of the hotel where I'll be staying. But the choice is now hers. She gave me an out, and now, I'm returning the favor.

I walk over to Daisy and Commando Ken, offering them both my hand. "Goodbye. All the best for the future." They both shake it, and Daisy grins. She's won. I was merely there to entertain her until something better came along. I was simply the fill-in.

Axle looks happier than a pig in shit, and without a doubt, my future with A&G Publishing is now ruined. But when Gerry emerges from the dining room, I realize the saying rings true—one door closes and another literally opens as Axle shows me the way out.

Regardless of the fact he's a pompous arse, I extend my hand. "Thank you for your hospitality. Merry Christmas."

I'm surprised when he shakes it, but I'm left speechless when he says, "Have your agent email me the first five chapters of your new manuscript." That's it. He doesn't promise me anything, but he's offered me the bait.

I lock eyes with Gerry who stands behind Axle, clearly anxious to see how I will respond.

It appears for Axle to show me a lick of decency, I was to leave his daughter alone, which is ironic because that's all I really wanted. However, I'm pretty sure his offer is akin to a pity fuck, and I don't take too lightly to being treated that way.

At this moment, I vow my next book will be fucking victorious, better than any before it, and I refuse to settle for second best. Returning my attention back to Axle, I grip his hand and smile. "Thank you. However, with my contract up, I think it's time I see what else is out there. As they say," I very arrogantly declare, intent on using his own words as ammo, "you snooze, you lose. Nick will be in touch." That's it.

Gerry looks five seconds away from offering me his fist in a celebratory fist bump, but he knows that applies to him as well. My mind isn't made up either way, but one thing is clear. As I lock eyes with Carrie, who stands tall and proud that I stood up to her father and finally did the right thing, I know she is the reason I can call myself a writer again.

Without further ado, I turn my back on the past, ready to embrace the future with both hands. The waiting Uber is the lifeline I've longed for, and after I hop into the back seat, rattling off the address to my hotel, I pull out my laptop, eager to forget and focus on tomorrow.

7
Seven

My entire body aches, but this feeling is one I happily embrace because it's one I haven't felt in a very long time. Leaning back in my seat, I lift my glasses and rub the bridge of my nose.

After leaving the house of horrors, I check into my hotel, place my laptop onto the small desk, and write like a man possessed. I haven't left this spot for hours. Scrolling through the pages, I'm in awe of the fact I have managed to write over five thousand words.

The storyline is still vague, but I can't help but draw the similarities between my heroine and Carrie. She was, after all, the reason I was able to write in the first place, so it seems fitting that I would shape my character after her. Her name is Bailey. The hero, however, is still unnamed, but it goes without saying he's a strapping brute with a great arse.

Happy with the direction of chapter one, I decide to reward myself by raiding the minibar.

Standing, I stretch, my muscles thankful for the reprieve. Looking at the clock, I see that it's just before midnight. Merry Christmas to me. Thinking back to last Christmas, I remember the white gown Liz wore, hugging her exquisite curves. I thought she was the most beautiful woman I had ever seen. Now, all I see is what a fucking twat I was.

We had Christmas Eve dinner at our house, a tradition we started once we married. It was a grand affair, and Liz invited anyone who was anyone. Jerking open the minibar, I gather the three tiny bottles of whiskey and unscrew the lid of one, needing the burn to douse the rage within.

I can't believe I didn't see it, see *her* for what she was.

Tossing back bottle number one, I relish in the bitter aftertaste before immediately needing a chaser. I loosen the lid, memories of Liz and her red smeared lipstick assaulting me as if it was only yesterday.

I was blind to her wandering eye, but I should have known. I should have listened to my gut because Eduardo wasn't the first. She was unfaithful for a long time before I caught her. I never had any proof, but that night, that Christmas Eve when she emerged from my study looking less than perfect with some arsehole whose name I didn't even know, I knew she was fucking someone other than me.

Instead of confronting her, I played it off, arrogant or blinded, most likely both, unbelieving she would find comfort in someone else. I gave her everything she ever wanted, so what reason was there for her to stray?

But a comment Carrie said rings true: "*I have a feeling she'll never be happy anywhere.*" And she's right.

Since that Christmas, my life has slowly turned to shite. The cracks became craters, and alas, here I am, alone. But I would rather this than live a lie, which is what Liz and I were for so long.

Refusing to waste another moment of my time, I throw back the remaining liquor, intent on writing until the sun comes up. I still have yet to hear from Nick, but that's no surprise really. I have no doubt he's standing under every mistletoe he can find. As for me, the only thing I intend to wrap my lips around is a bottle of Jameson.

Wondering if room service delivers whiskey by the bottle, I don't hear the knock until it sounds louder. Turning to look at the door, I question if my need for booze has conjured up such a noise, but when a rap thuds once again, I know that someone is, in fact, outside.

I refuse to entertain the notion that it's Carrie because she would have been here hours ago. And besides, why would she come? But tell that to my cock as it's doing push-ups and getting ready to impress. Putting a lock on the infernal beast, I focus on answering the door.

When it swings open, however, all bets are off, and my body demands to get up close and personal with the woman who stands before me.

"Merry Christmas," Carrie says, blowing a party horn, the colorful ribbon elongating like something else.

"Carrie?" I very ungracefully spit. She's changed into jeans and a sweater. She's also carrying her overnight bag.

She smiles, lifting a bottle of whiskey. I can't help but grin at the pink bow tied around the bottle's neck. "I bought you a present. I thought you might need it after today."

I almost interlock my hands and thank the lord above for granting my Christmas miracle—Carrie on my doorstep, holding a bottle of Jameson. Getting my shit together, I gesture for her to enter. "Thank you. Come in."

The moment she steps past me, I'm winded by her strawberry and cream scent. My god, how is it possible a smell alone can work me up this much? But when my eyes feast on her womanly curves, I know her entire being is what whets my appetite.

She takes note of the open laptop, looking back over her shoulder with a sassy smile. "The drought has broken, it appears."

When she walks toward it, poised and ready to read my work, I sprint over and slam the lid shut.

That playful smirk tugs at her supple lips as she arches a brow. "Or are you looking at porn?"

A rumble erupts from me. "As of today"—I make my way over to the desk to retrieve the two glasses resting on the surface—"I have decided to follow your lead." She cocks her head to the side, curious.

Extending my hand, I wait as she hands me the bottle. I unscrew the lid, taking my time to pour the amber liquid. "I, too, intend to quit booze, boys, well, women, and sex," I explain, referring to our conversation on the plane.

However, when the smell of the pear and ripe apple of the whiskey hits my nostrils, I know I will probably need lots of booze to deal with the absence of the other two. "Two out of the three isn't so bad," I backtrack, passing her a glass.

She accepts, drawing the tumbler to her nose. A girl who loves her whiskey—who needs Shakespeare because that is poetry within itself. "Let's make a toast then."

I raise my glass, ready to toast whatever she has in mind.

"To our very boring yet chaste life. May we both find what we're looking for."

What I'm looking at right now is exactly what I'm searching for. But I quash down the urge to strip her bare and nod. We clink glasses and take long sips. It appears we both need to revel in a little depravity before we turn virtuous.

When she licks the whiskey from her top lip, however, I know I'm going to need another drink to drown out the wickedness stirring within. "I haven't had a chance to thank you. Your evil genius should scare me, but I'm impressed. Daisy and Isaac were a thing then?"

I pour myself another drink as I need the alcohol to numb the vision.

"Yes, for about two years. He was the only guy who broke her heart. I knew he was your get out of jail for free card because she never got over him," she explains, kicking off her sneakers and making her way over to the sofa. She plunks onto the couch and reaches for the remote.

I can't deny I love seeing her so comfortable in my presence.

Snaring the bottle of whiskey, I make my way over to where she sits with a leg tucked beneath her. As she's channel surfing, I attempt to make sense of how a woman like her can be single. She is smart, beautiful, and incredibly witty. What the hell is the matter with the men of America?

She must sense me staring because she turns her cheek to look at me. When she brushes over her nose self-consciously, I smile at her adorability. "So you escaped the asylum too?"

She sips her drink while rolling her eyes. "Yes. If I had to listen to Daisy calling Isaac her poopie one more time, I would have rendered myself unconscious. And besides, you shouldn't sleep with a concussion. I wanted to make sure you were all right."

I'm touched.

"Did you mean what you said to my dad?" she asks, reminding me of my parting words to Axle.

"Yes. I did." Taking a drink, I decide to tell her about Gerry.

"I had an interesting conversation with Gerry Williams." She pauses mid sip, eyes wide as she peers at me over the rim of her glass. "He's going rogue, and he asked that I follow suit."

"*Oh, my god*. No fucking way." I nod while her mouth hinges open. "I don't blame him. My dad is a complete narcissist. But holy shit…who knew Gerry had a pair. Did he proposition you?"

"Yes." I don't see the point in being vague. With those business cards readily available, it's clear he's been scouting for other heads besides mine. It's only a matter of time until the cat's out of the bag.

"What are you going to do?" she asks, shuffling her position to get comfortable.

Finishing my drink, I lean forward and place it on the coffee table before undoing the lid on the bottle. "I want to talk to my agent, but first and foremost, I need to write something that isn't rubbish. The pressure is really on, especially if I do jump ship. I need this book to be fucking groundbreaking."

"What idea do you have in mind?"

Taking a swig from the bottle, I shrug. "I don't know. I've started working on something, but it's still early."

Carrie throws back her drink, making a pained face as she swallows. "How about you write a self-help book for single ladies to snare the right man? You must have some insight, considering you're a man and all," she proposes as she leans forward, placing her glass on the table.

The proverbial light bulb flashes as I take her suggestion on board.

"I was joking," she says with a laugh, but I raise my finger, shaking my head.

Words, images, scenarios come to mind. Fuck me. "No, no, this is genius. The context would work. But it would have to be fiction." My heart begins racing, the blood whooshing through my veins, and it has nothing to do with the whiskey.

"So what are you suggesting?" She reaches for the bottle sitting limply in my hand.

"This writer's block is because I have been so shut off from life these past six months, but what better way to beat it than by experiencing life in ways I never have?"

She curls her lip in humor, certain I've gone mad.

"All this time, I've been looking in all the wrong places. I thought sleeping with random women would give me the inspiration I sought, but that theory had a major plot hole. To write romance, I need to experience the romance instead of counting how many orgasms I can have in a week."

She tugs at her lip while the apple of her cheeks turns a deep crimson.

"And to do that, what better way than experiencing romance in its purest form." Oh, my fuck. I jump up, unable to sit still. I can't believe I didn't think of this sooner. I have been lacking inspiration because yes, I'm a physical being, but at heart, I want my happily ever after. I'm a writer, for fuck's sake. Give me my soppy ending and I can go home one happy man.

"What, are you planning on being a voyeur or something, peeping in on other people's relationships in hopes that their love, passion, and lust rub off on you?" she asks, tongue in cheek. But that's exactly what I plan to do.

"Yes," I reply, ceasing my pacing as I turn to look at her. "But not any relationship will do. I need something fresh. New. I need to relearn the basics because I've forgotten what the butterflies feel like. And to get that back…I need to go back to the beginning." I'm talking a mile a minute, vocalizing everything in my head before I forget.

I can see the moment when she pieces together what I'm proposing. She sips the whiskey, her cheeks bellowed as she swallows the liquor in thought. Once it's down, she smirks. "You're going to spy on people having their first dates, aren't you?"

Not only is she beautiful, but she's a true genius as well.

"Yes," I reply, running a hand through my hair as I blow out a breath.

When she's quiet, I look over my shoulder at her, wondering what's going through her mind. "Let me help you," she says, throwing me for a complete loop.

My curiosity is piqued.

Taking another mouthful of whiskey as if she needs the Dutch courage, she finally explains, "You told me that you haven't been able to write a single word…that is, until meeting me. So"—she lowers her eyes, toying with the frayed hole in her jeans—"let me come with you. I can detail what I'm seeing from the woman's point of view while you do the same for the man's. I don't want to be sexist, but it might help to have a different perspective. I could give you insight into what the women are thinking and hopefully help..." She leaves the sentence unfinished because I'm completely on the same page, the same line as she is.

This is brilliant; not to mention, she is offering to spend more time with me. Where do I sign up?

"You can help me understand how women think, so I can write a convincing heroine?"

"Exactly," she says, raising her eyes. They glimmer in exhilaration. "And maybe down the line, I can use your expertise to find my Mr. Right."

I almost choke on the wheeze that escapes. I have no desire to help her find a Mr. anything. Shoving a pineapple head first where the sun don't shine sounds far more appealing than that. But who am I to stop her from finding her HEA?

"So this little experiment will benefit us both," she states, coming to a stand. "You did say this book needs to be groundbreaking. I will be brutally honest, steering you clear of clichés." The moment she says those words no author wants to hear, she chews the corner of her mouth while I check my pulse.

"Clichés? What makes you think I write anything that's remotely clichéd?" Asking her this question just affirms her point, but I want to know her reasoning.

Now she's chewing her lip for an entirely different reason, and that's to hold in her amused giggle. "No woman wants to read a sentence involving the words *throbbing member.* That may have worked back in Fabio's days but not now."

I blink once. "Are you calling me…old?" I ask, horrified.

"Well…" she replies with a lopsided grin and a slight shrug before guzzling down the whiskey.

That cheeky little minx. Two can play that game.

Gently ensnaring the bottle from her lips, I watch in utter interest as the brown liquid spills down her parted lips. She goes to wipe away the fallen drops, but I beat her to it. Using my thumb, I swipe along her bottom lip, taking the whiskey and her essence with me.

Her eyes widen, and she gulps loudly when I place my thumb into my mouth, sucking slow. Who knew a Carrie laced whiskey could taste this good? "You have yourself a deal." Her taste lingers on my tongue, and it takes all my willpower not to go in for another sip.

The rise and fall of her chest reveals that the next few weeks will be interesting. And her sassy comment confirms we're both in wickedly grave danger. "Just so you know, I'm not going to sleep with you." Dear lord, visions of Carrie writhing naked beneath me assault me from every angle, but I pull it together.

"Good," I reply before taking a long sip of whiskey. "Just so *you* know, I don't want to sleep with you. I'm a reformed man slut."

She bursts into magical laughter. "When do we start?"

"Tomorrow," I counter without thought. Thinking back to our conversation earlier today, she mentioned art school. "Or whenever works for you. You said you were in school?"

She nods nervously, reaching for the bottle of whiskey, but we've drained it dry. "Yes, I am. My passion is photography. I hope to make a career of it one day, but I don't know." That explains her taking the photo of us. "The beauty in the unseen is what I attempt to capture. It's the imperfections that make life beautiful," she confesses sadly. I wonder why.

"So it would appear we're both hopeless romantics at heart."

She nods, appearing a little off balance. I know it's the whiskey. It takes a lot for me, but her hooded eyes and shallow breathing all point to her being intoxicated. Her bag sits innocently by the door. "Do you want to stay here? I'll take the couch," I quickly add, not wanting to sound like a hypocrite after my earlier comment.

She sways when she stands, and I wrap my hand around her bicep to stop her from falling. "Holy shit. I think I'm a little drunk. So much for my no booze rule." She finishes her comment with a giggle that turns into a hiccup, then slaps her hand over her mouth, horrified. "I wouldn't want to impose."

"There is no imposition," I reply. "You look beat, so if you want to crash, please be my guest. I have some work I want to do anyway."

There is no way I can sleep. I need to draft out all my ideas and brainstorm possible storylines. Carrie peers over at the bed, which looks like a mammoth cloud. In the end, the thought of sleeping on a cushy mattress wins her over. "Thank you so much. I might freshen up and change."

"Of course. The bathroom is over there." I point in the direction of where it's located, which is absurd as it's fairly obvious, but I'm suddenly nervous.

Carrie nods, and it must be all the whiskey going to her head because she too appears a little flustered. Before I can question it further, she quickly turns her back and practically runs into the bathroom. I exhale, but that breath is taken in vain because the door opens a second later, and Carrie emerges looking a little sheepish.

"I forgot my bag," she explains, making a beeline for it. I watch as she shoulders it, her fingers toying with the strap. She appears to want to say something but changes her mind. *Why is she so nervous?*

The bathroom door closes, putting an end to further discussion. Not that I'd know what to say.

Blowing out a breath, I toss the empty bottle in the trash and decide to get a start on brainstorming my new book. As I take a seat at the desk, my eyes wander to the bathroom door. The sound of the shower running evokes images of Carrie naked, standing under the misted spray.

My body is telling me to man the fuck up and tell her how

I feel, but her comment about not sleeping with me or her eventually finding her Mr. Right hint at the fact she doesn't see me in the same light. Just because I have a schoolgirl crush doesn't mean she does. This insta-love nonsense is stuff you only read about in books. I really need to get a grip.

When the water switches off, I get my head back into the game and open my laptop. Deciding to start a new document, I peer at the blinking cursor, wondering what exactly to call my WIP. For the moment, I decide to name it the obvious—Mr. Right.

My fingers type frantically as I take all the ideas I expressed aloud to Carrie and put them in words. I keep circling back to the notion that this story should be completely different from my other novels. Maybe Carrie is right. My formula has worked for so long, but should I break away from what I'm used to and delve into the unknown?

This might work, especially if I take Gerry up on his offer.

Leaning back in the seat, I tap a pen on the edge of the desk, deep in thought. Seeing as this is my first book after Liz, I toy with the idea of writing under a different pseudonym. I want to distance myself from her because she comes with bad juju.

"That's the face of a man who has the ability to change the world." I glance over my shoulder to see Carrie emerge from the bathroom towel drying her hair. She's in sleep shorts and a T-shirt with a large banana printed on it. How appropriate.

When her pearled nipples push against the tight fabric, I

almost moan aloud. But thinking of my ninety-five-year-old neighbor, Agnes, naked stops me from poking Carrie's eye out. "I was just toying with the idea of writing under a different name," I explain, curling my fists so I don't accidentally reach out and run my fingers down the curve of her neck.

She saunters over to where I sit, rigid and counting sheep. I know that's supposed to work for falling asleep, and that's what I'm hoping—for my raging hard-on to fall into a comatose slumber. "You've worked so hard for that name, though. It seems a shame. You're a brand now," she says, her scent of strawberries and cream amplified tenfold.

Talking about work helps an iota, and I nod. "You're right, but that name makes me want to maim myself." She bursts into laughter, which doesn't help the predicament in my pants.

She peers over my shoulder, looking at what I've written. "Mr. Right. I like it," she says while I measure my breathing and don't inhale too deeply for fear I'll overdose on her fragrance. "You want to steer away from your typical formula of boy meets girl, they fall in love, there is conflict, a misunderstanding, but eventually they find their way back to one another and live happily ever after?"

"Maybe," I reply, eyes focused on the screen.

"Hmm."

Such a noncommittal word but it leaves me questioning my decision. After all I've been through these past six months, writing something like that seems so…unrealistic. I know fiction is just that, but in the real world, the good guy doesn't always get the girl. I want to connect with my readers and write a story that is gritty, raw, and real.

By watching new love flourish, I have a beginning. The middle and the end—I'll be able to fill in the blanks. "I want to write a story that encompasses the trials and tribulations of what being in a relationship is truly like. And what better way to connect with my readers than by stripping back the bullshit fluff and writing what we all want to read. The highs and lows, the good times and the bad. How love can turn to hate. Or how love can lead to obsession. Love in its purest form is what I intend to capture. Love isn't always smooth sailing. It's hard work, and most times, it fucking sucks, but when you find it—true love, I mean—you'll do anything to keep it. That's the type of story I want to write. Something real and relatable and by starting from the very beginning, I can map out where things went wrong or right. Not everyone has a happily ever after. And I want to detail that. I want my readers to know that it's okay if you fail because love is a battlefield. Whoever said all you need is love is a fucking twat."

Carrie's silence hints that I've just vocalized all this out loud. The idea may be rough, but I like it. I like that after being surrounded by superficial bullshit, I can finally shed my skin and write something that will hopefully be cathartic for both the reader and the writer.

Risking a look over my shoulder, I'm uncertain what I'll

see. Carrie stands behind me with the towel hanging limply by her side. It's clear she's deep in thought, but when she meets my eyes, I can see it—I'm onto something.

"Jayden." My name has never sounded so wicked. "This is brilliant. But may I suggest something?"

Spinning in my seat, I raise my brows and gesture that I'm listening.

"Instead of only observing first dates, how about we people watch? Watch people not only in love, but watch people hate. Get every angle of a relationship and write about that. That's the only way you can comprehend every side to love. I'm sure you're able to write from experience on that too."

Steepling my fingers in front of my lips, I ponder her suggestion. She's right. For this to be real and raw, I need to understand the good and bad side to love because let's face it, you can't have one without the other. I can definitely write from experience, but seeing it from all different sides will give me a broader understanding and not conclude my story with the hero being a reclusive drunk. If I only wrote from my experience, that was where my Mr. Right would end up.

She shifts from foot to foot, drawing my attention to her supple legs. I've been good thus far, but holy shit, she is perfection. "You hate it?" she finally says, breaking my trance.

"No, on the contrary. I love it."

"You do?"

I nod and stand.

I want nothing more than to step closer, but I don't trust myself if I do. "Thank you. I haven't felt this…inspired in so long."

She brushes a piece of damp hair behind her ear. "I'm glad I can help."

That undeniable pull bounces between us once again, and I know Carrie senses it too. Our pheromones are ready to perform a strip tease, enticing the other to the dark side, but for this to work, I need to keep my head in check.

I value Carrie, and yes, she is fucking delectable, but neither of us has the best track record with the opposite sex. I won't ruin this feeling by giving into a night of wanton passion—no matter how badly I want to because that's all I can offer her. I come with baggage, lots of it, mainly named Elizabeth Evans. Until I can rid myself of her memory, I won't drag Carrie down with me. She's had her fair share of assholes, so I won't add my name to the shit list. Long story short—she deserves someone better than me.

"I'm going to get back to it." I hook my thumb toward my laptop, and Carrie nods quickly.

"Are you sure it's okay for me to take the bed? I'm happy with the sofa."

"Take the bed," I insist as there is no way I'll have her sleeping on the couch.

"Okay, well, good night." A static lingers over our heads, and as Carrie stalls, I wonder what exactly she's thinking.

"Good night." She smiles shyly and makes her way over to the bed. When she pulls back the covers and settles in, an urge to join her sideswipes me, but I remember why that can't happen. "Merry Christmas, dove."

She turns on her side to face me with a sleepy smile touching her lips. "Merry Christmas, Jayden."

Her soft breathing is the lullaby which inspires me well into the night, determined to start anew.

Stuck in the middle with you (pronoun)

8
Eight

I wake to the most delicious scent—strawberries and cream.

Cracking open an eye, I find myself topless and sprawled out on the leather sofa. The sweet fragrance reveals Carrie is close by. That thought has me opening both eyes, blinking quickly to adjust to the morning light.

I have no idea of the time or when exactly I collapsed face first, but I do remember my fingers being possessed as I wrote out a storyline I didn't hate. It detailed a couple from their very first meeting to their last breath. I intend to delve deep and show the many sides of love.

Running a hand through my snarled hair, I sit upright, searching the room for Carrie. I want to run my ideas by her because she does seem to get my creative juices flowing.

Sweet holy fuck…speaking of juices.

She emerges from the bathroom looking freshly showered and dressed. Her auburn hair tumbles in soft waves around her face, which seems to be dusted in a light coat of makeup. I like that she's a natural beauty. She's in white jeans and a baby pink fluffy sweater.

When she sees me sitting upright, she smiles. What a way to start the day. "Good morning."

"Mornin'. What time is it?" I ask, yawning.

"A little past nine. What time did you go to sleep?"

Shrugging, I come to a stand, stretching my arms over my head. "I have no idea. The last I looked, it was about four a.m."

"How'd it go?"

"Good. I have the idea down pat. Maybe we can discuss it over breakfast?" I suggest, scratching over my tattoo absentmindedly. "I'm famished."

Lost in the vision of fried eggs and golden hash browns, I don't realize Carrie is staring until a breathy sigh leaves her. This happened yesterday when she tended to my wounds. And just like yesterday, my body was the subject of her clear appreciation.

Everything below the belt is screaming at me to throw her over my shoulder and toss her onto that unmade bed, but I silence that voice. However, a small part of me is fucking victorious that she doesn't find me a repulsive troll.

Carrie lifts her eyes, and an adorable blush spreads from

cheek to cheek. I don't see the point in playing coy as I grin. There's nothing wrong with a little harmless flirting. And besides, it seems only fair that she find me attractive because she is the most stunning woman I have ever seen.

"Breakfast sounds good," she says, breaking the silence.

"Excellent. I'm just going to take a shower. I won't be long." I walk toward my bag, deciding to take it with me into the bathroom. Even though I've made peace with the fact we're only friends, that doesn't mean I have to look like a hobo.

"When are you flying back home?"

Her question has me reaching for my cell off the desk. Scrolling through my texts and emails, I see that Nick has yet to reply. "I have no idea. I'm waiting on my agent. If I don't hear from him today, I'll book the first flight I can get. How about you?"

She swallows and nervously hunts through her overnight bag. Finding a pair of white socks, she sits on the edge of the bed to slip them on. "I don't know. I thought I'd at least survive until the new year at the lake house and deal with my decision then."

Thinking back to our conversation yesterday, I say, "Ah, you're currently homeless, aren't you?"

"Yup," she replies, popping the P. She laces up her sneaker with a sigh. "So I guess I'm in no real hurry to return to Seattle." There is a bite to her tone which has me wondering why.

Her comment gives me an idea, but I decide to think on it

before I blurt it out.

Gathering my belongings, I make my way into the bathroom, sampling the air inside because remnants of Carrie's perfume wafts through the air. I undress as I wait for the shower to heat; my mind focused on what Carrie said.

The moment I step under the shower spray, my knotted muscles unwind, and my idea begins to take shape. Carrie is in no hurry to get back to Seattle and, honestly, neither am I. Maybe Seattle and the memories that come with it have been the issue these past six months.

I can't help but associate the city with Liz, so maybe it's time for a change of scenery.

I can write whenever, wherever, and people watching can be done from any place in the world. Both Carrie and I need a break from Seattle, and it seems fitting to start this new book, one completely out of my comfort zone, in a place where everyone is a new face.

The more I think about it, the more sense it seems to make.

Once I'm scrubbed clean, I turn off the faucets, excited to venture on this journey. I just hope Carrie wants to come along for the ride. Wiping down the mist from the mirror, I peer at my reflection. I really need to shave. My stubble is thick, but as I rub a hand over it, I decide to leave it.

Opening my bag, I shove aside the shirts and ties and opt for a pair of dark denim, a fitted gray crewneck sweater, and a black blazer. I want smart casual because I have no idea where the day will take us.

Once I've brushed my teeth, I spray on my favorite cologne but don't bother with any hair products. I run my fingers through it, allowing the longer strands to fall naturally. Satisfied, I zip my bag and exit the bathroom.

Carrie is where I left her, but she's donned her knitted beanie and a scarf. When she looks up from her phone, her mouth parts as she visibly examines me from head to toe. I'm glad I went with the blazer.

Tossing my bag into the corner of the room, I hunt for my boots, attempting to ignore Carrie. I'm trying to be good, but holy shite, she's testing my patience with her ogling. "When do you start back at school?" I casually ask as I take a seat and put on my socks.

She wrestles with how to reply before answering, "Not until after the new year. But I don't even know if I'll go back."

This is news to me. I'm about to ask why that is, but she beats me to the punch.

"Why?"

Always so inquisitive. One of the many things I like about her.

Tying the laces on my boots, I smile. "I wanted to run something by you, but how about we grab some coffee first?"

Once both my boots are tied, I risk a look her way, smothering the urge to reach out and brush the hair from her cheek. My memory has done a poor job remembering her because each time I see her, it's like the first time.

She licks her lips, then nods. She clearly trusts me, which just ticks another box. "Okay, sounds good. Can I leave my bag?"

"Yes, of course. I've booked the room for two nights as I wasn't sure when I would be leaving."

We both stand, appearing to appreciate the space between us. I need caffeine before I can deal with this constant longing.

We exit the room and make our way toward the elevators. The Christmas carol playing softly over the speaker reminds me that today is Christmas Day. The doors open, and I'm thankful a family is already inside because I don't trust myself in a confined space alone with Carrie.

The lobby is lit up with Christmas cheer and jovial faces, and although this time of the year is a reminder of the beginning of the end, being with Carrie seems to take some of the doom and gloom away.

The moment we step out of the revolving doors, the bitter wind and icy temperatures have us both hurrying along the sidewalk, eager to find a warm place and a hot cup of coffee. We stumble upon a vintage looking diner just down the block.

It's crowded, but the kind waitress cleans a table, then waves us over. Carrie unwinds her scarf and slips off her beanie. She shakes out her hair, before sliding into the booth. I remember to swallow and follow suit across from her.

The waitress pours us each coffee, then walks away to allow

us time to read over the menu.

Carrie reaches for the folded menu, smacking her lips when she sees the stack of pancakes the lady at the next table hacks into. Reaching for my coffee, I don't bother with creamer or sugar and take a sip.

Carrie watches me, a mischievous smile flickering across her lips. "Okay, so now that you've had your coffee, what did you want to run by me?"

I smile behind my white porcelain cup, amused by her eagerness.

Placing the cup onto the saucer, I lean back in my seat and watch her closely. If she says no to what I'm proposing, I think I might cry. "If you could go to any place in the world, right now, where would it be?"

She arches a brow, clearly not expecting my question.

She mulls over her response as she reaches for a sugar packet and begins to flick a corner. "Paris," she finally reveals, and I'm unable to hide my approval of her reply.

She really couldn't have chosen a better place. The City of Love. If France doesn't inspire me to write a kick arse book, then I may as well give up now.

Leaning forward, I place my forearms along the tabletop and pin her with my most serious look. "Carrie…"

"Jayden…" she counters, mimicking my pose. It's the ultimate standoff. I only hope I don't lose.

The color of her eyes is electric, drawing me into a hypnotic emerald bubble. Here's to hoping that bubble isn't about to burst. "Let's go to Paris."

Kudos to her for not flinching. "Now?"

"Yes, right now." I nod, my confidence building.

She purses her lips in thought, which is far better than a fuck you. "What will we do in Paris?"

"What won't we do?" I reply, loving this playful banter. She may only be humoring me, but I'll revel in make-believe for as long as I can.

She slowly leans back in her seat, eyeing me closely. I know this is a big request, considering she hardly knows me, and under the circumstances of how we met, I wouldn't blame her if she ran for the hills.

Just as I'm about to play it off and pretend I was merely joking, she smiles. "Okay."

"Okay?" Pulling back, I wonder if I'm hearing things. "Okay as in yes, you'll come?" I need clarification.

"I don't know what okay means in London, but yes, I'll come," she quips, her excitement contagious.

"I left the UK over sixteen years ago, but that's beside the point…I can tell you all about that on the flight to Paris!" My voice raises an octave because I can't believe she said yes.

She giggles, covering her mouth, while I wonder what I did to deserve her. But a thought suddenly occurs to me, dousing my enthusiasm. "How quickly can you get your passport?" Mine is already packed; I wanted to be prepared in case I needed to flee the lake house for Canada in the dead of night.

"I never leave home without it," she replies, reaching for her coffee. "It's a habit I've had since I was a kid. My family has been known to fly around the world at the last minute to snare the latest literary 'rock star.'"

"Really?" This is too good to be true.

She tears open the sugar packet with a smirk. "For someone who is a supposed master of words, you sure as hell lack them at times."

I can't stop the rumble from erupting because she is absolutely right.

This is so spontaneous, so unlike me, which is exactly why I reach for my cell from my inner breast pocket and dial Nick. He answers on the fifth ring.

"Ho, ho, ho! Did Santa empty his sack?"

I roll my eyes at his not so subtle innuendo. "You are one sick fuck," I say with nothing but love.

"And don't forget agent extraordinaire. How's Daisy? Was she naughty or nice? Please say naughty." I can just see him winking in an exaggerated manner as he nudges me in the ribs.

"Correction. You are the world's worst agent. If you actually looked at your phone instead of playing Santa so every lass could sit on your lap, you'd have seen that I left there last night, intent on never returning."

"What?"

Carrie bites her top lip to stifle her laughter.

"Axle is a fucking twat, and Daisy is insane. Between the two of them, I would have become an alcoholic by the new year." I mouth a sorry to Carrie as I did just insult her family, but she waves me off. It appears she agrees.

"Jay…you can't just do that."

"I did just do that, and now, it's time to move on. I'm going to Paris."

"Sweet baby Jesus. You're killing my hard-on."

I turn my lip up, suddenly feeling the need to burn the phone, especially when I hear a nameless woman call out to "Nicky" for a quickie. "Look, all you need to know is that I'll be in Paris. I don't know how long for, but when I come back, I will have a manuscript that will kick your fucking arse. Oh, and by the way, email Gerry Williams. He is starting his own publishing house, and he wants me as his prized pig. Merry Christmas. Don't say I never give you anything."

"What? Jay…" But I hang up before he has a chance to finish.

Pocketing my cell, I watch Carrie's eyes flash in animation. "You're a man who knows what he wants." Oh yes, I certainly do—starting with those plump lips.

"Ready to order?" The waitress saves the day because after the past five minutes, adrenaline is coursing through me, and I might do something stupid like lean over this table and kiss the living fuck out of Carrie.

I'm certain Carrie is privy to my thoughts, but she doesn't

say a word. She simply orders her breakfast.

"When do we leave?"

"Right after breakfast," I reply, not seeing any reason to wait.

We're both packed and have our passports—what's stopping us?

"This is fucking crazy," she says, shaking her head in humor.

"Yes, it is." I can't keep the smile from my lips.

As I reach for my coffee, I observe a dashing young man, no older than eight, take a seat at the table beside us. He looks positively debonair with his red bow tie and white suit. He places the pink glitter gift bag on the table and adjusts his bow tie as he confidently scans the room.

Carrie also notices our very chic neighbor and watches him with an amused grin.

When a blonde girl, similar in age to our Casanova, strolls over wearing a sparkly pink dress and a silver tiara, I know that, without a doubt, she's his date. She holds a small box wrapped in red and green paper and topped with a gold bow.

"Merry Christmas, Max," she says, catching him unaware. He quickly stands and presents her his hand. They shake while I hide my broad smile behind my hand.

"Merry Christmas, Aubrey," Max the Casanova replies. "Here." He reaches for the bag, offering it to her. "I picked it out myself."

"Thank you. This is for you." She hands him the wrapped

box. "My mom helped me pick it out." Mention of her mother has Aubrey glancing over her shoulder, waving her little fingers to two women who sit huddled in a booth, smothering their grins behind their cupped palms.

Audrey unwraps her gift first— a Disney princess snow globe. She squeals, shaking it vigorously, then watches as the white speckles fall.

Max's gift, a science kit featuring a microscope, is also a hit.

As they take their seats, Max very sensibly tucks his white napkin into the collar of his shirt. Audrey reaches for the menu, her innocent blue eyes scanning over the contents. They talk about what gifts they got for Christmas and how their teacher, Mrs. Ironbark, falls asleep in class. They giggle, and the conversation is never stilted because this is a connection of the purest form.

I watch on in awe, wondering if these two youngsters will ever tire of one another or if they'll grow apart. What happens in ten years' time when both go off to college? Will they remember this particular Christmas and regard it as a cherished memory of their first crush?

Watching them inspires me, and I suddenly wish I had my laptop.

I wanted love from the very beginning, and this right here is exactly that. As the waitress takes their orders, I can't help but feel a melancholy sink low. Liz blamed her infidelity on the fact she couldn't get pregnant, and after seeing Max and Audrey, I can't help but wonder what our offspring would have looked like.

The two mothers who watch their children from afar radiate something I quite possibly may never experience. There is no doubt these mothers would protect their kin unconditionally because that's what good parents do. They pave the path for their offspring, wanting nothing but to protect, teach, and love.

Love.

At this moment, it becomes clear that love isn't always what you see because most times, it's the unseen, the insignificant moments that embody the simplicity of what love means. Max and Audrey's paths may sever, but in this split second, no one else matters but them. And that's what love is.

Love is whatever the fuck you want it to be. It doesn't have any rules. No right or wrong. It's belonging to the moment. It's belonging to yourself.

Carrie is watching me closely because she understands the significance of this. This is what I wanted—to experience love in its many forms.

When we lock eyes, an epiphany hits. Those who love are brave warriors because nothing is more terrifying than putting your heart on the line. But when you meet your match—the breath to your soul—you can conquer the world.

So…watch out, world. We're coming.

9
Nine

I'll give it to Nick.

Although I most likely took about ten years off his life and killed his hard-on, he came through when I needed him to. Within thirty minutes of informing him of my decision to go to Paris, he emailed me my flight and hotel details.

Kudos to him for not asking questions when I requested he book another ticket for one Carrie Bell. I don't know how he managed to organize two tickets on such short notice, and on Christmas Day nonetheless, but at midday, we were headed for Paris.

Thanks to the time difference, we arrive at eight in the morning, but neither of us can sleep. "Merci beaucoup," Carrie says to the taxi driver as she pays for the ride.

She insisted she pay for her plane ticket, but I wouldn't have it. She is my guest, after all. We grab our bags and make our way to my favorite hotel in Paris—the Shangri-La Hotel. It is completely overpriced, but I figure when in Rome…or in our case, Paris.

The moment we step foot into the lobby, the open archways and beaming chandeliers remind me of when I was here last. It was to promote my book *The Last Breath.* Liz, of course, insisted we stay here, saying the views are unmatched, and she was right.

Peering around now at the bright opulence and the grand staircase, I wonder if maybe I should have chosen another hotel.

Carrie notices my apprehension, sparking my honesty. "The last time I stayed here was with my ex-wife. If that makes you feel uncomfortable at all, we can stay someplace else. I just wanted to be honest."

I've caught her off guard.

She removes her black woolen gloves, appearing to mull over her response. Just when I'm about to suggest we stay somewhere else, she wraps her warm fingers around my wrist. A friendly gesture even though I wish it was something more. "No, I want to stay here. Let's replace your memories with new ones." She squeezes lightly, affirming her claim. "And besides, holy shit, this place is amazing."

A laugh escapes me.

We make our way to the front desk, and when I pull out my wallet, Carrie slaps my hand away. "It's on me."

I shake my head because this place costs a fortune. "Dove, your money is no good here."

The attendant, a gorgeous woman with silver gray hair and striking violet eyes, smiles when she hears Carrie and I arguing. *"Bonjour. Bienvenue."*

"Bonjour. Réservation pour Jayden Evans et Miss Carrie Bell," I say, all but shoving Carrie out of the way as we race toward the counter.

The lady nods as she types away at her computer.

Carrie elbows me softly, blowing her hair from her cheeks. "At least let me pay for half."

"Don't be ridiculous," I scoff, pulling out my Mastercard.

The attendant lets out a low, "Hmm," before reaching for her glasses. She continues typing, but it soon becomes apparent something is wrong. I'm thankful I'm fluent in French. *"Désolé. Mais je ne peux trouver que votre reservation, monsieur."*

"Vraiment?" I ask, confused. I'm about to explain to Carrie that the attendant has just said she can only find my reservation and not hers. Nick assured me via email that he booked two rooms.

But it appears no explanation is necessary. *"C'est pas grave. Une chamber, c'est bien."*

I turn over my shoulder to look at her, mouth slightly parted because I am so fucking turned on to hear her speaking French. It's no secret I have a love affair with everything French, so when Carrie reveals she's fluent in my favorite language, I have to wipe the drool from my chin.

But I can deal with that later because she just agreed to share a room with me.

As tempting as that offer is, I don't think I can spend whatever time we stay here sleeping on a couch. And more importantly, I don't trust myself with Carrie. Merely standing this close to her is enough to leave me a slobbering fool. I have no chance of keeping my hands to myself if I share a room with her.

The attendant looks at us, clearly mortified about the mix-up.

Retrieving my cell from my pocket, I send Nick a quick text. Within seconds, the screen lights up, and I curse the day we bonded over 80s hair metal bands.

Oopsie. Silly me. I only booked one room.

Sighing, I slap my phone against my palm, wondering how I'm going to detail my friend's attempt at playing cupid. I explain to the attendant that it's my fault, and that I only booked one room. Carrie has every right to be mad, but she isn't.

"At least I don't feel so bad about you paying for the room now."

The attendant stifles a giggle behind her clamped lips, but it's apparent she's as spellbound by Carrie as I am. Her glasses are perched on the edge of her nose as she types something into the computer. She smiles a moment later.

Once the paperwork is taken care of, she hands over our

keys and points at the elevator. “Enjoy your stay,” she says in a broken accent.

“*Merci.*”

We pass a young couple walking toward the front door, hand in hand. Their love shines. But one can’t help but be swathed in the emotion because this city is bursting with it.

“Have you been to Paris before?” I query as we wait for the elevator.

“Yes. Many times. The last time I was here I was twenty-four.”

“How long ago was that?” We both crashed on the plane, which limited our getting to know you time.

“Two years ago. I came here with my boyfriend at the time,” she reveals with a snicker. “I thought it would inspire me to feel something for him because after being together for three months, I was lacking that…”

“Spark?” I fill in, and she nods.

We enter the elevator, and Jesus Christ, it’s a tight squeeze. I need to think of anything other than her body inches from mine. “What was his name?”

Seeing as I’m invading her personal space, I figure I may as well invade her privacy as well.

“Albert.”

My brows shoot up into my hairline. “Albert? That sounds like a very mature name. I was expecting something a little more…modern.” My jealousy soon subsides because what dashing male lead is named Albert?

"That's because he was forty-five."

"Fo-forty-five?" I spit out, and she nods. "So you don't have any issues dating older guys then?"

"No. I'll try anything once," she replies with a sassy grin. I almost swallow my tongue. She is bound to give me a heart attack come nightfall.

Once the elevator stops at our floor, she exits, cool as a cucumber, while I subtly rearrange my pants. I'm trying, I truly am, but holy fuck, this woman is something else.

"What room are we in?" she asks over her shoulder. I can't help but think back to our conversation on the plane. She confessed to never being in love.

I still find it hard to believe that someone this terrific has never experienced the big L. Maybe she's incredibly fussy. Although I've only known her for such a short amount of time, I don't take her for the shallow type. I wonder what sort of men she's dated. From the two I know, one was an utter tosser while the other was old enough to be her father.

She did say she's dated a lot of guys. Therefore, it appears she doesn't have a type. I wonder if I'm her type? Whoa, this train of thought needs to end now. We're not here to worry about such trivial matters. I'm here to write, and Carrie is here to forget about the Alberts and twats of this world.

"Two hundred and five," I reply to her earlier question.

We walk the elaborate hallway, appreciating the true beauty

of this place. Carrie stops by our door, and her energy to enter is palpable. I unlock the door, gesturing for her to enter first. A gasp leaves her when she steps foot inside. Following behind, I relish in witnessing her reaction.

"Holy shit. One can easily see this was formerly a palace," she gushes, turning in a circle as she examines our home for the next few days.

The spacious room is decorated in golds and whites, showcasing the elegance. A large living area is separate from the master bedroom. The king-size bed to the right is draped in gold silk and throw cushions.

I have no doubt every room in this hotel is stunning, but I now know what the attendant was smiling about. We got the upgrade. This is clearly a suite with a…

"Oh my god…the view," Carrie coos, opening the terrace doors, which confirms my assumption that we got a suite with our own private terrace.

I walk to where she stands by the balcony, mesmerized by the skyline of Paris, and at its center, the Eiffel Tower—the nucleus for so many worldwide.

"Wow."

"Wow, indeed," I confirm because this is some view.

Even though the fog casts gray clouds over this magical city, it doesn't take away from the magnificence that is Paris. If anything, it amplifies the fact that beauty can be found in the most unexpected of places.

I leave Carrie to her private thoughts and go to unpack a few things.

As I step into the master bedroom, my eyes land on the well-dressed bed. This will be the first time I've slept beside someone—just sleep. The thought is unnerving. It also reminds me of the number of women I've slept with over these past six months.

"What side of the bed do you sleep on?" Carrie asks, snapping me from my thoughts.

"I don't mind." Running my fingers through my hair, I hope to disguise my nerves.

"I'll probably end up on your side anyway," she reveals, dumping her bag by the right side of the bed.

"Oh?" I wet my lips.

"Yeah. I've been told I'm a restless sleeper. I end up in all sorts of positions."

Bloody hell.

She smirks, knowing damn straight what her comment is doing to me. This innocent flirting is sure to leave me walking with a limp.

"I'll be sure to stay on my side then."

She bumps me with her shoulder playfully. "Where's the fun in that? Are you hungry?"

"Ravenous," I reply in a tone that reveals I'm not only hungry for food.

Small victory for me when her cheeks blush a sweet pink.

At least I'm not the only one affected by our flirting.

She chews her bottom lip, her confidence soon replaced with the bashfulness she shows from time to time. It's becoming. Like her whole persona.

When I don't shy away from staring at her, she nervously crouches down to unzip her bag. She retrieves a coat and her camera. "You can capture your beauty, and I'll capture mine." She loops the strap around her neck after slipping into her white coat.

I stand transfixed as she untucks her long hair from the collar. Our eyes meet, and a knowing gaze bounces between us. But neither of us wishes to address it and make things awkward.

"Shall we?" I suggest, suddenly needing fresh air. When she nods, I grab my jacket and laptop, and then we're out the door.

As a silence overcomes us when we enter the elevator, I wonder what she's thinking. Our attraction has been present since the first moment we met, but this silence is new. Is she having second thoughts?

She had no qualms flying to Paris with an almost stranger, so I don't understand why she's clamming up all of a sudden.

"I know a great café not too far from here," she says, breaking the silence.

"As long as they have coffee and croissants, I'm sold."

"Their pastries are delicious. Paris is not good for one's waistline." We exit the elevator and brace ourselves for the punishing weather.

Once outside, we commence a quick walk as the morning air is bitterly cold. "There is nothing wrong with curves," I say, remarking on her comment.

She rubs her gloved hands together, blowing them as she's still evidently cold. "Oh, so you like girls who aren't wafer thin then?"

Pulling up the collar on my leather jacket, I reply, "That doesn't matter to me. It never has. Confidence and independence is far more appealing than a pretty face."

She doesn't look convinced.

"Why, you thought otherwise?"

She shrugs, but that's a yes.

"Go on then. What do you think my type is?" This should be fun.

"Judging by your ex-wife, I'd say your type is a superficial, spoiled princess with a stick up her ass."

I trip over my own feet, almost kissing the pavement.

Carrie makes no apologies. "You asked."

"Yes, I did," I reply when I find my voice. "I just find it interesting to hear your opinion of her."

"I'm sure I'm not the only one who thinks that."

I mull over her comment and decide to set the record straight. "She wasn't always this way."

"Uh-huh," Carrie replies, hinting she doesn't believe a word I say.

I have no idea why I feel the need to defend her, but I soon realize I'm defending myself and not her. "There once was a time when I was enough. But after being together for thirteen years, the passion, I suppose, it dies."

"That's bullshit," Carrie counters, huddling into her coat as the wind blows.

"Excuse me?" I can't keep the humor from my tone.

"That's bullshit," she repeats, not at all bothered. "Regardless of how many years together, the passion dies because the love was never there." She seems quite passionate about this topic, so I listen with interest. "Time should *strengthen* what you have, not tear it apart. I hope I'm still doing the dirty with my husband well into my nineties, if I live that long.

"Yes, we may not fuck like rabbits, but I'd imagine I'd still want him as much as I did when we first met."

"So you don't think you'd grow bored?" I ask, genuinely curious.

"No." She turns serious. "I think my love would grow more and more each day. That's what love means to me… which is why I'm still single, so what the fuck do I know."

She's deflecting her emotions, but I stop her by gently gripping her upper arm. We're standing in the middle of the sidewalk, covered in white flecks of snow, but it's small moments such as these that make the most impact. "Don't disregard your feelings like that. They matter. And as it happens, I agree with you. Being in a relationship is a partnership, and I thought I'd found my partner, but it appears I'm still looking."

Her chest rises and falls, her cheeks rosy from the wintry breeze. A snowflake lands, perching on her long lashes, and just like that, inspiration hits.

She is unique, different, just like every snowflake that falls from the heavens.

"Let's go." Her lower lip quivers, and I'm unsure if it's the cold or if it's something else. I suppress the need to bundle her into my side when a shiver passes through her.

We walk the rest of the way to the small café in silence. The smells catching on the morning chill are mouth-watering. Carrie enters the quaint café, which is simple in design but so very Parisian. As she peers around, looking for a table, a waiter immediately spots us, and I instantly want to tear off his arms and beat him to a bloody mess with them.

"Bonjour. Table for two?" the young waitress asks.

Carrie nods while I watch the preppy Ken doll make a beeline for her. "*Salut.* It's okay, Anna. I'll show them to their table," he says with an American accent.

Carrie seems to only just notice him as she looks up and smiles.

"Follow me. I've got a booth in the back under a heater." He winks as though he's doing us a favor, and I have to refrain from reminding him it's his job.

We follow as do the eyes of every patron in the café. Yes, I can admit, he is clearly appealing to the opposite sex if you like that perfect hair, perfect teeth kind of look, but I know Carrie won't fall for the optical illusion. She knows better.

He places our menus on the table, that interested grin still attached to his face as he stares at Carrie. Then at me. Is he sizing me up? She shyly pushes past him to slide into the booth, but nothing is reserved about my manner as I clear my throat very loudly and almost send him three feet by shoving him out of the way.

The violence alerts the creep to stop staring. "I'm Mason, by the way. I'll be back to take your order." He flashes a white, toothy smile, then leaves us alone.

I sigh. Even his name is flawless. Why can't he be called fucking Albert?

Carrie removes her gloves and coat, and I reach for the menu. There is no denying this wave of jealousy clouding my rationale, but I squash it down because it has no right to be there.

As I scan over the options, everything suddenly looks so bland. But Mason is the reason for the bad taste in my mouth. I toss the menu onto the table, deciding on just a coffee as I've lost my appetite.

As Carrie studies the menu, I peruse the room, and my gaze lands on a young couple two tables over. They too are reviewing the menu, hinting they just arrived.

"What will you have?" asks the beau to his woman companion in French.

He wears a blue dress shirt and slacks, and his blond hair

is styled neatly. Peering down at his shoes, it's apparent they've been shined clean. I examine the lovely woman's attire, which is a tight green dress and brown heeled boots. Her makeup is a little too heavy for a casual catch-up.

His bouncing foot is a dead giveaway he's nervous. Her hair flicking and licking of lips shows this for what it is—a first date.

Without thought, I unzip my bag and pull out my laptop and glasses. As I wait for it to fire up, I peer over the top of my glasses and meet Carrie's eyes.

"What?" I ask when she appears to have seen something astonishing.

"I like that."

"Like what?"

"The look you get when inspiration strikes," she explains.

"Well, that seems to happen a lot when you're around." It's out there before I can put a lid on my outburst. But Carrie seems flattered.

"I've never been anyone's inspiration before."

"That's a damn shame and an indication of the *boys* you dated. They were just that—little boys who wouldn't know their nose from their cock. Even Albert." I have no idea where this bout of Tourette's has come from, but I don't regret a word.

Carrie's mouth twitches as she leans back into her seat. "Them're some fighting words."

"I only speak the truth."

"Speaking of truths…how many women have you been

with then? Seeing as you're a big man and all."

This is dangerous ground we tread, but she makes it clear she won't let this slide when she arches a challenging brow.

Matching her pose, I brace my arm across the top of the leather booth and shrug. "Before my marriage turned to shite, I had only ever slept with one other woman before Liz. We got together when I was twenty."

She blinks once, clearly stunned by my revelation. "Wow. Her cheating seems all the more worse now."

I know exactly what she means.

"So getting back on the horse, so to speak, wasn't high on my to-do list. But Liz's infidelity plagued me, almost mocked me at times…so I guess I…"

"Fell into someone's vagina?" she offers when I'm at a loss for words. A hoarse chuckle escapes me because I love how candid we are with one another. "Stop stalling. What's the closing number?"

"I honestly don't know." And that's not because I have endless victorious notches on my bedposts. It's because I never wanted to keep count.

"Ballpark," she presses, pursing her lips.

There is no way I can avoid this topic without answering her. Math was never my strong suit, but I do a quick calculation in my head. I was hooking up with random women, some more than once, others a one-night-only deal, about two weeks after I left Liz. The number of women would be roughly two a week, maybe three.

So, off the top of my head, I…*holy shite.*

That's a lot of women.

"More than thirty?" Carrie says, giving me a lifeline. But I am utterly ashamed. When grouped together, that number confirms what a manwhore I am.

During those six months, I never really gave much thought to the final number, but put on the spot like this, I suddenly feel the need to neuter myself. "Yes, more than thirty but no more than fifty. I don't think," I add, scratching the back of my neck.

Carrie sits quiet. She has every right to want to spray me with Lysol. "Wow. I'm impressed with your stamina." Her comment is supposed to be playful, but an underlying bitterness breaks the surface.

I understand completely. I am disgusted with myself too.

She senses my revulsion. "Hey, I'm not one to judge. Believe me."

Before I get a chance to ask what exactly that means, Mason strolls over. "What can I get you?" He has his notepad and pen poised, ready to take Carrie's order.

She shakes her head, most likely to dispel such heinous thoughts of my gluttonous cock from her mind. "I'll have a café au lait and a pain au chocolat." She purses her lips in thought. "And an éclair. And also a lemon and sugar crepe."

Mason writes down her order with a smirk. "Good choice. They're all of my favorites."

Good thing no one asked you, I silently add.

"And for you, sir?"

The word sir has never sounded so…old. But I suppose compared to Mason, I am. I would guess him to be in his mid to late twenties. Not that much older than me, but when I was his age, I thought anyone over the age of thirty was ready for retirement.

"Just a coffee. Black."

Carrie clucks her tongue. "You can share my breakfast. But can we get two forks?" she asks Mason, batting her lashes playfully my way.

Mason doesn't get the banter but laughs anyway. If this dude had one intellectual thought, he'd be dangerous.

When he lingers, I know he wants to talk to Carrie. I have one of two options. I can either break both his legs, or I can focus on the reason I came here, and that is to write. Much to the horror of my testosterone doing push-ups and primed for a fight, I decide on the latter.

Opening a new document, I title it as first date and watch the couple closely as they awkwardly make conversation. They discuss in great detail how cold it's been of late.

Strike number one.

Discussing the weather is skywriting the fact that you're bored because, unless you're a meteorologist, no one cares if it's fucking cold or not.

My fingers type frantically, not wanting to miss a thing,

but what I hear next has me pausing and tempted to slap some sense into our young beau. "What is your favorite food?"

Dear god, did he get the dos and don'ts of first dates mixed up? This is a train wreck. I can barely watch. I'm counting on him to inspire me with newfound wisdom, not bore me to death with how many carbs are in a breakfast baguette.

However, I continue watching, hoping this will turn around for the young couple.

"What's your favorite animal?"

This just goes from bad to worse.

Groaning, I slap a hand to my forehead. The only thing it appears I will be unearthing today is a headache.

Carrie's light giggle is a welcome reprieve because at least this exercise wasn't a complete waste of time. "Don't be so mean," she whispers from behind her hand.

"He's being mean to my brain," I counter, only half joking.

"He's nervous."

She defends while I opt for, "He's a twat. That poor girl is looking at that knife as if it's her lifeline."

Carrie bites back her smile as she turns in the booth to subtly examine the woeful pair. All I see is failure with 20/20 vision, but Carrie sees something else.

"Look at their body language."

I tilt my head to the side, but all I see is his awkward fidgeting.

"Seventy to ninety percent of our communication is

nonverbal. What's her body telling you?"

"That she's wishing she swiped left?" I offer, but Carrie ignores my quip.

"Look at her face. It's friendly. She's smiling. She's listening intently..."

"To him boring her," I add, wondering what his next horrible question will be.

"She's pointing her body toward him, she's opened up, and her arms are not crossed. There is a comfortable amount of eye contact too. He looks nervous. Is that good or bad nerves? What do you think?"

Her comment has me surveying the scene, attempting to make my own observations. He is fiddling with everything on the table, so unless he has OCD, I dare say he's trying to focus on anything other than how hot his date is. Some guys seem cool, calm, and collected, but it appears this dude wears his heart on his sleeve.

"Why is he so...sweaty?" I ask, connecting the dots of his sweat marks to form a map of Italy.

"'Cause he's into her," she reveals as though it's a no-brainer.

I thought our Casanova was merely a poor conversationalist, but it seems his nerves are getting the better of him.

"You're good at this," I say, typing out her observations.

She sighs. "Too bad I can't apply that knowledge to my own love life. If I were on that date, I'd have thought he was sweating it because he was devising ways to escape."

Pausing from typing, I peer up at her from over my laptop. “I stick by my affirmation that these were little boys.”

She smiles.

“So we’ve established they both like one another. They just need a helping hand?”

“Yes, they definitely like one another. I think this is our perfect first specimen.”

“Second,” I correct. “Did you forget our young Casanova?”

“How could I forget,” she replies, beaming at the memory of Max and Aubrey.

Mason decides to ruin a nice conversation by breathing. “Your café au lait. And your black coffee.” He huddles close. He clearly has never heard of personal space.

I’m seconds away from throttling this gigantic dickhead, so I decide to put my hands to good use elsewhere. Standing, I begrudgingly leave Romeo to talk to Carrie and make my way over to the couple in need because he’s losing her. The ultimate deal breaker has just occurred—she’s scrolling through her phone.

I can’t let technology win.

“Excuse me. May I borrow your sugar?” I ask in French.

The young woman looks up, her brown eyes sparking in interest. Her date instantly sees her curiosity, and finally, his balls come out of hiding. He reaches for her hand, which startles her.

Hallelujah.

I make a point to look at their connection and coo like a clucky mother. "How long have you been together?"

Her cheeks pinken as she passes me the sugar canister. "It's our first date. We know one another from school."

"Really?" I fake horror, mouth agape. "First date? I wouldn't have guessed. I thought you'd been together for a long while. You're one lucky man." Just as Hulk Hogan is about to come out of hiding, I turn her way and wink. "And you're one lucky girl." She giggles, while the guy looks like he's just inflated to double his size. Nothing like a little flattery to break the ice.

He's like fucking Superman when I turn to leave, so my work here is done.

"He's right. I am lucky. I've liked you since I first saw you in class. You were wearing that red dress with the white lace."

This is so in the bag.

"I can't believe you remember what I was wearing. I liked you too."

I leave the lovers to whisper their sweet nothings and return to my table, thankful it's Mason free.

"Well played," Carrie says as I slide my ploy sugar onto the table.

"He just needed a little push," I reveal, "and to defend what's his. You see, at heart, we're all just cavemen fighting for our primal needs—food, shelter, and to procreate.

"Interesting," she says around a mouthful of her crepe. "Write that down." She gestures to my laptop with her fork.

I do as she says.

As I'm sipping my coffee and reading over my notes, Carrie pushes her plate my way. I see it as a peace offering. "Mason invited us to a bar tonight."

I scoff. "I think you mean he invited you."

"No, actually, his words were you and your older brother should come tonight." She smothers her giggles as I seek out Mason and envision him writhing in a ball of flames. "This will give us loads of people to watch. Think of all the research we can do," she reasons.

A small voice inside me is screaming that I say yes. She clearly wants me to go with her. She wouldn't have told me otherwise. But the issue I'm faced with is I don't know if it's because she wants to spend more time with me, or if she wants me to be her wingman.

Regardless, my words come back to bite me in the arse.

*You see, at heart, we're all just cavemen…*and when I look at Carrie, I see her as mine. Houston, we have a problem.

Reaching across the table, I steal her fork en route to her mouth. It shouldn't tempt me the way that it does when I place the fork into my mouth, knowing it had the lucky pleasure of being enveloped between her lips.

The tartness versus the sugariness of the crepe is bittersweet—a perfect analogy of how I feel when I say, "Okay. Let's go."

Eating in silence, we see that the couple seems to have finally gotten their shit together, and they end up leaving arm in arm. I'm happy for them, I truly am. It's good to see someone will leave this café with the girl in tow.

10
Ten

After breakfast, Carrie and I did some sightseeing and people watching. The snow and the subzero temperature made it hard to determine if people were huddling close for warmth or love. But we made our own assumptions. No surprise Carrie was convinced they were all long-lost lovers.

We were both in our element as Carrie was off taking pictures, and I sat on a park bench watching passersby. There is something almost forbidden about watching other people interact because you're a voyeur on their life's journey, wondering which way the chips will fall.

After a couple of hours, Carrie and I decided to head back to the hotel because her nose rivaled Rudolph's. The thought of her red button nose has me smiling, which just confirms what I knew from the first moment we met.

I like Carrie, and the more time I spend with her, the more that like only seems to grow.

Today at the café with Mason, I knew that I was jealous—the violent need to maim him validated this. But this is ridiculous. I haven't even known this woman a week, and I'm ready to throw down and mark her as mine.

This has never happened before. Even with Liz.

Yes, the attraction was there, but what I feel for Carrie, I just can't explain it…and it has nothing to do with my writer's block because coming here has unplugged the mental drought. Well, for now anyway.

After we came back to the hotel, Carrie crashed, but I couldn't sleep. I was dog tired, but I had so many thoughts bouncing around my head, and I had to get them down. Three hours later, my first chapter was complete.

I stared at the screen for about twenty minutes, unbelieving that I actually did it. After being shrouded in nothing but doubt, seeing your words before you—words you don't hate—is the most rewarding feeling in the entire world.

I felt lighter somehow.

Feeling victorious, I knew a drink was in order, but the moment I stood and my eyes landed on Carrie's sleeping form, I knew my thirst could only be quenched by her. Her auburn hair contrasted the crispness of the white pillow, and unable to stop myself, I walked to where she lay.

Her chest rose and fell, sweet breaths fanning the strands of hair from her rosy cheek. She looked so peaceful, so innocent, but nothing was innocent about this fierce woman. She is far braver than I am.

And just like that, I was once again struck with inspiration, which led me to write half of chapter two. I'm currently three thousand words in.

The story stars none other than our heroes—Max and Audrey. It seems fitting to begin with them. What Carrie and I witnessed was just too priceless not to put into words, so my story begins in a diner on a cold Christmas morning…

It's dark out, and my shoulders and fingers are begging for a reprieve, but I promise myself another thousand words, and then I'll be done.

"Hey." Carrie's sleepy voice stirs the beast within.

"Hey. Sleep well?" I ask, quickly finishing my sentence because once I turn and look at her, I doubt anything coherent will follow.

"Yes, I did. That bed is like sleeping on a cloud," she replies with a yawn. "Wow. Did you write all that?" I hit full stop and turn in my swivel seat.

"Yes." When I see her, it's as if I hit another punctuation mark, and that is Carrie is fucking delectable. *Full stop.*

Her ruffled hair tumbles around her rosy cheeks in messy waves. "How long was I asleep?" she teases, standing on tippy toes to examine the screen.

Unsure of the time, I look over my shoulder to see the clock on the laptop reveals it's just after 8 p.m.

"Do you want to get dinner before we head out?"

The thought of her going anywhere near Mason leaves me with the vicious need to break something. But I remind myself that Carrie and I are just friends.

"Sure. Sounds good."

She smiles, and I know she's hiding something, but I don't have time to uncover what. "I'm going to take a shower."

She carries her bag into the bathroom, leaving me with the very explicit image of her about to get naked. Needing something to quench my thirst, I stand and make my way to the minibar. The whiskey will be a poor substitute, but it's better than nothing.

As I unscrew the lid, my cell chimes. Thinking it's Nick, I take a swig of booze and reach for it off the table without looking who the caller is.

Shame on me.

"Hello?"

Sniff. "Why didn't you call and wish me a Merry Christmas?"

Suddenly, all the whiskey in the world isn't enough to deal with my soon-to-be ex-wife. "Why on earth would I do that? It was only last Christmas you were fucking god knows who on my desk. I thought you'd be busy. You know, history repeating itself and all."

"How long must you torture me?" Liz says, her voice quivering. A small part of me—a stupid, fucking insane part—

feels the need to comfort her, but I soon squash that part and all the memories that come with it.

"*You're* torturing yourself. This is over. It was over the moment you cheated, Elizabeth. The sooner you accept it, the better it will be for us both."

"How many times must I say I'm sorry? I made a mistake."

"Mistake?" I scoff, finishing off my bottle of whiskey, then hunting for another. "A mistake would mean you slipped up once. And if that were indeed the case, I could maybe, *maybe* get over this, but you were screwing around long before I caught you, weren't you?"

She never confirmed my suspicions, but now, her silence says it all.

I should feel relieved, but I don't. I feel like a fucking failure. How could she cheat? Why wasn't I enough?

"I'm human," she offers as some plausible explanation to why she cheated. "After thirteen years, I needed…"

"I don't fucking care what you needed!" I shout, anger bursting the seams. "All I ever needed was you, and in return, you go and break my fucking heart!"

As she sobs, I throw back the contents of my whiskey bottle, but I need so much more.

"I'm sorry, Jayden."

"I'm sorry too, Liz. I'm sorry for ever giving a damn about you." And I mean it.

"I lov—" Before those vile words can pass her traitorous

lips, the phone is yanked from my ear.

I almost fall over my feet when I see Carrie standing before me in nothing but a towel. Her hair is twisted into a high bun, and beads of water cling to the slope of her neck. Although she's in nothing but a white bath towel, she owns this room.

"This must be the elusive Elizabeth Evans. Well, soon-to-be ex-Evans. You're ruining our evening, so would you kindly take a hint and leave Jayden alone?"

My mouth opens and closes uselessly as Carrie puts the phone on speaker.

"Who is this? Are you the little slut my husband was with when I called last?"

Carrie examines her nails, clearly bored. "Nope. That was probably my sister."

A winded chuckle leaves me.

"He will grow tired of you soon enough. Mark my words. And then he will come back to me. We belong together."

"Too bad you didn't feel that way when you were screwing anything with a pulse. It's women like you who ruin it for everyone else. Your behavior warrants men treating us like commodities, nothing but a warm body to do with as they please. You're an appalling human being, and Jayden is too good for you." Carrie expresses all this without tearing her gaze from mine. Wow, this seems kind of personal, and I wonder why that is.

This woman is fierce, and she is someone who will soon

pervade every inch of my soul.

"You're right. He *is* too good for me, which is all the more reason to fight for him. I don't give up easily, little girl."

"Well, guess what? Neither do I. Now, if you'll excuse me, I have to get dressed."

Game. Set. Match.

Liz bellows out a string of profanities before Carrie ends the call. She calmly hands me back my phone. "So what do you feel like for dinner? I'm starved."

Food is the furthest thing from my mind. I am standing mute, processing everything that just happened. Carrie completely crushed Liz, but her comment has left me wondering what she won't give up.

Fuck me, I need a drink.

"Bathroom's all yours," Carrie says, reminding me she's standing inches away in nothing but a towel. She's by the foot of the bed, clutching a red dress to her chest—a subtle hint for me to leave so she can get dressed.

But I take a moment to appreciate this delicate anomaly.

The face of a warrior queen, I scan downward, transfixed by her erratic pulse which throbs at the side of her throat. The tops of her breasts are milky smooth, rising and falling in a hypnotic manner with each deep breath she takes.

The towel is wrapped tightly around her, but if she moved in just the right way, the split would reveal a glorious vision of her supple stomach and inner thigh. Continuing my journey, I admire the supple shape of her calves and the fine gold chain which sits snug around her ankle. I've stooped to a new low—who knew, an anklet has the ability to make me hard.

Even her goddamn toes are delicious.

Needing to get the hell away from her, I quickly grab some clothes and make my way to the bathroom. The moment I shut the door, I tip my head toward the heavens and sigh. I need a shower. A cold one.

I am so screwed.

Taking a long, cold shower does nothing to alleviate my throbbing hard-on, but rubbing one out with Carrie in the next room feels as perverse as it sounds. Though so is poking her eye out with this boner I'm sporting.

As I wrap my hand around my dick and begin to stroke it, I think of that fucking anklet and how I have the urge to rip it off before I sink into her honeyed sex. I would take my time with her, meeting her needs first. I would cherish every part of her.

Her lithe body would feel like heaven beneath me, and her pussy…holy shite…I can't even. Oh, shite.

With a few quick strokes, I spill my seed all over the shower wall with a deep guttural groan. I slam my fist against the marbled tiles as I slump forward. My orgasm tackled me from out of nowhere because I just came in under a minute. I should be ashamed. What a two-pump chump.

Once I catch my breath, I wash away my shame of coming like a pubescent teen.

Stepping from the shower, I dry off and slip into what I grabbed in my haste to flee from Carrie—my ripped blue jeans, white V-neck T-shirt, and the black blazer from earlier. I run my fingers through my hair and apply some cologne.

Once I'm done, I exit the bathroom and see Carrie standing before me in a tight-fitting long-sleeved red dress. As I watch her zip up her black heeled boots, I roll my tongue back into my mouth. "Ready? What do you feel like eating?"

I refrain from expressing my indecent thoughts and smile. "Your choice."

Once I've laced my Chucks, I peer up and almost come in mere seconds once again when Carrie watches me with a hunger in her eyes. It's gone as quickly as it appeared. "I feel like something spicy."

You and me both.

♥ ♥ ♥

After feasting on Brazilian cuisine and two bottles of wine, we caught a taxi to Brooklyn, a cocktail bar located around *rue Oberkampf* in the 11th. Seeing Paris by nightfall is like experiencing something out of this world. Carrie's nose was all but pressed to the window, spellbound by the lightened magic.

I love this city, but being here with Carrie is like seeing it for the first time.

She saw the beauty in everything and appreciated the smallest of things. I'd almost forgotten how exquisite the Eiffel

Tower looked when illuminated by the millions of twinkling lights, but being with Carrie has opened my eyes to a lot of things.

I pay the cab driver and offer my hand to steady Carrie as she steps out on the frost-coated curb. She accepts with a small smile. I expect her to let go, but she doesn't. Her warm fingers interlace mine as she drags me down the busy sidewalk. I play off her affection as her one too many glasses of wine with dinner.

After talking to Liz, I'm thankful we're coming here because Google told me this place is notorious for its whiskey. They apparently have over thirty different types to try, and I intend to sample each. Beneath the bright orange fluorescent sign stands a mass of people, smoking or chatting with their friends.

With our hands still locked, Carrie leads the way, and we enter the very cool, trendy bar. I can't remember the last time I was in a place like this because Liz wouldn't be caught dead in a bar like this. I instantly relish in the thought.

"Drink?" Carrie yells over her shoulder to drown out David Bowie blaring from the speakers. I pull a face because it's a no-brainer.

We wait in line, both taking in our environment, and even though this place is pretty spectacular, it pales compared to the feel of Carrie's hand in mine.

Like Carrie, it's the simplest of things that mean the most to me, which is why I haven't kissed another woman or wanted to kiss another woman after Liz. But as I peer down at Carrie's pink glossy lips, I want nothing more than to break that rule.

A busty blonde gestures us over to order our drinks, and the moment we reach the bar, I know she's interested. She studies me from head to toe, uncaring that Carrie is by my side. "What can I get you?" she asks in a thick Russian accent.

"Your finest whiskey and…"

"Make that two," Carrie says, bopping to the music.

The barmaid doesn't shy away from giving me a final once-over. Reaching for the top shelf whiskey, she's uncaring that her ass cheeks are hanging from her short shorts. Once upon a time, I probably would have gotten completely pissed and taken her back to my hotel, but now, I wish she'd hurry up.

"Whiskey? We're in for a big night then?"

Carrie smirks, and it's too endearing for words. "Oh, there's a table," she says, pointing at a small circular booth at the back of the room. "I'll go grab it. You'll be okay?"

"I think I can manage to carry two whiskeys without your help," I tease, but I should have known there is always more to Carrie than meets the eye.

Standing on tippy toes, she leaves me winded when she whispers into my ear, "No, I meant you'll be okay defending your junk from the barfly making fuck-me eyes at you. I don't want her to spit in my drink."

"Why do you think she'd spit in your drink?" I ask, turning slowly so our faces are mere inches apart.

Even in her boots, I'm still a head taller, but the temptation seems greater because those lips…those fucking lips. "Because"—she peers up at me through her long lashes—"I'm pretty sure she's the one who wants to be holding your hand. Or something else."

Instantly, my fingers squeeze gently around hers because she feels it too. I thought she was oblivious to us holding hands, but clearly, I was wrong.

"Your drinks," the bartender says, snapping us from a moment, which stuns us both.

Carrie almost collides with the man beside her as she severs our connection. The disappointment drags me under because I don't understand what just happened. And I will apparently never find out because Carrie makes a beeline for the booth.

Digging into my back pocket for my wallet, I pay for our drinks and suddenly wish I'd ordered ten more.

My heart is in my throat when I make my way through the noisy crowd. On any other day, I'd have paid attention to my surroundings, but right now, the only thing I can focus on is Carrie. She appears flustered and nervous as she shifts in her seat. What is she hiding?

Whatever that was back at the bar has left her uneasy. When she meets my eyes, she smiles, but it's forced. Not wanting to make it a big deal, I present her with her whiskey. "Bottoms up." She accepts and scoots over so I can sit.

The booth barely sits one person, but I slide across the

leather and hope to god whatever this awkwardness is between us fades. When our thighs innocently touch, she downs almost half her drink but then splutters it back up, coughing loudly.

"Dove, careful. Whiskey is like a kiss—best enjoyed slow." Damn me and my mouth. It was supposed to be a joke, but Carrie's scarlet cheeks reveal I have embarrassed her. I probably sound like some perverted creep.

Not wanting to be boxed in with all the other men she's spent her time with, I take my own advice and sip my drink, scanning the room. We have a fantastic viewpoint, and my interest instantly falls to three people sitting at a long table across the room from us.

Their backs are to the brick wall, so I can see their legs and hands. And both are telling me a scandalous story. Leaning back, I watch in interest as a flaming redhead is wedged between two men who look like brothers.

The redhead leans toward the more robust looking of the two men, linking her arm through his as she whispers something into his ear. Whatever she says has him grinning as if he's just won the lottery. I notice they're both wearing wedding rings.

Waist up, one would be forgiven for thinking they've just witnessed a tender exchange between man and wife, but waist down, it's an entirely different story. The redhead may be canoodling with one man, but she has no qualms about playing footsie with the other.

The man to her left, the younger and far more attractive

man, plays aloof, sipping his drink, but there is nothing aloof about his hand sliding up her leg. She's wearing a very short dress, and when she shifts her legs, I can see why. Easy access for bachelor number two.

Carrie follows my line of sight, gasping when she sees what holds me captive.

The room is shadowy enough for your average partygoer not to notice the wicked activities after dark, but when you're looking, it's hard to miss.

"Oh my god," Carrie says, shifting closer to me for a better view. I'm thankful our bout of uneasiness has escaped us for now because she doesn't hesitate to press her body to mine. "Is he…yup, he is." She answers her own question when the redhead's mouth parts as do her legs.

The man continues delving his fingers in deep, and when he hits her sweet spot, she buckles and leans into her husband, biting the side of his neck. He thinks she finds him irresistible, but the poor sucker, he's got a lot to learn.

This is like a train wreck—I need to look away—but I'm mesmerized at how someone can openly cheat with their spouse literally feet away. This is the ugly side to love. The love I have been faced with these past six months.

But something about this doesn't make me clam up; it does the complete opposite. It inspires me to never, ever shape my characters into selfish, philandering arseholes. It makes me want to write a story for every person who has been cheated on.

My hand is curled into a fist, a fact I'm unaware of until Carrie places her cool hand over my very angry one. "Dance with me."

It's not a question but rather a statement, and when she downs her whiskey and stands, I know she means right now.

I follow suit and toss back my drink as I'll need all the Dutch courage I can get on that dance floor. We pass the threesome, the redhead clearly climaxing as her oblivious spouse strokes her neck. I am suddenly so fucking angry.

But Carrie leads me and my rage toward the dance floor.

I have no idea of the song or when the last time I danced was, but the moment Carrie presses her body to mine, all reservations are long forgotten. I know what she's doing; she's distracting me so the memories I've tried so hard to erase from my mind don't drag me back under.

The song suddenly changes into something slow and sensual. The change of pace surprises her, but now that I've got her, I don't plan on letting her go. Wrapping an arm low around her waist, I tug her forward so not even a wisp of hair can pass between us.

The sharp movement stuns her as her eyes widen, the pupils instantly flaring to alert me to her heightened state. But she started this, and now, it's time I finished it. She nervously places one hand on my bicep and wraps the other around my shoulder. Unable to help myself, I wrap my fingers around her nape, drawing our faces together, and then we move.

Her body molds perfectly to mine as she slides against me, allowing the music to rule her. We never break eye contact, both watching the other closely, not knowing what comes next. Her breath is laced with whiskey; combined with her trademark scent of strawberries and cream, it's a fragrance I could easily become addicted to.

When she rubs against me, I know I already have.

I'm rock solid, and she can feel it as I'm pressed against her center, but that fact only seems to spur her on as she grinds down and groans. Her skin is on fire, and when I gently tighten my hold around her neck, pulling us even closer together, I'm certain she detonates around me.

Her lips are a hairsbreadth away. I could close the distance and give in to temptation, but once we connect, I won't be able to stop. Her fingers toy with the strands of hair curling at my nape, and when she licks her lips, I know she wants it too.

Our bodies move in sync, and this dance elicits images of me throwing her onto our bed and burying myself between her legs for hours. I want those strong thighs wrapped around me as I eat her out before fucking her into submission. I want to be gentle. I want to be rough. I want to take. I want to give. I want it all. With her. And I want it now.

My cock springs against her, desperate to escape its confines, but Carrie's arousal soon turns to dread when her eyes pop open. "I think I'm going to be sick." Untangling her body from mine, she races through the throng of people with her hand over her mouth as she finds the bathroom.

Well, this is a first. My cock rocks under a blanket in the fetal position, unsure what just went wrong. I've sickened many women before but not to the point of physically being ill. Leaving my pride on the dance floor, I push my way past gyrating bodies to go find Carrie.

Once I push open the bathroom door, I don't have far to look. The retching coming from the last stall is a dead giveaway to where she is. "Sorry, ladies. I'm not looking," I call out, cupping both hands by my temple to protect their modesty. This is Paris, however. No one seems to care.

"Dove?" I knock gently on the door and am greeted with an echoed groan. "Let me in."

"No," she manages to say between vomiting.

"Come on. Let me prove to you that I'm not that bad of a dancer." It was supposed to be a joke, but when I'm greeted with a groan and more retching, I don't hesitate to slip my finger through the gap in the door and unlatch the flimsy lock.

"Oh," I say when I see her slumped over the toilet bowl, her beautiful hair cascading around her. "Let me help." I don't exactly know how I'm supposed to do that, but I drop down beside her.

"Go away," she says, her voice echoing off the porcelain.

"Nope, that's not going to happen." I pull back her hair and gently rub the back of her neck.

"This is so embarrassing."

"Nonsense. It happens to the best of us." Been there, done that. But what she says next has me wondering what the hell is happening.

"Even to your ex-wife?"

A wave of utter confusion passes over me, and it takes me a moment to find my voice. "What has Liz got to do with this?"

"Everything," she replies. I am so sodding confused right now. I wish she'd face me, but I know that won't be happening anytime soon. Rubbing her back, I gently brush back her hair. "Stop being so nice."

"I'm not nice," I rebuke because I wasn't nice a few days ago when her sister was riding my face.

But she won't hear a word of it. "You're the nicest person I know."

"You clearly need to get out more then."

She laughs, but it's strained. I need to know what's going on.

But when Carrie continues to vomit up her wine and dinner and the chaser of whiskey, I know this conversation will have to wait.

11
Eleven

Once Carrie was done throwing up her guts, she allowed me to help her from the bathroom and out of the bar. She was embarrassed, and in turn, she barely looked at me. She washed up and then fell into a deep slumber.

I was exhausted because I'd been awake for well over twenty-four hours, but I was too restless to sleep. However, Carrie's deep breathing soon lulled me into submission as I slept beside her—but on top of the blankets and not underneath.

I woke around six and showered since Carrie was still out like a light. I decided to get us some coffee because no doubt she'd be waking with a hangover. I quietly open the door when I return, unsure if Carrie is still asleep, but when I hear the low hum of the TV, I know she's awake.

I don't know what to say to her because last night, something clearly upset her. I just don't know what that was. And when she mentioned Liz, I was confused even more. When I enter the living room, Carrie sheepishly looks up at me. She's dressed and looks a lot better than I thought she would.

"Hey. How are you feeling?" I pass her a cup of coffee, which she accepts with a small smile.

"I'm okay. I'm really sorry about last night. I had way too much to drink. This is why I made my New Year's resolution. Me and alcohol have a love-hate relationship. It won't happen again."

A big fat elephant remains in the room, and I have no idea how to address it. Does she not remember the things that were said? Or done? I decide to ask her.

Sitting on the armrest of the sofa, I sip my black coffee, gathering the balls to ask her something she may not want to talk about. "What happened last night?"

The cup trembles as she draws it to her lips. She takes a sip of coffee before replying blankly, "I don't want to talk about it."

I figured as much. "Carrie, that isn't fair. Clearly, whatever happened had to do with me. Did I upset you somehow?" I'm grasping at straws.

"No, of course not."

"Then what is it?"

She lowers her eyes, tugging at the frayed hem of the blanket wrapped around her. "You're wrong." I wait for her to continue. "It had nothing to do with you. This is all me."

Now, I'm even more baffled.

The harder I press, the further she will retreat. In this instance, I can't help but compare her to a wounded animal. Whatever secret she's guarding is one she won't reveal anytime soon.

"Can we just drop it?" she asks, lifting her eyes and appearing hopeful. "Please."

Every bone in my body is screaming at me in protest because I feel something for this woman, and I want to know if she feels something for me too. But I can't force her to unburden her soul because if I push, Carrie will run.

I think back to her admission on the plane when we first met. How she said she'd had twenty-one boyfriends and that she was a serial dater. Each to their own as I clearly am in no position to judge, but I can't help but now think there's a reason for that number. I want to ask her what was wrong with these men she dated, but I don't.

"Okay," I begrudgingly reply. I can't force her to talk to me, but I'm disappointed she won't.

"What shall we do today?" She is clearly happy to change the subject.

My mood is a little flat, but we are in Paris, and I'm here to do a job. "How about we do more sightseeing?"

She nods happily and stands. "I'll just brush my teeth."

And just like that, this conversation is over.

When the bathroom door closes, I blow out an exasperated

breath. Reality sinks in and reminds me that even though it feels like longer, I've only known Carrie for four days. I thought I knew her, that she would share almost anything with me, but I was wrong.

Her cell chimes on the coffee table, and without meaning to, I look down at it to see who has sent her a text. When I see Mason's name flash on her screen, I squeeze the paper cup in my hand.

C'ing as u bailed on me last nite. C u 2nite? You kinda owe me LOL. Besides...I wanna talk.

I pale because not only did he just butcher the English language, but he's texting Carrie for a date. When were numbers exchanged? And talk? About what exactly?

This is absurd and needs to stop now. Just because I have an unhealthy obsession with Carrie doesn't mean she feels the same about me.

I pack my laptop, eager to forget these pathetic woes and focus on making some headway with this book. That's one thing I feel good about. Carrie appears, bundled up in her coat and scarf. I attempt to busy myself but can't help but notice when she snags her cell from the table and sees the text from Mason.

She instantly looks my way, but I play it cool. "Ready?"

Quickly slipping her cell into her coat pocket, she nods.

The staleness between us has me shouldering my satchel and heading for the door. Once we're in the elevator, I can't help but compare this ride to the one we took only yesterday.

It's bloody freezing out, so I suggest we ride a tour bus. Carrie happily agrees.

Armed with her camera, she takes pictures of everything and anything while we ride the bus for hours. It appears the quieter she is, the more vocal her photography becomes. It's hard not to admire her as she is a true artist at work.

When we're stopped at a light, she crouches to one knee and points the camera upward. I wonder what she's doing. We're on the top level of the bus, but it's undercover, so I have no idea what she's doing until I crane my neck to see what has captured her attention.

A butterfly with bright orange wings has somehow managed to hitch a ride. It's clinging to the clear roof, appearing to be trapped on the wrong side.

The moment we reach our stop, Carrie leaps onto her chair and cups the creature into her palms. Tourists think she's mad, but I can't help but compare her to that butterfly. A colorful, spirited creature clearly trapped. Is she waiting for someone to set her free?

We step from the bus with Carrie's hands still interlocked gently. I have no idea where we are, but ahead is a small patch of greenery, and Carrie immediately heads for it. When we reach the modest park with a bench seat and small rotunda, Carrie unclasps her palms, and the sight of the butterfly taking flight is breathtaking.

She watches mesmerized, almost jealous that this creature

can fly free. It flies high and strong, and it's pleasing to know we had a hand in its liberation. Carrie begins snapping photos, appearing happy with the silence.

Looking around, I scope out my surroundings and soon realize where we are. Morbid to most, but to me, this place pays homage to many who changed the world.

"Père Lachaise Cemetery is up ahead. Would you like to take a look with me?"

Carrie turns to look at me through her viewfinder. I wonder what she sees? Charm or a damned soul?

She clicks the shutter release and takes a picture. It pleases me that I am now a memory. "Yes, I'd love to."

We walk toward the stoned main entrance and regardless of the dismal weather, the place is packed with tourists. I don't know what it is about the dead that appeals to the living. I suppose it's the sense of the unknown. They've experienced what we're bound to sooner or later.

I've come here many times; the last time was with Liz. She bitched and moaned the entire time, saying the winding potholed paths were giving her motion sickness.

Shaking my head to dispel such thoughts as I don't want my ex to ruin my experience a second time around, I walk over to the signage that details the layout. There are so many final resting places, and many of these individuals have inspired me throughout my life. We decide to start at the beginning and make our way around at our own pace.

This place is tragically beautiful, and if the towering trees could speak, what a tale they would tell. It's hard to believe some of the dates on the headstones. When we reach Oscar Wilde's tomb, Carrie gasps and instantly focuses her camera.

This happens for the next countless hours, us stopping by each grave—some well-known, others not—but each name represents a life that once lived. I wonder what purpose they served and if they died happy.

My inner rock child comes out to play when we stop by Jim Morrison's grave. It's merely rubble now, but that doesn't matter. Its symbolism is what people come here for. Surrounded by all this death makes me appreciate the life I have, but it also has me wondering who will pay their last respects for me. What will my headstone say?

He was loved…but loved by whom?

We turn a corner and come to a small passage where an elderly man kneels by what looks like a relatively new grave. He's in a suit and bow tie; his tan hat hangs limply in his hand. There is nothing but sorrow and reflection shrouding him.

We've encroached on a private moment because this place isn't home to just famous poets, rock stars, and actors; it's also the final resting grounds for people just like me. Carrie senses my thoughts, and we attempt to turn to give this man some privacy, but he smiles.

"My wife is buried here," he explains in French. "She passed away two years ago."

"Je suis désolé," I reply, expressing my sympathy.

But he surprises me when he shakes his head. "Don't be sorry. We all die, but it's what we do when we're alive that matters. My Gaelle, she lived life to the fullest. She had no regrets when she died. Not many people can say that."

Carrie sniffs beside me.

"Never take one moment for granted. *La vie est belle.*"

And he's right—life *is* beautiful. Each breath proves that.

He blows her a kiss with his weathered hand, promising he'll see her soon.

The sight is beyond touching, and I don't realize how much it effects Carrie until she chokes out a strangled, "Excuse me," then sprints away. I bid the man farewell and go to follow Carrie.

She hasn't gone far. I find her hidden beneath a tree, her back turned as she clearly wipes her eyes.

"Dove?" I don't know if she wants me to leave her alone because today has been full of surprises.

"I'm sorry, Jayden," she says, her voice wavering.

"There's no need to apologize. I just wanted to make sure you're okay." I stop a few feet away, unsure if my touch would be welcomed.

"That was so sad. You wanted to see all the sides to love, and that was so beautiful. To find that sort of love…" She leaves the sentence unfinished because there's no need for her to explain.

Her shoulders rise as she takes a deep breath, and when she feels better, she slowly turns to face me. Her eyes are rimmed red, tears sticking to her lashes. I want to console her, but I don't. "How about we get out of here?"

She nods, quickly wiping away a fallen tear.

We walk in silence, both lost in our heads, but that's Paris—*Je ne sais quoi.*

Deciding to take a break from this ominous cloud that hangs over our heads, I'm struck with a brilliant idea. Carrie is scrolling through the pictures she took, oblivious to what I'm doing on my phone.

When I see a cab, I hail it down. "We're not getting back on the bus?" she asks, peering from left to right, attempting to decipher what she's missed.

"No, we are not." I open the door for her, hinting if she wants to know why that is, she needs to get into the cab. She slides in without a second thought. I rattle off the address to the driver, thankful Carrie hasn't figured out where I'm taking her.

Thanks to Paris traffic, a half an hour ride takes close to an hour, but it's perfect because where I'm taking Carrie, the magic truly comes alive at nightfall.

The mood has finally lifted, and whatever was troubling Carrie seems to have settled for now. She sits taller in her seat, the slightly grungier feel to the neighborhood piquing her interest. However, when the unmissable red glow from our destination lights up our faces, Carrie squeals and claps her hands.

"No?"

"Yes," I confirm when the driver pulls up in front of Moulin Rouge. I pay him while Carrie can barely wait as she bursts from the cab.

The vibe is electric and fun. It's exactly what we both need.

When she peers up and examines the flaming red windmill, the blades shining brightly, she smiles wide. I have missed that smile. "Are we going in?"

"No, I thought we could stand out here in the freezing cold and hope to catch a glimpse of those smashing topless dancers."

She playfully slaps me in the stomach and winds me. I love her spunk.

Seeing as I purchased the VIP tickets, we skip the line and are welcomed by our host. The moment we enter, both Carrie and I gape as we look around because this place is pretty remarkable. Moulin Rouge is the one place in Paris I've always wanted to go but have never been. Liz said it was filled with prostitutes who shamefully shook their can-cans for everyone to see. It wasn't a fight worth having.

So being here, it makes me happy that I'm experiencing this first with Carrie.

Everything is red and dimly lit, and it's fucking sexy. Our host leads us upstairs and shows us to our own private balcony. The view from up here is beyond words. We take a seat at our table, and when I see the expensive bottle of bubbly and macaroons, ripe for the picking, I know we're in for a great night.

Carrie's excitement is palpable. "The stage is like, right there." She points, unbelieving. "How much did this cost? Let me pay you back."

"It's my treat," I say, shaking my head as she will not be paying me now or ever. I pour us a glass of champagne, unsure if she'd want to drink after last night, but she accepts.

She fluffs her hair and unwinds her scarf as it's a lot warmer in here than it is outside. "If I knew we were coming here, I would have worn something a little nicer."

She peers around self-consciously, examining the furs and jewels. But her modesty is far richer than she'll ever know. "I'm sure you'll be wearing a lot more than the dancers."

She rolls her eyes playfully. "Is that why you brought me here? To gawk at boobs and asses?"

"It's not the only reason," I tease, relishing in Carrie's snort giggle.

The snobby couple to the right of us purse their lips, clearly not accustomed to having fun. If Liz were here, she'd fit right in.

"What's the other reason then?" she asks, snatching a macaroon from the table and popping it into her mouth. She moans when the sweetness hits her tongue. That lucky, lucky macaroon.

"I've always wanted to come but never had the chance." I refuse to mention Liz because after last night, I don't fancy a trip down misery lane.

But Carrie can read between the lines.

"Well, in that case, let's make a toast." She raises her glass, so I do the same. "To new beginnings."

"To new beginnings," I affirm as we clink glasses. "I couldn't have phrased it better myself."

"I'm honored, considering you're supposed to be a writer and all." And just like that, the sassy minx is back. We drink, unable to break our stare as we peer at one another over the rim of our glasses.

The ripple of her throat as she swallows the champagne stirs a longing in my loins. My fuck. I need to get a grip.

Her cell chimes, and just like that, my good mood fizzles.

"It's fine. You can answer it." I down the contents of my glass, desperate to drown this dread in the pit of my stomach.

But she firmly states, "No, I'm here with you. There's no one I want to talk to anyway."

Well, that's interesting.

I shouldn't press, but I'm tenacious and curious. I have to be—look at my day job. "Not even the waiter?"

"Mason?" she asks, the rise in her tone indicating she's nervous.

"Yes, *Mason*." His name feels like venom eating away at my vocal cords.

"He's texted me a couple of times. That's all."

"You do realize he has a massive hard-on for you, don't you?" I almost give everyone in earshot a heart attack, including our server, who makes a beeline for another table.

"What?" she says, curling her lip and shaking her head. "I don't even know him. And besides, it's not like that."

"It's *so* like that." His grammatically riddled text comes to mind. I'm surprised he didn't send her an emoji of an eggplant and a winky face.

"He wanted to hang out tonight," she reveals, and I'm thankful for her honesty. "I haven't replied, though."

"Why not?" I lean back in my seat, watching her closely. She's flustered, and it's not from the wine.

"Because I didn't come to Paris for romance. I came here to get away from it. I've made some mistakes, ones I can't take back."

Arching a brow, I pose, "That seems a little strange, considering that's *why* we came here."

But she stubbornly presses her lips together. "Romance from afar, not involving me, is why I came. I wanted to help you because you clearly have zero clue when it comes to women. Your track record proves this."

She instantly bites her lip and reaches for her glass. She's said too much. On the contrary, *Cherie*, she's said just enough.

"Well, we are a pair then. Your stellar list of losers also hints at the fact we'd be better off single. I am awfully curious, however, as to why *your* twenty-one beaus didn't make the cut. Care to share? Call it research." And this has nothing to do with my book.

She shakes her head with a smile. "Nuh-uh. I'm not your

lab rat. I don't want you dissecting me."

"Why not?" I counter because the more she talks, the more intrigued I become.

"Because you won't like who you see." She lowers her chin, embarrassed.

The playful banter simmers.

"Carrie"—I hesitantly reach for her hand—"that's impossible. I've known you for three, four, five days, I don't know, and it doesn't matter because regardless of what time zone we're in, I've liked you from the beginning. A lot."

"Why?" She's not asking for an ego booster. She's asking because she's genuinely curious.

"Why do I like you?"

She nods.

Running my thumb over her knuckles, I smile. "Because you're unlike anyone I have ever met before." I could list a dozen other reasons, but that sums it up.

She's still not convinced. What happened to her to leave her this untrustworthy? "I'm no one special," she expresses with a limp shrug. There is no way in hell I will have her saying such blasphemy.

"Well, you are to me."

A gasp leaves her. "Th-thank you, Jayden."

The waiter finally gathers the nerve to approach our table and announces what's on the menu. But as Carrie's hand sits snugly in mine, I'm suddenly ravenous for something else.

♥ ♥ ♥

Regardless of the fact I was surrounded by bouncing, jiggly supple flesh all evening, all I could focus on was Carrie. Dinner and the show was absolutely spectacular even though at every corner I turned, I was faced with boobs and more boobs, and they did nothing, zilch, nada for my libido.

Carrie in her skinny jeans and sweater turned me on more so than the girls who were dancing around in costumes resembling dental floss.

The way her eyes lit up as she leaned forward in her seat, spellbound by the music and the dancing, held me so captivated, I barely watched the show. When it ended, she discreetly wiped away the tears from her eyes and thanked me for taking her.

All in all, it was a perfect evening, and the moment we slid into a cab, that spark that has been ever present since we first met sparked brighter than it ever has before. I literally sat on my hands to stop myself from reaching out and touching her.

We exited the taxi and rode the elevator to our room, ensuring we stood on opposite ends of the cart. Not that it made much of a difference because, in the small confines, I was certain I could hear her heart thrashing wildly within her chest.

She all but flung herself from the elevator when the door opened and ran to our room.

She excused herself, saying she needed to use the bathroom, and that is where she's been for the past twenty minutes.

It's bloody freezing out, but I can't stay inside, so I'm out on the balcony. Sipping my scotch, I'm hoping I'm struck with some revelation as to why Carrie is hiding from me. I thought things were going well, but it appears I was wrong.

"Hey. What are you doing out here? It's freezing." Her voice is like a salve to my constant ache.

"I grew up in London, dove; this is summer for me." I'm attempting to deflect the situation with humor, but the strain shows.

"Is your family there?" she asks, her footsteps slow as she walks toward me. I don't move an inch.

"We moved to the US when I was sixteen, but my parents moved back to London about five years ago. My younger brother lives in New York."

"What's he like?" She's making small talk, which betrays her nerves.

With elbows resting against the railing and my scotch glass sitting loosely in my right hand, I give off the appearance of being aloof and uncaring. But the closer she gets to me, the harder it is for me to control myself.

I don't even know what I want. I just know I want more.

Raising the glass to my lips, I take a long drink before replying. "He's an even bigger mess than I am. At least I attempted to stay on the straight and narrow."

Elijah is not only proud of his bachelor status; he's also proud of the fact he's slept with half of New York and its surrounding boroughs.

"You haven't strayed too far off the path," she says, coming to a stop a few feet away from me. "There's hope for you yet."

"I like to think so. At least I can still hold on to a small scrap of my dignity." Her gentle breathing hints that she's listening. "I may have shagged my share of women over the past six months"— I don't see the point in being coy—"but I didn't kiss a single one. I know that's not something to be awfully proud of, but a kiss is something treasured."

Realizing what an utter wank I sound like, I raise my glass and drink my damn scotch to stop the whimsical dribble.

"I respect that," she reveals a moment later. "Having sex and having feelings are two entirely different things. I thought Donny was different, but he proved to me that he wasn't. He's just like all the other guys I've dated."

"So the twat was the only man who ever came close to being your Mr. Right?" I peer at her over my shoulder, hoping she doesn't flee.

She doesn't.

"I suppose so."

"You suppose so?" I question with a smirk. "What sort of noncommittal answer is that?"

She shrugs. "I don't have anything to compare it to. I know my feelings for him were different, but I don't know why that was. He was the only guy who challenged me, I suppose."

"It sounds like you dated a bunch of duds," I claim, and she covers her smile.

"I second that. I just haven't found anyone who…who sets my world on fire. I want the crazy, chaotic love that leaves you breathless and impatient. I want the type of love which isn't a man dominating a woman. I want a man who will walk by me in a partnership."

"That's a fair request. That's what a relationship should be." I try not to press too hard because she's openly sharing, and I want her to continue.

"Is that what you had with Liz?"

Peering into the starless sky, I try to ignore my feelings, but I can't. "In the beginning, yes. She was my everything. But things change. Clearly."

Carrie seems to ponder over what I've just shared. "She's a fucking idiot."

I blink once, unsure if I've heard her correctly. But I have.

"Tonight, when you said you've never met anyone like me…" She wrings her hands together. "Well, I feel the same way about you. I feel like I've know you forever. I shouldn't feel this way…"

"Why not?" I coax, attempting to suppress my happiness over her sharing this with me.

"I just shouldn't," she says on a rushed breath. I'm losing her, and when she goes to turn, I grip her forearm, trapping her.

"Why not, dove?" My voice is dangerously low. And Carrie senses it too.

"Don't, Jayden," she warns in a timid whisper.

"Don't what?" I pull her toward me. She comes willingly.

"I can't."

"These half-arsed answers will not do. What. Can't. You. Do?" I pause between each word, hovering close, needing her to know that the next few seconds and the many that will follow will be entirely based on her answer.

She wets her lips. "I can't do *this*."

Oh god, my rule of no kissing is completely obsolete because I want nothing more than to kiss the living shite out of her.

"Last night, when we were dancing, and today, I just...I am so—" But she doesn't finish her sentence. Instead, she is moments away from fleeing. But it'll be a cold day in hell before I allow that to happen.

My body reacts before my brain can comprehend what's happening, and I close the distance between us, once and for all, slamming my lips to hers.

A whoosh of air escapes her because I've caught her unaware. It fills my lungs, and a strangled groan catches in the back of my throat.

Neither of us moves. We're caught in a stalemate, and the pinnacle of no return is within reach.

I've forgotten what it feels like to be locked with another this way. But it could just be that with Carrie, everything feels brand new.

I brush my lips against hers from side to side, tasting, sampling, and relishing in the foreign intrusion. Our eyes are locked—hers frantic but trusting. As far as first kisses go, this is chaste and also a little unorthodox, but with Carrie, I don't want to rush a thing.

With scotch on my breath and strawberries and cream on hers, I inhale, nudging her nose with mine. She whimpers, threading her fingers through my hair. We haven't actually kissed as there is no tongue or open mouth connection, but this encounter is far more erotic than groping and going in for the kill. The chase is what excites me.

I press my palm to her cheek, our mouths still fused together as I lick the seam of her plump upper lip. A hoarse grunt escapes me when she tugs at the strands of my hair. She isn't gentle, but who wants a docile lamb when I have this.

The energy thrumming through my veins animates me with a fierce need to consume this woman like she is my last meal. I want all of her—consequences be damned. Just as I tilt my head and open my mouth, ready to be lost in her, she severs our union, her lips trembling.

"Jayden, no, I can't."

And there's that word again.

I blow out an exasperated breath because I don't understand.

She stumbles backward, her eyes mirroring nothing but regret. "I can't like you," she finally explains although I am still no closer to knowing why.

Interlacing my hands atop my head, I take a minute to process what she just said. "Why not?"

It's a simple question, but her answer is not.

"I don't want to ruin our friendship." She may as well have kicked me in the balls because she just boxed me in the friend zone.

"Why can't we have both?" I ask, and she looks at me like I'm fucking insane. What she says next, though, has me questioning her soundness.

"Look at your ex-wife and look at me." She sweeps down her body as though that's supposed to make any bloody sense.

"I *am* looking," I say, not understanding why she would bring Liz into this and ruin something enjoyable.

"What she did?" She sniffs. "You can never forgive her for."

"Yes and…? What has that got to do with you?"

And there it is. I see it. Carrie has a secret. But what does that have to do with Liz?

"I don't think you're completely over her," she says in a rushed tumble of words. But I know that's not what she originally wanted to say. I actually recoil and acid rises. "I can't get hurt again. Not by you. I can't be your rebound."

She's spewing forth this poison, and I can't keep up because none of this makes any sense. "I am *completely* over Liz. Trust me. I was over her the minute she cheated," I stress, but it suddenly lacks ammunition. "And there is no comparison. None." But she doesn't listen because this doesn't just have to do with Liz. This has to do with Carrie's demons—all twenty-one of them.

"I'm embarrassed," she confesses, averting her eyes. "I have a pattern. I always fall for the wrong guy, and I don't want to do that with you. I like you too much. Take Donny, for example. I can't do that anymore. I need to look for someone stable, sensible. My Mr. Right."

I think she means Mr. Boring, but potato, potahto.

"We will only end up breaking each other's hearts. You're the first guy I actually like. So, trust me, I'm doing you a favor. We would never work."

This entire time, I wondered what was wrong with the men of America. But now I know it's Carrie with the problem. She's scared of…love. Of being vulnerable. And because of that, she's shut herself off from opening her heart fully. This pattern she says she follows—she finds flaws, so it's easy to say goodbye. But even though I'm different, that doesn't seem to make a difference.

No matter what I say or do—I will never be her Mr. Right. Look at how we met. I was going down on a complete stranger, only to go and fuck her sister in a limo, and then ogle her naked mom. I am history repeating, and she said on the plane, she's quitting boys…well, more specifically, boys like me.

Her eyes well with tears because she can see she's clearly wounded me. "I'm sick of being single. I'm always the bridesmaid, never the bride."

Unable to hold back my sarcastic snigger, I reply, "Being the bride is overrated."

"I'm sorry if I've hurt your…"

But I thrust out my palm, not wanting her apologies. "Don't make apologies for how you feel." Her winded breaths emit white plumes of sadness. "Come on. Let's go inside. You're cold."

"Really?" she asks, stunned. "You don't want me to leave?"

"No, of course, I don't. I'm not a complete bastard." Low blow, but it's the truth. I knew my depraved ways would eventually catch up to me, but I just never anticipated they'd come back this way. I have no one to blame but myself.

Carrie is looking for someone who doesn't come with a shitload of baggage. Not to mention, someone who didn't once shag her sister. But what she said about Liz—that upsets me the most. Carrie would never be my rebound. I am well over Liz. But my subconscious is shaking his head. He can fuck right off.

I suddenly need a drink.

Turning, I walk inside, the fire proving the perfect beacon to thaw out my chill. But I can't help but feel there will always be a chill to my bones after Carrie just friend zoned me.

Pouring myself a glass of scotch, I drink in pensive silence, wondering how exactly I go about being Carrie's friend. I want her—more than I've ever wanted anything—and now that I've had a small taste, I've been cut off.

"So we're okay?" she asks from behind me.

"Yes." Downing my scotch, I turn and extend my hand.

Carrie looks down at it as if it's some trick. But when she sees I'm serious, she shakes it lightly. "Friends?"

"Friends," she confirms, but the quiver to her shake reveals we both know actions speak louder than words.

12
Twelve

Running is my outlet.

I ran for miles every day after I caught a man balls deep in my wife. I ran when I couldn't write a single word. So it's no surprise I've run for the past two days like a man possessed.

After Carrie took a sledgehammer to my pride, we went to bed, but sleep has evaded me these past two days. What Carrie said may have been the truth, but it fucking sucked. No one wants to hear they're nice but not nice enough for the person they want. And I do. I want Carrie, but she doesn't want me. She wants someone stable, someone who hasn't slept with her sister. Someone she can enter a room with without fearing a horde of angry scorned women lurks in the shadows, primed on getting revenge on the manwhore.

This shouldn't hurt so much, but it does. And because of that, my flow of words is now a trickle.

Unable to run away from the mess my life has suddenly become, I amp up the speed on the treadmill, hoping to fall into an exhausted sleep. My cell chimes, and I know I can't avoid it any longer. It's been off for the past forty-eight hours, and it's been blissful.

"Hello," I breathlessly say as I turn the phone to speaker.

"Oh? You're alive?"

"Don't sound too excited about that fact. What do you want, Nick?"

"Why are you so out of breath? Did I catch you in a threesome?"

I choose to ignore him. "Again, I ask, what do you want?"

"Someone woke up on the wrong side of the bed."

I don't bother correcting that I haven't yet been to bed.

"If you'd bother to check your emails, and voicemail, and text messages, you'd know I spoke to Gerry."

"And?" Just the mere mention of Gerry has me running faster.

"And Jesus Christ, Jayden, he's driving a hard bargain. The terms are excellent. But they're a new publishing house. It's risky, especially because Axle is so respected among the industry. People won't take too kindly to Gerry backstabbing Axle, and you'll look like an ungrateful bastard if you change publishers."

He relays everything I already knew. “So what happens now?” The line suddenly becomes filled with overhead announcements and chatter. “Where are you?” I ask, slowing down so I can strain my hearing.

“Enjoy your flight,” says a mysterious female.

“Nick?”

“See you soon, mate,” is his ambiguous reply.

“Hang on. What?” I switch off the machine and come to a standstill.

“What kind of agent would I be if I wasn’t there when you’re offered the biggest deal of your life?”

“We’ve already established you’re the world’s worst agent,” I tease, reaching for my water bottle.

“Please. You know you love me. I’ll see you tonight when I land. Gerry will be at your hotel around nine p.m. to talk business.”

I almost spit out my water. “Tonight?”

“Yes. I told you. If you actually checked your phone like a normal person, this wouldn’t come as a surprise. Make sure you have something to show Gerry. Au revoir.”

The line goes dead.

Bollocks.

The one time I decide to switch off from technology, this has to happen.

I have nothing to show Gerry. Well, nothing I would be proud to show him. Looking down at my watch, I see I have fourteen hours to cram thirty-three thousand words into coherent chapters.

With no time to waste, I take the elevator to my floor, wondering if I can pull off this miracle. Carrie is still asleep when I enter the room, so I quickly shower and dress and am ready to tackle this book and win.

As my laptop powers up, I take a sip of scotch, rocking back in my chair. I have words and notes throughout the pages and need to make sense of it to compile three decent chapters.

Who knew—I'm a complete masochist.

Groaning, I place my palms on my face. There is no way I can do this and be happy with the result. Especially since writer's block has raised its ugly head again.

"Is everything all right?"

"Fine," I lie, unmasking my face. I ignore the stirring in my loins when Carrie stands before me in her pajamas.

"*We would never work,*" she said, which is the reason she's been distant these past two days. We both have been. She's taken off on her own, camera in hand, only to return late at night. I refuse to entertain the notion that she's off with Mason or some other French beau.

When I've managed to catch half an hour of sleep, it's been on the couch. The thought of sleeping beside her kicks me in the guts and leaves me with indigestion.

"So have you got plans for tomorrow?"

"Tomorrow?" I ask, brow scrunched.

"It's New Year's Eve," she clarifies when she reads my confusion.

"I have to get through today first," I reply, opening my Word document, which resembles a dog's breakfast.

"What's happening today?"

"My agent is on his way to Paris. So is Gerry Williams."

"Holy shit!" she declares, eyes wide.

"Indeed."

She comprehends my disquiet instantly. "Does he want sample chapters?"

"Yes, he does. And all I have to show him is the ramblings of a madman."

She covers her smile. "It can't be that bad."

Sweeping my hand toward my laptop, I say, "Knock yourself out."

She takes me up on the offer and leans over me to read the gibberish on my screen. If I wasn't so bloody anxious, I would take the time to bask in her scent.

"The sunlight was kindling across the horizon as she looked into the heavens, begging for a…burrito?" She cocks her head to the side while I slip further into despair.

Oh, god.

Running a hand through my damp hair, I blow out a despaired breath. "I was clearly hungry."

"You were clearly something," she adds, lips twitching.

"Oh, fuck it. I should just give up now. I've had my heyday.

It's time to face reality." I attempt to stand, but Carrie places her hand on my shoulder. It's the first contact we've had in two days, and my body grows lax, like an addict taking his first hit in days.

"Stop doubting yourself. That's your problem. You're a good writer, but if you don't believe it, then how is anyone else supposed to?"

Well, put that simply, I suppose she's right. But self-doubt is public enemy number one not only to writers but also to most people. What I've written doesn't suck, but I'm terrified Gerry will look at it and ask if a five-year-old now writes under the pseudonym J.E. Sparrow.

"How do you know I'm a good writer?" I ask, watching her cheeks turn a cherry pink. She's so busted.

"I've read your books," she confesses. "They're good, Jayden. I sobbed my eyes out when Christopher died. Did you really have to kill him?"

She's referring to my eighth book—*Your Lover's Last Breath.*

It exhilarates me to know she's taken the time to read my work. "Yes. His death was meant to signify the characters coming full circle."

"I know but have mercy on a girl's heart. I've been a mess these past two days." The moment she confesses her actions, she bites her top lip, but it's too late. She just let slip that even though we weren't particularly talking, she was thinking of me nonetheless.

I suddenly feel like fucking Hercules.

"Find that inspiration. Draw from it and write the best fucking sample chapters you have ever written."

Her pep talk has the desired effect, and I drag myself from this slump and man the fuck up. I *am* a good writer. I thought I needed Liz as my muse, but in reality, that need was really just believing in myself.

"I will dedicate this book to you on the proviso it's not a load of shite."

She laughs. "It won't be. I'm going to take a shower and then come back with some coffee and loads of food so you have no excuse to leave that desk."

I appreciate the gesture. "And what do you plan on doing all day?"

She peers out the window, and when she sees it's snowing a storm, she smiles. "Read. Someone gave me their book. I suppose I shouldn't be rude, so I'll read it."

I have the urge to beat my chest in pride because there is no greater feeling than having a person you respect and admire read your work.

Unable to contain my smirk, I turn in my seat and face the screen, ready to make this manuscript my bitch. "I know how the story ends."

"I bet you do."

♥♥♥

When continuous thumping pounds against my door, I know without a doubt my agent and best friend has arrived.

Carrie is getting ready in the bathroom as she thought it best to make herself scarce tonight. She didn't want Gerry to see her—in case he feared she was Axle's spy—and change his mind about the deal.

I tended to agree with her. Even though I wanted her by my side more than I cared to admit.

Today, she did what she said she would. She read my book. I couldn't help but peer over every so often, wondering what she thought. Or what part she was up to. When tears welled in her eyes, I knew she'd reached halfway—the scene where the heroine's husband returns from war when she thought he was dead.

Watching her read my book did something to me. My feelings for Carrie, regardless of how she feels about me, are growing each day. I know she said she just wants to be friends, but I can't stop this pull I feel toward her. She has the ability to just…take my breath away. And when these feelings erupt, I write my best stuff.

With Carrie curled up by the fire, reading my book, I smashed out words like a madman possessed. It felt like I was writing for her because I wanted to see her reading this new book. I wanted her to be the very first person to read what meeting her had done for me. She is the inspiration behind every word, so I'll be damned if it's anything but perfect.

So on my table lies three fucking good chapters. I nailed it. I cut out all the bullshit and pulled back the layers to deliver an honest, relatable story. Our leads—Bailey and Leyton—meet when they are kids, and this story will detail their life. I used all the experiences thus far to shape my story, and I can't wait to add more.

But that will have to wait because now, I have to tend to my best mate.

I won't lie, the moment I open the door, I'm happy to see this bloody bastard. "Fuck and you," he says as he shoulders past me. "You couldn't have chosen someplace warmer to write?"

"Hello to you too." I close the door and wonder how long it'll take him to ask about Carrie.

I give him three…two…

"So…?"

And one.

"Where's the other Bell daughter? Is she as hot as Daisy?"

Rolling my eyes, I walk toward the table and pour us some scotch. "There is no comparison. And I'm not talking about looks. Carrie is…something else."

I pass Nick his glass, but he narrows his eyes, cocking his head. "I recognize this look." He sweeps his finger up and down.

"You've finally lost the plot, mate." If he's going to torture me, it seems only fair I drink his scotch. But he smacks my hand away.

"Someone has a crush," he singsongs while I really need that drink.

"I don't have anything, and would you lower your voice? She's in the bathroom." I regret my admission instantly because I've just thrown poor Carrie under a bus.

"Oh, Carrie," he croons, sauntering over to the bathroom. There is no point in trying to stop the inevitable, so I reach for the bottle and take a seat on the sofa.

The door opens and out comes Carrie, looking beyond gorgeous. It's actually comical to see Nick at a loss for words. But I suppose Carrie has that effect on everyone.

She meets my gaze from across the room with a smile. I raise my glass. "Meet Nicholas West. My agent."

"And don't forget best and most attractive friend," he adds, extending his hand. When she places her hand in his, he raises it to his lips and kisses the back of it. This man has no shame.

A tiny giggle escapes her. It appears she's not immune to Nick's charisma.

"It's nice to meet you. I've heard a lot about you."

"Don't believe a word of it. Unless it involves—"

"All right," I interrupt, shooting up before Carrie is introduced to Nick's charm. "Shall we?"

Nick is still holding Carrie's hand. "Are you coming with us, *ma chérie*?"

I shake my head while downing my scotch. He has no

shame.

Carrie gently removes her hand before replying, "No. I'm catching up with a friend."

"You are?" My ears prick up as this is the first I've heard of this.

"Yes. We're just going out for dessert."

"My favorite kind of meal," Nick says, tongue in cheek. I pale, wishing I'd opted for another question.

Carrie shrugs into her coat and slips on her leather gloves, indicating she has no intention of revealing just who this friend is.

I need to take a chill pill and calm the fuck down. She can have dessert with whomever she likes. *We're just friends*, I remind myself for the ten thousandth time. But it doesn't stick. The fact she won't divulge just who this friend is has me guessing it's a man. Maybe Mason?

A grinding fills the room. It's not until my jaw aches that I realize the grinding is coming from my jaw.

Nick is onto me and wears that damn smug smile once again. Screw him.

"Well, good luck," Carrie says, coming over to where I stand and giving me a hug.

The softness of her curves and the delicacy of her scent on my palate has me wishing she'd just waved goodbye because being her friend is a lot harder when we embrace this way. But pulling my shite together, I break from our union gently. She seems surprised but recovers before I can question her.

"Have a nice night." And there's that word again. Nice. Just how I'm a *nice* friend.

This exchange is nothing short of awkward, so I slap my hands together. "Where are we meeting Gerry?"

Nick stands on the sidelines. Carrie clears her throat as she brushes back a curl of hair behind her ear.

"He was going to come here, but I told him to meet us at that amazing dumpling place, Siang Kitchen. Liz..." But his sentence comes to a halt when he realizes he just mentioned the she-devil.

Carrie's gaze instantly drops to the floor because Liz appears to be a touchy subject for us both. She's not even here, yet she still manages to ruin my life. "That's fine. Let's go."

I grab the stack of papers off the desk and avoid looking at Carrie, but I can feel her watching me. "Bye, dove." I nudge Nick, hinting it's time to leave.

He thankfully gets the hint but not before he mouths, "Dove?" with an arched brow.

"It was nice meeting you."

"You too," Carrie says, a sadness echoing in her words. But I can't let that worry me. We're friends, and if she wanted to share what's wrong, she would. Just as she'd share who she's seeing tonight.

This shouldn't irk me, but it does. And the moment we step into the hallway, the Dr. Phil in Nick emerges. "You are falling for that girl. Or should I say dove."

"Please. Don't be ridiculous. I hardly know her." Even to my ears, I sound like a pathetic twat.

"Jayden, you're a lot of things, but a liar isn't one of them." This is true. Lying is my hard limit. A deal breaker.

"It doesn't matter either way," I say, stabbing at the elevator button, "because she just wants to be friends."

"Oof." Nick makes a pained face, mimicking my inner turmoil perfectly. "Why did you get friend zoned?"

"I don't know. Maybe because I was fucking her sister and lots of sisters before I met her. She asked me how many women I've slept with, and you know what, I don't even know. What kind of person doesn't have a rough estimate of how many people they've shagged?"

"A fucking rock star," Nick offers while I groan.

"Stop being such a pussy. Before Liz, you were a fucking saint. You're allowed to run a little wild."

"But that doesn't seem to matter, mate, because the afterburn will be my legacy. I need a fucking drink," I mumble, running a hand down my face.

The elevator opens, and we squeeze inside, talks of my whoredom forgotten for now.

"So how are the sample chapters?" Nick asks, flicking through the pages.

"I'm pleased to say bloody brilliant." I'm thankful for the change in pace.

The doors thankfully open because Nick was seconds away from kissing me. "That's my boy. What's it about?"

When we hit the sidewalk, we hustle into our jackets and walk the three blocks to the restaurant.

"Love," I reply as I place my hands into my leather jacket pockets.

"Loving what? I love blueberry bagels. So you have to be a little more specific. I can't pitch a book without a hook."

"It's about the innocence of love. A simple story of boy meets girl, and the obstacles they face. They've known one another since kids. But I want to detail how, in the real world, the good guy doesn't always win."

"Oh, god. You're going to rip out my spleen, aren't you? This better not be an autobiography."

We sidestep groups of people because regardless of the weather, someone is always taking a photo. This is Paris, after all.

"It's not. I came to Paris because I needed a change in scenery. I've drawn inspiration from mere strangers who have helped me look outside the box."

"And Carrie wouldn't happen to be one of these people, would she?" Nick may come across as a raging hard-on most of the time, but he's not stupid, by any means. He's also a persistent bastard.

Thankfully, we arrive at the restaurant, avoiding any more heart-to-hearts.

Gerry is sitting in a booth in the back, frantically typing on his cell. “Remember, play it cool. Let me do the talking. We don’t want him to know how eager we are.”

I nod because honestly, talking shop is a fucking bore. I’d be happy with a handshake over a beer, but Nick is a stickler for the rules. “Gerry, great to see you again.” Gerry peers up from his phone and shoots up when he sees me behind Nick.

“Nick.” They shake hands, then I offer mine to Gerry. “And J.E. Sparrow. Hello.”

“Jayden is fine,” I correct, not interested in being treated like some rock star.

We take our seats, and I look over my shoulder, hoping to attract the attention of a waiter. I need a drink.

“Are those for me?” I almost forgot about the stack of papers I was holding.

“Yes, sorry.” I place them on the table, about to slide them over to him, but Nick slaps his hand onto them. Let the games begin.

“Not so fast.” Gerry shifts in his seat. I feel sorry for the poor bastard because Nick drives a hard bargain. “Before we show you Jayden’s next bestseller, which will be sure to make millions, let’s talk business. What makes you so special?”

Now I’m the one to squirm. Alerting a waitress, I indicate I need three drinks. I don’t care what she brings me, but anything is better than doing this sober. “As you know, I am a massive fan, Jayden. When we signed you over ten years ago, I knew you were headed for great things. Your success is no surprise. You have that something special most authors strive for. But under Axle, your talent is being squashed. He's giving you the same covers, the same marketing. He's not willing to evolve. This market is changing. Romance is a harder genre to crack. It's saturated with J.E. Sparrow wannabes, and Axle will soon enough replace you with someone who would accept a quarter of the advances we've given you. Talent doesn't matter. Money does. He's cutting corners and scooping up every author he can just to build an empire."

When the waitress places three beers in front of me, I almost kiss her in gratitude.

"So how will Williams Publishing be different?"

"I'll invest not only my money but my time in each author we sign." He emphasizes his point by jabbing his finger onto the tabletop. "And as I mentioned, Jayden will be one of our main authors. We won't be saturated with authors. We will focus on the talent we have."

I sit back and sip my beer, wishing Nick would just put Gerry out of his misery. And besides, he may hate the sample chapters. No point in talking numbers until he actually reads what he's investing his money into.

"So half a mil advance is where we're sitting at?"

I spit up my beer. "For one book?" I ask, incredulously.

Nick kicks me in the shin, which is my cue to shut the hell up. But this is madness. Gerry needs to read the damn chapters before he goes and throws that sort of money around.

"No, per book. I'm wanting to buy your next three books, with a fifty-fifty split."

"Gerry, that's—"

"Not good enough." Nick cuts me off, kicking me once again. "The risk Jayden is taking by signing with you is vast. He has been loyal to A&G Publishing for so long that he would look like a disloyal bastard if he were to come over to Williams Publishing. And you know how this industry loves a good scandal. This has the potential to ruin his name if your company were to fold. You're new, and there are no guarantees. It's risky." Nick leans back, unruffled, while Gerry looks seconds away from having a heart attack.

I feel sorry for the poor chap. But Nick is like a dog with a bone.

"A six hundred-thousand-dollar advance per book. I can't do any more than that."

Gerry is clearly on crack.

"Mate, just take a read before you offer that kind of quid." I slide him the chapters, ignoring Nick's evil glares. I can't take that sort of money. It would ruin Gerry if I didn't deliver.

He accepts but is firm when he replies, "I have no doubt this will be phenomenal. I will read it tonight and let you know what I think. And while I'm doing that, maybe you could think about my offer."

"Will do. Thank you, Gerry. Whatever happens, I want you

to know that I appreciate your belief in me." I sound like a soft cock, but it's the truth.

He nods. "And that's exactly the reason I do. You haven't let your success go to your head. You're humble, and humility is hard to come by these days."

"I had enough arrogance in the form of my ex-wife."

Gerry bursts into a rowdy roar while Nick ceases from bruising my shin for now. "I hate to chat and run, but I have a Skype call in fifteen minutes. These time zones are impossible." He goes to stand. "I will be in touch." My chapters are clenched in his hand as if he's holding the Holy Grail. I hope I don't disappoint.

We say our goodbyes, and when he's out of earshot, Nick slaps me on the back of my head. "Ouch. Motherfucker. What was that for?" I ask, rubbing my skull.

"We had him. Hook. Line. And sinker. Sometimes, your integrity is sickening."

I can't help but laugh.

Nick talks big, but he knows I did the right thing. If Gerry signed me and my books sucked balls, that would be the end of my career.

"I need to be to make up for your lack of social grace." Nick steals my beer, proving my point.

We order some food and more beer, and I go into detail about what occurred with Axle and Daisy. Out of principle, there is no way I want to sign with Axle. But Nick's concerns are warranted. Changing from the publisher who nurtured your career isn't taken too kindly. I have to be prepared for some bad press.

As I'm explaining how I saw a little too much of Nora, I notice Nick looking over my shoulder. When he continues looking, I give in and turn to see what's so exciting. I don't see anything. "What are you looking at?"

I turn back around, hands turned upward, hinting he give me a clue.

"You're fucking serious?"

"Are you high? Actually, don't answer that. Yes, I'm serious."

Nick looks at me like I've just grown a second head. "You missed those two hot babes behind you who are ready to offer you their own dumplings?"

I curl my lip as his analogy just put me off my food.

However, I subtly turn back around to see who exactly he's talking about. Two pretty brunettes sit a few feet away. The one on the left waves and giggles. I wave back, but it lacks the oomph and resembles a flaccid penis.

That analogy is indeed valid this time because that's exactly how I feel when looking at two women who would usually wet my whistle.

"Should we invite them over?" Nick asks, sitting taller in his seat and flashing his killer smile. Nick has no trouble with the ladies. He's dark-haired, blue-eyed, and successful. He also oozes confidence. But I have no interest in making this a foursome.

"You can do whatever you want. Once I'm done eating, I'm going to sleep." I reach for my beer, watching as Nick's mouth gapes open in horror.

"Don't you mean going to search for your balls? What is the matter with you?" He appears horrified, and I can't help but chuckle.

"You know, you offend the English language every time you open your mouth."

"Well, you offend my cock by being a cock blocker. So fuck you."

Our food arrives, but I've suddenly lost my appetite as memories of Liz assault me. I push away the plate and nurse my beer instead. Nick has no issues eating for two.

"It's Carrie, isn't it?" he says around a mouthful of food.

"It's Carrie what?" I've been good thus far, but now that he's said her name, I can't help but wonder how her night is going.

"You clearly only have eyes for her because normally, you'd be all up in those girls' faces. Not to mention, other parts."

"Well, I was a stupid wanker for thinking with the wrong head."

Nick chews pensively, but I know he's only gathering ammo to throw my way. "I bet if Carrie wanted you to think with the wrong head, you'd have no issues bowing to her command."

He's right. Fuck him.

"I kissed her. Well, sort of."

His fork slides along the table and swan dives into my lap. It takes him three attempts, but he eventually spits out, "You *what?* What about your no kissing rule? And what does sort of mean? You forgot how to use not only your dick but your mouth as well?"

Seeing him this riled up humors me. "We didn't kiss per se. I pressed my lips to hers..."

But Nick cuts me off as he waves his hands in the air. "Okay, stop. Now you're just embarrassing yourself. You either kissed, or you didn't. It hasn't been so long that you've forgotten."

"Of course not. It wasn't tongue and groping and me smacking her arse. It was soft and tender, and I was so fucking hard, I wanted to throw her over my shoulder and fuck her into next week."

Nick fist pumps the air. "There he is. My boy. So why didn't you step it up?"

"Because that's when she friend zoned me."

"In the middle of your sort of kiss?"

I nod, drowning my sorrows in my beer. "She said she's not interested in being my rebound. That I'm still in love with"—I swallow down the vomit —"Liz. I didn't want to tell her I shagged the rebound from my system fifty something women before her because it didn't matter. I'm not her Mr. Right, if there even is such a thing."

Nick shakes his head as he folds his arms. He's clearly up to something. "Rebound kiss."

"What in the ever-living hell are you talking about?"

"You need to have a rebound kiss. Yes, you've fucked plenty of women but never kissed them, right? So really, the rebound is still kind of an issue? Fucking we can do, but you seem to get attached, hence the no kissing."

I want to scoff at his theory, but I'm listening.

"For you, a rebound isn't just physical, it's emotional, and Carrie still thinks you're attached to your cunt of an ex. So that's why she pushed you away. She's scared, which means she likes your handsome ass. Oh, my fuck. I'm in the wrong industry."

Bad language aside, Nick just may be onto something.

Technically, if I kissed Carrie, she *would* be the rebound kiss as I haven't kissed anyone after Liz. I told her what a kiss means to me.

I haven't kissed a single one. I know that's not something to be awfully proud of, but a kiss is something treasured.

So she's scared because…could it be, she likes me?

No, I can't allow myself to be wrapped up in something that probably isn't true. Nor can I take my best friend up on his offer as he leans across the table, pursing his lips. "Come on then. Let's make it quick."

"Thank you for the offer, but I'm not kissing you. I'm not drunk enough for that."

He slumps back into his seat with a dramatic flair. "I feel so unloved."

Standing, I seek out the bathroom. "Never say never, mate."

I leave Nick gloating in his seat. I fucking love this guy.

Once I'm done in the restroom and have washed my hands, I reach for my cell from my pocket. I want to text Carrie and explain that she could never be my rebound. I know she just wants to be friends, but I need her to know how I feel. Before she writes us off as a DNF, she needs to know that this, *she* means something to me.

With that as my driving force, I storm from the bathroom, intent on going back to the hotel and telling her how I feel. Sadly, the only thing my lips will be doing is kissing some random stranger who latches onto my face like a depraved octopus.

I'm stunned as she literally catches me off guard and tackles me from out of nowhere. She slams her lips to mine, molesting my mouth as she thrusts her tongue inside like an epileptic slug. I don't want to be rough, but I grip her upper arms and attempt to push her aside. But she latches on tighter as she wraps her arms around the back of my neck. Holy shite. This woman has lockjaw.

"Nick!" I call out. "A little help!"

"I love you!" my admirer gasps, sucking my face while I attempt to breathe. "You're my favorite author."

"Thank you," I say from around her lips, prying her fingers from my neck. "However, a simple hug would have sufficed."

This isn't the first time a zealous reader has kissed me, but kudos to this woman, as she's the only one who's held on for so long.

"Hey, break it off. Back off, lady," Nick says, yanking her off me. "You break, you pay."

"Oh, I'd pay anything for a night with J.E. Sparrow," says the blonde woman smugly while I wipe my lips. Her red smeared lipstick is a trophy she sports with pride.

She goes back to the table of her giggling friends while I feel like I need a shower. Stat.

Nick bursts into a husky fit of laughter, and I deadpan him. "This isn't even a little bit funny. I think she impregnated me."

My comment sets Nick off, and he bends at the waist, holding his ribs in laughter. "Oh, it so is. You wanted your rebound kiss. There you go."

"Fuck you. I need a new best friend." I leave him to his laughter as I turn to leave, but I stop dead in my tracks. "Dove?"

Nick's cackles soon die in his throat when he shoots upright. His silence is confirmation that I'm not imagining her here, looking at me like she's moments away from bursting into tears.

"Wh-what are you doing here?" My falter gives away my guilt. My lips, even though taken against their will, were just pressed to another woman's. What a rotten scoundrel.

"That's n-not your co-color," she spits, reminding me of our conversation when we first met. This time, however, it's laced with utter contempt.

I have no idea what she's talking about until she walks over and stands on her tippy toes. My heart is in my throat when she wipes her thumb across my lips, and it comes away with hooker red lipstick.

Fuck.

"Carrie, I…"

But she shakes her head, wiping her thumb with disgust. "I came to see how things went with Gerry. Obviously, they went well."

She's angry, but more so, she's hurt. Her pain kills me, and I want to drop to my knees and beg she listen. But she doesn't owe me anything. I've just confirmed her fears.

We will only end up breaking each other's hearts.

"The lipstick, it's—"

She holds up her hand, stopping me from explaining. "I don't care. I'll be staying elsewhere tonight."

"Where?"

"What does it matter?" She looks over my shoulder, curling her lip. I hear giggling. It's akin to Satan's doorbell. "I'm sure you can find someone to keep the bed warm."

"I don't want anyone else. Just stop. Listen to me." I attempt to reach out and touch her, but she jumps back as if I've just asked her to sell me her soul.

"Mason is waiting for me outside."

Motherfucking Mason.

I was right. She was having dessert with that abbreviating dropkick and here I am feeling guilty for something that wasn't even my fault. "We wouldn't want scholar Mason waiting," I bite back, my jealousy baring its teeth.

She crosses her arms, quick to jump to his defense, which pisses me off even more. "He's actually studying law."

I scoff, then burst into a bitter laugh. "Well, that's a waste as he clearly should be studying English seeing as he can't spell for shit. By the way, LOL is not a word! You can tell him that from me."

Oops. In my rage, I just gave away the fact I read her text message, but it's too late to take it back.

She marches forward, jabbing her finger into my chest. "So now you're reading my text messages? What else have you been doing? Spying on me in the shower? Watching me sleep?" The watching her sleep was only that one time, but that's beside the point.

"I can't believe I agreed to come here with you. I must be out of my mind." She pins me with those fierce eyes, not backing down.

"It does run in the family." Fuck me and my quick wit.

Her ferocity soon simmers, and she steps back, swallowing.

That was a low blow, and I immediately need to apologize. "I was out of line. Please…"

But she shakes her head, not interested in a word I have to say. I've said enough. "I was stupid to think you were actually different."

"Dove…" I call out, but she wipes away one betrayal tear before turning to leave.

Sighing, I raise my face to the ceiling and close my eyes.

What the fuck did I just do?

"Dude…"

"Nick, just don't," I say, not in the mood. I just fucked up epically.

"I just wanted to tell you Gerry texted. He loves the chapters. He said he'd pay anything to sign you."

This should be good news, but it's not because the reason those chapters are any good just walked out that door, and like a fucking wanker…I let her go.

13
Thirteen

Christmas. New Year's. It's all horseshit and can sod right off and blow me. I know, not the most eloquent of phrases, but no other words describe how I feel.

Last night was a fucking disaster.

Carrie stuck to her word and stayed elsewhere. Not that I slept, but the bed felt empty without her. These things shouldn't happen. You shouldn't fall in deep with someone you've only known for seven days. But that's what happened.

A week shouldn't have the aptitude to change your life in unfathomable ways, but it has.

I called Carrie endless times, but no surprise, her phone was switched off. I needed to explain myself, but the radio silence was a clear indication she wished to be left alone. Ironically, her walking out on me showed me just how much I cared. And I was prepared to tell her that, but sadly, I was molested before I had the chance.

The only good news is that Gerry loves what he's seen. It appears I've gotten my mojo back, but I wish I could share that with the reason that is.

"Dude, seriously, if you thought about writing as much as you did Carrie, you'd have written a trilogy by now," Nick says from my sofa. He's been here all day, organizing the contract to email over to Gerry.

I would be stupid not to accept Gerry's offer. And it's not just the illustrious terms. It's the fact I can cut ties with Axle.

"I've written over eight thousand words today," I defend, lifting my glasses and rubbing the bridge of my nose.

"And how many of those words were inspired by Carrie? Hmm?" he adds when I flip him off over my shoulder.

He's right. The only reason I was able to write was because she never strayed far from my mind. I wondered where she was, but most importantly, I wondered why she reacted the way she did at the thought of me kissing someone. She was the one who set the rules, so that makes no sodding sense.

Nick's rebound kiss theory floats to the surface, but I refuse to pay heed to it.

Groaning, I reach for my coffee cup, only to find it empty. Today can go to hell.

"Right, we're going out. We're in Paris, and it's New Year's Eve. I need to find a hot Parisian and bring in the new year with a bang—and I mean that literally."

Rolling my shoulders and cracking my neck from side to side, I reach for the bottle of whiskey behind my laptop. "I'm happy right where I am. But you go out."

"I need my wingman," Nick counters.

"And I need to finish this book. Go, have fun. Get laid. I will live vicariously through you." I hate to be such a buzzkill, but if I go out, I may quite possibly end up stabbing someone in the eyeball with a party horn.

Nick won't take no for an answer, though, and I know my best friend. If I don't go to the party, he'll bring the party to me. Strippers and copious amounts of alcohol will fill this hotel room before I'm finished with this chapter.

My cell chimes from the coffee table. Turning in my seat, I see that Nick is holding my phone with the biggest shit-eating grin plastered across his cheeks.

I instantly get the feeling my plans of staying in for the evening have just gone up in flames.

"I don't want to spend New Year's without you," Nick reads, while I rock back in my seat, unsure who the sender is. He reveals who a moment later. "Meet me at *Le Bateau de L'amour*. I miss you. And the sender is none other than the lovely Carrie."

The seat is like a trampoline as I spring upward and hustle toward a grinning Nick. "Give it here." I curl my fingers, indicating for him to pass over my cell because I don't believe him.

But when he complies, I know he's not lying. And the proof is right in front of me.

"Holy shite," I say, shaking my head in awe. "Why would she send this? The last time I saw her, she couldn't get away from me fast enough."

Nick shrugs, appearing just as baffled as I am. "I've given up on understanding women. What I do understand, however, is my desperate need to get wasted. And I won't do that without you. This isn't negotiable."

Carrie texting is a whole different ballgame because I miss her too. But more than anything, I need to apologize for being a gigantic dick. Knowing I've upset her tears a hole straight through me.

"Fuck it. Let's go."

"Atta boy!" Nick exclaims, all but fist pumping the air.

I sweep the room for my coat, but Nick is soon to point out the obvious. "How about you shower first? You wouldn't want her to think your new cologne is *I rolled in dogshit*."

Looking down at my sweats and white tee, I wonder when I ate spaghetti 'cause I seem to have splatters of marinara all over me. Or maybe it was the Bloody Mary I had for breakfast. I can't really tell.

Either way, he's right. I don't want to give her any more reasons to stay away.

Grabbing my jeans and a button-down shirt, I dash into the bathroom, intent on washing the hobo from me. Twenty minutes later, I'm dressed, looking and smelling better than I did. I can't deny both my nerves and excitement at seeing Carrie.

However, the fact she texted me is a good sign. I try not to overthink it by focusing on what I plan to say to her. I need to clear the air between us, and for that to happen, I just may have to divulge my feelings.

Nick and I decide to walk to the rooftop bar Carrie is at because the traffic is madness. The streets are filled with partygoers eager to start the new year with wine in one hand and a fetching suitor in the other. The vibrant atmosphere is contagious.

I wrap my arm around Nick's shoulders. "Thanks, mate. For everything. You may be a pain in the arse, but you're my pain in the arse."

Nick chuckles. "If I was going to annoy anyone for the rest of my life, I'm glad it's you." The mood lifts, and I'm thankful to be bringing in the new year with my best mate.

When we get to *Le Bateau de L'amour,* the line extends around the block. But when I peer up and see the building soar into the skyline, I know the view will be worth the wait. Nick, however, doesn't share the same sentiment.

I watch as he moseys up to the bouncer and taps him on the shoulder. When he has the buffoon's attention, he says something behind his cupped hand before they both look up and make eye contact with me. The bouncer nods once, and

Nick waves me over.

I feel like a right royal arse for cutting in the line, but the thought of seeing Carrie has me promising to buy all these people drinks. The bouncer, who could be The Rock's cousin, snaps up the red velvet rope, indicating we're to enter.

"*Bonsoir Monsieur* Eastwood." I almost trip over my boots, but Nick grips me by the elbow before shoving me inside.

"Really?" I question as we enter.

"What?" He feigns ignorance. "It's not my fault you could be a body double for Scott Eastwood. Blame the good genetics on your parents."

I don't bother arguing.

As we wait in a short line to catch an elevator to the seventh floor, which is where the bar is actually located, I check my cell, wondering if I should send Carrie a text to let her know I'm here. I decide to surprise her.

When the elevator doors open, I'm pleasantly surprised how chic this place is. The huge circular bar is situated in the center of the floor, lit up by wreaths of colored lights. There are sofas and wicker chairs decorated with massive throw pillows and blankets draped over the arms.

Candles and outdoor patio heaters provide warmth and light and set the comfortable vibe.

"What are you drinking?"

"Beer is fine." Nick heads to the bar while I subtly scope out my surroundings, hoping to see Carrie.

The place is packed, so I decide to grab a table and do my hunting with Nick because two sets of eyes are better than one.

The view from up here is incredible. The 360-degree view of the twinkling Parisian skyline has me suddenly wishing I was seeing it with Carrie. Retrieving my cell, I scroll to her message and read it over with a smile.

"Of all the gin joints in all the towns in the world, he walks into mine."

My head snaps up and every part of me backflips in excitement because standing before me is Carrie. She is a vision. Her soft waves tumble around her shoulders, highlighting her breathtaking face. Her lips are coated in a pink gloss and visions of tasting that mouth tackle me from behind.

I want this woman more than I've ever wanted anyone. I'm so screwed.

"We'll always have Paris," I finally say, unable to hide my admiration of the fact we're quoting *Casablanca*—one of my favorite movies.

She brushes a strand of hair behind her ear, a nervous habit of hers.

I want to say so many things, but more than anything, I just want to tell her how much I've missed her. Sadly, all talking is put on hold when Mason appears out of nowhere. "Here's your mocktail, party pooper."

Carrie's cheeks redden, and it has nothing to do with the subzero temperature.

When Mason sees me, he clears his throat. Looks like he wasn't counting on me to rain on his fun parade. Well, tough luck. "Hello, Mason. We haven't formally been introduced. I'm Jayden, Carrie's *friend*." The word, supposed to denote unity, sounds like profanity.

Carrie lowers her eyes while chewing the corner of her lip.

I thrust out my hand, which he shakes firmly. "I know who you are, Jayden." That cocky bastard. His tone is swimming in victory because Carrie is here with him and not me.

Nothing but tension bounces between us, so when Nick arrives with our drinks, I almost kiss him in gratitude. This was a bad fucking idea. "*Ma chérie.* Where have you been? We've missed you."

Carrie seems thankful for Nick's appearance also. "I've been around. Besides, I thought I'd give you and Jayden some privacy." Her tone is dripping with vicious innuendo, coupled with avoiding eye contact with me.

I wish she'd allow me to explain what actually when down last night. But when a group of men surround her, it appears she's readily moved on. When the three men high-five Mason and draw in for a group hug, it's apparent they're his friends. That's all I need—more competition. I'm man enough to admit that these dudes are bangable.

Nick senses my retreat, but he nudges me forward with his elbow—a not so subtle hint to man the fuck up. "Hi, I'm Jayden." I offer my hand to the blond Adonis first. He shakes it, but his lopsided grin hints he too knows who I am. So do his other two friends who have similar responses when they shake my hand.

I feel like everyone is in on a little secret, bar me, and that could be because I'm the butt of everyone's joke. I gulp down my beer, suddenly wishing I had stayed in my hotel room where it was warm, and I wasn't questioning my manhood.

"How's the new book going?" Mason has the audacity to ask. I'm not here to make chitchat. But I refuse to allow him to get the better of me.

"It's going great. Looks like I'll be signing with a new publishing house."

"You are?" It's Carrie who speaks, her surprise clear.

Finally making eye contact with her, I nod, trying my best not to sound like a bumbling fool. "Yes. Gerry loves the chapters."

"Jayden, that is incredible. I'm so proud of you." For a split second, she lets go of this animosity she feels toward me and smiles. I die a thousand deaths. That smile gives me purpose; it gives me hope. But it's gone as quickly as it appeared.

Mason and his entourage are watching closely, but they mean nothing to me. I desperately need to clear the air between Carrie and me because I can't stand this bitterness. I feel out of sorts knowing she thinks I'm some raging manwhore.

"I have you to thank. If it wasn't for your encouragement, then none of this would have fallen into place the way it has."

And I mean that in more ways than one.

Mason shifts beside her, clearly uncomfortable with my honesty, but he can sod right off.

The DJ gods are looking down at me because the reggae music quiets, and a golden oldie takes its place. The makeshift dance floor soon fills with amorous couples, which is my cue to offer my hand to Carrie.

"Dance with me."

Just how when she asked me. It's not a question but rather a statement.

She peers down at my hand, biting her lip, but I'm done waiting. I take her hand, savoring the connection, and lead her toward the dance floor. She's nervous, and her heaving chest confirms this. Her face is downturned as she stares at the floor, but that won't do.

Placing two fingers under her chin, I gently coax her to look at me. Each second is excruciating, but when those warm green eyes meet mine, everything fades into the background, and we focus on this tether, this electrical current which has captivated us since the first moment we met.

I draw her into my arms, not satisfied until we're pressed chest to chest. Even in her heels, she's small, but she stands tall, daring me to make the next move. And I do. I lead her, swaying to the gentle rhythm, unbelieving how right this feels.

"I missed you last night," I declare, not seeing the point in being evasive.

"I doubt that," she counters, but she's wrong.

"What you saw, it was a misunderstanding," I press, hoping it doesn't sound clichéd.

She rolls her eyes, but her sharpness seems to be subsiding. "It doesn't matter. You can kiss whomever you like. It's none of my business."

"Cut the bullshit," I bite back, sick and tired of these games.

"Excuse m-me?" She licks her lips, enticing me further.

"I don't want to kiss anyone else. I want to kiss"— here goes nothing —"you. And even though the feeling isn't mutual, I need you to know that last night, I walked out of the bathroom and got mauled by a reader. I know that's the oldest excuse in the book, but it's the truth."

Carrie appears shocked by my revelation, but I don't know which part has surprised her the most.

"You want to be friends, and I respect that. But you need to tell me why you reacted the way you did last night." When she opens her mouth, clearly flustered, I intercept. "Don't. Don't you dare lie to me. Tell me. Whatever you have to say, I can handle. Just please, don't lie to me."

She attempts to break from my hold, but her efforts are weak. She knows she's bound to lose a fight that has the ability to change everything between us.

"I-I"—she takes a steadying breath—"I told you. I can't do this with you."

"Why?" I press. If this is it, then I need to know I tried my hardest to make her stay.

"Because you don't just have the ability to break my heart… you would ruin me," she confesses, her lower lip trembling. "And I'm scared! What I feel for you…"

"What?" I pull her toward me, relishing in the whoosh of air that leaves her and bathes my cheeks.

Her eyes search mine, frantic for me to assure her that I wouldn't do as she fears. But I can't. We're both fucked up—our emotional baggage outweighing each other's—but that's why we take risks. That's why we jump into the deep end with our eyes closed. When we break the surface, the daylight gives us new meaning, hope to go on.

"What I feel for you doesn't make any sense, and that's the worst kind of…lo—"

"Love?" I offer, filling in the blanks. "Isn't that the reason we're here? At the end of the day, it all comes down to love. Loving yourself and allowing yourself to love another. I may not be ready, but I'm willing to try. And so are you. Why would you text me otherwise?"

Something awful happens, something that has me second-guessing if I know Carrie at all. She lies—the ultimate deal breaker. "I didn't text y-you," she says, but her stutter gives her away.

I understand she is scared, and she has every right to be. I'm scared too. But I can't accept her deceit. What does that say about myself because I've come to realize the most important love is loving yourself.

Releasing her, I run a hand through my hair. I'm done. "For once, how about you stop hiding behind your fears? You told me you're a hopeless romantic, but the truth is, you're afraid of love. You're not who I thought you were."

I've hurt her feelings. "I didn't text you," she presses, but it doesn't even matter anymore. The truth is, I don't even care. I don't have time for liars. I've had enough deceit to last me a lifetime.

Carrie is not the woman I believed her to be, and whatever feelings I believed to have for her are evidently for someone who doesn't exist.

"You don't believe me?" she asks, her eyes wet with tears.

"No, I don't," I cruelly state, done with these games. "You've not given me a reason to."

A betrayed tear slides down her cheek, but she wipes it away with the back of her hand. "I should be enough of a reason," she whispers, "but clearly I'm not."

This was never going to be a long-winded affair. So I put us both out of our misery. "Clearly."

She nods once, biting her lip to stop the tears, and no matter how much I want to console her, I can't. With nothing further to say, she pushes through the crowd while I watch something that could have been beautiful slip through my fingers one final time.

An ache throbs in my chest, but I won't chase her, not this

time. I don't like liars.

Without a doubt, Nick has beared witness to this clusterfuck of events. I need a moment to clear my head. Making my way to the balcony, I remain hidden behind the greenery, happy to remain incognito for a little while.

I have no idea why Carrie just lied. I could have shown her the proof on my phone, but what would have been the point? Her dishonesty speaks volumes. I just don't understand why. I don't understand anything anymore. And this is confirmed when someone casually stands by me.

"Want a smoke?" Turning over my shoulder, I see Mason light up a Marlboro coolly, while offering me his open packet.

This motherfucker has some nerve. But I suppose he's come here to gloat.

When he makes clear he has no intention of leaving, I decide to humor us both. "Why the bloody hell not?" He offers me his lighter with a grin.

When I take the first drag, I savor the nicotine hit. "It's been about five years since I had my last cigarette," I reveal. "My ex-wife hated the smell."

Blowing a smoke ring and watching it dissipate into the atmosphere, I add, "I hated the feel of her Botox lips, but I still managed to tolerate it."

Mason listens quietly. "I don't understand women, mate." Why am I confiding in him? The world is clearly ending.

"Neither do I," he replies, snapping me from my pity party

for one.

"Carrie left." I state the obvious.

"I saw. What happened?"

I can't contain my sarcastic chuckle. "*She* happened." That's his cue to leave me alone to wallow in my self-pity and chase after Carrie, but he doesn't.

"You really like her, don't you?"

Not bothering in pretenses, I take another drag before replying, "Yes, I really do."

"That's a shame."

All touchy-feely, heart to hearts come crashing down around me. "Excuse me." I turn to face him, about ready to give him an earful, but what he does next has me giving him something else.

He kisses me.

I'm in a state of complete shock, and as far as first kisses go, this is bloody horrible. But what the actual fuck.

"I can't leave you alone for five minutes," says a playful voice behind us. Mason breaks the kiss, while I stand like a deer in headlights.

What just happened?

"I'm sorry," he says, appearing beyond triumphant. "I've wanted to do that since the first moment we met."

My mouth opens and closes like a stunned goldfish. When I finally find my voice, I squeak, "*You have?* Why?"

"Because you're fucking hot," is his simple reply. But I've

never been more confused than I am right now.

"I am?" I ask, pulling back. As far as conversations go, I am appalled at my lack of articulation. But what the bloody hell is going on? "What about Carrie?"

"She's hot too, and if I swung that way, I'd be all over that cream puff."

It takes me a minute, actually two, but when I finally catch up to speed, I ask, "You're gay?"

"Yes." Mason looks at me like I'm daft, and at this moment, I too am wondering the same thing.

How did I miss this?

However, in spite of his response, I question, "So you've never been interested in Carrie?" because my brain can't catch up fast enough.

"No. She's a great gal, but I caught up with her to ask about you. Seems we've both got the same taste in men."

Mason's friend, the tall blond, comes and stands by us. He offers me his hand. "It's nice to finally meet you. Mason has been kind of obsessed." Mason elbows him, blushing. "He's read all your books."

Feeling like a sodding, arrogant arse, I state, "So this entire time you've been into…me?"

"Yes. You didn't know?" Mason replies, eyebrow cocked.

"No. I had no clue." *No fucking clue.*

"I thought Carrie told you?"

"Our relationship hasn't been of the sharing sort of late," I reveal, shaking my head in regret.

"I know. She told me…which is why I stole her phone and texted you where she'd be. She's been miserable."

His admission winds me, and I almost give myself whiplash as I turn to look at him. "*You* texted me?"

He holds up both hands in surrender. "Guilty as charged."

I am such a douchebag.

"Did I do something wrong?" Mason asks when he reads my inner thoughts. But this is all my fault.

"No. This is all on me." Mason waits for me to elaborate, but I don't have time to explain.

I'm about to excuse myself because I owe Carrie a huge apology, but I can't leave with that god-awful kiss as my legacy. "By the way"— I smash my lips to his, leaving *him* stunned this time —"give someone a little warning the next time you kiss them," I conclude smugly because that's a legacy I'm proud to leave.

Mason's cheeks are flustered as he gushes, "Will do, Mr. Sparrow."

I leave Mason and his friend chuffed with my farewell and seek out Nick. He's pulling the moves on some blonde, but I won't be long. "I'm going to find Carrie."

Nick nods, shooing me away. But he soon narrows his eyes. He so can smell the depravity on me.

"Yes, mate, if your theory is right, I just had my rebound kiss; therefore, I can tell Carrie everything."

Nick almost falls over his feet. "Who?" he asks, his tone filled with accusation and disbelief.

Reaching for his beer, I take a sip before announcing, "Turns out Mason is a bloody good kisser."

His jaw hits the bar. "I'm not drunk enough for this, but just remember"—he holds up his finger—"I'm your number one bae."

"Always," I counter, laying a big ole kiss on his cheek.

"Go, go," he says, playfully wiping his cheek. "Go get the girl." The sound of that sings to my senses, and I take off like the devil is at my heels.

The line for the elevator is a mile long, so I make a mad dash down the flight of stairs. Once I hit the pavement, I continue with my wild sprint. I don't bother calling Carrie because I know she won't answer me.

So I lead with my gut, hoping for once, I'm right.

The streets are bustling, hinting it's almost time to bid farewell to 2017 and hope for a better 2018. But I don't have time to reminisce.

I use my cardio prowess to make it back to the hotel in record time. My boots skid along the polished floors, but I press on because it's a race to beat the clock. Once the elevator arrives at my floor, I burst out the doors and continue my sprint.

I hope I'm right because every part of me is telling me that Carrie is here, packing up her stuff, hell-bent on leaving. That's what she does when she's scared. She runs.

But not this time.

The moment I open the door, I know she's in here. Her familiar bouquet whets my senses. "Carrie!" I shout, searching the room frantically.

Please let me not be too late.

"Carrie!" I call out once again, running into the bedroom. "No!" I cry when she's not in here. I'm too late. I let the best thing that's happened to me in a long time go.

The thought leaves me winded, and I rub over my chest in distress. However, when a gust of wind sweeps into the room, my heart kickstarts again.

"Carrie?" I step out onto the balcony and exhale in relief when I see her standing by the railing.

She doesn't turn around.

Measuring my words and steps, I decide to throw caution to the wind. "I'm sorry, dove. I fucked up. I know it wasn't you who texted me. Please forgive me for not believing you. I just have an issue with trust." No need for me to detail why.

Her shoulders sag as she dips her chin to her chest. "It doesn't matter."

"Yes, it does," I press, refusing to play this game any longer. "Look at me." Her hand swipes at her cheek as she sniffs. I feel like an utter arsehole for making her cry. "Please."

She inhales, before giving in to my request.

When I see her tears, I immediately march toward her, wanting nothing more than to wrap her in my arms. But she shakes her head. "Don't. Please."

Her anguish is clear, but I don't understand why.

"Talk to me. I fucked up. Royally. I should have believed you. After Liz"—I huff, running both hands through my hair—"I have an issue trusting people, but you're not any person. You're you. The person who has…" Here goes nothing. "The person who has stolen my heart from the first moment we met."

Sadly, my honesty has the opposite effect. "Jayden, don't. I can't do this with you." She squeezes her eyes shut, but I won't allow her to shut me out.

"Do what?"

"This," she replies, gesturing with two fingers between us. "I promised myself I wouldn't do this. Remember?"

I know she's talking about her promise on the plane. *"My New Year's resolution is to quit booze, boys, and sex."*

"Yes."

"And what do I do?" She throws her arms out to the side. "The complete opposite. I'm a fucking idiot. A complete glutton for punishment."

"Why would you say that?"

She crosses her arms and shivers. I want to offer her my coat, but I don't know how she'll respond. I don't know anything anymore. "Because, Jayden, I did what I said I wasn't going to do."

"And what's that?" I take a step forward, while she takes one back.

With a quivering lower lip, she confesses something that is sure to change everything. Forever. "I've fallen for you when I promised myself I wouldn't. And now I'm acting like a crazy person again—something I promised myself I wouldn't do. But it appears all of that is void 'cause when it comes to you..." She pauses, biting her lip.

"When it comes to me, what?" I coax, fisting my hands by my side.

With the emotions swirling inside me, and her confession, I don't trust myself. I don't trust that I won't drag her into my arms and claim those plump lips as mine.

When she lifts those eyes, I'm done for. Nothing will ever be the same. "When it comes to you, nothing else exists, and I'm scared. I'm scared of feeling this way because I've never felt *this* before."

And there it is.

The woman I am smitten with has just confirmed that this is real. No matter the small amount of time we've known one another for, this ever-present, undeniable pull grows stronger every day.

And yes, it's scary. It's fucking frightening but running from this is even more terrifying.

Besides, I'm sick of running. From now on, I only plan on moving forward. And with no time like the present, I charge over to where Carrie stands and smash my lips to hers.

The deed surprises us both, but that soon turns to wanton

desire. I've been reborn.

Threading my fingers through her silky hair, I tug softly, angling her mouth so I can devour every inch of her. I lick the seam of her lips, before diving in deep and dueling my tongue with hers.

Her moans mingle with mine, and I'm certain I'm lost forevermore.

Our mouths move in unison, a perfect meeting of give and take. I'm trying to be gentle, but holy fuck, I'm so worked up. I've clearly been doing this wrong all these years because I don't remember kissing feeling this way.

Our tongues circle the other, an intricate dance of what my flesh is craving. I bite her bottom lip, before suckling it the moment she whimpers.

She stands on tippy toes and loops both hands around my nape, tugging at the longer strands of my hair. I'm going to eat her alive.

I thrust my body into hers, humming when a whoosh of air escapes her. I'm so fucking hard, and I have no doubt she can feel me pressed rock solid into her. Tiny, impatient mewls and her sweet taste just add to my heightened state, and suddenly, kissing is not enough.

Her taste, smell, her entire being is my new addiction, and I need another fix. I lift her up and die a small death when she comes willingly, wrapping her legs around my waist. Our lips never miss a beat as I walk us inside and into the bedroom.

With one final taste of her mouth, I sever our connection. Her eyes flutter open.

The sated look in them, combined with her swollen, pink lips unleashes my inner caveman, and I toss her onto the bed. She yelps as her delicious arse bounces on the mattress, but that soon turns to a mewl when her eyes drop to my tenting hard-on.

The tip of her tongue wets her bottom lip, stirring this out of control inferno from within. "I broke your no kissing rule," she quips, rubbing her legs together.

That naughty little minx.

Placing a knee on the foot of the bed, I strip out of my coat and boots and commence to prowl toward her. She falls onto her back, her spectacular chest rising and falling rapidly. I grip her ankles when she attempts to scramble up the bed.

Dragging her toward me, I lower my chest to hers until we're face to face. "Actually, Mason was the first one to break my rule." Her eyes widen. "Why didn't you tell me?" Bending low, I bite behind her ear. She lets out a low moan.

"Because like I said, I'm not here for romance. Especially romance that involves someone interested in the same man as I am."

My cock jerks. "You drive me crazy."

"Ditto," she counters.

Done with talking, I paint a trail of kisses down the length of her neck. Sadly, her sweater gets in the way, and I realize she's wearing way too many clothes. Kneeling between her legs, I reach for her foot and unlace her sneaker. I do the same with the other shoe.

My eyes zero in on the top button of her jeans. They then descend lower to the junction between her thighs. I thumb the corner of my mouth, unable to take my eyes off her. She is beautiful. And she is all mine.

"Now is the time to tell me to stop," I say, feeling certain that if she does, I just may cry. As I flick over the button on her jeans, I skim my finger along the sliver of flesh just below the hem of her short sweater and watch as tiny goose bumps prickle her milky flesh.

When she remains quiet, watching me with those stormy eyes, I take that as my cue to continue.

I flick open her button, never breaking eye contact with her as I unfasten her zipper. She lifts her hips in a silent invitation to continue. Dragging the jeans down her thighs, I almost come in my pants when I see the small triangle of white cotton covering her pussy.

She doesn't need to be cloaked in silk, lace, or leather. This is far more of a turn-on than her parading around in sexy lingerie because this is real. This is just a man and a woman, barriers stripped back, who are about to embark on a journey that is sure to change everything.

Once I've stripped her of her jeans, I sit back on my heels and take a moment to appreciate her beauty. She shyly attempts to draw her legs together, but my hand snaps out as I grip her inner thigh.

"Own it," I hoarsely declare, running my thumb over the soft flesh on her leg. "Do you know how incredible you look right now?"

She smiles timidly. "Thank you." When her flesh turns the same sweet pink as her cheeks, I'm unable to control myself and walk my fingers to the outside of her underwear where her wetness has soaked through the cotton.

With eyes locked, I circle two fingers over her entrance, groaning when she bucks into my touch, demanding more. My pace is slow, sluggish; I can do this all night, but Carrie grunts in the back of her throat, frustrated.

"Please," she begs on a whimper, opening her legs wider.

She places her hand over mind, coaxing me to give her what she wants. But I intend to savor her and only surrender when she's at the pinnacle of no return.

"I've never wanted anyone more than I do you. I don't know if I can be gentle," I confess because just the feel of her through her underwear has me grinding my teeth.

"I don't want gentle," she breathlessly replies. "I just want… you." Those words are ones I've been waiting to hear since the moment we met, and now that she's said them, there's no taking them back.

I cup her mound, then hook my fingers into her underwear. "I hope you're not attached to these." Before she can ask why, I rip them clean from her body. She yelps, and a hum leaves me when I see her bare center.

I need a minute. Actually, make that two.

Her womanly curves and supple, creamy flesh seem to highlight the softness of her ripened sex. "Holy fuck," I gasp, eyes feasting on her bare core. "You are so beautiful."

She turns her cheek, embarrassed.

Reaching for the hem of her sweater, I gently lift it from her body and strip her bare. Her breasts rise and fall as she inhales and exhales deeply, watching me watching her. The smooth flesh spills from the cups of her bra, and it takes all my willpower not to bury my head between those pillows of perfection.

Cupping her throat, I gently arch her head backward, and her surrender is music to my soul. With splayed fingers, I glide my hand down her chest, skimming my fingertips against the curve of her breasts, and she whimpers. I almost keel over from the sensation of touching her so intimately.

As I caress the tender flesh of her stomach, I take a detour and circle her belly button. She shivers.

It's sensory overload because I want nothing more than to sink into her heat and be lost for hours, but I honestly don't know where to start. It's a smorgasbord to my senses, and when she shifts, and her sweetened smell hits my nostrils, I know I need so much more.

Never taking my eyes off her, I walk my fingers down the dip of her lower stomach before sliding my finger along her slick entrance. Her back bows from the mattress as she moans. I repeat the action, only faster this time, and increasing the pressure.

Her arousal is the perfect lubrication, and before long, wet, delicious strokes fill the fervent air. The moment she arches her back, I sink a finger deep into her. She's hot and wet and so fucking delicious, I'm unable to help myself as I begin to move faster and deeper.

She sighs loudly, her body bucking into me as she desperately chases a release. Her breasts sway like a hypnotic pendulum, and I am utterly under her spell. I can't get enough and neither can she when I insert another finger.

She's stretched full as she rides my hand, gasping for air. "Oh god."

The sight is beyond words and will forever be ingrained into my memory. Carrie is writhing, a flush overtaking her pale flesh, and I quickly merge the sight with her signature fragrance—strawberries and cream.

The sight, no matter how visually satisfying, is suddenly not enough because I need everything—I want it all. With fingers buried deep inside her, I flick over her needy clit, and a quiver overtakes her. She rides my hand as I punish her with a reckless rhythm.

A winded exhale leaves her, which is my cue to remove my fingers…only to replace them with my mouth.

Carrie doesn't have time to protest because I slither down

her body and come to rest at her sex. Hooking my elbows behind her knees, I drag her legs over my shoulders and press my lips to her honeyed heat.

She screams; the sound is a blissful melody to my ears.

Her taste is unlike anything I've ever sampled—her sweetness burns my tongue. Her flesh is scorching, but I welcome the burn because I want more.

I lap at her entrance, suckling the smoothness and relishing the way she tastes and feels. She tugs at my hair, her aggression an utter turn-on, and I finally give in to what she wants. I suckle over her clit, circling the engorged bud, before delving in deep.

She bucks against my face, my hair still coiled tight in her fists as she moans over and over again. I fuck her with my tongue and mouth, opening her up like a rosebud in bloom. I'm without mercy and will only be satisfied when she's screaming out my name and coming wildly.

Her body is wound tight. She's close. I know what she wants. It'll only take a small swipe of my tongue, and she'll be done for. I bury myself deeper between her legs, her essence engulfing me as she rides me wildly, incoherent gibberish spilling from her lips.

Her mewls reveal she can't take it any longer, so I rear up and bite over her clit, before sucking it deeply. She screams, and her body grows lax. The sight is a glorious one. Carrie comes with a well-sated moan while my hard-on drives a hole straight through the mattress.

Arching, I watch her come undone. Her stomach quivers. Her flesh is a blossoming rosy pink. She thrashes about, tiny mewls passing through her parted lips, and I feel like fucking Superman knowing I am the reason behind her gratification.

It takes a few moments, but eventually, her breathlessness calms.

I lay one final kiss over her sex before crawling up her body, unable to wipe the smirk from my cheeks. Her eyes are closed, but she wears a satisfied smile. "Wow," she gasps as I kiss the corner of her lips before rolling onto my back.

This position showcases my raging hard-on, but I honestly don't care. Going down on Carrie and seeing her explode in that way was more than enough. Sadly, however, tell that to my impatient dick.

Carrie shivers, and I automatically reach for the blanket to cover us. But her hand snaps out. "I want more," she very boldly confesses, unhurriedly opening her eyes.

Something different reflects in them, and it's simply beautiful.

"What more do you want?"

She smirks, leaning up on one elbow. "I want it all."

This woman will surely be the death of me, but when she reaches behind her and unfastens her bra, I can't help but think what a way to go.

The material falls from her chest, revealing the most delectable pair of breasts I have ever seen. Dusty pink areolas and pearled nipples are inches from me, and I blink once to ensure I'm not dreaming. But with Carrie's arousal still slathered on my lips, I know this is very real.

Not masking my appreciation of her body, I watch as her skin breaks out into goose bumps. After what we just did, her bashfulness is too sweet for words.

Her mussed hair falls around her shoulders, setting off the pinkness to her cheeks. She is truly a vision. Running my thumb over the apple of her cheek, I confess, "I knew you'd shake up my world. I just never anticipated how much so."

She leans into my touch, and just when I think she can't take the wind from my sails, she goes and says something like, "Don't break me. I'm not perfect. I'm just me."

At this moment, Carrie exposes her fears and vulnerability, but never has she been fiercer than she is right now.

Cupping her cheek, I relish in our connection and smile. "I won't." And we seal our deal the only way we can—with a kiss.

I can't believe I went without for so long, but the key to this kiss is that it's shared with Carrie. It starts out slow, both exploring once again, but when she presses her chest to mine, I'm done for.

I roll on top of her, never breaking our union as we steal the air from each other's lungs. Her fingernails scratch over my beard before she slides her hand down my neck and fists the neckline of my T-shirt. She wants it off. And I do too.

Reaching behind me, I tug at the back of the collar and

yank it off. We only separate long enough for me to toss it aside before we're desperately reaching for the other. Carrie moans into my mouth as she skims her fingers down my chest and over my stomach. When she tugs at the hair painting down my navel, I hum low.

With fumbling fingers, she unfastens the top button of my jeans. Her eagerness has my cock jerking against her hand. She gasps and suddenly breaks our kiss.

"I want to see you," she nervously confesses, licking her swollen lips. I'm unsure what she means, but I'll give her anything she wants.

She gently pushes my shoulder, hinting she wants me to roll onto my back. I comply.

She sits up in all her naked glory, and it takes every ounce of strength not to rear up and suckle those incredible breasts. But this is her show. She glances down at me, inhaling when she examines my tattoo.

Running her fingertip over the cursive font, she asks, "What does this mean?"

"Where there is life, there is hope," I reply, watching her closely. She nods in understanding and continues her exploration.

Toying with the light dusting of hair between my pecs, she follows the trail down my chest and stops when she reaches the waistband of my boxers peeking out from my jeans. "I like this scruff." She tugs at it while I bite down on my tongue to stop from raising my hips, demanding more.

"Thank you," I manage to choke out, barely holding it together.

"Holy shit," she gasps, brushing over the top of my V muscle.

I don't have time to gloat because she brushes her hair over one shoulder and lowers her lips to my abs. I barely breathe when the tip of her tongue traces over the outline of each one. Fisting the blanket beneath me, I steady my breathing and watch in awe as she slowly runs her fingers over my hard-on.

We both hiss—me in relief, and I can only hope Carrie in happiness.

I need these jeans off like now.

Carrie continues her exploration, touching me over my jeans while I almost rip the linens to shreds. She rises, those inquisitive eyes watching me as I respond to her touch. I don't care that I'll come in my pants like a two-pump chump because nothing has ever felt this good.

However, when she walks her fingers into my boxers, I stand corrected.

She timidly grips my shaft, appearing to familiarize herself with my girth. I swallow, trying to hold it together. But when she works her small hand downward and runs her thumb over the end of my cock, I groan, almost losing it.

"Wow," she gushes, eyes alight. "That's so fucking hot."

My reaction to her touch spurs her on, and she begins a slow and torturous voyage of exploring me. I raise my hips when my jeans get in the way. She almost rips them and my boxers clean off. My cock springs free, and she wets her bottom lip.

I'm barely holding it together especially when I peer down and see her hand working my length. She fingers the curls at the base of my shaft, teasing me just how I teased her because I want more…so much more.

I thrust into her grip, desperate for a release, but when that happens, I intend to be buried deep within that delicious sex of hers. Her breaths turn raspy as she gasps for air, and the way she watches what she's doing to me hints she'll stick by her affirmation that she wants it all.

"Oh, fuck," I growl, arching into her strokes. She continues her onslaught, and I love every minute.

On the cusp of exploding, I almost cry out for her to stop, but when I hear fireworks, I almost think it's too late. But when those fireworks grow louder, and Carrie's movement slows pace, I know what we hear is us bringing in the new year in the best possible way.

"Happy New Year," Carrie says with a smile and her hand still wrapped around my cock.

"And what a way to start it," I reply, before gently prying myself from her grip and hunting the room for my wallet. She watches me closely as I retrieve a condom and boldly tear open the packet and roll it onto my shaft.

I don't waste a second and crawl onto the bed as she falls

onto her back. She shuffles up the mattress, placing her head on the pillow. I want to savor this moment, but if I don't sink into her right this second, I will lose my fucking mind.

Smashing my lips to hers, I dip two fingers into her heat to ensure she's ready. She is.

We kiss like ravenous beasts all the while I shift my hips and line us up in the most intimate way possible. Unlike all the previous times I've done this, this feels different, and I realize it's because it's with someone who has the power to change my world.

Slowing the kiss, I pull away, wanting to look into Carrie's eyes when I do…this.

She gasps and arches her neck when I sink into her all the way to the hilt. I remain still, allowing her muscles to accommodate to my size. Only when I feel her relaxing do I move.

I pace myself at first—slow and steady as I want to ensure she's enjoying this as much as me. She feels fucking incredible, and the fireworks sounding around us pale in comparison to the explosion budding within.

She raises her hips and wraps a hand around my nape, encouraging me to go faster. "Fuck," I hum, sinking into her heat over and over again.

Unable to help myself, I peer between us and am enthralled by our bodies becoming one. The sight kicks me in the balls, and the need to come overthrows me.

My rhythm becomes faster, but as Carrie's pearled nipples abrade my chest, I drive into her deeper and harder, showing no mercy. She surrenders, moaning hoarsely as her body grows lax. I smash my lips to hers, kissing the ever-living fuck out of her as I continue my reckless tempo.

Gripping her leg, I wrap it around my waist and deepen the angle.

Her eyes pop open. "Oh, god," she whimpers, my vicious thrusts moving her up the bed. The more savage I am, the harder she cries, and before long, she is groaning and thrashing uncontrollably. Her sex grips me tight.

Sweat coats our bodies, and the sound of the raw slapping of flesh has me reaching down and circling her ripened clit. She cries and appears to lose all control of her body. I wrap both hands around her waist and slam into her until she is coming with a glorious scream.

"Jayden!" she yells over and over again. My name spilling from her lips is my undoing, and when the final tremor wracks her body, I let go and come so violently, I arch back and roar. My hips have a mind of their own as I continue sinking into her heat, desperate to milk every last drop.

Once I'm spent, I fall on top of her with a well-sated grunt. She wraps her arms around me and cradles me to her heaving chest. We stay this way for several minutes.

When I finally catch my breath, I realize I'm probably squashing her and attempt to move. But she tightens her hold.

"Five more minutes," she sleepily says, nuzzling into the crook of my neck.

Pressed against her, both sticky and spent and still rooted deep inside her, there is no place I'd rather be. So I cocoon my body around hers and get lost in the feeling of being united with Carrie because with a new year comes New Year's resolutions, and for me, I will do anything to ensure this feeling never ends.

I came to Paris for romance, but I'll be leaving with so much more.

14
Fourteen

I wake to the most delectable scent on my pillow and lips—strawberries and cream.

It takes me a moment, but as soon as I stretch and realize I'm very naked, the truth smashes into me—Carrie and I had sex, and it was fucking epic.

Rolling onto my side, I reach for Carrie, but my eyes pop open when the bed is cold beside me. Shooting up, I scan the room, wondering where she could be. The en suite door is open, hinting no one is inside.

"Dove?" I call out.

Silence.

Reaching for my cell off the bedside dresser, my fingers brush over a note propped up against the lamp. Without delay, I open it, and a wave of relief passes over me.

Gone to get breakfast. Didn't have the heart to wake you. Be back soon.

Carrie xx

Those two innocent kisses remind me of the many not so virtuous kisses I laid all over her body.

Memories assault me, and I can't help but reminisce about the way our bodies united as one. A perfect yin to yang. All the meaningless sex I've had in the past feels like a distant memory because I haven't felt this way in a very long time. I feel happy.

I thought sleeping with endless women would help make the pain go away, but instead, each warm body I had lain with chipped away at the one thing I never thought I'd have again—hope. Carrie has given me hope from the first moment I met her, and now, I feel fucking invincible.

With that as my mindset, I strip back the blankets and decide to shower before she gets back. Yes, we had incredible sex, but now, the morning talk is inevitable. Last night meant something to me, and I'm pretty certain it meant something to Carrie. But I need to know what happens next.

I take a quick shower and dress in ripped jeans and a T-shirt, a casual choice as I'm not too sure what the day holds. It is New Year's Day, after all. We should do something special to commemorate our new beginning.

A knock sounds at the door.

It's a little too early for housekeeping, so it's surely Carrie. Maybe she forgot her key. I know my brain is scrambled after last night's strenuous activities.

Unable to wipe my smug smile clean, I saunter toward the door, opening it, all but ready to lay a thousand kisses all over Carrie's beautiful face. But who stands before me has me wanting to render myself unconscious.

"Hello, Jayden."

I blink twice because there is no fucking way she is here. But when she steps forward and attempts to hug me, I know this is real.

Dodging her advances, I recoil backward, fearful for my soul. "*Liz?* What the fuck are you doing here?" My sharpness still stuns her. "How'd you know where I was?"

Toying with her pearls, she attempts to play off my insolence. "Is that any way to say hello?"

"The only salutation I wish to give you is a goodbye." I try to shut the door, but she wedges her heeled boot in the doorway.

"I'm not going anywhere, Jayden. Not until you listen to what I have to say."

"I've heard enough," I reply, still attempting to close the door, but she won't budge.

"I will stay here for as long as it takes."

"Well, you'll be waiting a while then." It's a struggle, us both pushing—a true reflection of what our marriage was.

"I'm sure your little tart won't appreciate your wife camping outside your door."

"Ex-wife," I correct, pushing harder on the door. But she

has touched a nerve because she's right. Carrie and I are in a good place, and Liz being here will just undo any progress we made.

"Not yet," she counters, sensing my surrender as she fights harder to make her way inside.

A curious guest passes by, watching the strange tug-of-war. I give him a strained smile, but he walks by quickly, on his way, I'm sure, to tell security of the spectacle he witnessed. Not needing any more bad press, and wanting Liz gone before Carrie returns, I have no other choice but to give in.

Letting go of the door, Liz topples forward but saves herself from face planting when she grabs the doorjamb. Uncaring, I turn my back and make my way toward the bottle of scotch on the coffee table.

The door closes behind me, the noise akin to a prison door sealing my fate for good. I don't bother turning but instead unscrew the bottle and take a large sip.

"Starting a little early," Liz says, her judgmental voice grating on my nerves.

"What can I say? You drive a man to drink." She exhales, but she has another thing coming if she thinks I'm going to make this easy for her.

"The least you can do is look at me." Her hurt is apparent but so was mine when she cheated.

"I owe you nothing, Elizabeth," I stubbornly counter, taking another drink.

The room falls silent.

"I want you back."

Tipping my head toward the ceiling, I sigh as a frustrated groan leaves me. "No. For the millionth time, no. The answer will always be no. N.O. No."

Here's to hoping if I repeat myself, it'll finally sink in. But that's wishful thinking.

"I will do anything, Jayden." She advances, gripping my arm and coaxing me to look at her. But the feel of her hands on me reminds me of the fact her hands have been on many others before.

Ripping from her grip, I spin violently, pinning her with a fierce glower. "No, you clearly won't because the only thing I want is for you to leave me alone. Yet here you are. How did you know where I was?"

Her lower lip trembles. "I have my ways."

I don't even want to know what that means because I am done conversing. But it appears she's only just begun.

"I miss you so much. I miss us. I can't sleep. I can't eat. I'm miserable without you." Taking a closer look at her, I can't deny she looks thinner, sicker, and her usual flawless appearance is marred with dark circles under her eyes. Her casual outfit of skinny jeans and a pink sweater is also not one I would expect to see her in. But knowing Liz, she's done this with intent—to display her inner turmoil, she's unable to dress like a prized poodle because she's so heartbroken.

But I'm not fooled.

"Well, I'm miserable with you, so too bad. You need to move on."

"Never," she rebukes, tears stinging her eyes. A small part of me feels sorry for her, but I promptly quash that part. "I made a terrible mistake, one I will never forgive myself for. My therapist—"

I cut her off with a snicker. "Therapist? Since when do you see a shrink?"

"Since I fucked up the best thing that's ever happened to me!" she exclaims, stunning me with her emotion. "Please, Jayden. I'm better. I'm sorry." She advances again, hands interlocked, begging me to listen. "I will never forgive myself for what I did. I just wanted a baby…"

"Stop." I thrust out my hand, shaking my head. "Enough." Memories begin to pour into me of the day she tore out my heart, and I can't take it anymore.

"It's not an excuse, but it's part of the reason I did it."

"And what's the other part?" I bitterly ask while she turns her cheek. "Eduardo wasn't the first, was he?"

Her silence speaks volumes.

"And the other part is clearly because you're selfish, and narcissistic, and no matter what I gave you, it was never enough." I fill in the blanks while a tear falls down her cheek. "You fucking ruined me, Liz! You took everything, *everything* from me. Not only did you shit on everything we had, but you also took away my will to write. My only savior was tainted by the memories of what you did."

I clutch her upper arms, anger spewing from me. "So don't you come here and tell me you're sorry because you're only sorry you got caught!"

"That's not true," she sobs. "I love you. They meant nothing to me. You're the only man I've ever loved."

She lunges forward, her lips headed for mine, but I draw back in disgust. "That makes it all the more worse."

If she had feelings for any of them, then maybe, maybe, one day I could forgive her. But her cheating just because makes her betrayal worse.

Liz slumps onto the sofa with her head in her hands and cries while I once again just feel numb. She is the only woman who can provoke these feelings from me, and I want no more. "Get out," I say, exhausted and so done with this conversation.

"What can I do? How can I make this right?" she asks, raising her eyes. I've never seen her more distraught than right now, but I think that's because she's finally realizing this is over for good.

"You can sign the divorce papers."

Harsh, but true.

Her sniffles make me feel like an utter bastard because no matter what she did, I don't like seeing her cry. But this needs to end. Now. I have other pressing matters to deal with, like Carrie.

"Jayden?" Carrie stands by the doorway, her confusion apparent. I don't blame her. She's just walked into hell.

The moment she hears Carrie's voice, Liz looks over her shoulder slowly. The room drops to artic temperatures. "Are you the homewrecker? The whore trying to steal my husband."

Carrie pales and tears sting her eyes. I lunge forward, enraged. "Leave. You are not welcome."

Liz snickers, standing proudly. However, she has no intention of going anywhere. "Jayden will tire of you, little girl. Look at him…and look at you." She scans Carrie up and down and laughs. "I can't believe *you're* the rebound. Shame on you, Jayden. I thought you'd at least attempt an upgrade. But it appears you've gone blind."

Low blow and completely untrue.

Carrie storms forward, primed on ripping into Liz, but I beat her to it. "On the contrary, Liz. I *was* blind, blinded by your bullshit. But the moment I met Carrie was the first time in a long time my eyes were opened. I was simply sleepwalking through life, but Carrie has changed that. You may think she's a rebound, but she's so much more. You're not even half the woman she is. Now, if you'd kindly leave. Otherwise, I will throw your arse out myself."

Liz stands her ground, swallowing down her rage. "You will regret this."

The only thing I regret is allowing her in. "I won't ask again."

Liz's tears soon dry as she pulls back her shoulders,

arrogantly. "Carrie…the name of my successor." I suddenly get punched in the stomach, and I don't know why. "Things just got interesting."

Carrie grins, not at all intimated by Liz. She saunters forward, standing her ground. "Yes, they did. It was a pleasure meeting you. It's put my mind at ease."

"At ease?" Liz asks, pursing her lips.

"Yes, at ease," she confirms with a confident nod. "I was worried I had some stiff competition. Looks like I was wrong."

Liz's eye twitches, but she keeps her cool. "I'll be seeing you around."

"Not if I can help it," I reply, thankful to see the back of her and even more grateful when she walks out the door.

Carrie and I are quiet, both needing to digest what just happened. Even though Liz is gone, I have a sneaking suspicion that's not the last we'll be seeing of her. "Dove, I…"

But I don't have a chance to finish because Carrie steals the air from my lungs when she presses her lips to mine. Although she catches me off guard, it doesn't take me long to catch up to speed. There is a hint of aggression to her kiss, an almost ownership as she coils her fingers through my hair and pulls.

My cock instantly stirs.

We kiss like starved beasts, clawing and biting, and if she doesn't stop pressing that delectable body into me, I won't be held accountable for my actions.

"Thank you," she says from around my mouth, suckling my

bottom lip.

"Why are you thanking me? I should be the one thanking you for having such a glorious derrière," I reply, slapping her on the arse playfully.

She yelps and propels forward with a giggle.

As much as I want to continue, we need to discuss what just happened. Pulling away is beyond blasphemous, but so is allowing Liz to taint this moment with Carrie. "Sorry about that." There is no need for me to elaborate.

Carrie sighs, pressing a hand to my cheek. "You have nothing to be sorry for. How did she know you were here?"

I shrug. "I have no idea."

"I can't believe you were married to her. She's horrible."

"I can't believe it either." I shudder at the thought.

Carrie averts her eyes, weighing up what to say next. "Thank you for saying what you did."

"I meant every word." I know she's referring to my rebound comment.

She smiles, and the sight is really just spectacular. However, what she says next takes my breath away in a whole different manner. "Liz coming here wasn't a complete disaster."

I curl my lip in confusion. "Care to explain? Because from where I stand, her coming here has just jinxed this room. I'm not above bringing out the sage."

She laughs and explains. "I just meant she kind of forced us to have the awkward morning-after talk."

My mouth forms an O because she is absolutely right. "Well, I suppose it's not a total train wreck then."

She tugs at her lip, clearly wanting to say something else. But she's said enough.

Thumbing her bottom lip, I pull it free, and the hazel in her eyes turns a molten honey. "I suppose not," she whispers, watching me closely.

A tremor passes through her, and I hum in response.

"Let's get out of here," I say, leaning forward and nudging her nose with mine.

"W-where?" Her falter has me wanting to beat my chest in pride. She feels this too.

"Let's just go wherever the wind takes us. That's how this all started, right?"

She nods, closing her eyes with a sigh when I press a gentle kiss to her cheek. "Yes," she finally replies, which could be a response to my question as well as to what I'm doing to her body.

Detouring over to her throat, I kiss her throbbing pulse as she tips her head backward. Unable to help myself, I slip my hand between her legs and begin massaging her sex. She's wearing thin yoga pants, so I can feel her wetness and heat.

What a smashing combination.

I increase the rhythm but pull back when she gets greedy and grinds down on my hand. "Jayden," she groans, frustrated, while I chuckle.

"What, dove?" I can't keep the smirk from my lips.

"Don't dove me. Oh, god." She whimpers when I bite her neck.

My cock is rock hard, but this isn't about me. It's about Carrie and evoking those breathy sighs over and over again. She spreads her legs and grips my wrist, demanding I stop fucking around, or maybe that's exactly what she wants.

She controls the speed, and I'm more than happy to be her puppeteer. With two fingers, I stroke along her entrance before coming back up and circling over her center. She moans and slumps forward, burying herself in the crook of my neck.

I continue my delicious torment, feeling her body tighten. I could do this all day, but the need to touch her in the flesh overthrows me, and I slip my hand into her pants. Bypassing her underwear, I go straight for the kill and curse when I feel her succulent heat.

"Bloody hell," I murmur when I insert two fingers into her.

She lets out a cry, riding my hand. "Stop talking. I'm going to come from your accent alone," she pants, driving her hips forward. "It drives me crazy."

"Oh, dove. Don't be saying things like that," I counter, ensuring I talk more often from now on.

The sounds coming from her are beyond sexy, and I plan on eliciting them from her any chance I get. I sink in deep, savoring the connection because this isn't just sex to me; it's so much more. It's always been so much more between us.

"I want you inside me," she breathlessly confesses, attempting to unbuckle my belt with frantic fingers.

But this is all for her. This beautiful woman who has set my world on fire.

Dancing from her grip, I sever our connection, only to drop to my knees while tugging down her pants. A whoosh of air leaves her, then that turns to a sated moan when I bury my head between her legs.

I want her all over me—always.

Peering up at her, I grin. "Later." Before the string of protests can leave her, I suckle at her aching clit. "Now it's time to learn our ABCs."

She half grunts in question, only for me to show her just what I mean.

With the tip of my tongue, I draw the letter A over her aching mound. "A," I smugly state while her body quivers beneath me. "B."

"Oh, my god…" she mewls, threading her fingers through my hair. "I can't—"

But I interrupt her. "What do you know…that's our next letter. C." Just in case she's forgotten what that letter looks like, I grip her upper thighs and arch upward, reminding her. "C is for cat."

"Christ…" she adds, groaning and writhing against my tongue.

"Good girl," I praise, rewarding her by sucking her… "Clit."

"Crap," she cries, thrashing against me. I honestly could do this all day.

"But the most important word of all," I say, sweeping her entrance in one long lick, "is Carrie's captivating cun…"

"Oh, my god!" she screams, riding my face. "I'm coming."

Chasing her release, she bucks against me while I eat her out with a ferocious appetite. "Another one of my favorite words," I grunt out between raspy breaths.

She whimpers, her orgasm guttural and raw. "Now…I know my…ABCs," she pants, collapsing in a messy, beautiful heap.

❤ ❤ ❤

"You do realize you're sunbaking in winter?"

Carrie's smile brings back the memory of her well-sated body lying beneath me earlier. "Yes, but we're on a beach in Morocco. Anything goes." As if on cue, she reaches behind her and unties the thin strap of her red bikini. She tears it from her body, leaving me to salivate in silence.

Her luscious breasts are sunny-side up and so is my dick. Dear god. I am insatiable when it comes to her. But I attempt to be a gentleman and continue working on my novel.

We left Paris this morning, and it appears the wind took us to Morocco. I have no idea when she has to return to the US, and I'm afraid to ask. I don't want this bubble to burst. Not yet anyway.

Reading over the chapter I just wrote, I can't help but think that I'm back. After six months of utter silence, I can't seem to stop the words from spilling out of me. I never thought I'd get back to this place, but it seems even better than before.

This inspiration has without a doubt been because of Carrie.

Gazing down at her, I wonder if there is such a thing as love at first sight. The notion every hopeless romantic wishes for. But it's almost a myth because, out of all the couples in the world, who can honestly say they've experienced this phenomenon?

Lust at first sight, sure, but love? That's a whole different ball game.

Which brings me to my next question.

What exactly do I feel for Carrie?

It's definitely past the point of merely liking her, but I bypassed that stop the moment we met. The thought of us going our separate ways when we get back home gives me heartburn. I rub over my chest, the burn rising.

"Are you okay?" Carrie asks, peering over the top of her Ray-Bans. "I told you not to eat all that spicy harissa sauce."

Playing it off, as I don't want to alert her to my love-sick thoughts, I grin. "I'm fine, Mom."

She opens her mouth playfully, which just evokes those sinfully delicious images all over again. However, when she rises and crawls onto my lap, straddling me, I decide to make a whole different set of memories.

"Mom? I'd be worried if you did the things we've done with your mom." To emphasize her point, she presses her breasts to my bare chest.

My dick instantly twitches, the gluttonous bastard. She smirks, thrilled she's able to get a rise out of me—literally. "How's the book coming along?"

"Great," I reply, clenching my jaw when she rubs her hand over my hard-on. On the flight over here, I told her about my meeting with Gerry and how I most likely will screw over her father. She played it off, but deep down, she has to feel like it's a betrayal.

We steered clear of the topic because Carrie now has the inside scoop on J.E. Sparrows doings. Although she supports me as Jayden, fucking over her father as J.E. may be an issue down the line. I hope not, but I suppose only time will tell.

"That's good to hear. How about you take a break?"

I'm pretty certain by break she means fucking my brains out, which sounds like a fabulous idea.

Just as I'm about to dip my fingers into her skimpy bikini bottoms, a camera flash sparks to my right. I turn to see what it was, which is a complete rookie move because standing before us is none other than the paparazzi.

Thankfully, it's only one chump with a camera, but that's one chump too many because he just snapped a picture of Carrie topless. "Motherfucker," I curse under my breath as Carrie yelps, wrapping an arm around her as she fishes for her top.

"Is this your new squeeze, J.E.?" he has the gall to ask, still snapping away. In the past, the paparazzi have never been an issue as Liz loved the attention, but now, these photos could ruin us both.

I'm pretty certain Axle has no idea his daughter is sleeping with the enemy. If these pictures see the light of day, Axle will disown her, especially after I dump his arse and sign with Gerry.

As she's frantically getting dressed, I lift her from my lap and settle her on the sand. She looks at me, working her bottom lip. She knows what this will do to both of us. But it'll be a cold day in hell before I allow this parasite to ruin our future before it even begins.

"Mate, give me your camera." I stand, brushing the sand from my legs casually.

In response, the arsehole takes another picture, no doubt capturing my tenting erection. This wanker is going down.

"This is going to go one of two ways," I state confidently. "You either give me your camera, or I take it from you. And trust me, option two will not end in your favor."

This guy barely looks out of diapers. This may be harsh, but it's an introduction to the real world. If you want to spy on people, then there will be consequences.

Now that he's got his happy snap, he seems to realize I have about sixty pounds on him and that I'm not messing around. "I can't. My boss will kill me. This is my first real scoop," he says with a quiver to his voice.

"Listen, kid, your boss is going to take credit for the photo and pay you a fraction of what he'll sell it for," I explain as I know how these scumbags work.

"That may be true, but I can't go back empty-handed. I'm already skating on thin ice. I'm trying to put myself through college," he says, talking a mile a minute when I'm totally unmoved by his sob story. "I'm an English Major."

That explains why he spotted me out of the crowd.

"Is that a Nikon?" Carrie asks, appearing beside me, thankfully dressed.

The kid looks at her, then down at his camera suspiciously. "Yeah. How did you know?"

Carrie reaches into her bag and produces her own camera.

The kid's eyes widen. "Wow, is that the latest Canon?"

Carrie nods, toying with the strap. "I'm in art school. It took me months to save up for it." Even though her family has millions, I have no doubt she's telling the truth. Carrie works for what she wants and doesn't sponge off her father.

"That photo you took…" she explains, frowning, "It'll destroy everything I've worked hard for. I know you don't understand why that is, but just trust me."

She's appealing to his humanity while I'm picturing all the ways I intend to break every bone in his body.

His gaze flounces back and forth between us, but he's not budging. "I'm really sorry, but if I don't have anything to show Yale…"

The moment he says that name, I gesture with my finger

that he's to stop talking. "Hold up. You work for Yale Kent?"

He nods quickly.

"Oh, mate, my condolences." Yale is a bottom feeder. I feel sorry for the kid.

Yale doesn't care whose life he ruins. He would sell out his own mom if it meant he could make a quick buck.

I'm suddenly struck with a brilliant idea. "How about you erase every photo you took of us, and I'll give you a real headline. One Yale will love."

There is no love lost between Yale and me, and quite frankly, I think he's the one who leaked the photos of my very naked ex-wife to the press. However, I doubt any skill was needed on his behalf as I'm certain Liz mailed him the pictures.

It was right after her boob job. She wanted the world to see what book number eight of mine bought her.

"I'm listening," he says, drawing the camera against his chest protectively.

Not seeing the point in dragging this out, I ask, "Is there a pharmacy close by? And a doctor who would prescribe me some…Viagra?"

Carrie bursts out laughing but quickly reins it back in when she sees I'm serious. "What do you need Viagra for?" she whispers from behind her hand, looking down at my crotch. "I know for a fact you don't need it."

I can beat on my chest like the barbarian I am later because right now, I have to sacrifice my self-pride to save the woman

I...like? Adore? *Love?* I scoff at the notion and focus on the task at hand.

The kid weighs up my question before a lopsided smirk replaces his frown. "Hypothetically speaking, if I said yes, I did, what exactly would you do?"

Without a stutter, I reply, "I would walk out of the pharmacy with the bottle of Viagra in hand as you snap all the shots you want of me reading over the label."

The kid's eyes widen while Carrie mutes her giggle behind her hand. "That won't exactly win you any favors with the ladies."

"There is only one lady I'm trying to impress," I state, peering over at Carrie, who blushes. "Besides, Yale will lap this up. Trust me. Anything to prove who has the biggest dick... even though there is no competition."

The kid ponders my offer, then nods. "Your funeral," he says, walking over and showing me the viewfinder. When I see he has the delete prompt all geared up, I nod. He deletes everything off the memory card and passes Carrie the camera so she can double check the evidence is gone.

Once she's checked it twice, she passes it back to him.

The way her lips are pulled in reveals she wishes there was another way. But I meant what I said. I couldn't care less what this does to my reputation. If anything, it might put this bad boy, manwhore image to bed once and for all. Nick is going to be pissed, but he'll see reason after I write him a bestseller.

"Shall we?" I say, interlacing my fingers through Carrie's. She squeezes my hand, expressing her gratitude.

The kid leads the way, and Carrie and I follow.

"This will completely ruin your cred on the street," she says, leaning into my side. God, she smells amazing.

"This will ensure incidents like the one on the plane and in the restaurant and wherever else will never happen again," I counter, shuddering at the thought.

Carrie's spine straightens as her grip on my hand tightens. "Maybe you could ask for double the dose." When I turn to look at her, unable to keep the smirk from my cheeks, she adds, "Just in case he can't get a good shot of what you're holding."

This is clearly an excuse because there is a little thing called a zoom button, but I nod. "Good idea."

She smiles, before reaching down and fondling me subtly. "I'll make it up to you." She accentuates her promise with a wink.

Shaming my manhood has never felt more victorious.

❤ ❤ ❤

The kid whose name turned out to be Terry left Morocco one happy camper. He got what I promised, and that was to announce to the world that J.E. Sparrow was a limp dick.

Who would have thought my lack of a hard-on would bring Carrie and I closer together?

The moment Terry left, she dragged me into an alleyway

and fucked my brains out—no Viagra needed. Once we were done sneaking around like love-sick teenagers, we decided to grab something to eat and then explore the beachfront markets.

As Carrie was trying on a dress she had spotted and loved, I waited for her by the jewelry case and happened to see something that instantly made me think of her. Without a second thought, I bought it and hid it in my back pocket.

We walked back to our hotel, Carrie unsuspecting of the gift I had buried in my pocket. When we got to our room, she said she was going to take a bath, which is where she's been for the past hour.

I've been focused on my book because with the crappy internet connection, I haven't been tempted to check the football scores. Even my email cutting in and out isn't a huge loss. Switching off from technology suddenly doesn't seem like such a bad thing.

I have everything I need—scotch, my laptop, and the woman who utterly spellbinds me.

I don't know the exact moment I passed the point of no return, but was there any other way? I don't remember feeling anything other than this longing for Carrie, and with each moment I spend with her, my feelings only seem to grow. Like today.

There was no questioning my decision because I would happily sacrifice my reputation to save hers.

I don't ever remember feeling that way. And it terrifies me.

"That felt amazing." Carrie emerges from the bathroom. Bundled up in an oversized bathrobe, she's drying her long hair.

I can't take my eyes off her. She looks positively delicious with rosy red cheeks and freshly painted pink toenails. I'm trying not to stare, but holy fuck is she a vision.

My cell chimes, interrupting my gawking. Peering at the illuminated screen, I see that it's Nick. I really should answer, but when Carrie places her foot on the edge of the bed and commences rubbing lotion on her legs, I do the complete opposite. I turn it off.

"You're not going to get it? It could be important," she says, oblivious to the effect she has over me.

Sitting up higher against the headboard, I watch mesmerized as she massages the white cream into her defined calf and over her knee. The split in her robe reveals the flesh of her inner left thigh. Her supple creamy flesh reminds me of the gift I bought her.

Reaching into the bedside dresser drawer, I retrieve the blue velvet pouch the shop assistant placed her gift into. Carrie pauses, eyeing the bag. "So I got you something…" Her surprise is clear, which suddenly makes me nervous. "If you hate it, that's totally okay. I just—"

"I won't hate it," she interrupts softly, capping the lotion. "Thank you so much."

I offer her the bag, not seeing the point in dragging this out.

She leans forward, stroking her fingers over mine as she

accepts. She unfastens the gold string and reaches into the small pouch. The moment the silver charm bracelet catches the light, a small gasp leaves her. She holds it up and examines the charms hanging off the thin chain.

She's silent, and I don't know if that's a good or a bad thing. If I were to give this twenty-dollar piece of jewelry to Liz, she would be silent too, but her silence would be due to disgust because the charms were silver and the stones were not real diamonds.

But this is Carrie, not Liz, and when she meets my eyes and smiles, I'm reminded that they are universes apart.

"Jayden, this is beautiful. I love it." She fingers over the dangling airplane charm. She goes on to examine the others—the Eiffel Tower, a camera, the letter C to match the one hanging from her neck, a bird to represent a dove, and a strawberry. She fingers the strawberry, a smirk tugging at her lips. "Why a strawberry? I understand the meaning of the others, but a strawberry?"

Unable to stop my grin, I place my laptop on the bed and rise. Walking toward her, I slowly lean down and inhale, sampling the length of her neck. An intake of breath escapes her. "Because you smell like strawberries and cream." And now is no exception.

"I do?" She gasps as I pull away.

"Yes, you do," I confirm, reaching for the bracelet. Opening the clasp, she turns her wrist over and offers it to me. Unable to help myself, I bend down and lay a gentle kiss over her racing pulse, before putting the bracelet on her.

Once it's fastened, I can't help but admire how good it looks. Rubbing my thumb over the crease in her wrist, I smile. "You can always add more. I just thought this was a good start."

My comment suddenly takes on an entirely different meaning.

She lifts those eyes, which slay me, and pins me to the spot I stand. I have no idea what she's thinking. "Thank you."

"I'm glad you like it."

But she shakes her head, chewing her lip. "Not just for the bracelet, but for everything. Since I've met you, my life has been…"

Her pause has me filling in the blanks. "Has been what?"

"Has been good. I can't remember the last time I've felt this happy." She quickly lowers her chin, appearing embarrassed for sharing too much.

But that won't do.

Placing my pointer finger under her chin, I coax her to look at me. She does. "Ditto. It doesn't make any sense, but I suppose no great love affair does."

She appears horrified and frowns. "Is that what this is? An affair? When we go back home, does this all end?" Her sadness crushes me.

It takes a moment for me to reply. "No, Carrie. Not for me it doesn't. I don't know what that means for us, but the most important thing is that I want there to be an us. And I hope you do too."

I wait for her response, watching as she carefully considers her words. I won't push her because I know this is a lot to digest, but I want her to know how I feel. This isn't just a holiday romance for me. It never was. This is real.

She toys with her bracelet, appearing deep in thought, and just when I'm about to change the subject because I don't want to pressure her, she catches me unaware and pushes me onto the bed. My arse hits the mattress, and I don't dare move a muscle.

My heart is in my throat as Carrie unhurriedly unfastens the sash around her waist and peels the robe from her body. It pools by her feet, leaving her completely bare. I need a minute.

Even though I have feasted on her flesh, seeing her naked is like witnessing a miracle. Her wet hair falls around her shoulders, drawing attention to the fullness of her perfect breasts. Her nipples instantly pebble, and I suppress my guttural moan.

Continuing my visual journey, I wet my lips when I remember licking a path down her toned stomach and over her ripe sex. Her honey was succulent and sweet, but there was a fire to her taste, one that collided with my smoldering need for her.

"Take off your shirt," she commands.

As I comply, I'm instantly hard, and the straining against the front of my jeans seems to please Carrie. She grins, and the sight is fucking devious.

"Touch yourself."

I wasn't expecting that, but I'll play along. "You want me to show you how hot I am for you, dove?"

She nods coyly.

Seeing no point in delaying what we both want, I unfasten my button and reach into my jeans. Gripping my shaft, I never break eye contact as I begin to stroke myself. It feels great, but it's not my hands I want.

Carrie watches me closely, her cheeks blistering as she rubs her thighs together.

"Don't be shy. I know what that pussy feels like. Don't deny yourself." My permission sparks a deviant to emerge because she does as I say and begins to stroke herself.

The image is almost too much.

When she slips a finger into her heat, a breathy moan escapes her.

"Feel good?" I ask, pumping my cock.

"Yes." She gasps, opening her legs wider to gain deeper access. "How about y-you?"

"Yes, but I would much prefer your hands. Or better yet, my hands in you."

She groans, tossing her head back.

Her fingers work fervently, and the sight of watching her get herself off is so fucking depraved, I almost come at the image. But when she suddenly stops, I rein it in because I know she has only just begun.

With her pussy glistening, she saunters over, her sweetness lingering in the air. I attempt to draw her toward me so I can slam her onto my face, but she stops me. She slowly drops to her knees and draws my jeans down my legs.

I'm still jerking myself off, and when she sees me in the flesh, the tip of her tongue skims along her bottom lip. She places her hand over mine, watching closely as my strokes increase and the drop of pre-cum catches the light.

She instantly leans forward and catches it with her tongue.

My hips jerk off the bed and a grunt catches in the back on my throat. "Dove?" I question in a strained voice; this is her show, and I have no idea what comes next.

But apparently no words are needed because in this case, actions speak a lot louder than words. She sweeps her hair over her shoulder before bending down and sucking the tip of my cock.

Sweet baby Jesus.

I stop jerking myself off as the sight of her lips wrapped around me is just too good to miss. Brushing her hair aside, I watch as she slides down my length. When she gets a quarter of the way down, I remove my hand, but she quickly retracts and breathes steadily through her nose.

I don't dare move a muscle as she becomes accustomed to my size and goes back for round two. She licks and sucks, and my fuck, I don't remember a blowjob ever feeling this good. She splays both hands against my upper thighs as she bobs up and down between my legs.

Each time, she gets deeper, her rhythm quicker, and before long, I am fisting the blankets while she moans around my cock. When she reaches between her legs and begins a hypnotic dance, I grunt, thrusting my hips upward and hitting the back of her throat.

"Oh, fuck, sorry," I pant, attempting to withdraw myself as she gags, but she surprises me when she holds on tight and doesn't let me go.

Her touch is almost punishing, and it's exactly what I need. She suckles me deeply, using her tongue to circle my tip before licking all the way down my shaft. As her actions turn wild and desperate, so do her fingers as she sinks them deep into her heat.

The vibrations of her moans pulsate all the way up my cock, and it takes all my willpower not to explode. Her breasts sway between us, and if there was ever a more erotic sight, then I don't know what it is.

"Carrie," I growl, gently stroking her hair to coax her to let me go before I make a mess. "Dove…when I come, it's going to be inside that hot little body of yours."

She moans, her fingers working a mile a minute, and holy shit, I could just come from watching her get herself off. She's pumping two fingers inside her but finally comes up for air when I run my thumb along her wet bottom lip.

I don't give her time to catch her breath, however, because I reach into the bedside dresser and hunt for protection. Once I'm suited up, I lift her, and in one fluid movement, she sinks onto my length. We both moan at the connection.

We take a moment to savor the union because being face to face this way warms my heart. She loops her hands behind my nape and begins to rock slowly. I circle my hands around her waist, allowing her full rein as she arches backward, controlling the speed and depth of her movements.

We never break eye contact, and there is something profound to her touch. She bends and kisses me, whimpering when our tongues duel sluggishly. Being inside her this way is unlike anything else, and when she increases the tempo, bouncing on my lap and lowering her inhibitions, I know that I am falling in love with Carrie Bell.

Never have I felt this alive.

Her body quivers, hinting she's close, so I tighten my grip around her waist and rock her against me. Each stroke hits her ripe center, and it's not long before she's bucking wildly.

When she arches backward, I circle her pink nipple with my tongue. "Oh, god," she whimpers, slamming onto my dick over and over. "I want—"

"What do you want, dove?" I ask, sinking so deeply into her, I don't know where she begins and I end.

"I want there to be an..." she cries, bowing back as I reach down and rub over her clit. "An us too," she finally declares before coming with a guttural groan.

Her hot, sticky flesh sends me into overdrive, and with the smell of her sweet arousal on the air, I pump once, twice, and am fucking done. I come with a roar, squeezing her so tight, I'm afraid I've milked her dry.

She collapses in my arms, breathless and completely spent because what just happened wasn't just sex, it was a game changer.

Now that we're on the same page, the question is, what happens next?

This is the end…my only friend, the end (noun)

15 Fifteen

Three Days Later

As I peer out the airplane window, I can't help but compare my arrival to my departure. I left Seattle a shadow of the man I once was, but I return the man I remember myself to be.

Yes, what Liz did was unforgiveable, but in a way, if it wasn't for her indiscretion, I'd never have met Carrie. I intrinsically slip my hand around hers, marveling at how two weeks can change your life forever.

Over the past three days, we talked, we laughed, and we made love. It was incredible. Due to the shitty reception, I switched off from the real world—literally. My phone has been off, as has my Wi-Fi on my laptop.

But truth be told, I haven't wanted to join the real world because my reality was so much better than anything outside the bubble Carrie and I lived in.

My novel is almost complete. I can't remember ever feeling more excited over a manuscript. So, although Morocco was our own private oasis, coming home feels good because I have so much positivity to come home to and that hasn't happened in a very long time.

Carrie has made a few calls and will stay with a friend until she figures out her living arrangements. I offered her my home, seeing as there is more than enough room, but with our "relationship" being so new, she decided it was best if she stayed somewhere else.

That doesn't mean she can't stay over. And I plan on her staying over more nights than she is away.

Peering over at her, I can't suppress the swell of emotions I feel for her. She has been my sustenance and nurtured my soul.

She looks up from her photography magazine, sensing my thoughts. As usual, when we lock eyes, I'm hit with the inspiration bat, and words come pouring out of me. She really did quench my thirst in every possible way that there is.

When the captain announces our descent, I stow my laptop, looking forward to calling Nick and discussing my book. He's going to be pissed I've been MIA, but what could've possibly happened in three days that can't wait?

Carrie sighs, lost in thought. "Everything okay?" I ask, rubbing my thumb over her bracelet she hasn't taken off since I put it on.

"Yes, but I think I'm going to miss you."

I can't help but laugh. "You think?"

An adorable smirk tugs at her lips. "I will," she amends. "Maybe we can have a sleepover?"

"Of course. Although, I don't think much sleeping will take place." I bury my nose into the curve of her neck, unbelieving her smell has the ability to leave me hard.

"Surely, not again? After this morning?" She's referring to when I ate her out for an hour before ensuring every surface of our hotel room was christened.

I shrug while she bursts into laughter. But it seems strained.

Once the plane lands, everyone is in a hurry to disembark, but Carrie and I seem to want to prolong our goodbye for as long as we can. I can't shake the feeling that now that we're back, Carrie wants to tell me something. All along, I knew she was guarding a secret, and it seems Seattle has brought that to the surface.

When we can no longer avoid the inevitable, we exit hand in hand.

An awkwardness swarms around us because no one likes goodbyes, especially when our hello was so memorable. Deciding to distract myself, I reach into my back pocket and turn on my phone. The moment it powers up, it beeps continuously, which is no surprise.

"Someone is a popular boy," Carrie comments, peering over at the illuminated screen.

When it finally stops chiming, I see that I have sixty-eight voice messages and one hundred and seventeen text messages. All are from Nick.

"I hope everything is okay."

"Yes, it's just Nick being a drama queen," I reply, scrolling through the texts quickly. They are all of the same nature—name-calling and him demanding I call him. But it can wait.

Carrie's friend lives about an hour from me in the opposite direction. We step outside and wait in the taxi line in silence. It's evident neither of us wants to part ways, but for life to go on together, we have to live it apart.

A driver gestures that the next cab is ours. I drag her suitcase toward the idling taxi and place it into the trunk.

"So…I'll call you when I get to my friend's?" she asks, struggling to figure out the right protocol when it comes to a new romance.

But there are no rules when it comes to Carrie and me. That's been evident from the first moment we met.

Threading my fingers through her belt loops, I draw her toward me until we're only inches apart. "You can call me the moment you get in the cab," I correct, and she smiles.

The impatient cabbie slams the trunk shut, hinting we're to wrap this up.

"Okay."

She chews the corner of her mouth, which drives me wild. She is wrestling with what to do, but there is only one thing we can do. And that's for me to devour her whole.

We kiss unapologetically as she stands on her tippy toes to keep up with my fierce demands. I fist her hair, humming into her mouth as she melts against me. My senses sing in delight; she is a delicacy on my palate, and I will never tire of her taste.

But when the driver honks twice, this sample will have to do for now.

"I'll talk to you soon." I brush the hair from her face, running my thumb over the apple of her cheek. She leans into my touch with a sigh, but something is stirring in her eyes.

"Before I go, I need to tell you something…" She gulps, and my heart rate picks up speed.

"What? You can tell me anything," I assure her, but she doesn't seem so sure.

This is hardly the place for confessions, so instead, I soothe the furrow lines between her brows. "Tell me tomorrow."

She chews her lip, lowering her eyes. She's harbouring a secret and coming back here has clearly opened old wounds. But whatever she has to tell me won't diminish my feelings for her.

Neither of us wants to make the first move, but knowing I'll see her soon and preferably in my bed has me kissing her forehead and saying goodbye.

I watch as she gets into the cab, taking a small piece of my heart with her.

Only when the taillights are no longer visible do I turn

and join the back of the line. I figure it's the least I can do for holding it up.

My cell chimes, reminding me of the endless voice messages I have to listen to. Unable to avoid Nick any longer, I answer on the third ring.

"Hello, mate…how—" But he doesn't let me finish.

"Where the fuck have you been?" His serious tone is so not like Nick.

"I was in Morocco. With Carrie. I had shitty reception and my Wi-Fi—"

He's not interested in excuses. "Get your ass over to my office ASAP. We need to talk."

I'm waiting for a wisecrack, but I get nothing. This can't be good. "Okay. I'll be there in twenty."

♥ ♥ ♥

Fifteen minutes later, I'm exiting the elevator and making my way to Nick's office. His secretary, Denise, peers up from her computer when I walk through the door. "He's expecting you." She gestures for me to enter, but from the look on her face, it's apparent she wants to be nowhere near me when that happens.

What the hell is going on?

Not bothering to knock, I push open the door. Nick is sitting behind his desk on the phone, but when he sees me, he quickly hangs up on whoever he was speaking to. Standing, he runs a hand through his uncharacteristically messy hair. "You need to sit down, man."

"I'd rather stand," I counter, crossing my arms. Whatever he has to say, he needs to do so now.

Sighing, he steeples his fingers over his mouth as if wrestling with the best way to tell me his news. "Dude, there is no easy way to say this, so I'm just going to come out and say it."

"Okay," I reply, drawing out the O. He's clearly lost his mind.

Rounding his desk, he stands in front of me, before finally perching on the edge. "Liz is blackmailing you."

It takes me a moment to process what he just said because it's simply ridiculous. *"Excuse me?"* I can't keep the humor, or maybe it's surprise from my voice. But when Nick doesn't blink, I know this is serious.

"She visited you in Paris, right?"

"I wouldn't say visited. More like gate crashed," I correct, shuddering.

"Well, whatever the technicalities, she knows about the deal with Gerry."

"What?" If it wasn't for my immaculate hearing, I'd swear I misheard him, but his demeanor of us being royally fucked confirms this clusterfuck as being real.

"Gerry's wife…she and Liz play badminton together. They also happen to be in the same social circle, you moron. She didn't look familiar?" Retracing my steps, I think back to the night I saw Gerry and his wife.

My stomach drops.

"Fuck me," I moan because I remember thinking at the time she did look familiar. I just couldn't place where I'd seen her. Now I know.

"That's not the worst of it. She told Liz that Gerry was in Paris talking to us about the deal."

And that explains how she knew where I was. But so what. "Who cares if she knows? It'll be public knowledge soon enough." But when Nick reaches for the bottle of whiskey from his desk, I add, "Right?"

He unscrews the lid and takes a long sip. "Actually, no. This is where the blackmail part comes in."

I pinch the bridge of my nose.

"You didn't happen to tell Liz that you've suffered writer's block, did you?"

"Of course, I…oh, bugger," I curse, remembering that, in fact, I did.

"Jayden, why?" Nick asks, shaking his head as I slump into the leather chair.

Not only did you shit on everything we had, but you also took away my will to write. Those were the words that signed my death warrant.

"So she knows I couldn't write, big deal. How's that enough to blackmail me with?"

"She is threatening to tell Gerry, and well, that's not what any publisher wants to hear. Especially someone pushing the boundaries as it is."

"We can tell Gerry the truth. I can show him the manuscript. It's almost done," I reason, but Nick's grim reaction alerts me to how naïve that suggestion is.

"It won't make a difference. You know how these publishers are. If she tells him this, and if his wife backs the soulless she-devil, he will pull the offer. Especially since you were all *read the manuscript, mate*," Nick says, mimicking a poor sounding me.

"So let him pull it then. If he doesn't have faith in me, then I don't want to work with him," I stubbornly argue, but Nick frowns. There's a catch. There's always a fucking catch.

"She's threatening…Carrie."

I take a moment to compose myself before I rip the arms off this chair. "How?" It's all I manage to say, but it's enough.

"She knows Carrie is Axle's daughter. She is threatening to tell Axle about Gerry opening his own publishing house, and that he's trying to poach you, and that well"—he rubs the back of his neck — "that Carrie knew this entire time and didn't tell him. She is going to implicate Carrie, and I'm sure Axle won't be too happy to know his daughter helped ruin him."

That conniving so and so…I'm going to kill her.

No matter what Carrie says, this will ruin her relationship with her family. Axle will see this as the ultimate betrayal and cut Carrie from his life. This is a fucking mess.

"So worst-case scenario is Gerry will pull the offer, and Axle will drop you like a hot potato and tarnish your name. You'll be without a publisher, and I'm sure the literary world will think you're a literary limp dick. You'll be ruined," Nick concludes, clearly not in the mood to sugar-coat anything.

Placing my head in my hands, I take a minute to digest this because it's a lot to process. I should have known she wouldn't leave without a fight. There is only one way to fix this. I'll be damned if she drags Carrie into this, and I plan on doing anything it takes to save her from the evil clutches of Elizabeth Sparrow.

Standing, I steal the bottle of whiskey from Nick and gulp down the amber goodness. "I'll take care of it," I announce, handing him back the empty bottle.

"How?"

"Don't worry about it."

"Jayden..." But I wave him off.

"This is my mess. I'll fix it."

"How?"

"The only way I can. Giving her what she wants."

Nick tsks me, shaking his head. But it's too late. "And what's that?" He humors me in case there is another solution. There isn't.

"Me," I state, realizing this is the beginning of the end. But if it's a fight she wants...it's a fight she'll get.

♥ ♥ ♥

Coming back here to a place I once called my home brings to light just how much I've changed. The three-story mansion was once my sanctuary, but now, the superficial monstrosity is an eyesore.

Parking my car across Liz's manicured gardens, I don't bother closing the door as I make my way toward the front door. I bang on it, then press the bell and allow it to ring in one long-drawn-out shrill.

"Excuse—" However, when Liz yanks open the door, ready to give whoever is disturbing the peace an earful and instead sees me, her mouth gapes open. "Jayden?"

"Hello, darling wife," I sarcastically quip, my finger still pressed to the doorbell.

Her shock is apparent, but she quickly composes herself. "Please, come in." She steps from the doorway, granting me permission to enter.

Only when I tap out AC/DC's "Highway to Hell" on the bell do I come in.

She clears her throat, clearly concerned for my well-being, but there is a lot more crazy where that came from. "Can I get you a drink? I have your favorite scotch."

"Sure, why the hell not."

She nods, pleased with herself, but her happiness will soon turn to shite. That's the plan anyway.

She leads the way to the kitchen, looking over her shoulder to ensure I follow. I do.

Her heels click along the polished tile, highlighting the differences between her and Carrie. But I quickly push her from my mind because if I'm going to do this, I can't allow her to distract me.

The house is exactly how I left it, and when we step into the kitchen, my gaze instantly drifts to the hot tub. I thought I'd feel something when I saw it for the first time—I don't. Liz reaches into the cupboard and retrieves a crystal goblet and the bottle of whiskey.

I take a seat at the breakfast counter, ensuring to scrape the chair across Liz's precious flooring she has Juanita scrub daily. When she passes me the glass, I reach across for the bottle instead. "Jayden? Is everything all right? You're acting strange."

Unscrewing the lid, I throw back the whiskey, wiping my mouth with the back of my hand. "Strange?" I purse my lips, cocking my head in mock confusion. "Really? I think I'm acting perfectly fine for someone being blackmailed."

She tugs at her pearls. "Blackmail is such an ugly word."

"Try being on the receiving end of it," I refute, leaning back in my chair and placing my boot on the counter. She wants me? Well, she can have me because this is the man I will be if she forces my hand.

My insolence pisses her off, but she doesn't let it get under her collar. "I only came to Paris to give us another chance. But then you had to flaunt your little whore. What other choice did I have?"

Counting to five, I calm the fuck down before I ruin my plan. "You could leave me alone. That's a choice you've had these past six months. But instead, you insist on punishing me. This is a new low, Elizabeth, even for you."

This is Plan A. I hope I don't need to resort to Plan B.

But trying to appeal to her compassion is a dead-end. She has none. "I want things to go back to the way they were."

A laugh erupts from me, but it's not a pleasant sound. "I'm not sure if you remember, but things were fucking horrible. You were screwing anything that moved, and I was too blind to see you for the adulterous slag that you are."

"How dare you. What has gotten into you?"

"The better question here is who *haven't* I gotten into?" She pales while I sip my drink victoriously.

"This isn't you. The Jayden I knew wouldn't be dressed like a homeless person, speaking such vile things."

"This is the new Jayden, poppet. Get used to it because that's what you want, isn't it? You'll keep quiet if I come back home." There is no point in dragging this out. I came here for answers.

Her long blonde hair is twisted into a high chignon, and her once delicate features now look pointy and harsh. I suddenly miss the smell of strawberries and cream.

"Yes, you have my word. I don't want to do this, but you'll see it's for the best."

I've heard enough. "Fine. But if you break your promise, I swear to god, I will find every man you fucked and tell their wives their BFF screwed their husbands on our ten-thousand-dollar Persian rug. We clear?"

She gulps as my threat isn't empty. Neither is the fact my promise holds merit. God knows how many of her pretentious friend's husbands she blew.

"We're clear," she states, reaching behind her back, and the unmistakable sound of a zipper being lowered fills the air. "Now, fuck me." Her black dress pools at her feet, revealing a lacy underwear set with garter belts.

Once upon a time, I would be salivating at the sight, but now, I can't help but wonder who the hell wears something like this around their home. She unfastens her hair, shaking it out like a primed lioness.

But it'll be a cold day in hell before I ever touch her again. Looks like I'll have to resort to Plan B.

"Sorry, wifey, but I can't. I'm having issues downstairs." Just in case she's lost in translation, I point at my groin.

She gasps, horrified. "That's impossible."

Although I'm flattered, I shrug offhandedly. "It's very possible. Check out Yale's website."

There is no further direction needed as she dives for her cell off the counter while I casually sip my whiskey.

I went into this with no real definite plan other than saving Carrie. I intend on telling her everything, but not before I gauge Liz's motives. She said she wants me back, but I know Liz. If I don't put up a fight, she will eventually figure out she's being played. This will buy me some time to devise a plan that saves both Carrie and me.

I need to be where I can watch Liz, and what better place than her abode.

When her horror-struck eyes flick up and meet mine, I smirk. It appears she's stumbled across the photos Yale posted of me emerging from the pharmacy with two bottles of Viagra in hand as I read over the label. Who knew my supposed impotence would save my manhood.

"Oopsie. I have whiskey dick, after all." To accentuate my point, I drink the remaining liquor and slam the bottle onto the counter.

It's a challenge to her. One she accepts.

Sauntering toward me, I try not to laugh at her attempt to seduce me. She runs her fingernail down my shirt, toying with the button on my jeans. When she gets to my junk, I resist the urge to jump up off the chair as though it's on fire.

"That's just because you've forgotten the touch of a real woman. Here, let me remind you." Before I have a chance to back the fuck off, she thrusts her hand between my legs and begins massaging my dick.

My skin crawls and bile rises, but I push it down. This is what she wants. She wants to be in control. If she thinks she is, she thinks she's winning, and Carrie is safe for now. My cock goes into hiding as it has no interest in coming out to play.

After a few minutes of her rummaging around, she gives up. She purses her pink pumped lips, which look like flailing hot dog buns. “This isn’t part of the deal, Jayden. For things to go back to the way they were, we have to act like a normal married couple.”

When she attempts to manhandle me once again, I latch onto her wrist, stopping her. My aggression turns her on, and she gasps. Slowly coming down from my perch, I stand, towering over her as I pin her with a glare. “There is nothing normal about this, Elizabeth.” Her name has never sounded so dirty. “Maybe for us to go back to the way things were”— I begin to stalk her as she steps backward, her arse hitting the counter, trapping her —“you should watch me fuck somebody else. An eye for eye and then maybe, maybe, we can think about going back to what we had.”

Her chest rises and falls. It sickens me that this is turning her on.

“Now if you’ll excuse me, I’m going to sleep.” I don’t wait for her to reply and leave the kitchen, needing to put as much space between us as possible.

There is no way I’m sleeping in her bedroom, so I take the guest bedroom down the hallway. For good measure, I lock the door. Needing to take a literal breather, I inhale, filling my lungs with air that isn’t tainted by Liz.

What the fuck am I doing? I’m in way over my head, but I’ll figure something out. I have to.

My cell vibrates in my back pocket. If this is Liz paging me, I’ll throw the infernal thing out the window. However, the caller is my savior. "Dove," I say, watching my volume as I push off the door. I don't want prying ears to hear.

"Hey. Where are you? Why are you whispering?" Just the sound of her voice confirms what I'm doing is right.

There is no way I'm going to keep this from her, but I decide not to tell her everything until I've figured out a solid game plan. "Can you talk?" I ask, sitting at the foot of the bed.

"Yes," she replies, her suspicion shining. "But let me tell you something first. I've wanted to tell you this since we met. I—"

But whatever she has to say can never compare to the bombshell I'm about to drop. Exhaling, I can't believe this is my life when I reveal in a rushed breath, "Liz is blackmailing me." If I didn't say it now, I was afraid I'd chicken out.

"*What?*" she says after a short pause.

"I know how clichéd this sounds, but it's the truth." I'm about to pull the phone from my ear to see if she's still on the line.

"How?"

"She knows about Gerry and his deal. She also knows I haven't been able to write…until I met you. She's threatening to tell Gerry. If she does, he'll no doubt run. He won't take the risk."

"What does she want?" she asks in vain.

"What do you think?" I give her the time she needs to process this because I know it sounds like an episode of *Days of our Lives*, but god help me, it's not.

"You're not going to give her what she wants, are you?" she questions, horrified.

"Of course not!" I declare, leaping from the bed, needing to move before I hurl. "But dove, she knows you're Axle's daughter. She's not just threatening me…she's threatening you too. She is out for blood and apparently just mine won't do. She said she will tell Axle you knew about the deal. I'm sorry. This is all my fault." I run my fingers through my hair, exhaling in frustration.

I'm expecting anger, maybe even for her to hang up on me, but what she does next just cements how incredible this woman truly is. "So we tell my dad then. Get to him first." But we both know it's not that easy.

"He won't be so understanding. We both know this. He will make sure I don't work in this town again. And god knows what he'll do to you. He'll disown you and probably make your life hell."

"I couldn't care less about me."

"Well, I do," I argue.

It's no surprise when she asks, "So your career is more important than me? Than us?" I can hear the hurt in her tone.

"No, I just need to figure this out."

"How?"

"I need to prove myself," I reply, the wheels in my head turning.

"And how do you intend to do that?"

"By writing a kick-arse book." A light bulb flickers. I need

Liz to believe that my writer's block is back and worse than ever before. This will buy me time to blindside her when I give Gerry my motherfucking masterpiece.

"Well, you're already there."

I pace the room as a plan begins to flourish. "You're right. I just need to finish it." What I say next, winds us both. "Give me some time?"

"Time? Time for what?"

She has every right to be suspicious, but she is a distraction, and I need my head clear, especially where Elizabeth is involved. "Just trust me." I know it's asking a lot, but this will ensure she's not dragged into Liz's twisted plans.

"I don't like this."

"Well, I don't like ruining your relationship with your family because of me. I'll fix this. I promise."

She sighs, clearly not happy with my plan. "Can I come see you?"

My heart aches. "I'd love that, but I need to focus on finishing this book now more than ever."

I feel like a bastard for lying to her, but what she doesn't know won't hurt her, which is exactly the reason I don't tell her where I am. I won't make this an issue. I will deal with it, and it'll be over before we both know it.

"Okay, you're right." She doesn't sound happy about it, but she knows I'm right. "Be careful. I have a bad feeling about this."

An ominous premonition maybe?

Her fear springs me into protection mode. “Don’t. Liz is harmless.” For the most part. “Let her think she has leverage. It’ll buy us some time.”

“I miss you.” She’s finally surrendered but at what price.

“I miss you, too. Now, sorry, I cut you off. What did you want to tell me?”

Silence.

“It’s fine,” she finally says. “It can wait.”

“Okay. I’ll talk to you soon.” I wish she was here, but I hang up, afraid Liz has her ear pressed to the door.

For this to work, I can’t flaunt Carrie in her face. That’s how arrogant she is. She believes I’ll just forget about Carrie now that I’m “back.” She clearly thinks the magical potion to saving our marriage is blackmail.

Sighing, I kick off my shoes and fall face first into the mattress. Welcome to my hell.

16
Sixteen

I wish I woke oblivious to where I was, but sadly, no such luck. I'm still in hell.

Reaching for my cell, I see that I mercifully passed out last night, and it's now just after six a.m. Thinking back to my conversation with Carrie, it's obvious what I have to do. I have to finish my book and show Gerry that my drought is over, proving Liz wrong.

In regards to Axle, I can only hope once I deliver the manuscript to Gerry, Liz's plan will fizzle, and she will go away. Besides, Axle is going to be so pissed at me, he won't want to talk to anyone associated with me. Liz won't even see the inside of the foyer before security throws her arse out.

All in all—everything is riding on me finishing this book.

It's a weak plan, but it's a plan nonetheless.

Rising, I quickly shower and change into the only clean pair of clothes I have left. Sadly, it looks like I will be forced to stay here and make sure Liz believes this bullshit charade of hers has actually worked.

I am about fifteen thousand words short of finishing my novel. At the longest, I'll be here for three days. Those three days will amount to ten thousand, but I have to do it for the greater good. Carrie can't know I'm here because I know what she'll do—she'll tell Axle the truth. She won't care what that means for her, but I refuse to cause her harm. Lying to her is the lesser of the two evils, and besides, it's only for a couple of days.

With a new mindset to start the day early and write at least five thousand words, I decide to do a load of washing, seeing as I'll be staying. There is no way Liz is up at this time, which has me venturing out of my room, intent on doing what I have to before she stirs.

Walking the hallway brings back memories—some good, some bad. No matter that Liz has tainted these walls with her infidelity, there are still some memorable moments I'll never forget. Like sitting in my office, completing a manuscript I'd worked on for nine long months. I don't remember ever feeling more victorious than I did that night.

Or the time Nick threw up all over Liz's hideous abstract art piece that looked like an elephant taking a shite after one too many shots of tequila.

Good times.

Speaking of Nick, I decide to send him an email, informing him of my plans. If he has a better idea, I'm all ears, but for now, this will have to do.

The laundry is equipped with high-tech apparatuses, but I doubt Liz would even know how to turn on the washing machine. Dumping my clothes into the drum, I pour in the detergent and set it to a quick cycle.

As it's doing its thing, I send Nick an email.

Gone into the lion's den. I have a plan. Stall Gerry. Give me three days.

Not exactly informative, but he'll get the gist.

As I close my email, I can't help myself as my finger hovers over my photos app. The need to see Carrie is overwhelming, and for the next few days, this is all I'll have—stolen moments. Opening the folder, the first photo I see is a candid shot I took of Carrie in bed.

I stroke my finger over her face, tracing her lips which are parted mid laugh. She's wearing my Manchester United T-shirt, which is about five sizes too big, but it looks perfect on her nonetheless. Our time together has been nothing short of epic, even the times when I wanted to throttle her.

Her free-spirited nature breathed new life into me, and before we met, I didn't realize how stagnant my life had become. What I feel for her, is it something like love? This insta-love stuff only happens in my novels, not in real life. But could I be the person to test that theory?

I wonder what she wanted to tell me last night. Nothing she could say would change my feelings for her. Nothing.

Groaning, I run a hand through my damp hair because it's not even been a day and I'm already having Carrie withdrawals.

"Good morning."

There is certainly nothing good about it now.

"You're up early. Did someone die?" I ask, not bothering to look up from my phone. I do close my photos, however, as I don't want Liz seeing me fawn over her archnemesis.

"Very funny," she replies. Who said I was joking? "Juanita could do your laundry. She'll be here soon."

"It's okay. I'm quite capable of doing my own laundry. I have fended for myself these past six months, you know." Casually making eye contact, I try not to gag when I see her in some netted white nightie that makes her look like a Christmas ham.

"Fair enough." She takes the jab as I knew she would. For this to be believable, I have to behave like a scorned husband. And eventually, she'll believe with enough begging and parading around in dental floss that I'll forgive her and all will go back to normal.

To any sane person, this is absurd. But that's how self-absorbed Liz is. She can't believe I would want anyone but her. She does think she's perfect, after all. She all but threw that in my face when she blamed me for her infidelities.

The thought has me wanting to flee from this horror house, but I man the fuck up and remember why I'm here.

"I wanted to invite a few of our friends over. Tell them the good news."

This woman really has some balls.

That sounds beyond torturous, but I know this isn't up for negotiation. "Fine. I'll be writing for most of the day, so you can organize it all."

Her smile almost looks genuine, but I know she's only happy she can show me off like a prized pig and wear some overpriced ensemble. "Great." She claps her hands together. "There is so much to do. I better get ready."

"Great," I repeat, thankful she'll be busy for most of the day and leave me the hell alone.

"Coming back here will have those creative juices flowing again in no time. I just know it. Gerry will be most happy to hear your newest bestseller will be in his hands soon enough." And there she is, the evil slag I married.

"So you're on Gerry's side? What about Axle?" I ask, crossing my arms.

"Faye told me how much money Gerry is offering you. There is no way Axle would match that, and besides, Axle is the past, isn't he?" She pointedly looks at me.

This isn't a trick question as there is only one answer. By the past she means Carrie and I suppose Daisy as well. As long as I'm her prized pig *and* cash cow, she won't resort to blackmailing me and ruining my life.

She is certain that with Carrie out of my life, she has

leverage because I all but told her Carrie was the reason behind my sudden flood of words. But now that she's gone, Liz believes the mental drought will return.

Good. This is exactly what I need her to believe. My plan is working. I just need to survive three days and then all of this will be over.

However, when she saunters over with a glimmer in her eye, those three days suddenly feel like a lifetime. She runs the back of her finger along my jaw. "I like this scruff. It's so sexy."

I refrain from recoiling. *Think of the greater good*, I chant over and over. But when she edges forward, intent on kissing me, I can only think of getting the hell out of here. When she's a hairsbreadth away, I blurt out, "I haven't brushed my teeth."

She stops mid assault, curling her lip in mild disgust. Lucky for me, this is one of Liz's many pet peeves. She thankfully retreats, and I breathe a sigh of relief.

"Make sure you brush them tonight then." She winks, before wiggling her arse as she exits the room. Once she's gone, I unclench my fists, my heart rate returning to a semi normal pace.

I may have dodged a bullet, but I know it's only a matter of time. Three days have suddenly never looked so long.

❤ ❤ ❤

I've been locked in my room all day, writing like a madman. Thankfully, Liz has been too busy planning god knows what to check in on me.

I've sent Carrie a few text messages, but I haven't disclosed where I am. Her sad face and broken heart emoticons nearly killed me, but I kept reminding myself I'm doing this for the greater good. She was insistent she would tell Axle about our predicament, but I made her promise not to.

This is under control. As long as I can dodge Liz's advances and finish this damn book, all will go back to normal by next week. That's the only thing motivating me as I peer at my reflection in the mirror and knot my tie.

I've decided to wear my ripped jeans as I know it'll piss Liz off. I have on a white shirt, so I'm not completely wayward, but the fact I'm not dressed in my Sunday best is sure to irritate the hell out of her. Running my fingers through my hair, I splash on some cologne and prepare myself for whatever Liz throws my way.

I have no idea who she plans to invite, but I can only hope it isn't Roger and his wench of a wife, Demi. Demi is everything you'd imagine a walking, talking Barbie doll would look like. Roger is an okay dude, but he isn't someone I have much in common with. That could be because he thinks what I do is a "woman's job," and the fact he's about fifty years his wife's senior.

Unable to put this off any longer, I lock my laptop in my suitcase because I don't trust Liz. As far as she knows, I'm months away from finishing my book. Gerry has three chapters, and that's all I'm certain she thinks I've done.

The moment I close the door and hear Demi's unmissable hyena cackle sound from downstairs, I groan. Fucking great.

Trudging down the stairs, I almost trip down the last two steps when I see that the foyer has been transformed into some sideshow circus. She said a few friends, not her whole address book. This is a disaster.

My palms begin to sweat as I wonder if she'd be that diabolical and invite Gerry. They haven't attended many of our functions in the past, which is why I didn't recognize them, but I wouldn't put it past Liz to do some fucked-up shite like this.

When I pass a server, I snare two glasses of champagne off his silver tray. When he attempts to leave, I stop him with one hand as I throw back a glass, then the other. I then steal the tray, and in return, I give him the two empty glasses.

As I carry my tray of bubbly, I look around Liz's home and wonder if it's always looked this shallow. These people dressed in furs and expensive designer brands look like complete wankers. I can't believe I ever associated with them by choice.

My gaze drifts across the room and lands on Liz. She's hard to miss, seeing as she looks like she's clubbed a baby seal to death and worn its skin as her outfit. I'm sure she thinks she looks stunning. To me, she looks like vacuum-packed salami.

Dear god, give me strength.

When she sees me, she stops talking to Lionel, a guy I once believed to be my friend, but now, I'm suspicious of everyone. Just how many men in the room know Elizabeth a little too well? Awful thoughts to have, but Liz was the one to put such notions in my head.

"There he is," she gushes, rushing toward me like we're a long-lost couple in a Danielle Steele novel. She hugs me while I stand limp with the tray of drinks still in my hand.

When she finally unwraps her tentacles from me, her attention flutters to my jeans. Her horror shouldn't please me so, but it does. But it appears nothing will ruin Liz's perfect evening. "I will make sure Juanita does all your washing tomorrow." Of course, that's what she'd assume. I opted for this look because everything else was dirty.

I make a mental note to give Juanita the day off.

A few of our friends mosey over, not wanting to pry, but it's obvious they're only here to get the inside scoop. I haven't spoken to any of these twats because none of them could care less when I left. It was just another day. So I have no idea what Liz has told them. For all I know, they probably think I was in rehab. The tray of drinks I hold would point to the epic fail that stay was.

"So glad you're back, Jay," says Tom, slapping me on the back. Tom is the type of guy you want to punch in the face. I only tolerated him because I'm friends with his wife. Karen appears from behind him and offers me a genuine hug.

"I tried calling you," she whispers, but Liz's sonar hearing doesn't miss a thing.

"He was working through some issues, but he's back now,

and it's for good." I glare at her over Karen's shoulder.

I break the hug and place the tray of drinks on the table. I need something stronger.

The convoy continues for way too long, but I smile and play along. When they finally grow tired of welcoming me back, Liz announces it's time for dinner. She loops her arm through mine while I grit my teeth. "I've missed this smell," she declares, snuggling close.

Her touch is wrong, so wrong, and I want nothing more than to bathe for a week, but I suck it up and refrain from stating I certainly didn't miss her heavy-handed floral perfume.

When we step into the dining room, I scoff. It's decked out like Christmas.

My thoughts drift to the last time I was greeted with a sight—it *was* Christmas, and it was the night which kick-started my rebirth. If I knew then what I know now, I wouldn't be in the predicament I'm in.

Liz leads us over to the head of the table. After I take my seat, I mouth to the server to inquire if we have any scotch. He nods and disappears.

Everyone is chatting happily as they fill their plates with food. I'll give it to Liz, she knows how to throw a party, but beer and pizza would have sufficed. When she fills her glass with water, I arch a brow. "No wine with dinner?"

She smiles, attempting to be coy. "Not anymore."

Demi, who is conveniently sitting to Liz's left hears her

strange response, and her mouth drops open. "Oh, my god. Are you…pregnant?"

I choke on air and thump on my chest to dislodge the bullshit I just swallowed.

"Not yet," she replies, placing a hand on my leg. "But we're trying."

We are?

The table hears the commotion, and it's celebrations all around while my temper spikes. She really has no shame. I once saw her determination as an admirable quality, but now I see her for the psychopath that she is.

A bottle of scotch appears, but instead of filling my glass, I reach for the bottle.

The more she speaks, the angrier I become. She is playing off her infidelity as though it never happened, and in turn, I look like the arsehole who left her. I unscrew the bottle and fill my glass full.

"Starting a little early, mate," teases some cockhead who needs to stop talking.

"Michael." I'm presuming it's his wife who nudges him, shaking her head. She's in tune to the fact I'm seconds away from ripping off his head.

"I need something to dull the pain, *mate*," I mock. However, when his gold cufflinks with ruby stones catch my eye, I'm suddenly transported to that Christmas Eve when Liz emerged from my study with some asshole. At the time, I didn't remember his name, but I do now. It's Michael.

I will never forget those cufflinks. And I'll never forget that smug look on his face—the one he wears now.

He laughs as he thinks I'm playing, but I am done playing. I refuse to sit here as the villain while Liz portrays the role of doting, supportive wife who has stuck by her husband who up and left her. I'm seething.

She places a few lettuce leaves and a minuscule portion of chicken on her plate, making a scene to support her apparent baby making claims. Her body is her temple and all that bollocks.

Not only is Michael a smug asshole, but he's also a noisy eater. Every chew of his filet mignon has me wanting to stab him with my fork. I can't sit here and not say anything. I know I have a moral code to abide by for the greater good, but if I don't say anything, I'm sure to explode.

"So Michael…" Liz peers up from her meal, stopping mid chew. "Remind me again how you know Elizabeth."

He swallows down his mouthful before reaching for this wine. "I'm her yoga teacher," he explains.

"Ah, so you're the one I should thank for Liz's ability to twist herself into a pretzel." The table falls silent the double meaning behind my words can't be missed. There is no gratitude directed toward him, just sheer animosity. "God knows she's put her talent to good use."

Demi gasps, covering her mouth, horrified.

I deadpan Michael as I want him to know that I'm onto him. He shuffles uncomfortably. "Lizzy is a very dedicated pupil."

A loud rumble erupts from me. "Is that what the kids are calling it these days?"

"Jayden, enough!" Liz whispers, tugging on my arm, but screw her. She's embarrassed. Too bad her scruples weren't an issue when she was shagging this tool in my office.

"What's the matter, *Lizzy*?" I hiss, yanking from her grip. "We're just having a friendly conversation about your uncanny ability to twist your puss—"

"Okay, that's it!" She stands, tossing her napkin to the table. This is the first genuine response I have seen from her since this charade started. "You've clearly had too much to drink."

"That's the problem, poppet. I haven't had enough." I reach for the scotch and throw back the liquor straight from the bottle.

Gasps and quiet whispers sound from around me, but I don't care. Let them judge. They already have. This is all bullshit anyway. "You're all a bunch of sad, lonely arseholes who thrive on each other's misfortunes to make yourself feel better about your miserable lives. Except you, Karen." I raise the bottle in salute. "I'm done pretending."

"He's clearly lost his mind," Demi mumbles under her breath. "Maybe it's all the Viagra?" Her jab can blow me 'cause I'm fairly certain she's mistaking Viagra for steroids. But who knows.

Standing, I kick back my chair, causing it to fall to the floor with a thud. "Let's make a toast." Everyone looks at one another, unsure what they should do. But I'm more than happy to drink alone. "To my darling wife." I hold the bottle of scotch out to Liz whose chest is rising and falling in utter contempt. "Thank you for reminding me why I left. And to Michael." I turn toward him. "Fuck you."

His mouth hinges open. Maybe he's practicing one of his yoga deep breathing techniques.

As his wife gasps, holding him protectively, I smirk. "By the way, love, my wife fucked your husband, but he mustn't have been anything special because she was shacking up with the pool boy too."

The room erupts into pandemonium.

Michael stands, ready to take me on, but his wife has other plans when she whacks his cheek. "How could you?"

"He's lying!" he cries, attempting to defend himself, but his deceit is transparent.

With scotch in hand, I bow to the room, so done with this sham. "Namaste." I leave a trail of destruction in my wake as I walk up the stairs with a smirk spread from ear to ear.

As I enter my room, I go about collecting my things because I refuse to stay here a second longer. I thought I had it figured out, but there is no way I can see this through. I will work something else out because this isn't a solution; it's a fucking train wreck.

The door booms open and in strolls the she-devil in heels. "How dare you!" she shrieks, slamming the door shut behind her.

I don't even bother looking at her.

"You embarrassed me!"

"I'm pretty sure wearing that frock did that, not me."

She ignores my jab. "But more importantly, you embarrassed yourself."

"I'm way past that," I counter, shoving past her and making a beeline for my suitcase.

"You promised me."

"Yeah, well, I lied. You should be familiar with that concept, seeing as our whole marriage was based on a fucking lie!" I scream, finally facing her.

"You seem to forget I have the ability to ruin you." She arrogantly folds her arms. My maniacal laugh surprises her.

"You already have, Elizabeth," I state coolly. "The day you took our vows and shitted all over them. So go ahead and do your best."

A small victory for me, but that soon turns to dread.

She walks…no, she stalks toward me, but I stand my ground. "I wasn't born yesterday. I knew you'd never come back without a fight. But you're either in or out, and you know what happens if you're out. This is your last chance."

The more she speaks, the more entertained I become. "Please, so what?" I yawn, bored. "Tell Gerry. I'm done playing your sick, twisted games." I know Axle is also a factor, but maybe Carrie is right. Maybe we could get to him first. But it appears Liz has thought about it all.

"I'm sure Yale would love to know all about Axle Bell, CEO of one of the world's biggest and most influential publishing house's eldest daughter having an affair with her well-respected photography teacher."

The world stops spinning. "*What?*"

"Oh? You didn't know?" she says, faking surprise, peering at her nails, bored.

"You lie," I press out between clenched teeth. But deep down, I know that she's telling me the truth. This is her lifeline. If I turned rogue, just how she knew I would, she would use this against me and blindside me. This is her ace in a hole.

"No, I'm not. I believe his name was"—she taps her chin in contemplation—"Mr. Donny Adell. He is married and has two beautiful children. I told you she was a little whore."

The walls begin closing in on me. There is no way this is true. But how does Liz know his name?

This explains her reluctance to go back to school and why she fled Seattle the way she did. She was running away from the horrible mistake she made.

At the airport, she wanted to confess something. Was this it? It would explain why she was so apprehensive about letting me in. Why she kept seeing herself as unworthy. And why she hated Liz so—she saw herself in Liz because didn't she do the same thing to Donny's wife?

Bile rises. I think I'm going to be sick.

"Don't believe me? Call her," Liz taunts, reaching for my cell and extending it my way. "Your perfect little angel isn't so perfect after all."

It's the imperfections that make life beautiful, she once said. And this entire time, that's how she viewed herself—an imperfection.

Unable to stop myself, I snatch my phone from Liz's clutches and dial Carrie. I don't care that Liz is still here. She knows how this is going to end. We both do.

"Jayden." Her voice brings back so many happy memories, but what I'm about to do will shatter every single one.

"Who was Donny?"

Silence.

"Wh-what do you mean?" Her falter says it all.

"Was Donny your…your teacher?" Her staggered breathing tears me into two, but I need to know. "Dove?"

"Yes."

A winded exhalation escapes me. "Why, why didn't you tell me?"

"Because I was embarrassed," she cries, sniffling. "I knew you'd judge me."

This is the question which will make or break me. If she answers yes, then I don't know what happens next. "Did you know he was married?"

"Jayden, I need to..."

But it's a simple question. "Did you know?" I repeat, watching Liz as she grins in triumph.

"Yes...but—"

There are no buts in this equation. What she did, I know what it feels like to be on the receiving end. I thought I knew her, but I don't know her at all.

"Did you know he had children?"

"Yes."

I press my eyes closed, wishing I could shut out the truth.

"Can I come over? Please let me explain." I wince, her words the same words Liz used when I caught her cheating. History seems to be repeating itself.

"Now isn't a good time," I reply, sighing, utterly defeated.

Liz chooses this precise moment to speak. "Now or *ever* is not a good time."

"Who is that?" Carrie asks. I can just imagine her wise eyes widening in horror.

"It's no one," I respond honestly.

"You're with *her*?"

Sick and tired of the lies and games, I sigh. "Yes."

"Oh, my god," she cries. "Have you been with her this entire time?"

My silence is all the answer she needs.

"How could you? Did you...sleep with her?" She sobs, breaking my heart all over again.

What does it matter? This is all fucked up, regardless of my response. "No, of course not."

"Then why are you there? Why?" She chokes on her tears.

"I thought I was doing the right thing, but I don't seem to know what that is anymore."

"Leave her. Come here. Let's talk. Please."

Her pleas are too much, but I can't leave, and it has nothing to do with the fact Liz is blackmailing me because that all seems obsolete now. "I can't, Carrie. I'm sorry. I can't be with you. What would that say for everything I've experienced these past six months if I were? You lied to me. You cheated with a married man. You did what Liz did to me." This is my hard limit, and I don't know if I can forgive and forget.

"When I spoke to Liz, I was talking to the past me who fucked up epically. I know I'm no better than she is. Hell, I *am* her." Remembering the phone call, I now understand why it felt so personal…because it was. "That's why I was so afraid to tell you. I knew you'd never forgive me."

"You should have told me," I mutter, defeated.

"I wanted to tell you. So many times. But you hate Liz for what she did, so how could you not hate me? We're both… cheaters."

"No," I utter, shaking my head, unable to hear the awful truth. This entire time, she had me believing we weren't right for one another because of *my* past…but it was *her* past that was the issue.

“So that’s it? Everything you said to me…it was all a lie? You won’t even let me explain.”

“No, I meant every word, but I just wish you’d have told me. This is something I needed to know.”

“Like you telling me you were spending the night with your wife,” she counters, wounded.

I understand her pain, but this isn’t tit for tat. Two wrongs don’t make a right. I was here to protect her and save her from the shame, but it appears I can’t save her from herself and the mistakes she’s made.

“I’m not perfect. I never said I was. But I told you everything. I never lied.”

“Until now,” she whispers.

“It seems we’re both liars then,” I counter, sealing our fate for good. “You knew I had issues with trusting people. I asked you never to lie to me because whatever you’d done, I could deal with as long as you were honest. This is my deal breaker. You know that!”

“I kn-know. I’m s-sorry.” Her remorse is clear, but I need some time. I’m not angry about her poor choice. We all make mistakes. I’m wounded by the fact she didn’t trust me enough to tell me the truth.

“I am too.” So many emotions are running through me right now. I don’t know how to feel.

“So, th-this is i-it?” Her stuttering is crushing every fiber in my body, but I need time.

"For now." Until I can figure this out, I need to distance myself from Carrie, and I think she needs the distance too.

"Are you getting back together with Liz?"

Looking at her, at her smug, pretentious being, I finally shed this skin for good. "No, never. I can't be with someone I don't trust."

I've never meant that more than I do now.

Carrie is holding back her tears, but it's too late. We're both broken. Something beautiful has shattered us both. "Goodbye, Carrie."

"Jayden, no. Please…" She sobs, but her pleas…they are just like Liz's. I can't do this again. I don't have the strength to do this and come out sane.

"I'm sorry, dove. I'm sorry…I just…I just need time to think. Goodbye." Her tears tear a hole straight through me, but I hang up before I lose the strength to.

I crush the cell to my chest, closing my eyes, unbelieving this just happened. I don't know what to feel.

"So you see, I did all this to protect you." For a few glorious minutes, I had forgotten Liz was here.

"Protect me?" I snicker, ready to end this once and for all. "You did this all for your personal gain." When she attempts to refute, I walk toward her, steady and slow. "But I'm done. No more games."

My confidence diminishes hers. "I'll ruin her. I'll ruin you." But her threats, they're empty—just like her.

"Go ahead." I spread my arms out wide. "Tell whoever the fuck you want. Tell Gerry. Tell Axle. Tell Yale. Tell the world. It doesn't matter anymore. I was trying so hard to make this right, but there is no right in this situation. We're all sinners. And it's time we make amends for our sins."

"I lo-love you," she falters, launching forward, but I reach out and grip her upper arm. It's the first voluntary touch I've made. It will also be the last.

"No, you don't. All I am to you is one of your fancy jewels." I flick at the thick gold necklace around her neck. "I'm someone to show off because, god forbid, you enter a room alone. But that's all you'll ever be, Elizabeth. No matter how much money, men, and materialistic shit you buy, it will never fill the void because you're running away from the one thing that scares you most in this world—being alone."

Tears fill her eyes, but she sniffs them back. "I me-mean it. I'll tell them."

Lowering my face toward hers, I smile. "Tell them, I dare you. Because if you do, I have some stories of my own to tell."

"What stories?" Her eyes widen, and I see something I haven't seen from her for a very long time. Humanity.

"I'm sure your friends would love to know how you screwed most of their husbands. I mean, by Michael's wife's reaction, I dare say you may need to find some new friends."

"They won't believe you," she says, showing me her colors by not even attempting to deny my claims. I had my suspicions all along, but she's just confirmed them.

"I think that they will. The fact Michael got bitch-slapped proves it. Maybe they've suspected all along." She clenches her jaw. "What's the matter? Don't like being on the receiving end for once?"

This is the ultimate standoff. The gloves have come off.

"And you will sign those fucking divorce papers. If you don't, I will give Yale a juicy story which just happens to be true." No one knows the exact reason we separated—it was none of their business—but I have no qualms about divulging it all. Hell, it might even win me brownie points with whoever my new employer might be because after tonight, I have no doubt my career is over.

Our "friends" undoubtedly will be leaking the information to whatever source they can find. You know the anonymous "friends" you read about in gossip magazines who love to spill the confidential beans about their "friends." I was just sitting in a room full of them.

My woes will be tomorrow's headlines. But funnily enough, I've never felt freer.

"Okay, fine, you win."

I shake my head, letting her go. "This was never a game. Well, to me it wasn't."

"I did love you," she says, and the real Elizabeth Evans, the one who walked into that Starbucks before all this heartbreak occurred, shines.

"And I loved you, too. Remember that. Not this. Because this is ugly—and I know you're not. Beneath everything, you're still beautiful. You just need to find that beauty again. Goodbye, Liz." No matter if that is true or not, I choose to believe it is. I choose to believe she will keep her promise and I will keep mine.

I believe that when I leave her standing in the middle of the room, sobbing into her palms. I hold that belief when I make my way downstairs, suitcase in tow. Liz's friends quieten down when they see me, but I don't care.

Today is a brand-new day—the death of J.E. Sparrow and the birth of someone new.

17
Seventeen

One Month Later

"A skinny tall cappuccino and an extra hot latte," says the hipster, Barry, who just happens to be my boss. "Got that, old man?"

He's lucky I like the cheeky bastard.

"Yes, I'm not deaf," I reply, passing Wanda, my 11a.m. regular, her mint tea.

"Not yet anyway," Barry quips, laughing.

This is my life now. Working for twelve dollars an hour at a coffee shop and getting picked on by a boy with a curly moustache and trouser braces. But it's a life I've chosen, and it feels fucking terrific to shed my skin.

After the night I said goodbye to J.E. Sparrow for good, I called Nick and told him everything. I needed a break from the crazy. I asked him to call Gerry and tell him the deal was no longer on the table. He begged me to sleep on it, but there was nothing to sleep on. My decision was made.

It had nothing to do with Liz blackmailing me. It was all me.

When it came to Axle, however, I had the pleasure of telling him I would no longer be writing for him, or anyone else for that matter, because I was on hiatus—effective immediately. He asked if it had anything to do with Daisy, which made me happy. Why? Because that indicated he knew nothing of Gerry's offer, meaning Carrie was in the clear.

This also meant that Liz kept her promise, and I knew she'd stick to it when I received the signed divorced papers in the mail. I thought I would celebrate when the day came, but I didn't. It was filed away with another part of my life that I moved on from.

I thought I'd be missed, but it's amazing that another hundred up-and-coming authors are ready to take your place. I was yesterday's news.

I left behind the person I was for so long and became this unnamed face in a sea of many. My job is pouring coffee, or if you want to get fancy, I'm a barista. It seemed fitting I go back to the beginning and uncover what's next for me.

A day doesn't pass when I don't think of Carrie and the error of our ways. What we had was real—a whimsical romance that one reads about in books. It's no surprise the day we stopped talking was the day I stopped writing.

I haven't written a word since. And I'm okay with that.

I was trying so hard, believing she was the magical cure, but all along, that cure was me. Yes, Carrie may have inspired a new lease on life for me, but in the end, I wrote those words for me. But now, I don't want to write. And I don't know if I ever will again.

So I spend my days working, watching life pass me by. Things may be slow moving, but it's a nice change of pace.

When I hear, "I'll have a beer," I look up to see Nick harassing Barry, just as he always does.

"For the tenth time this week, we don't sell alcohol. Just coffee."

Nick blows a raspberry while loosening his tie. "What kind of an establishment is this anyway?"

"A respectable one," I reply, shaking my head at my best friend. He rounds the corner, as he seems to think he works here too.

"Is that for me?" When he attempts to reach for the cappuccino I just prepared, I elbow him in the gut. He grunts on impact while I smirk. I live for these moments.

I pass the two ladies their orders. One of them has been giving me flirty eyes, but I simply smile. "Enjoy your day."

She clears her throat, as no one likes being shot down, and once upon a time, I would have most definitely returned the affection, but not anymore. I am done with relationships for the moment because I am focusing on the most important relationship of all—the one with myself.

After Liz and I split, I self-medicated on sex when I probably should have seen a shrink instead. I never thought Carrie was my rebound, but I suppose in a way she was. No matter what Liz did, I loved her, and she broke my fucking heart. I should have dealt with those feelings before becoming a walking hard-on.

"Oh, no. You're having one of your touchy-feely moments with yourself, aren't you?" Nick says, ruining the moment.

"Why are you here?" I ask, slapping his hand away when he reaches for a chocolate chip cookie.

He pulls out his bottom lip. "I can't visit my best friend? I miss you."

"You literally saw me an hour ago." It just happens where I work is around the block from Nick's office. Convenient or a curse—I'm still undecided.

"Fuck you. Let's go out tonight. It's Friday. You do remember what your Friday nights used to entail, right?" he poses with a grin.

To shut him up, I pass him a cookie.

It doesn't stop him, though. "One beer then. Just because you've given up on life doesn't mean we all have," he says around a mouthful of food.

"On the contrary. I'm embracing life," I argue with a smirk. I know what he's doing, and it's working.

"You're embracing boring," he counters, pointing his half-eaten cookie my way. He looks at Barry for moral support, who nods. Fuck them both.

"He's right, Jay. You get hit on at least ten times an hour, and you hardly seem to notice."

"Ten times an *hour*?" Nick cries, horrified. "What the fuck is your secret?"

"Not caring," I reply with a shrug.

"Now you're just being smug."

I burst into laughter while Barry goes back to the cashier to serve the line of thirsty patrons.

Nick leans against the counter, making it clear he's not going anywhere until I agree. "My morning is free," he explains, which means he will be here annoying me until he needs to go back to work.

Barry passes me the next order, which consists of about fifteen coffees. Nick may have all the time to chitchat, but I don't. So I have no choice but to cave. "Okay, fine. If I agree to come out tonight, will you leave me alone? Some people actually come to work to work."

Nick clutches his chest, feigning horror. "They do? And it's a deal. Now, I'll have a long macchiato. To go."

Rolling my eyes, I get to work, wondering what exactly I just agreed to.

❤ ❤ ❤

Nick texted me the address of some bar downtown.

I went home and changed after work, not really in the mood to socialize, but it might be good to go out after being an almost hermit for the past month. Besides, it's just for one beer. What's the worst that can happen?

The moment I step into the overcrowded bar, I want to step back out and go home. I'd much rather be a couch potato and binge watch the new season of *The Walking Dead*. But I suck it up and wedge my way through the throng of people.

No surprise, Nick is at the bar with a row of shots in front of him. When he sees me, he raises one in a salute. "You made it!" In celebration, he throws back the clear liquid and slams the glass onto the bar. "Here." He slides a shot over, but I slide it back.

"A beer, thanks," I order from the bartender. "Are you celebrating?"

Nick tosses back two shots, replying with a sluggish shrug. "I signed a six-figure deal for some little up-and-coming snot whose book is about two robots who fall in love. That's remotely exciting, I suppose. But I miss the days when authors wrote for the love of writing. Some manuscripts I read—" He scrunches up his face as though he's just smelled something bad.

"The literary world is changing. With self-publishing taking off the way it has, authors have to stand out in a saturated world," I explain. "It's not just about writing good stories anymore. It's about image and who's cool to read. An industry where we're not supposed to conform has become just that. Sad, but true."

Nick sighs, mussing up his brown hair. "Maybe I need a new job. It's no fun without you anymore. So you've given up writing for good?"

I've asked myself that question often, and I'm still no closer to uncovering what exactly the answer is. "For the moment, mate, yes. I used to love writing, but now, I feel like a phony. How can I write about something I have no idea about?"

"She really fucked you up, didn't she?" There is no need for him to elaborate who that is.

The bartender chooses this moment to place the beer in front of me. He clearly can sense my dire need to forget my woes when he places a shot of whiskey beside it. "I don't know what she did, but this feels different than it did with Liz. Carrie and I shared something…unique. Two ships at night, desperately seeking the solace of a lighthouse to welcome them home."

"When you say shit like that"—Nick wipes away his imaginary tears—"it confirms that no matter what you're feeling, you will always be a writer at heart."

I suppose he's right.

"You still haven't called her?"

Reaching for my whiskey, I cherish the burn as it slides down my throat. "No, it's too late, and what would I say?"

"Hello?" Nick offers, making this sound so easy, but it's not. I know what I feel for Carrie. I think I knew from the first moment we met. But before I commit to someone else again, I need to make sure she won't be my rebound, and I won't be hers because that's what we both were.

A rebound kiss that turned into something else.

"Let's get drunk," I declare, needing to switch off for just one night. This constant ache I feel in the middle of my chest is because I miss Carrie—I miss her so much it fucking hurts. But if she wanted to call me, she could have. Just as I could have called her. But until I figure myself out, this is the only solution that makes any sense.

Nick almost springs from his seat with my suggestion, flagging the bartender down. "A bottle of your top shelf whiskey. We're celebrating."

"We are?" I ask, cocking an amused brow. "What are we celebrating?"

Nick wraps an arm around my shoulder and draws me to his side. "We're celebrating everything and anything and nothing at all."

Sounds good to me.

❤ ❤ ❤

Two bottles of scotch later, I am utterly wasted. So much so, I'm almost contemplating joining Nick on the dance floor as he dances to some 70s disco tune.

I needed tonight. I needed to realize that no matter what happened with Carrie, you live and you learn. I accepted that we both fucked up and the time we spent together was indescribable. Maybe that's why the writer's block has returned.

Whatever the case, I will only look forward and hope I uncover the reason the universe decided to throw Carrie in my path.

Needing to go to the bathroom, I stagger through the crowd, seeking out where it is. As I search the room, however, I get more than I bargained for because my eyes lock with someone who I'll never forget.

Those hazel orbs seem to have grown wiser, but her innocence is still there. She looks just as I remember—a ray of sunlight in a withering storm. My heart picks up the pace, and my palms begin to sweat. She's here; she's really here.

Standing feet away is Carrie Bell, the woman who has ruled my every waking thought since the first moment we locked eyes. I can't help but think of our bumping into one another in Paris. Although that wasn't coincidental, the relief of seeing her now is just the same.

No matter how much time we spend apart, my feelings for her never waver, they only seem to grow.

Everything around us fades into the background as we stand motionless, unable to look away. I'm transfixed, rooted to the spot, and if I died right now, I'd die happy because we've both changed. We've both grown.

She brushes a strand of hair behind her ear, evoking memories of what those curls felt like in my hands. I want to say so many things, but where do I start? Sorry might be a good place. Sorry I didn't give her a chance to explain.

But all chances of a reunion come crashing down around me when someone stands beside her. Our connection severs as she lowers her gaze to the floor. I don't know who the man is, but it doesn't matter. I got to see Carrie for the briefest moment in time, and it was enough.

She shyly lifts her eyes, leaving me breathless. If this were a movie, the swoony hero would swoop in and tell the heroine that he wants her to give him a second chance. But this isn't fiction, this is real. So, in light of that, I do the only thing I can—I raise my hand and wave.

An olive branch as such, one she accepts when she returns the motion.

We stand, hands raised, unmoving, as a silent gesture can amount to a million words. In that simple wave, we express sadness, happiness, regret, but most of all, it's a hello.

A burst of something explodes inside of me when the light catches the bracelet around her slender wrist—the bracelet I gave her. She's still wearing it. Could it be, she still feels it too?

The guy beside her gestures that it's time to go, and when she chews her lip, I know she's torn. But I do the most selfless thing I can do—I let her go. With a final wave, I say goodbye… goodbye for now.

Her surprise is clear, but she nods with a smile and leaves me standing with my hand and head held high.

"Dude! Carrie just left!" Nick nudges me so hard, I stagger sideways, breaking my trance, but that seems to open a door that has remained shut for weeks.

Nothing about this makes any sense, but that's how every good story begins…

Nick ceases with the violence, reading my response immediately. "I know that look. It's happening, isn't it?"

All I can do is nod, too afraid to speak because all the words I need are the ones in my head. Maybe sometimes, the good guy *does* get the girl.

18
Eighteen

Six Months Later

I've done this a thousand times before, but this time is different. So very different.

The night I saw Carrie stirred something in me, something I was too afraid to do—I wrote, and I haven't stopped since.

Seeing her inspired me, reminding me why I was on this journey they call life. I could have called her, but I didn't, and she didn't call me. What we had was enough because it was the start of something new for the both of us.

"Nervous?" Nick asks, looking his finest in a gray pinstripe suit.

Pacing the small back room, I wring my hands in front of me. "I am now."

"You'll be fine. They're here for you. If you fuck up, just sing

Elvis. Everyone loves Elvis."

"Not helping," I quip, wiping my sweaty palms onto my torn jeans. "This was a bad idea. What if she doesn't come?"

Nick grips my upper arm to stop me from pacing. "If she doesn't come, she doesn't come. At least you tried."

He's right.

This is by far the bravest thing I have ever done. I'm taking a gamble, but Carrie has always been worth the risk.

Karen pokes her head around the doorway, smiling. "You ready?"

"No," I reply, but it's now or never. People are waiting… waiting to see me. "How many are out there?"

"Two, three…" I exhale in relief, but it's short-lived. "Hundred."

I turn to Nick, cocking my head to the side. "How many people did you invite? I said small."

Nick shrugs unapologetically. "This is small. I had to turn people away. I'm pretty sure tickets were selling online for five hundred dollars." I don't even want to acknowledge that claim because it does nothing to settle the nerves. "It's your fault for being so secretive."

"I'll announce you, all right? They're getting restless. Break a leg," Karen says, excited I chose her bookstore to do this in. But it was never a question of where.

Exhaling, I nod. "Let's do this." Nick slaps me on the back and joins Karen, the proud agent that he is.

Tonight is opening night—the reveal of the new me, so to speak. Most know me as J.E. Sparrow, but that man is no more. Yes, we're here to unveil my new book to the masses, but this book is different. My characters aren't flawless. They don't have an obscure name with perfect hair and deep blue eyes and a defined jawline.

They aren't without blemishes or wardrobe malfunctions because none of that is real. In real life, people don't wake up looking as though they just stepped off a runway in Milan. Real people have real problems, and those problems teach us life lessons. They make us. They break us.

Life is messy, but that's the best kind of life one can live.

For months, I've wanted to write something different. I thought the manuscript I started in Paris was the different I was searching for, but it wasn't. It was a good start, but to shed my skin, I had to start again—the rebirth of the real me.

"Put your hands together and welcome…Jayden Evans."

Yup, that's me. I may have made a name for myself as J.E. Sparrow, but just imagine what I could achieve by being true to myself.

With that thought as my compass, I walk out in front of the audience, head held high. The crowd erupts into applause. Karen wasn't lying. It's a full house. Some faces I recognize, some I don't. And the one face I'm desperate to see doesn't seem to be here. But that doesn't matter. It's because of her that this book exists, and it will honor her and honor us whether she is here or not.

I asked Karen for simple, and she listened. My stage is a wooden chair and a small round table piled high with copies of my book. Nick is standing off to the left, my forever supporter, cheering me on from the sidelines.

Taking a seat, I look out at the sea of people, so thankful they're here to celebrate life. "Hi. Thank you for coming. My name is Jayden Evans. Some of you may know me as J.E. Sparrow, but that's no more. This new book…it's different. I know all authors say that about their newest release, but this one truly is. There is a lot of secrecy surrounding this book because everything you're about to read is true."

Taking a breath, I can only hope she's here to hear my confession.

"I know a lot of rumors have surfaced over the past few months about me. Some are complete fiction, but sadly, most are true. Which is why I've decided to pen my life, in my own words, and put an end to those rumors. Who needs rumors when you have the truth? I used to write fiction. Love stories that ended in a happily ever after. Well, this isn't that. It's an autobiography about a man, and that man is me."

Gasps sound because this is shedding an image and starting again.

Reaching for a copy of my book, I open the page to the introduction. Here goes nothing.

"My name is Jayden Evans. I'm a thirty-three-year-old

Sagittarius who used to write about the miracle of true love and finding your forever soul mate. I'm a *New York Times*, *USA Today*, and *Wall Street Journal* bestselling author with over twenty-five million copies of my books sold worldwide.

My first novel, *Lost in Love*, was written when I was twenty-two. It was inspired by my whirlwind romance with my ex-wife, Elizabeth Sparrows. By twenty-four, I was one of the world's most beloved authors. All of this, all my accomplishments were because of Liz. She was my muse…but things change.

"That change came when I met someone…someone who didn't just change my life, she changed me. We met when I was caught in a compromising position, one that I found myself in more times than I care to admit. Nothing but a cliché, I'm sure that's what you're all thinking, and you're right. My wife cheated on me, and in turn, I became a man seeking inspiration in a world where I felt so lost.

"You see, I suffered from something every author dreaded—writer's block. I couldn't write a single word. I've done some deplorable things, ones I can't take back, and at the time, I thought being a raging manwhore would unearth the inspiration I so desperately craved. But all it did was drive me further away from who I was."

Pushing my glasses up the bridge of my nose, I continue.

"I was caught at a crossroads as such…a crossroads in life. So when I met her, she brought with her the breath of fresh air I was searching for. But she had her own demons. Fuck, who doesn't. But it appeared her demons danced with mine. A deadly combination, one I didn't fully understand until it was too late.

"I thought she was my savior, that she was the reason I could write again. But when I lost her, I realized *I* was the reason, and that's the only reason that should matter. Because how can you make someone else happy when you're not happy with yourself? But I'm happy now, and I hope wherever you are, you're happy too. I know it's too late. Months have passed, but I need you to know that I'm sorry. I'm sorry for judging you when you never once judged me.

"This entire time, you were searching for your Mr. Right, and finally, I can offer you that. I'm your Mr. Write.

"So this book is dedicated to you, dove. I wasn't afraid of telling you that…I love you. I was afraid of what your answer would be. Thank you."

I close the book, unsure how that went down because it's so quiet, I can hear my racing heartbeat. Nick nods, his eyes glossed over with what appear to be tears. But that's impossible; there is no way he would cry. But when the crowd stands, exploding in pandemonium, I realize that it's very possible because this book…this book is a fucking hit.

The next few minutes pass by in a blur. Strangers congratulating me, and publishers begging for five minutes of my time. But I seek only one face, and as I scour the crowd, I don't see her.

I invited Carrie because, regardless of everything, I wanted her here. I wanted her to know that I'm sorry and that I now know what that feeling I constantly questioned was…it was love. I have loved Carrie from the moment we met, and I'm a convert. Insta-love, love at first sight, although rare, exists. She is the one, the only one I want. But she clearly doesn't feel the same.

"Jayden, it's time to sign your books." Nick shoos away the vultures, who couldn't care less when I hung up my literary boots. But I showed them. Gerry was right. The publishing world is changing, and it's time I caught up to pace.

Mr. Write, the name of my new book, is published by me. I'm now an indie author—I think that's what they're calling it. I oversaw the editing, formatting, cover, and everything else that goes into self-publishing, and it was bloody hard work. Anyone who thinks being an author is simply penning words to paper needs to spend a day in our shoes.

The bloggers may state they wanted this and that, but in the end, we write for ourselves. If anyone else likes it or connects with our words, then we are truly blessed.

I follow Nick to the table set up with piles of my book and endless Sharpies—an author's best friend. The line is insanely long with budding readers, but the face I long to see isn't among them. Nick sits beside me, slapping me on the back.

Somehow, he managed to secure foreign rights in twenty-one different countries. It's still hard to believe my autobiography will be translated into Bulgarian. When I wrote this book, it was a form of therapy because I started from the beginning, and the end…well, I can't give the ending away.

I didn't know what I wanted to do with it, but the more I wrote, the clearer things became. I overcame this mental block. It wasn't writers block; it was me afraid of failing. So with nothing left to lose, I wrote a story detailing what it's like to be human. A story that translates in every language.

Nick passes me books as I sign each one, chatting with my readers. They express their excitement over my new work and share their own personal stories of love. The night is truly magical.

As I'm chatting with a reader who has been with me since day one, I hear Nick wheeze and kick me sharply under the table. I pay no attention to him as Jackie is detailing the ups and downs of her forty-year marriage, and I don't want to be rude.

"Would you mind posing for a photo?" she asks while Nick kicks me once again. He's gone mad.

Standing, I ignore his outburst and round the table to stand in front of a banner of my book. I smile for her daughter, who snaps a few pictures. As I'm thanking Jackie for coming, the hair on the back of my neck stands on end. The air sizzles. I disregard it, however, as it's probably the fact I'm in a room with hundreds of people.

Once I bid Jackie farewell, I take my seat. Nick passes me a bottle of water and an antacid. "I don't need that," I say, referring to the antacid.

"Trust me, you will," he says, passing me a book to give to the next person in line. He clearly needs some fresh air.

"Hi." However, my greeting lodges in my throat when I look up and see the one person I had given up on seeing ever again. I now understand Nick's madness because, on cue, my heart begins to ache.

"Hi, Jayden."

"Dove?" I ask in case my mind dreamt her up. She smiles while I instantly reach for the antacid. Nick passes me the bottle of water, which I gulp down in one mouthful.

During my mini meltdown, I hear hushed whispers.

"Is that *the* Dove?"

"Oh my god. The girl he dedicated his book to?" But I can only focus on one thing at a time.

"Congratulations. You did it." She toys with the silver C hanging from her neck. I need a moment to speak as I take her in.

She wears her long dark hair down, highlighting the crimson on her cheeks. Her face is natural with just a hint of gloss coating her plump lips. She's in a red summer dress and ballet flats. I notice her attire not only because she is the most beautiful woman I have ever seen, but because many seasons have passed since we last met.

"Thank you. Thank you for coming," I add, suddenly tongue-tied. I want to pull her aside and talk, but I have a line of people waiting.

She notices my dilemma and takes a deep breath. “I won’t take up much of your time.”

I quickly stand. “Let’s go somewhere private.” But she waves me off.

“No, if I don’t do this now, I’ll lose my nerve. I should have done this months ago. I’m sorry, Jayden. I should have told you from the beginning about Donny. I was just so…ashamed of what I’d done. When you told me what Liz had done, I hated her because she was me. Not that it makes a difference, but I want you to know the truth.”

She has my complete attention, and it appears the room is also under her spell. “Donny told me he was married…” Gasps and murmurs sound, but I ignore them. “But he said they were separated. He only stayed because of the kids. Oldest excuse in the book, right? But I believed him because I wanted to. He said his marriage was over, which was the only reason I started the affair.”

“Carrie—”

“No, please, let me finish. This has been eating me up these past few months.” I nod, shoving my hands into my pockets to stop myself from reaching out and holding her. “I thought what we had was real. But when I found him in bed with Natalie, well, you know what happens next. I boarded that plane with the intention of never falling in love again. But then…I met you.

"I wanted to tell you so many times, but I was scared." Her eyes twinkle with tears. "I was scared you'd never forgive me because I couldn't forgive myself. Everything happened so fast, but the more time I spent with you, the more in love with you I fell. But I know I hurt you, and that it's too late—"

"Dove, shh," I interrupt, which catches her unaware. "It's now my turn to talk."

The masses coo and laugh, watching my book come to life.

"I forgive you because I'm sorry too. I should have told you I was staying with Liz. But it was only for one night, and I was doing it in hopes I could finish my book and prove her wrong. I needed to watch her to make sure she didn't ruin your life as well. I know it was a stupid idea, but it seemed like the only solution at the time.

"So I want you to know that I understand why you did what you did. Sometimes, we lie to protect the ones we love. It's not an excuse, but it is an explanation. And it's what forced us both to let go of our demons and love ourselves again."

Nick sniffs—the big softie.

"We needed time to get over the past and focus on what's important—the future. And I want that future to be with you. I now know that you were right. You would have been my rebound kiss, and I would have been yours. But no more..."

Before she has a chance to reply, I round the table and press my lips to hers. She gasps, stunned, but that soon turns to a moan when I conquer her mouth with a feral possession. I don't care if she's seeing anyone or who that guy was the night I saw her six long months ago. All that matters is now.

We kiss as though the world is going to end, but as she duels with my tongue, I know this is just the beginning. I thread my fingers through her hair, angling her so I can dominate her—mind, body, and soul.

When her familiar scent of strawberries and cream assaults my senses, I growl and almost pin her to the table. However, Nick clears his throat, reminding me that I am molesting Carrie in a room full of people.

I pull away, which is nothing but a sin, and rub my nose with hers. "Sorry, I had to do that. I know you've probably moved on…"

But she presses her finger to my lips. "It's always been you. The guy you saw me with, he's in my cooking class. Just a friend."

"Cooking?" I ask, unable to stop my smirk.

"Yes, it's time to try something new." A double-edged sword. "Besides, photography shouldn't be learned, it should come from here." She presses her hand over my racing heart. "Just how your book did."

I'm unable to mute my gasp. "You heard it?"

She nods. "All of it." So she was here all along. She heard my admission that I love her. So what she says next seals our fate for good. "And my answer would have been…I love you too."

And there it is…my reason to smile.

"So what happens now?" she asks.

My loins stir, but there is the small issue of the fact we're not alone. I look down at Nick, who rolls his eyes. "Jayden will be back in fifteen minutes," he announces to the crowd. "For the inconvenience, you all get a free copy of his book."

Whether everyone cheers in celebration of a free paperback or the fact I have finally found my true north, I'll never know. But I bend down and kiss him quickly. "Thanks, mate. I owe you."

He wipes his lips wildly, shaking his head, but there is nothing but happiness behind his smile. "Just be quick."

However, when Carrie slips her hand into mine, I know that'll be an impossible task. "Make it twenty." I don't wait for him to argue. Instead, I lead Carrie through the crowd, who congratulate us as I make a beeline for the back room.

The moment we step inside, I lock the door and lean against it as I watch in utter desire as she undresses. "So does our story end in a happily ever after?"

"I don't know," I reply, unbuckling my belt. "You'll have to read it and find out."

When she's completely bare, I smash my lips to hers. "But for now…I promise to give you a different kind of HEA." And I make good on my word. Twice.

So how *does* our story end? Well, what you hold in your hands is our story, and how we wrote…

THE END.

Acknowledgements

My wonderful husband, Daniel. I love you. Thank you for believing in me even when I didn't believe in myself.

My ever-supporting parents. You guys are the best. I am who I am because of you. I love you.

My agent, Kimberly Brower from Brower Literary & Management. Thank you for your patience and thank you for being an amazing human being.

My publicist—Nina Bocci. Thank you for organizing my life. Your support means the world to me. Thank you for always being there.

My editor, Jenny Sims. What can I say other than I LOVE YOU! Thank you for everything.

My proof-readers—Rosa Sharon from iScream Proofreading Services and Lisa Edward. You guys are the best!

Sommer Stein, you NAILED this cover! Thank you for being so patient and making the process so fun.

Christina and Lauren, Tina Gephart, Elle Kennedy, Lisa Edward, SC Stephens, Vi Keeland, Penelope Ward, Adriane Leigh, Pam Godwin, Natasha Preston, Beverly Preston, Natasha Madison, Len Webster, K. Bromberg, Rachel Brookes, Debra Anastasia, Stina Lindenblatt, Sylvain Reynard, J.L. Drake, Jay McLean, Heidi McLaughlin, Audrey Carlan, BJ Harvey, K.A. Tucker, Kylie Scott, Mia Sheridan, Helena Hunting, Tijan,

Kimberly Whalen, Gemma, Louise, Heyne, Random House, Kinneret Zmora, Hugo & Cie, Planeta, Art Eternal, Carbaccio, Fischer, Harper Brazil, Bookouture, Egmont Bulgaria, Brilliance Audio, Hope Editions, USA TODAY/ Happy Ever After, Buzzfeed, BookBub, Love Letters Convention—Berlin, Aestas Book Blog, Hugues De Saint Vincent, Nikki McCombe, Mary Matta, Romance Writers of Australia, Paris, New York—Thanks for the support and laughs.

To the endless blogs that have supported me since day one—You guys rock my world. A special shout-out to: Donna Cooksley Sanderson, Ria Alexander, Melissa Teo, Amy Jennings, Mindy Guerreiros, Gel Ytayz, Melissa Gill, Jennifer Spinninger, Vanessa Silva Martins, Cheri Grand Anderman, Lauren Rosa, Kristin Dwyer.

My reader group; My Sinners—sending you all a big kiss.

My beautiful family—Mum, Papa, my sister—Fran, Matt, Samantha, Amelia, Gayle, Peter, Luke, Leah, Jimmy, Jack, Shirley, Michael, Rob, Elisa, Evan, Alex, Francesca, and my aunties, uncles, and cousins—I am the luckiest person alive to know each and every one of you. You brighten up my world in ways I honestly cannot express.

Samantha and Amelia— I love you both so very much.

To my family in Holland and Italy, and abroad. Sending you guys much love and kisses.

Zia Rosetta and Zia Giuseppina—you are in our hearts. Always.

My fur babies— mamma loves you so much! Buckwheat, you are my best buddy. Dacca, I will always protect you from the big bad Bellie. Mitch, refer to Dacca's comment. Jag, you're a wombat in disguise. Bellie, you're a devil in disguise. And Ninja, thanks for watching over me.

To anyone I have missed, I'm sorry! It wasn't intentional!

Last but certainly not least, I want to thank YOU! Thank you for welcoming me into your hearts and homes. My readers are the BEST readers in this entire universe! Love you all!

About the Author

Monica James spent her youth devouring the works of Anne Rice, William Shakespeare, and Emily Dickinson.

When she is not writing, Monica is busy running her own business, but she always finds a balance between the two. She enjoys writing honest, heartfelt, and turbulent stories, hoping to leave an imprint on her readers. She draws her inspiration from life.

She is a bestselling author in the U.S.A., Australia, Canada, France, Germany, Israel, and The U.K.

Monica James resides in Melbourne, Australia, with her wonderful family, and menagerie of animals. She is slightly obsessed with cats, chucks, and lip gloss, and secretly wishes she was a ninja on the weekends.

Connect with
Monica James

Facebook: https://www.facebook.com/authormonicajames

Twitter: https://twitter.com/monicajames81

Goodreads: https://www.goodreads.com/MonicaJames

Instagram: https://www.instagram.com/authormonicajames/

Website: http://monicajamesbooks.blogspot.com.au/

Pinterest: http://www.pinterest.com/monicajames81/

BookBub: http://bit.ly/2E3eCIw

Amazon: https://amzn.to/2EWZSyS

Join my Reader Group: http://bit.ly/2nUaRyi